DANGEROUS

Secrets

AMY BARNETT

Dangerous Secrets

AUTHOR'S NOTE

This book is the first in the DeMarco family mafia series, and ends on a cliffhanger. The road will be trying, but Sage will eventually get her happy ever after.

Trigger warnings:

This book is intended to be a darker romance and may contain triggering situations and topics such as death, grief, child abuse, graphic violence and explicit sexual situations.

Prologue

SAGE

When I imagine how I would kill someone, I picture doing it with a knife to their jugular. Maybe a quick stab to the heart, then a swipe across the throat. We'd be face to face, so I could look them in the eye while they slip away.

I see a bloody battle. Adrenaline taking me like a wild animal as I fight rabidly for the killing blow. Teeth bared. Blood dripping. Something poetic and cinematic.

Of course, this is only an epic fantasy of a person I'm not. I'm far too weak to kill. A weakness I'm reminded of right now.

The house is dark as the night, with only the moonlight shining through the second-floor windows to light my path. My feet shake as I struggle to steady myself, stumbling down our hallway and smearing bloody handprints along the walls as I go. I can only see what's right in front of me, my breath coming in harsh pants that echo in my head.

I paste a bloody handprint on my chest as I gasp and double over in horror. *I* did this.

No. I shake the thoughts away. I have to keep going. I have to make it. Even if only my memory of my home guides me down the hall.

I pause when I see red dripping at my feet. I've left a trail of blood. Tiny crimson tear drops pave the way I came. Blood drips from my temple, down my chin and onto the tile.

There's more blood on my hands too. But that's not mine.

Masked men were waiting in my room, trying to grab me, when I snuck back inside through the window. One of my father's men tackled them to the ground before they could get a shot at me. The blood on my hands is his. I'd tried to help him; instead, he told me to run.

But running seems too risky. Running is loud.

I hear a thump somewhere behind me and turn panicked towards the sound. There's nothing there, so I continue forward on hushed feet. Just across the hall from Dad's office, I'm almost there when I pause. My father's pained groan reaches me from across the space. As does the sound of smacking flesh.

"Stay the fuck down if you know what's good for you, Dimitri."

I slap a hand over my mouth and press my eyes shut as I suppress a sob.

"Why are you here?" My dad's voice.

I peer around the corner and can vaguely see into Dad's office through the open double doors. Three muscled-looking guys dressed in all black stand over him where he's crumpled on the floor next to his desk. They all have guns; the main guy's out and trained on my dad.

"You know what we want," the main one says.

I recognize him. He's the one I opened the gate for. The guy holding a gun in Dad's face... I'm the one that let him in the front gate.

"Where's the girl?"

As I watch on, I can't bring myself to move. Overruling fear won't even allow me to hide around the corner. All I can do is stare and hope they don't see me. There's no fight in me. No flight. Just complete ice pinning me in place.

"One last time, Dimitri. Where's. The. Girl?"

The girl? They can't possibly mean me? Dad shakes his head. But I know he'd lie. If it were to protect me, he would never break. He would never lead them to me the way I led them to him.

Boots pound up the stairs, and finally gaining some sense, I scramble into the shadows to hide, feet slipping beneath me.

Another guy enters the room.

"Well?" the leader addresses him without looking away from my dad.

"She's not here."

The leader cocks his head. "You can't possibly know that. This place is huge."

The newcomer doesn't look nervous. "I couldn't get much out of them, but I'm told she-" They talk quietly enough that I miss the end of the sentence.

A few beats pass where no one speaks. All that can be heard is Dad's heavy breathing. He slumps against the desk, head resting skyward.

"Slippery." The main one finally breaks the silence, his voice a smile. He checks his weapon, filling it with bullets and no bother for a silencer.

He aims and fires into my dad's chest without warning.

I flinch, my gasp covered by the gun's echoing bang.

Dad's shoulders drop as he hisses, gritting his teeth and breathing through his nose in angry huffs. He's knocked aside when the main guy kicks him square in the jaw.

A tear traces my cheek and drips onto my chin.

Just like that, they're leaving. I barely get my body hidden, back pressed firmly against the wall around the corner, before they pass me, heading down the stairs. Whether the job is finished or they're continuing their search, I can't miss this chance.

I stand on shaky legs and rush across the open hallway, dropping to my knees beside Dad where he lies on his side.

"Sage?" he coughs, blood seeping out the sides of his mouth. I grip his shoulders and place him back in a sitting position against the glass window. "You need to get out of here. Hide."

"Not without you. Can you walk?" I hold his hand against mine and stare in wide-eyed shock horror, tears pouring down my face as his blood drenches our hands. The gaping wound in his stomach gushes.

"I - I didn't- this wasn't- Dad, I'm sorry," I say, scrambling to put my hands over his wounds and sobbing when I can't hold pressure on them all at once.

"Sage, stop," he says, trying to pull my hands away. "It won't help."

I sob again. "Why? What's going on?" I finally look around his office. The usually pristine space, equipped with leather chairs, bookcases and dark furniture fit for a mafia kingpin, is now in disarray.

Books have been pulled from the shelves, files discarded from their drawers and strewn about like confetti, rips and tears making a home on the upholstery.

It's ransacked.

"W-What were they looking for?"

"Me."

I look around again. He's lying. I know what I heard.

He must see the look in my eye because he says, "Don't. Let this one go, *anima mia*."

There's stumbling behind me that has me struggling and gasping, panicking that we've been found. But finally, Uncle Anton makes his way into the room. From wherever the fuck he's been in the middle of all this. His gray suit is disheveled, the white shirt tugged free and splayed with blood spatter, his fine dark hair running loose over his eyes, and his gun gripped tight in his fists.

He searches the space before his eyes land on us, softening only when he takes us in. "Fuck, Dimitri!" Anton says. He locks eyes with Dad.

Anton quickly joins us, kneeling on my dad's other side.

"Sage, are you hurt?" he asks. I shake my head. I'm so relieved to see him here. Scared out of my mind and way out of my depth, I can't handle this alone.

"Christ, Dimitri," Anton gasps, his gaze roaming the litany of Dad's injuries.

"I know, brother," Dad says, letting out a breath rattled with blood.

"They were-"

"I know," Dad says, giving Uncle Anton a hard look.

"Shit," Anton says, his nostrils flaring in a rare outburst of anger. "How did they even get through the fucking gates?!"

I avert my eyes and try not to look guilty and small. Sweat forms on my brow, coating my neck as the world around me suddenly goes very black. The edges of my dread close in on me.

"I don't know, Anton," Dad says. He closes his eyes, leaning his head back against the window. I can see his body fading, his skin paling. His mind is still there but working to keep up with us. I can see it behind his eyes, the desire to give up.

"Dimitri, if-"

"Just hold my hand, brother..." He gives my uncle a pleading look. "I don't have long."

"What?! Dad-"

"Ssh, it's alright," Dad coos, trying to comfort me.

We fall into stunned silence. Anton is no longer arguing, and I'm no longer pressing my hands against his wounds. Instead, I'm afraid to touch him, like my poison will only open him further. Bleed him out quicker.

"I love you, *anima mia*. I'm so proud of you. I always have been."

"Dad, just hold on a bit longer, you don't need to-" I choke on a sob.

When I imagined how I would kill someone...

I cannot - *cannot* - have done this. I'm only twenty-two years old. I'm meant to be living carefree and thinking about my future. I'm not meant to be responsible for letting my dad's murderer onto the property. I'm not supposed to be the reason anyone dies.

He opens his arms for me. "Sage, come here."

I dive into his arms without thought, glad for the welcome, and crush my arms around him as he holds me close too.

Anton grips Dad's hand in his. "I've got you. And her."

Dad nods once, gratefully, at my uncle. His mouth opens as if to say something else, but instead he takes his final breath.

I feel it as it pushes out of his lungs. I watch as his eyes glaze over. As he goes very, very still. I watch him die.

I want to scream, but my throat constricts. Freezes. Dries out in panic. Those men... they came here and murdered my dad. When I imagined how I would kill someone, I didn't imagine that it would be my own father I'd kill.

Now I have a secret that will have to go with me to my grave. That is, if I ever learn to live with myself.

I knew who those men were.

I let them inside the gates on purpose.

One

SAGE

I wake with a start, water splashing over my face. Sputtering to clear my throat, I jolt upright and find myself blinded by the sun from where I'm strewn about in the garden bed. With a frown, I catch my breath and wipe the water from my eyes before pulling my little white dress to cover my thighs.

The sky is clear over the grounds of our country-mansion estate. Birds chirp and fly happily in the periphery over the manicured lawns and cobblestone pathways that lead around the house. Vines crawl over the sandstone exterior, all the way up to the window that I clearly fell from when trying to sneak back in last night, leaving me passed out in the fucking plants with - *yep* - a garden hose pointed at my face.

The sun gets blocked by a shadow and a chuckle.

"Rise and shine."

The chuckle belongs to Freddie, the shadow to Nicholas. Who is standing over me with his corded arms folded and a frown on his perfect face while Freddie smothers a laugh in the background. Freddie's the fucker holding the hose.

"Freddie. Jesus, that was cold," I say. I groan as I sit up, pulling leaves from my hair and wiping dirt from my forearms.

Nicholas looks away and shakes his head. "The garden bed, Sage? Really?" He turns his surly brown eyes onto me, raising a brow as if he's expecting me to answer.

I won't.

"Your uncle is coming up the drive, *bella signorina,* best straighten up," Freddie says, dropping the hose and smacking his hands together to rid the dirt covering them. With an exaggerated glare, Nicholas picks up the hose and reels it back together to secure in its rightful place.

The second that I stretch my arms and stand, my CGM monitor starts beeping like crazy. I'm suddenly lightheaded, and my feet get stuck to the planter beds as I stumble and trip over my own feet.

Nic just manages to reach out and catch me in his arms before I hit dirt. I clutch onto his straining biceps and grimace when I turn my head up to him. Now I know I've really fucked up, because in this state, I'm not sure I *can* make it back inside.

If it's even possible, Nic's frown gets deeper before his eyes dart down to the monitor. He rights me and pulls me to him, scanning over the reading on the device's receiver.

"Less than fifty?! Sage, for the love of God." He doesn't release my arm. "That's nearly hypoglycemic. Where's your fucking insulin?"

Shit, fifty? No wonder I feel like I'm about to die. "In the kitchen."

Nicholas wipes at his forehead, turning a nervous look over his shoulder as the big iron gates to the estate open, signaling my uncle's impending arrival. "Carry her inside, Freddie, and give her a fucking candy before she kills herself."

"I can do it," I say, attempting to pull myself free from his grip but instead swaying on my heels.

Nicholas doesn't spare me another look as Freddie comes froward, his eyes downcast as he slings an arm around my waist and puts mine around his shoulders. Freddie lifts me and carries me bridal style into the house, moving slowly at first but speeding up when the inevitable sound of tires crunching over gravel gets closer.

"What were you thinking, *bella*," Freddie says.

After carrying me up the front porch stairs - not to be underestimated, since Freddie is tall, lean and built like a twig - he deposits me on the kitchen counter and goes for the cupboards.

From this angle, I can see Nic standing at attention in the driveway through the golden oak bow windows.

I can also see my uncle's limo and ridiculous entourage approaching, the gates closing securely behind his obnoxious posse of vehicles. There was a time, not long ago, when I would be here with my face pressed up against those windows waiting for my father to come home. Just to see him push out of the swarm of people and swoop me into a hug.

I'm a daddy's girl. Well...

I *was* a daddy's girl.

The reminder sears my heart and I drop my eyes, unable to take it. I was the daughter of one of the biggest crime bosses in the city. The name Dimitri DeMarco sent fear through the blood of the bravest of men. One look from him could turn you to stone.

Eight months later, it's like they don't even remember my father's name as they scramble to accommodate my uncle, who took on the leadership role after my father died.

"Eat this," Freddie says. He hands me my insulin pen and a dinosaur-shaped candy, which I munch on gratefully while I pull needles and packs from their wrappers. "You can't let your blood sugar levels get that low."

"I'm very well aware of the requirements, Freddie. I have been diabetic for twelve years now."

His sympathetic eyes eat into mine and nearly suffocate me. I *want* to feel alone since my father's death. I want to wallow in the pain and feel like there's nobody left in the world to look out for me. That's not true though. All of my father's men have rallied around me like the brothers they've always been.

All except one. Yeah, he could never be like a brother.

"You all need to stop mother-henning."

"I'm following orders, Nic's the hen," Freddie says, feigning his outrage.

"So you're not caring for me out of the love of your heart, Freddie? It's just orders?"

His flirty smile returns instantly. "Ahh, *bella,* these are orders I would gladly follow to the ends of the earth."

His genuine smile and kind words threaten tears from me as I deliver the dose to my stomach, the sting of the needle an oddity I don't even feel as I munch down on a candy snake.

I feel small as I curl my hands under my thighs and contemplate my place in the world. I have no idea who I am or where I belong. Daughter of Dimitri DeMarco? I'm not sure that ever defined who I am. Now? Well... I'm just a little lost.

Anton and Nic finally make their way through the house, coming up the porch stairs into the kitchen's side door through the same route Freddie and I followed.

"Pissed off is the understatement of the century, Nic," Anton says, barreling straight to the fridge.

"Can't make them do any more, boss," Nic replies, hands behind his back like a sentry. He's the only asshole that takes this work so seriously.

Nic used to be my father's third, but now he's Anton's second. Whatever it is they do, he's more dedicated than he surely needs to be. He's married to this job. This stupid lifestyle.

He's all sharp stares and muscles. Surly scowls.

It's hard not to notice him. Especially when he insists on walking around in those tight black shirts that sculpt to him like he's wet all. The. Time. The trousers that cling to him like a second skin. He's always standing up so straight, pulling his hands tight behind his back or folding them over his chest, muscles flexing and bulging with every slight movement. He's got that perfectly messy light brown hair that melts into my hands when I tug on it. The tense jaw with just a bit of stubble.

He's the only one that was brought on after I matured, and so I've never seen him as the brother I see in the others. He's always been a man to me. I smirk at the thought.

Nic and I have a secret. He hates it when I can't be as subtle as he is.

"You know, Anton, there's one way to get the Rushkoffs to hear you out," Freddie shrugs, appearing fully in Anton's face when the fridge door shuts. Nicholas shifts almost imperceptibly to glare at him.

Anton gives Freddie a tired look. "Shut *up,* Freddie. Not gonna happen."

"What's not gonna happen?" I ask.

"Nothing," Anton and Nic snap in unison.

My brows rise to my forehead before my shoulders slump in a clear sulk, my long dark hair - that probably still has leaves in it - falling out of its half-tie and down my back. "I never get to know anything."

"Don't sass me today," Anton says. "Don't think I didn't catch your escapade in the garden."

Freddie cringes and Nic tenses.

"Shit," Freddie laughs. Anton spares him a quick disapproving scowl before turning that attention back my way.

"You snuck out again," Uncle Anton says.

"I'm not sorry." I lift my chin and fold my arms for emphasis.

He rubs at his forehead like I'm very difficult indeed. I probably am. I can't bring myself to care, though. I can't bring myself to be or feel much of anything anymore.

"Why? Why, Sage?" Anton says, blowing out an exasperated breath. "You know the rules. Just take someone with you. I've never restricted where you can go."

"No, just that I'm not allowed to do anything alone." And that there is the catalyst. Being a crime boss' daughter is fraught with danger. Danger I know all too well. So I've never left this property alone. Never been to school. Never had friends. Never been to a party. Never been drunk. Never had more than a steady secret fuck. I'm twenty-two, looking at a future spent trapped in this house, without freedom and life continuing on *exactly* the way it is right now.

"Jesus, Sage. This was your father's rule too, you know. I'm just trying... trying to follow in his footsteps."

Anton lets out a heavy sigh. I admit, I start to feel bad. Anton has always been good to me. He's been a rock to me, all of them have. But rational thinking doesn't date a broken heart.

The mood in the room grows heavy.

"You're doing a great job, Anton," Freddie says, throwing me a hard look like I should say the same. Even though I want to - I don't actually *want* to be an asshole - my throat clogs and the words won't force themselves out.

I know I'm in the wrong. I do. Sulking for things that most people take for granted while I sit up here in this mansion estate with all its gauzy curtains and soft, expensive furnishings. I've never wanted for anything. Except everything I can never have.

I roll my eyes defensively, even though I want to apologize. To be good and offer comfort to someone else. I know as much as my heart hurts right now; theirs does too.

Anton's jaw ticks while Freddie gives me a disappointed look. I'm on the receiving end of too many of those, so sadly it's lost its sting.

"Don't sneak out again," Anton says. "It's far too fucking dangerous. Especially with what happened to Dimitri."

Anton stalks away, his Italian leather shoes stomping on the tiles as he returns to the foyer and heads upstairs with Freddie close on his heels.

When I turn over my shoulder, Nic is shaking his head at me. He gives me a rough look as he skates past me to follow them.

I slip a candy snake between my lips and suck hard. Hollowing out my cheeks and puckering my lips. Nic stops in his tracks to watch me, following the motion with a frown. He watches the candy disappear between my lips, tongue darting out to lick the remnants. When he realizes what I'm doing, his hungry eyes snap back to mine. I give him a devilish smile.

"Wanna lick, Nic?"

"That was immature," he says.

"The candy?"

He relaxes his shoulders, pointing in the direction that Freddie and Anton went. "The scene with your uncle."

"Ugh," I groan, pushing my dark hair over my shoulder and sliding off the counter to face him. "There wasn't a scene."

He grips my shoulders, forcing me left and right as he chases the eye contact I'm reverently avoiding. His lips are thin when our eyes finally meet. "You know you're not the only one hurting. I know you know that."

I gulp and paste an annoyed look on my face, but we both know it isn't sincere.

"Right," he says, removing his hands from my shoulders. "So, what are you doing?"

"I don't know," I admit on a whisper.

"Fucking figure it out," he says. He shakes his head at me and then sighs too, following my uncle upstairs. Most people seem to sigh or expel some sort of breath after dealing with me lately. Wonder what that says about me.

"I would if I could," I say, but he's well out of earshot and can't hear me now. How am I supposed to figure myself out now? I couldn't do it before. It certainly isn't going to happen now.

Not with less freedom and more security than before. None of the old labels seem to fit right anymore. As if they ever did.

Sage DeMarco - mafia princess?

Sage DeMarco - giant pain in everyone's ass?

Immature? Lonely? Lost?

Killed her father?

Or? Maybe just?... Terrifyingly and maddeningly in love with Nicholas Prince and denying it to the very core?

Yeah, that should do it.

NICHOLAS

By the time I reach Anton's office, he and Freddie are already getting comfortable. The massive space which used to belong to Dimitri, and still does in most everyone's mind, is decorated with oversized dark oak furniture, maroon leather chairs and bookshelves lining the walls. A desk sits along the back wall with two chairs in front of it. There's a bar on the left of the room and a lounge on the right.

It screams old money.

It screams *Dimitri*. Anton hasn't changed a thing about it since he died, and I think he probably should've. So he wasn't making himself feel like an intruder just by sitting in his big brother's chair.

I close the double doors behind me.

Anton is already staring out the big window that overlooks the back of the estate, worrying his lip as he's often known to do these days. My frown from my conversation with Sage is still firmly on my face when I chance a look over to Freddie, who just smirks at me. Smirks at me like he knows secrets.

I narrow my eyes, frowning harder. I like Freddie. No, I *love* Freddie. For all intents and purposes, in this life, he is my brother. But if he knows what he thinks he does, then he'd better shut the fuck up and keep it to himself.

"She sulking?" Anton says, drawing my attention back to him.

"Isn't she always?" I scrub at my jaw. Heading straight for the bar, I pour a shot that I sink back in one go. The alcohol burns its way down my throat and I relish the warmth it leaves behind.

"Harsh," Freddie says.

I look over my shoulder to see him wince. My shoulders drop before I sink back another shot. "I know."

The thing is, I can't help it. She works me up something shocking. Like she's slithered in under my skin and I can't fucking get her out. Being here around her all the time... Frankly, it's a fucking miracle that I don't spontaneously combust.

Freddie and the others don't see this side of her. They knew her when she was little. Watched her grow. But I came into this house when she was seventeen and all breasts and long dark hair and sultry green eyes. And damn if I didn't want to tear my brain out for the thoughts I had before she turned eighteen.

The legal age of consent here is seventeen. Yeah... knowing that was the only way to make myself feel less disgusting. Spoiler: it didn't work.

But now, she's twenty-two. Her tits have gotten perkier, heavier. Legs longer and more tan. Green eyes less innocent and more cutting. Lips fuller. Mouth... *smarter.* Hands wandering to places they shouldn't be. I can barely even look at her after I've...

Christ.

I've defiled the DeMarco daughter more ways than one in more places than one, and I'm sure if Dimitri had ever known he would've cut my cock off first and my head second.

That deserves another shot.

The others smile at her the way a father smiles at a toddler. Like she's giggling. But to me, her laugh isn't a giggle. It's slow torture. Sultry and smooth. Like a siren song.

Freddie clears his throat in warning before Anton can notice I'm in the clouds and my dick is half-hard. I manage to find my head, hint: it was in my ass. I promptly pull it out of there and put on my best game face.

"This isn't going well, is it?" Anton says, still worrying his lip.

"No," I say.

"Fuck," Anton says. He finally turns away from the window and slumps into the chair next to Freddie. "The Rushkoffs have gone eerily silent. I don't like it."

"What happened to the peace deal they had with Dimitri?" Freddie finally stops looking casual and starts paying attention.

"I thought they were open to re-negotiating a peace deal?" I ask.

"Yes. With Dimitri." Anton shakes his head. "Their lack of response is concerning."

The room goes silent as Anton leans forward, resting his forearms against his thighs and hanging his head between them.

"You think they've figured out our position?" I ask in a grave voice.

Anton looks up at me and quirks a brow. It's answer enough, but he follows up anyway. "We're weak right now. I'm pretty sure that's obvious. Our boundaries are being pushed."

"You think it's the Rushkoffs that're pushing them?" Freddie's brows rise to his head.

"Yes," Anton nods. "Maybe... I don't know." Anton jumps upright, beginning to pace. "The treaty has always been a sore point. Only held in place by the fact they think they can't take us."

"And now they think they can?" Freddie goes back to looking casual. Of course, he'd be in for a fight. It's literally his job in this machine. To fight.

"If there was a war right now, I don't know that we'd win it," Anton admits.

Freddie bites his knuckles and then looks to me. He's frustrated. Understandably in his position.

Our little slice of crime county, Bradford, VA, has always been divided in half right down the center. The DeMarco Family control and run the west side, with the open air and country landscape plus the western half of

Bradford City. While the Rushkoff's Russian Bratva control the east side, with its secluded forests, the lake and the east half of Bradford City.

A carefully constructed negotiation of peace to make sure that while we play nice, the Rushkoffs and the DeMarcos *never* have to cross paths.

The balance of power has always been in our favor. Dimitri DeMarco could've crushed the Rushkoffs with just his little toe. So what would they do if they knew that right now they could probably crush us?

"You know... there is another way," Freddie says, though to his credit he does cringe.

Anton's face turns to ice as my jaw clenches.

"Don't," is Anton's one warning.

"I'm just saying... Dimitri-"

"Would've *never* given them what it is they're asking for," I say through clenched teeth.

"But that document-"

"Is fucked," I say.

Freddie bats a hand at us. "It's probably why they won't return your calls."

Anton slams his fist down on the table, rattling the glassware. "I don't care what some fucking document says, Dimitri DeMarco never would've traded his daughter in marriage. Especially to a *Rushkoff.* Not even to avoid a fucking war."

The room falls into silence for a moment.

"Will they start one? Over this?" Freddie asks with caution.

Anton doesn't have an answer for that. I can see it in the hard set of his jaw. In the way he glares at Freddie before turning away and staring out the window.

Freddie takes the hint and stands up to leave.

Not because he's afraid, but because everyone here is aware of their triggers. As trained killers, we have to be. Sage might think Freddie is a big sweetie, but he's actually the best hitter we've got. The places his temper goes, the things he can do to people... I shiver. So Freddie wisely leaves the room before either his or Anton's nature takes over.

But of course, he has to get in that one last dig, grabbing my elbow and turning me to him. "I think she at least has a right to fucking know." Freddie slams the door behind him.

I make my way back to the bar and pour a scotch on ice. One for me. Another for Anton. I can see his posture has tensed from where he's standing. Hands clasped behind his back like they might snap.

"You hear that?" I ask as I join him at the window, handing over his glass.

"Hard not to. Freddie isn't discreet." We stand in comfortable silence for a moment. "You think he's right?"

"That Sage has a right to know?" I blow out a breath.

I know the answer. Of course, she has a right to know that upon her father's death, he wanted her handed off in marriage to our enemy.

But I want to tell Anton no. That we should hide this from her. My nature, however, does take over. Because the thought of it, that Sage might marry some fuckwit Rushkoff, makes my blood boil.

Even though she's not mine. As much as I wish she was.

And I do wish.

The glass in my hand forms a crack that brings my attention back to the room where Anton is looking at me with a quietly concerned look. I put the glass down on the windowsill.

"No," I say, getting the words out as little more than a growl. "She doesn't need to know."

Anton nods, but he looks like he's having second thoughts. I'd beat them out of his head if I could. I won't sit around while someone takes her. She'd never fall in love with a fucking *Rushkoff,* but I sure as hell won't watch her carted off to a loveless marriage either. That's probably worse.

My heart sinks.

"She's twenty-two. She's not a kid," Anton whispers.

"I know," I say, more calmly than I feel. Believe me. She's all woman.

"What if Freddie's right? What if she should be allowed to make this decision for herself?" Anton looks at me. Before I was his second, I was also his closest confidant. He said things to me he'd never dare to voice in front of Dimitri. Even though he's the boss now, that dynamic hasn't changed.

"You know what she'd fucking pick, Anton," I say. "For the drama, martyring, freedom, I don't fucking know. But if she knew, you know what she'd say."

Anton's fists clench. "Yeah. I know."

"You want her to do that? You want to watch that happen?"

He shakes his head. "No."

"We're not even *at* war. Not yet, anyway." I bite my bottom lip into my mouth, drawing blood. "She doesn't need to know."

Anton blinks once before he narrows his eyes. "I disagree." My heart stops, freezes over and snaps in two. A thousand emotions run through me in the time it takes for Anton to finish his sentence. "But for now, I'll take your advice. She doesn't need to know."

I take a breath but he pins me with a hard look which lets me know, on this issue, I'm later in for a fight.

"*For now,*" he repeats.

Three

SAGE

That night, I have a nightmare. Mask-covered faces pull up at the gates and I let them inside. In the dream, my smile is sinister. I take their hands and walk them right up to my father in his office.

When Dad turns and sees me with them, his face registers with shock before a gaping hole opens in his chest. His hand clutches his white shirt, washing with blood, and then he's falling to the floor to die. All the while screaming at me, 'Why did you let them inside the gates, Sage?! Why?'

Believe me, Dad, I ask myself the same question every day.

I shoot upright, clutching at my own chest as if Dad's wounds mar my skin too.

I wake with wet eyes, my gasps harsh but quiet enough that no one else will hear. I re-tighten the bun in my hair and pull my legs up to my chest to wrap my arms around them. My cheek presses against my knee as I stare out the window to calm my choppy breathing.

The early morning sun is already streaming in. I sleep with the curtains open now, so that I don't have to lie in the dark. But no one would ever know when the nightmares or the emotions become too much. When I cry, I cry silently. You'll never hear me scream.

Not even when my father was dying did I scream.

Resigning myself to another reluctant early start, I get ready for the day. Showering, washing my face, and pulling on casual house wear as I tame my dark hair into a high ponytail.

The others are always up at stupid hours, so it's not a surprise that the kitchen is dirtied by the time I get down there. I take my enzyme pill and grab a coffee with some dry toast from the kitchen before heading out to the back porch to eat with the sunrise.

Freddie is already there when I take my seat at the swirling iron table overlooking the expanse of gardens at the back of the estate.

I slip into the seat beside him. Three places are set, with three mugs of coffee still steaming, but Freddie is alone. Obliviously reading his paper. As if reading a physical paper isn't the weirdest fucking thing ever. "Morning," I say.

"Ah, there she is," Freddie says, dropping his paper to greet me. "Good morning, *bella.*"

My lips tip up and I roll my eyes as he fluffs the paper back up to read. It's far too early in the morning for his charm, anyway.

"What's the lo-down Freddie? You eating three breakfasts? Or have the other two abandoned you to their bickering again?" I spread a generous helping of butter onto the dry toast, which Freddie watches, but wisely doesn't comment on.

In fact, Freddie doesn't get to say anything. I get my answer only seconds later, without him even needing to speak a word.

"No way! You've not cooled down nearly enough to be going back there!" I frown when I hear Uncle Anton's voice from somewhere far away. I turn in time to catch Freddie clench his jaw. He doesn't speak, but his Adam's apple bobs as he focuses on his paper. I take a bite out of my flavorless toast and narrow my eyes on him.

"I've never disagreed with you before, Anton, but this. Is. Fucked!" Nicholas's voice.

I rise my brows to Freddie and while he acknowledges me this time, he just shakes his head. Wherever they are, I can't quite tell. But they've raised their voices enough that I can hear them clear as day.

It's no secret that Nic and Anton's bickering is at record level highs. But once again, whatever it's about, it's not something I get the privilege of knowing.

"Fortunately then, Nicholas, you're not the one in charge," Anton says, and I can almost picture him squaring his shoulders.

"You're pulling rank on me?"

I don't need to see it to know Anton's whole body slumps as he delivers the next line. I can hear it in his voice when he says, "Don't make me do this, Nic."

"You can't seriously be thinking this is a good idea?!"

"I don't have a choice, Nic," Anton says. "What if Dimitri-"

"Dimitri never would've wanted this!"

My father's name spoken aloud brings the dream slamming to the forefront of my mind. Blood on my hands. His? Mine? Was I bleeding that night? There *is* a scar on my temple that blends into my hairline. Though it's the smallest and least curious of all the disfigurements I have.

I slip up, dropping my cup onto the table with a rattle.

"Freddie-" I whisper.

"Ssh, *bella signorina,*" he says. "They're coming back."

That, at least, invites my frown back. How does Freddie do that? I swear he can hear their footsteps. I narrow my eyes and stick out my tongue in concentration as I, too, try to hone my ears on shuffling footsteps.

Freddie chuckles as I fold my arms and slump into my chair just as Anton and Nic round the corner.

Nic's eyes widen when he sees me.

"Sage, how did you sleep?" Anton asks.

"Good bu-" They hardly wait for an answer before settling back into their places at the table. Glares are exchanged, glasses are clinked about, and cutlery clangs as they engage in their epic stare down, smiling warmly at me each time one of them meets my eye.

I bite again into the toast, the crunch a violent sound that cuts into the tension.

"So," I lick my lips, "what was all that about?"

Anton's careful smile slips, but he doesn't look at Nicholas, who may as well be boring a drill into the side of my uncle's head with his stare.

"Nothing to worry about." Anton's smile is tight as she shoots another look at Nicholas.

It becomes painfully obvious.

They're hiding something from me.

Probably not something I *don't* need to know, wouldn't understand, shouldn't know. No... now it seems like something I should know. And they're hiding it from me.

I doubt anyone can see my skin heat, but it does. So much that it burns.

When Freddie thinks they're not looking, he quirks a challenging brow at me. Almost like he knows what I'm thinking and is goading me into doing something about it.

This, I can't have.

"Somebody spill," I demand.

"There's nothing to spill," Anton says. The fact that he doesn't even pretend to be shocked is a dead giveaway. He also can't look at me as he says it and that's the other big, fat red flag that pegs him as a liar.

Without saying another word, I shoot upright, my chair scraping as I stride through the door and towards the front of the house. Classic Sage DeMarco tantrum signs. Easily recognizable. I do it a lot. It's really the best way to get anything done.

"Oh, hell no!" Then there's the distinct sound of another chair being kicked away and big boots pounding in pursuit of me.

I'm halfway up the hall, arms swinging wildly as I power walk to the front door when Nic catches up to me, slamming his hand across me and into the wall to cage me in.

"Where the hell do you think you're going?"

"Out," I deadpan, giving him a challenging stare.

"Great," Nic deadpans right back, gritting his teeth. "Where we going?"

I push his hands off the wall and glare daggers at him, advancing on him so he has to take steps back from me as I point my finger at him. "You're not coming! I'm. Going. Alone."

He doesn't even miss a step on the checkered tiles as he backs away from my attack, avoiding the hall tables and sculptures without looking. Nic smiles a cruel smile. "Like hell."

I clench my fists. "You can't stop me."

I charge towards the front door, determined and not looking back. But he's there again and my body is pulled backward when he grabs my wrist and tugs me until I slam wide-eyed into his chest.

The contact presses me right up against his strong, muscled stomach. He holds me like a captive, watching my breath hitch when the electricity of him sends a shock straight down between my thighs.

I'm losing control. I have to put my game face back on *quickly.*

"Actually I can," Nic says. "It was your father's rule and now it's your uncle's. No going anywhere. Without. A. Guard."

"Fuck," I say, struggling to free my wrist from where he adjusts his grip to hold me. "How paranoid are you? We're not *that* important. And we're *not* on the verge of a mafia war either."

He narrows his eyes at me.

"Unless there's something you're not telling me?" I say, raising my brows in challenge.

He looks like he could kill me with that stare. But I stare right back. He takes one step toward me, then two. I'm not so much walking backward as I am *pushed* by the titan grip he has on my wrist. He doesn't stop until he's got me backed against the wall. His hands ball into fists and press softly, but with so much violence, into the wall beside my head.

I realize he's about to defile me against this crisp white wall with its gold trimmings.

Fuck yes.

He leans down to look me in the eye. "You go, I go."

I purse my lips, ready to refute. "There are plenty of ways to get past you."

He laughs a cruel laugh. "You may have gotten us once or twice, but I'll give you one last warning to fucking quit it-"

"Or. What?"

My reply stuns him. I can see it in the tiny crease that forms between his eyes. It smooths out as he leans further into my face, looking into my eyes with murder.

"Or...." I let the word draw out on the wind as I push forward until my lips meet his ear. "You'll sneak into my bed again?" I run my hand up his chest, feeling the muscles tense and flex underneath my hold like they're not sure whether to fight me or melt for me. "Or is the threat that you won't?"

I feel his growl in my ear before he grabs my hip and presses me fully back against the wall. This time with his hard body pressing into every inch of mine. He huffs and shakes his head. "You just can't help but bait me, can you?"

"Well, *your* bait is pressing into my leg."

Instead of pulling away, he rolls his hips forward, pressing his erection harder against my thigh. I do my best to keep my hard eyes trained on him, but they shutter as he rolls his hips again. He still looks like murder when his fingers begin inching up my thigh, teasing the skin and pulling my loose lounge shorts up as he goes. "This is what you wanted, isn't it? My hands on you again?"

"Yes," I breathe with an embarrassing air. God dammit, this is what always happens. Every time Nic gets his hands on me. Every time we get a little taste. Every time we turn rivalry into fucking.

I'll feel shameful about my needy wantonness later.

"If I put my hand on your little cunt right now, will you be wet for me?"

My voice is weak as I press my head back into the wall. "Try it and see."

His hand moves torturously slowly up my thigh until he finds the spot where my cotton underwear begins. His index finger slips up the edge and skirts back and forth.

"Look at me, Sage," he says. "If this is what you want, look at me."

I look right at him. His dark brown eyes have grown black and hungry. Every time we're together like this, I see this same change in him. When the mask slips off his face. The strong, stoic, protector face falls away and all that's left is an animal uncaged.

This part, I love.

His index and middle fingers turn into my panties, and he rubs the back of them against me. I know when he feels it. I can feel how easily his fingers slide back and forth across me. I can hear the wet trudge as he spreads me.

"Fuck," he breathes out, dropping his head to my shoulder.

He always stops looking at me at this point too.

In the foreplay, before he touches me, it's all 'eyes on me', 'look at me when I touch you'. But as soon as we get too close, as soon as he actually does touch me, he closes his eyes.

This part, I hate.

His fingers brush my clit, and I let out a soft sigh. He presses his mouth to my neck and begins nibbling on the skin there, sending me into overdrive. As his fingers move back and forth through my folds, brushing against my clit, his hips press harder into me. Giving me an impressive preview. If I look down, I can see him soaking his own pants with pre-cum.

The sight of perfectly controlled Nicholas Prince becoming unhinged is what always does it for me. "Oh shit, Nic," I pant. The visual alone could take me.

Nic caging me against the wall. One hand high above, steadying himself. The other deep in my panties rubbing back and forth. His hips pressing into me in his dress pants. The sight of his veined wrist as it pulses with every movement against my pussy.

Especially that corded tendon when it flexes as he pauses to slip a finger inside me.

I open my mouth to cry out, only to find his mouth there too, taking me in a brutal kiss that's meant to silence me. I kiss back for as long as I can. I'm not sure whether I'm trying to climb the wall or climb him, but my legs are floundering and I'm grabbing onto any object that will hold me upright.

My leg ends up hitched up around his thigh, my fingers grabbing at his ass through his dress pants.

"That's it, just like that," he whispers, and I let out little moans directly into his ear.

He pauses only a moment to add a second finger that slips inside easily, his thumb coming to press against my clit while his hips roll into me. Like the action is involuntary as he grinds himself on me.

I know he can feel it, how I tighten around him when I'm about to come, because his other hand flies from the wall and closes over my mouth just as I scream and convulse in pleasure.

I whimper against his hand as I calm down, his fingers continuing to draw gentle circles over me. He doesn't stop, even as I stop convulsing around him. He just keeps stroking, lightly curling his fingers inside me.

When I come down from my high, I'm left slumping against the wall.

Nic doesn't open his eyes. Even as his fingers come out of my pussy, leaving behind a sticky trail on my thighs like my dripping cunt wants to hang onto him as much as my heart does.

Still burying his face in my neck, he lifts his fingers to my mouth. "Suck."

He doesn't wait for me to reply, just slips them inside my mouth for me to gulp away my arousal. I kiss him clean, licking away the evidence of what he's done to me for him.

He rights my clothes for me. When he does open his eyes, he looks torn and conflicted. As usual, he takes an immediate step back.

This part, I hate too.

He runs a hand over his jaw but pulls it away like it stings. His nostrils flare and I know it's because he can smell me on him. It seems unspoken that I'm not going anywhere now. He's bested me with an orgasm.

Fuck, I'm pathetic.

He turns and starts walking away. Like every other time, though, I know he won't be able to resist sneaking a look back at me. He stops walking and cranes his head, looking over his shoulder and taking one last sweep of me from head to toe, where I'm sated and panting against the wall.

When he does this, he looks lustful and full of shame. Shame because he knows even though it's wrong, he's going to do it again anyway.

That part, I *fucking* love.

Four

SAGE

*P*redictably, Nicholas is avoiding me.

Ever since our... *interaction,* he's hidden himself away. From me, at least. That's usual, to be expected and, in my opinion, fucking childish. When he's finally brave enough to be in the same room as me again, he'll avoid looking me in the eye for a while.

He'll be back, though. He always is.

Another kind of tension fills the house. Whatever Anton and Nic were fighting about hasn't resolved. Whenever Nic's not running from me, he's curling his lip at Anton or trying to corner him for another argument.

Anton, while he's not been the same since Dad, seems exhausted to a new level. Especially every time he gets cornered by Nicholas.

And Freddie. Well, he keeps shooting me meaningful looks like he's trying to get me to figure out something that I'm missing. Whatever it is, it's clear now that these pussy motherfuckers aren't just going to come out and say it. No, I'm being kept very much in the dark on this one.

Which I know is *not* where I should be.

Sweaty and tense after my workout in the home gym, I head for the kitchen. My headphones slide down to rest at my neck when I pat my forehead with my gym towel.

The closer I get to the kitchen, the louder the muffled whisper of voices gets.

Dropping the towel and allowing the sweat to drip down my temple instead, I roll my eyes and shove the door open with an annoyed bang.

Anton and Nic's wide eyes swing over to me, mouths half-open like I've petrified them.

"Oh, for fuck's sake!" I throw my hands in the air. "Not this shit again, the both of you." I jab a finger at them as I come further into the kitchen.

They both pause to watch me.

I pull open the fridge and grab a bottle of water, uncapping it while I glare at them where they stand, still tense and silent.

They're waiting for me to leave. Fuckers.

When I take a big sip, a droplet slips over the edge of the bottle and slides down my bottom lip. Nic's eyes laser to the motion. I hide my smirk and do my best to refocus on the issue at hand. "Seriously? What's with the two of you? It's like you need marriage counseling."

Anton's jaw hardens when he turns back on Nic. He rests his tired hands on the countertop, leaning over like it's the only thing holding up his entire weight.

Nic tears his gaze from my lips. He takes a quick look at Anton and then rolls his eyes before turning his back on me like that will be enough to hide his shame. "It's nothing to do with you, Sage. Just leave it."

Anton stands up straight and folds his arms, clearing his throat. Nic shoots him a look so vile I have to remind myself which one of them is actually in charge. "Sage, why don't you jus-"

"No!" I stomp my foot. "I never get to know anything! Whatever you're hiding, just out with it!"

Anton sighs. "Sage, just let us sort it out."

"No, Uncle Anton, that's not good enough this time." I cross my arms. "You're clogging up the whole house with your tension. I demand to know what's going on."

"Sage-"

My monitor howls. Conveniently saving them by the diabetes. I check the levels and, in a huff, hoist myself onto the cupboards to reach the top shelf where the sugar candies are.

I really don't want to let them see me needing another candy hit so soon after the last one, but I'm not budging. My hands fumble for the handles. "I'm twenty-two, you know. It's not like I'm a little girl. There's a lot that I can handle."

"It's not that we think you can't hand-"

"I'm sick of being treated like a baby!" I climb down and shove a handful of candies in my mouth to chew violently. With my mouth full, I continue on a mumble. "Seh ooh of you, awways babying ee." I chew fast and barely swallow. "I'm so sick of you-"

Nic slams his fist on the counter. "You aren't a baby, but you are insolent!"

"You're not fucking in charge of me!" I rush at him until we're chest to chest, nostrils flaring. My chest rises and falls with my temper, and Nic's eyes glaze over with hatred. Or need. I can't be sure. They do actually look quite similar.

I take a deep breath in through my nostrils, straightening as I clench my fists. In my periphery, I see Anton throw his head back. Everyone can see what's coming. I've got a tantrum brewing.

I'm just about to open my mouth to let out my telltale tantrum scream when Nic one-ups me. "Go to your room, Sage. If you need to know, we'll tell you."

I widen my eyes. This motherfucker did not just tell me to *go to my room.* I throw my head back, let out a banshee scream and start stomping up the stairs, making as much noise as possible.

When I get to my room - *it's where I was going anyway!* - I slam the doors twice for good measure.

***

The tantrum serves as ample distraction.

It fell under the radar, like most truths about me that my family cannot see. One day I grew up, and they didn't notice. Instead of throwing tantrums like a child in need of an emotional outlet, I threw them as a distraction. I became manipulative.

Unfortunately, it was the only way to get things done.

When I'm finished stomping up the stairs and slamming the door, I turn on my angry boy band music and secure the lock. I meant every word I said to them. I've not been a child for a long time, but they can't seem to see beyond that.

I'm old enough to have sex. To vote. To drink.

To make critical life-changing errors in judgment that get people killed...

I stop myself there before my heart cramps so badly that I won't be able to follow through with my plan.

If they're not gonna tell me what's got their important-mob-boss knickers in a twist, then I'm going to find out.

I'm still in my workout gear, a crop top, sneakers and leggings, which turns out useful. I secure my hair again, brushing any flyaways back into my high ponytail. My CGM monitor looks good too. No nosy beeping.

Heading to the window, I click the buttons that I know reset the sensor. Which gives me a good two and a half seconds to open the window and block the sensor with sticky-tack.

Yeah, I'm that monitored around here. Makes my sneaking off successfully much more impressive.

In a heartbeat, I'm out onto the ledge that runs along the side of the house. It's a tiptoe with my back flat against the wall until I can finally make it to the open roof. As long as I don't look down, I'll be able to make it. After all, it's the middle of the day and this is much harder in the dark.

After what seems like an eternity of tiny steps I reach the low gable roof and can breathe a sigh of relief.

There's not that much further to go now. I'm not sneaking out today. I'm sneaking in.

To Anton's office.

Watching my step and walking carefully along the terracotta, I'm almost there when I see Anton and Freddie exit the house right below me.

Shiiiit.

I drop to my stomach and stay low. I'm just preparing to move again when they stop.

Oh, for fuck's sake.

They stop right in front of me.

Sure, while I'm laying down with this fucking roof digging into my gut, they won't be able to see me. But if I stand up, I'm a goner.

Come on. Come on.

I curse and chant in my head, begging them to move along quicker. But their conversation lingers.

Freddie clearly doesn't like something that Anton says because he lifts his head skyward in a *god help me* way and... yep. He looks right fucking at me!

Freddie's brows rise and then a smile forms on his lips.

He schools his features when Anton looks back at him. They continue to nod seriously for a moment, and then Freddie places his hand on Anton's shoulder and guides him away from the house. He gives me one last look over his shoulder, a challenging rise of his left brow before he continues walking Anton away.

I sit up and practically bolt the rest of the way, nearly slipping as I loosen some of the roofing.

I finally make my way to the office, but this is the tricky part. The office window is usually locked, and it's big. Big enough that there's no ledge to crouch on below, which means I need to hang down from the sill above it.

I haven't spent my time in the gym training for anything specific, but my grip strength doesn't fail me now. I grip the edge of the sill and hang.

There's a lock in the middle of the floor-length windows that works much like the one in my room. When I reach it, I switch from one hand to the other as I reach into my leggings and grab a credit card. I slide the card through the gap, struggling to latch it.

"Fuck," I curse when I nearly slip, needing to grab back on with two hands.

Finally, I slip the card into the latch, and slide the window open. I've got two and half seconds, but I make it, slipping inside and slamming the window shut before the sensor goes off.

I exhale and then stand to look at my surroundings.

I'm inside.

I'm not sure if my time is forever or fleeting, but I don't dawdle. Starting at the filing cabinets, I rip them open in search of papers. I thumb through them one after the other, failing to find anything damning. A litany of paper surrounds, but I leave it.

Next, I'm at the bookcases. Running my hands over the spines and pulling them out recklessly like it'll open a secret tunnel. Even though I know it won't. Be cool if it did, though.

"Sage!!"

Oh fuck.

Fleeting it is.

The roar of anger from my uncle has me bolting across the room to the desk.

"Sage! For the love of God!" It's Anton's voice still, only this time I can hear the heavy thump of footfalls climbing the stairs.

I trip over myself as I rush behind Dad's desk and hit the panic button *just* as there's a slam on the other side of the door. There's always been a panic button here to seal the office in case of emergency.

I just wish Dad had had the time or sense to use it.

I push that gut-wrenching thought away.

There's another two fists banging on the wood of the door, and I know I'm running out of time. Anton's got backup, apparently.

"For fuck's sake, Sage! You know I have an override code! Open the God damn door."

I panic then, running from one end of the room to the other, tearing at my hair, knowing I need to find something but not knowing where it is I should start.

I hear the pin pad outside the office buzz and freeze, my eyes widening.

"Christ, why didn't that work?" Anton belts from the other side of the door.

"They changed the codes after the incident with Dimitri," Freddie calmly says.

I run towards the desk and pull at the drawer-stack but it's locked too. With a code, though. That's okay, I can guess it.

"Then you unlock it!" Anton says.

"Alright..." Freddie says. I don't hear him hurrying to the door. In fact, I've tried two combos in my pin pad before I hear the first beep of his.

"Fuck yes," I whisper as the desk drawer pops open. It's my birthday. Of course, it is. Dad's a boomer.

I pull out the files and start skimming over them just as I hear the ping from outside the door that tells me Freddie has finished entering the override code.

Nothing, discard the paper.

Nothing, discard the paper.

In the event of the death of Dimitri DeMarco... Yep, that sounds like something *...security of the empire...* blah, blah, blah... *peace deals between the two dominant families in the territory...* YES COME ON! *Sage DeMarco is promised in marriage to Victor Rushkoff in a gesture of goodwill for the keeping of peace.*

Bingo.

The door buzzes and Anton and Nic burst into the room, comically fighting each other for first position while Freddie strides in behind them, not a care in the world.

My eyes are wide and frozen, my heart going a hundred miles an hour as I hold the document up in my hands like I'm presenting my heir to my kingdom. Anton and Nic both stop jostling each other long enough to look from me to the document in my hands. Nic visibly pales while Anton hangs his head.

I suck in a deep breath and then I belt, "What the *fuck* is this?!"

Five

SAGE

"Sit down and I'll explain everything."

Anton's voice doesn't crack, but his eyes do, giving away his nervousness.

I glance around the room at the three sets of eyes that watch me like I'm a wild animal. I hold the paper away from my body and they all follow the movement, like the document will detonate at any second.

"Explain everything, and I'll sit down," I counter, raising my brow.

Freddie catches on first. He purses his lips, nods and then taps Nic on the shoulder. "Come now, let's leave them to it."

Nic tears his shoulder back, jaw clenching, as he resists Freddie's pull. He doesn't want to go. He really wants to be here for this. My head tilts in contemplation. Was he against me ever finding out about this at all?

Freddie tugs on Nic's shoulder with more force. Nic gives me a once-over, sparing a scathing glance at the document, which is far too dramatic a look to be directed at an A4, before he squares his shoulders and storms out.

The door clicks closed behind them as Freddie sees himself out as well.

Uncle Anton's posture relaxes. "Come sit down, *anima mia.*"

My father's nickname for me stings, but I do as he says, taking the seat in front of his desk. Instead of stepping behind the desk, Anton takes the seat next to mine.

"I can explain," he starts, lifting his head in a wince.

Christ. He can't be serious.

"Great fucking start, Anton." I roll my eyes and fold back into my chair with a huff, insolently crossing my arms over my chest.

"*Sage*. Language, for the love of God." He rubs at his temples, and in this moment it's hard not to take pity on him. My father's shoes are hefty ones to fill and walk a mile in.

I stare down at the document in my hands, the carefully crafted words scrawled across it in dark black ink. When I lift my head, I notice Anton can barely look at me.

"You weren't going to tell me, were you?"

His eyes shutter. "Eventually, *anima mia*. Eventually..."

I should've been told about this. Really, I'm the only one it concerns. Betrayal stings deep into my blood. They're never going to see me as anything other than delicate. Made of glass. Ready to shatter.

The mutilated skin on my back and stomach says otherwise.

"Then tell me now." It's a command. "Don't leave anything out."

Anton's lip twitches, and he watches me like he sees someone else behind my eyes. To my surprise, he does as I say.

"Shortly after your father passed, this document showed up. His legacy, succession plan... whatever you want to call it."

I nod, urging him to continue.

"It's no secret that the treaty with the Rushkoffs has been flimsy at best. Caging at worst." He thumbs his jaw. "Your father had been working on a renewed peace deal. One that was supposed to be shot to hell when he-"

Anton stops himself, looking at the document in my lap before dragging his eyes back to mine.

"It promises you to Victor Rushkoff upon his death. As a peace treaty," Anton says.

It's then that he finds the courage to look at me, one hand pressed firmly over his jaw and the other nervously spinning his watch. I give him nothing in return. Not until I'm sure there's nothing he's conveniently leaving out.

"Yet I'm still sitting here. With you," I say.

His hands drop against his thighs with a large slap. "You haven't said yes to him."

I bark out a sarcastic laugh. "I don't think this specifies much of a choice." I wave the document in front of me before depositing it on the desk.

Anton's knee bounces. "Victor Rushkoff wants this to go ahead. He's a lunatic, *anima mia*. He's bought you a God damn ring and everything. In his mind, it's concrete," he says.

"Concrete?!" I jump out of my chair. "But what about-"

"Doesn't. Matter." Anton pins me with a look, and I know what he's asking me not to say. The fact he worries about saying it here, even in the privacy of his own office, is alarming.

"Well, he seems serious," I sigh.

Anton blows out a breath and then stands, beginning to pace. His words come out fast, like he has to push them out before his body explodes from holding them inside. "The document showed up out of nowhere a few weeks after your father's passing. It wasn't just sent to me, but to Victor too. He'd never heard of it before that day, and neither had I. I *refuse* to believe your father wrote it, but Victor wants it to stand. He won't take my calls. Now all he ever asks me for is your answer."

"And now I have to give him one?" I sit up, curling my arms across my stomach in a sad self-hug.

"I don't want you to worry about that, Sage," Anton says.

"Be straight with me here, at least. This could be my future we're talking about!"

Anton's eyes shutter but eventually he nods and continues. "War is an unspoken threat, but a likely one. Without Dimitri..."

"We can't take them," I finish.

"None of that matters," Anton says, dropping to kneel in front of me and clasping both my hands in his. "If it's war Victor wants, then he can have one."

"Comforting," I say, rolling my eyes. "This is a lot."

"I'm sorry you had to find out this way."

I give him an annoyed look and pull my hands from his.

"I know. It's just...this... It's a burden. But don't worry, we'll find a way to get out of this with Victor. He isn't having you. That much I can *promise*."

He stares at me with so much vehemence that I believe him. They would do it. They'd wage war on my behalf so that I didn't have to marry this *Victor* person.

But to me, it feels like I've only just lost my father. Because of something that I did. I won't stomach being the cause of war. I won't lose anyone else.

"I don't think that's your call to make, uncle." My voice is quiet and small. Foreign to me.

Anton reels back like he's been slapped. "This isn't something to be taken light-"

I stand abruptly, making him stumble to a stand too. "I'm not taking this lightly! I'm clearly taking this more seriously than any of you! You've known about this for *months*." I pause to shake my head. "This decision is mine. For once, *I* will be the one deciding what happens next."

***

The coarseness of betrayal rubs against me like sandpaper to my skin.

It's not news that they hide things from me. Keep secrets. Which may be only forgivable for the fact that what they hide has never been my business.

But this is absolutely my business.

It's got my business stamped all over it. Return-address-labeled, forwarding-mail-type stamped all over it.

I hide in my room for the rest of the day, snuggled up in bed watching old romance movies with my door locked and a grumpy 'fuck off!' for anyone who dares to knock.

It feels like I've had something stolen from me. Definitely freedom and probably my future.

It's after nine-pm when someone finally puts on their big boy pants and ignores my 'fuck off' warning when they knock on the door.

I'm sitting on the end of my bed, hugging a pillow, the TV playing in the background, when I hear the door click. I close my eyes and sigh. Someone's gotten a key.

Nic clears his throat and leans against the frame, arms folded over his chest as he looks at me with a frown. I regard him with barely a glance before turning back to the movie.

"The property is secure," he says, tone going hard. "So don't even think about sneaking off tonight."

My eyes narrow as I fold my gaze towards him with a sneer. "That doesn't sound like much of an apology."

He watches me for a moment, clenching his fists before he breaks our stare. "You're angry," Nic says. "That's expected."

"You were hiding a fucking *fiancé* from me."

"You'll get over it."

I rear back in disbelief, clutching my pillow as I contemplate chucking it as his head. I'm not sure what burns more; his dismissal, or that he was keeping this from me. And more importantly, *why* was he keeping this from me?

The full days' worth of emotion, and probably a lifetime more that I've bottled away, comes bubbling to the surface. Tears well in my eyes, but I refuse to blink. My throat becomes tight, strangling me as my lip quivers.

"Shit," Nic says. He drops at the end of the bed, fighting to wrench the pillow from my grip. He wins and throws the pillow back to the head of the bed. With a finger under my chin, he tilts my head upwards. "Talk to me."

I grunt and try my best to fight back the tears, shaking my head at the ceiling as if that will do anything to scare the emotions away. "Why should I?"

I feel the telltale sign of wetness against my cheek when the first tear falls and Nic wipes the errant drops away with his thumbs. "Because I'm here now. And I'm listening."

"*Now* you wanna know?"

He winces, thoughts running through his head that shine through in his eyes. "Yeah," he sighs. "From you, I want to know everything." He wipes more tears from my eyes and then scoots closer to me on the bed, pulling my fidgeting hand into his and massaging my palm.

"I'm scared," I whisper.

"Of war?" He asks.

I nod.

"Of marrying Victor?"

I nod again. He's close enough that I see the pulse jumping in his neck.

"Victor is pleasant. Kind. Ambitious," Nic says, but the words come out like they burn acid on his tongue. "I can't for the fucking life of me comprehend-" he stops his tirade when he sees its making me frown. "Sorry."

I watch him for a moment, but he continues, softer this time. "I don't understand why Dimitri would've done this. But... I've never doubted his wisdom before."

Nic's face is tense, brow scrunching. More things he's not saying to me.

"You don't think Dad wrote this?"

He whips his gaze to mine. "No. This document showed up out of nowhere. Anton didn't know about it. I didn't know about it. It's too convenient. It's too planned. I don't like it."

"And if it's real?"

"I don't fucking know," Nic says. He drops my hands, agitated and defeated. "Dimitri had lots of possessions and prizes. You were by far his most valued. He didn't want his life for you. Of blood and crime and murder. As the only DeMarco heir, was his only option to promise your hand? Maybe."

I drop my head.

Before this, I'd never once thought about marriage. I'd had many men at my feet, but never once had I considered committing to someone. Not for the short term, and certainly not for the long term.

Even if it didn't know it until this very moment, until my future stares me right in the eye and starts drifting away, I know I want to marry for love. Not for whatever *this* is. Wanting things seems so fickle and selfish when there are lives on the line. Lives that my decision will directly affect. Wars that will start if I make the wrong one.

"If this... *Victor* person... knew me. He'd-" I sigh. "Ugh, he'd hate me. He'd want to call it off and start a war, and then what?"

Nicholas cracks his first genuine smile then. "He won't hate you. He's already declared his intentions. He's ready to waltz over here like a reckless moron and drop the knee for you."

"That'll change. I'm rude and arrogant and brash and condescending and difficult." I roll my arms to emphasize my point.

"Yes," Nicholas says, a slight chuckle on his lips that has me widening my eyes at him. "But you're more too."

He opens his mouth to speak again but pauses, nervous. It piques my curiosity enough that I leave the silence open, hoping he'll speak, anyway.

"You're... everything."

He won't see anything other than the slight hitch in my breath as I stare into his eyes. Eyes that glisten with sincerity. He won't see my chest cave in on itself, my blood burn, my skin tingle.

But... maybe he does. Because he smiles, eyes casting downward before meeting mine again. "Goodnight, Sage." He gives me a lingering kiss on the forehead, leaving the room and not turning back to watch me fall apart.

***

I worry my lip as I hesitate to knock on the door to Anton's office, where I know he, Freddie, and Nic are inside with their breakfast.

For the past three days, while I've been going through the motions, replaying everything Nicholas said, confusing thoughts have echoed in my head. I could play meek, my usual move, and hide behind the might of my family's empire. I could come out swinging, igniting a war of my own. I could give Victor everything he wants. Fuck, I could run naked into the woods and never be heard from again if I really desired. All these choices swarm my mind until it becomes comfortable and easier to just do *nothing*.

When the fog clouding my decisions clears, I know what it is I have to do.

Something.

I'm not sure how big that something is yet. But I have a good idea of where it could start.

I puff a breath into my cheeks and raise my fist to knock when I hear Freddie speak, and decide to eavesdrop for a while longer, instead.

"She make a decision yet?" Freddie asks.

"You'll know as soon as I do," Anton replies.

The sound of cutlery smashes against ceramics. "You already know what she's going to do."

"There's no way to know for sure what she'll do."

Nicholas huffs, the sound anything but amused. "Then you don't know her very well."

There's a pointed silence in which I imagine that Nic has managed to either stun them or earn himself a death glare.

Of course, it's dead silent, so my blood sugar monitor chooses now to beep like its being robbed from a department store.

"*Shit, shit, shit,*" I chant under my breath, fumbling the device in my hand in my haste to shut it the fuck up. The door swings open with a force that blows air up into my face, fanning out my hair. Wide-eyed, I come face to face with a scowling Nic.

"Figures," he scoffs and then holds the door open, motioning for me to step inside.

I square my shoulders. "I was going to knock."

Nic takes his seat again. Following, I head over to the couches and take the space on the lounge next to Anton, sinking deep into the cushions.

I sit quietly with my hands in my lap, wondering how, exactly, I'm going to drop the bombshell of my decision on my family. When I look up, I notice that while their plates are still half-full, no one has resumed eating.

Great. They're expecting it.

I have to say something.

I clear my throat. "I - uhh - I've come to a decision."

Nic's nostrils flare. The only external sign that gives away his disapproval. I gather my inner strength and turn to look my uncle dead in the eye. "I want to say yes to Victor Rushkoff."

I don't break under Anton's heated stare or from the other one that I can feel burning the side of my face. I'm convicted and condemned to this choice and I'm going down swinging. Lucky for me, Anton breaks our stare first.

I let out a breath and dart my eyes to Freddie's, gauging his reaction. He gives me a proud half smirk and I smile back.

Anton's approval is the only one that matters, though. After an eternity, he says, "Okay."

The ensuing silence holds the pressure of an impending eruption.

"Fucking Christ! You can't be serious!" Nic jumps from his seat.

There it is.

"I swear to fuck, Anton, if you don't-"

"If I don't what, Nicholas?!" Anton seethes. "Sit the fuck down."

Nic's fists clench and unclench at his sides, but he does as he's told, slowly sinking back into the chair.

"I want to bring him here," I whisper. The tension in the room melts as they turn my way. "I-I know that's not typical. But, I want him to come here. If he wants to get to know me," I square my shoulders, "he can do it here."

A relieved smile spreads over Anton's face. I suppose he's been preparing for this inevitable choice ever since he gave me that document. I can't bring myself to look at Nicholas.

"Alright... Sage will say yes and we'll bring the Rushkoff boy here, where we can keep an eye on him. It's clever."

Pride fills me at that.

Nicholas leans forward to grip the arms of his chair. "Victor Rushkoff never goes anywhere without Alexei Rushkoff." He pins Anton in his sights. "And Alexei Rushkoff is a fucking psychopath."

"So I've heard," Anton says, and to his credit, he sounds nervous. "We're out of options, Nic. I don't like this anymore than you do, but bringing the Rushkoffs to us gives us an advantage. And we desperately need an advantage right now." Anton nods to Nic and I roll my eyes as I realize there's yet *another* hidden meaning beneath their conversation that I don't understand.

"I won't step out of her sight for even a minute," Nic promises, like I'm not even in the room to hear him. "I don't trust them. You bring them here I'm right on her ass 24/7."

"She's going to hate you for that," Anton says, side-eyeing me but playing along with Nic's charade to pretend I can't hear him.

"She hates me already."

"That's not true," I whisper.

Nic says nothing. The silence halts me, and I wonder if maybe he doesn't realize just how much I could never hate him.

"Sage?" Uncle Anton's voice comes to me. "You want to meet Victor?"

"I want to see what he's like. What this is all about. But I don't want to do it somewhere I don't know. So... tell him yes, and we'll go from there."

Anton nods again like it's perfectly understandable, though he doesn't look completely happy with the idea either. "Then we'll make it happen." Of course, Anton knows something the rest of them don't.

Whatever emotion was driving Nic is wiped from his face. He's composed now, sitting up straight and staring off into the distance like he's a shadow that's meant to blend into the walls.

"They won't want to wait," Nic finally says as he clears his throat.

"I know," Anton says gravely. "If I make the proposition," he checks his watch, "this afternoon. They'll be here within days."

Days.

Damn.

"You good, Sage?" Anton eyes me in concern and I'm sure I've gone white.

"Fine."

In my head, I'm playing with words like Mrs. Rushkoff. Sage DeMarco-Rushkoff. Mrs. Victor Rushkoff. Victor and Sage Rushkoff. I'm not sure if that sick feeling in my stomach is nerves or low blood sugar.

At least this should be interesting. I've never been the best judge of character.

"Just tell Victor I say yes."

Six

SAGE

Nicholas is hovering.

I stand in front of the mirror in my bedroom, putting the final touches on my hair and makeup as I prepare to meet my future husband. My future husband, who is a *Russian* and a *Rushkoff.*

A Rushkoff who works fast, since after hearing my decision, he's now due to arrive on my doorstep today, only two days later. Recklessly throwing himself into enemy territory on short notice seems like a poor decision to me, but hey, what do I know? I'm not a mafia boss.

From outside my door, Nic clears his throat for the hundredth time and I throw my head back in exasperation. Refusing to come inside, he stands in the hallway outside my room, tall and straight, with his hands clasped behind his back. I never set rules, but he seems to have set unspoken ones for himself to not look at me. Which he keeps breaking by checking me out over his shoulder every few minutes.

"Nic, stop being weird and just come in here," I say.

His head snaps back to the wall in front of him. "I'm not here for comfort. I'm here for protection."

"Nic," I tut. "I say put comfort first. I'm on the pill. We don't need protection."

"Fucking Christ."

I fidget with my necklace, making sure it sits center between my cleavage. "Come on," I whine. "You're acting like a bodyguard."

He sends a heated look my way. "From now on, that's *exactly* what I am."

"Oh my God." I roll my eyes.

I ignore him and check my attire in the mirror. I've chosen something simple and innocent looking. Anton suggested I do my best to not look bridal. So I've done the opposite and gone as close to bridal as I can.

I'm wearing a knee-length white sundress, my dark hair pinned half up in curls that fall against my mid-back. Strap sandal heels complete the look. The dress has a wide open back, but it's not so low that you'd see the scars across my back and belly where they removed my mutilated pancreas.

I pair it with a nude lipstick and a fuck-ton of mascara to highlight my green eyes.

"Ready," I announce, clapping my hands together as I swivel on the spot.

Nicholas turns on his heel and gives me a once-over, perusing me like a painting. Though I don't feel like a work of art under his intense scrutiny. On his visual journey back up my body, he meets my eye, raising his brow. His hands clench at his sides before he gives me his back again.

"How do I look?" I'm shy to ask.

"Fine," he says, once again abiding by the secret rule to not look at me. He just adjusts the front of his pants, gives a curt nod, and then blasts down the hallway without even looking back to see if I'm following him.

Okay, ouch.

Hopefully Victor likes what he sees more than Nic just did, otherwise it'll be rejection for lunch and war for dinner.

It takes me a moment to regain my composure before I'm rushing down the hall to catch up with him. My heels clack on the tiles, arms bouncing at my sides as I run after him as gracefully as I can without tripping.

By the time I catch up, he's standing at the top of the foyer stairs clutching the railing in a white-knuckle grip. Anton and Freddie flank his sides. All of them look ready to raise hell. The Rushkoff family has been our enemy for longer than I've been alive, so. This is a weird day for everyone.

Freddie turns, the molten look melting from his face when he sees me. "*Bella*, look at you. An angel. Victor will fall at the sight of you."

"Let's place him at the top of the fucking stairs then," Nicholas says, pushing back from the banister and blasting down the stairs as if he can't move away from me fast enough.

Everyone warily watches him go. Ignoring the foul mood he's clearly in.

"Are they here yet?" I ask.

Anton spins to face me. "They're rounding up the gate now." His eyes travel over my dress too. "You look beautiful."

"Why do you sound worried when you say that?"

Running his hands across his face and breathing a laugh, Anton says, "Oh, I am. I know you're grown up, but you'll always be our little girl." He brushes a lock of hair behind my ear, his eyes becoming distant as he toys with the strands.

Freddie moves past us, clapping Anton on the shoulder.

"Thank you," I say, my voice wobbling. I take his hand and smile, giving him a gentle nudge down the stairs.

The sound of cars rounding up the driveway reaches me, and through the double-story floor-to-ceiling windows I see an entourage approaching. There's at least six cars in the procession with a limo in the middle of the fold.

Mesmerized or petrified - anyone's guess - I forget to go downstairs and end up standing at the landing, hands braced on the railing, gawking at the processional.

The cars come to a stop, the limo right in front of the water feature that center's our circular turnaround driveway. When the limo door swings open, I feel as if there should be ominous music playing or something. My heart starts up the drum line.

An oxford-shoed foot steps onto the gravel, and with my eyes I scan upwards. Dress pants, a thick black belt, and a cream business shirt. Then, finally, the mountain of a man exits, having to fold himself almost in half to get out. He looked tall when he was sitting, but now he's enormous. Golden skin, muscles resting underneath that tight business shirt that's rolled up to the sleeve.

Yeah, fucking hell, that's a *man* if I've ever seen one.

He's got bushy blonde hair with a generous beard, and his tree-trunk like arms are full of thick hair too. Luckily, I stop myself before I can drool, regaining control of my mind and starting down the stairs to meet him.

Not even past the top step, I freeze. There's a second person exiting the limo. My hand grips the railing. Suddenly, it's the only thing holding me upright. My breath is robbed. Stolen callously from my lungs. Outright thievery is the only explanation for how this feels.

This man is the complete opposite of the first one, bar their height.

He's unreasonably tall too, but he's dressed in a dark shirt that, like the others, has the sleeves rolled up. Where the first man is light, he is dark. Clean skin versus tattoos. Sunshine versus brooding. Good versus evil.

Thick black hair sweeps across his head, slick and wet-looking. Tattoos cover every inch of skin. They're on his fingertips, up his arms, and even up his neck, only stopping at his jawline. A pulse starts up between my thighs.

Then he looks right at me.

I was wrong. *This* is what it feels like to be robbed of all air.

His stormy gray eyes lock on mine, and he stills. He's so far away, and surely can barely see me through this window, but I swear I see lightning in his eyes. In those eyes, I'm suspended in time.

He finds his brain first and severs our stare off with a sharp twist of his head.

The moment our eyes break, the rest of the world comes rushing back in around me as if the edges of reality are blurring back together at super speed.

Oh my God, what the *fuck* was that?

I wince and hurry down the stairs to settle in on Anton's right.

I'm such an embarrassing fool. I swear my panties are damp and that's just an unacceptable reaction to someone who's most certainly a *Rushkoff*.

"You good?" Anton quirks a brow at me.

"Great!" I cringe when I say it, but Anton just gives me an encouraging pat on the back that knocks me half a step forward.

Several underlings rush through the door first, fanning out around the edges of the foyer, and then the two specimens of men enter.

Standing side by side it's clear how right I was that they are polar opposites.

Dark and light. Night and day.

As soon as they step through the door, the blond surveys the foyer and its occupants, his eyes critical and assessing, like he's looking for threats. The dark-haired man, though, locks his eyes onto mine like he's already found all the threats worth worrying about.

He's looking at me like he wants to kill me. *And fuck, why is that hot?*

"Victor," Anton greets.

"Anton." The blond one steps forward and shakes my uncle's hand.

My stomach sinks, my mouth parting slightly as I shutter my eyes away from the dark one and latch onto the *blond* who I'm supposed to marry.

"Quite the predicament we've found ourselves in," Victor says. He booms out a smile and it's all over-confident charm. I can see he'd melt the panties off the girls any day.

"My niece, Sage." Anton gestures to me and I step forward.

"Sage," Victor smiles, taking my hand and placing a kiss on the knuckles. "How wonderful to finally meet you."

His eyes linger on me as he retracts back to his full height and takes longer to let go of my hand than necessary.

"My men, Freddie Fallon, Nicholas Prince." Anton continues the conversation.

Victor nods at my boys before gesturing beside him. "My brother, Alexei."

Alexei takes his eyes off me for the first time since he entered the room, nodding at my family in a way that should look complacent but comes across as hostile.

"Thank you for coming to stay with us, considering the terms of the contract," Anton says.

"Well," Victor smiles. "I think it blindsided us all a little, didn't it? Dimitri was sneaky when he wanted to be, but I'm sure we can all play nice for a few weeks. Can't we, boys?" He folds his arms, relaxing his stance.

"I appreciate you being accommodating," Anton says. "But know this is temporary. I don't give a single fuck what some contract says. If Sage doesn't want to marry you, then she won't."

Victor remains calm, as if he expected this reaction. Even though I told my uncle that I was going to say *yes.* I shoot an annoyed look his way to remind him of that.

We suspend in a standoff for uncomfortable moments, only to be broken when Alexei's nostrils flair and he rushes forward like he's going to charge us. Victor's hand snaps out at lightning speed, blocking his brother.

"A breach of contract. For you, that could mean war." Victor finally drops his smile.

Anton doesn't budge. "I'll die before I force her into something she doesn't want."

Anton and Victor stare each other down, all the while with Victor holding a hand on Alexei's chest as if he's a bull that's liable to tear the place down at any second.

Finally, Victor smiles again. "I wouldn't expect anything less. I can agree to those terms. I'm not in the business of forcing women to marry me." He turns to me. "Looks like our lives are in your hands, pretty girl."

Great, no pressure then.

Then Victor tries to prove his point. By doing the most surprising, but probably stupidest, thing he can in this moment. He drops to one knee.

"Oh shit," Freddie says, and it sounds suspiciously like a chuckle.

Victor pulls out a ring box and holds it out to me.

"Whaddya say? Marry me?"

Doubt slams into me.

Even though I'm sure I'm going to say yes, several moments pass while I stare wide-eyed down at the ring.

A fucking ring. Jesus. And the only crazy-ass thought that's floating through my head right now is that I'm way too young and pretty to marry a man named Victor.

"Sage?" Anton prompts.

I shake my head and put on a fake smile. This guy is fucking crazy. I've known him two seconds?! In fact, these are the *first* words I'll ever say to him.

"Um... yes? Yes!" I say. Victor smiles. He goes to open the ring box and I'm presented with a jewel that looks like a family heirloom. There's no diamond on it. It's a simple metal on metal piece with an enormous skull in the center. It looks like a candy ring.

"Yeah, I'm not fucking wearing that." I frown, pointing at the ring. "You can consider this a tentative acceptance of your proposal. No wedding planning until I'm sure we're both willing to hold up our ends of this bargain. And get off the fucking floor."

"Shit, you've got a mouth on you," Victor laughs as he stands, but he doesn't push it and instead pockets the ring, seemingly happy that I've accepted his proposal, anyway.

"Now that all the cock-measuring has been done, let me show you to your rooms," Freddie says, clapping his hands.

Nicholas comes to stand at my side as Victor and Alexei, with their people, follow Freddie to their rooms. But they don't watch Freddie as they follow him.

No, their eyes lock on me through their entire journey up the stairs.

Both Victor's eyes *and* his brother's.

Seven

VICTOR

My brother paces restlessly, cracking his tattooed knuckles as he alternates between glaring out the window and rushing to the door like he's off for a confrontation. "This was a fucking terrible idea," Alexei finally says, pointing a finger at me.

I barely hold in my sigh, standing from the bed in the DeMarco guest suite that was assigned to me. This mansion the DeMarcos have been hiding in all these years is certainly something. Now that I'm finally inside, I see they are not wanting for space. My brother and I have been given separate suites and not one of our men has to bunk up. Not to mention all the finest trimmings and furnishings. It's luxe, ostentatious and refined. It's old mafia money.

Alexei continues, as if he hasn't made his position on my engagement clear already. "Rolling right into enemy territory. It's insane, brother. Insane. You've finally lost your mind."

I drink my vodka straight from the bottle, wiping at my beard. "A document like that shows up out of nowhere you don't just ignore it." The same spiel I've given him every single time he's overreacted about this.

"You dense motherfucker," Alexei growls, snarling at me.

Alexei is, and always has been, perpetually agitated. Where I'm calm no matter the stressors, Alexei cannot keep his cool for even a moment. In a way, he's an open book. Every shift of his eyes, every flare of his nostril, is easy to read.

It's why he's not the one in charge.

"Why the fuck would they want to give us their precious daughter? Peace cannot be worth *that*," he spits, before continuing his disconcerting pacing.

"Alexei, for the love of God, calm down. They're being hospitable, and they're just as confused as we are about where this came from."

"And that's a *good* sign?" Alexei pauses his pacing to challenge me.

I shake my head at him, choosing to ignore his immature outburst as I head to the window and pull the curtains wider. Alexei is inches from my face when I turn around, his unsettled eyes pinning me to the spot. "You actually want to marry that girl?"

I see now he's going to pretend she isn't exquisite. It's easier for him to compartmentalize that way.

I slide past him. "She's said yes. I'd be a fool not to."

"You'd be a fool to fucking do it!"

Icy rage tickles over my skin, the kind that only my brother can draw out of me. I grind my teeth and turn a deadly look on him. "I'm done warning you, brother." A low growl slips into my voice. "I won't say this again. It's decided. It's done. Shut up about it."

Alexei folds his arms and runs his tongue over his teeth, giving me that testing look he's known for. Unnameable emotions cross over his face before he huffs, and drops his sour attitude, letting me know I've won. "I'll be so fucking pissed at you if this gets us killed," he says.

My mood instantly lifts. "I know you will."

I swig the last of the vodka and slam the bottle down on the dresser. Alexei is caught at the window again, staring down into the gardens with a scowl. Curious this time, I step up to his side.

Ah.

The girl is in the garden. She's sitting on a bench in the middle of the flowers, picking at the edge of her sex-on-legs white dress. One of their men, Prince I believe, is standing stoically nearby, making me wonder if they've given the girl a bodyguard.

"Dimitri had been working on a peace deal for years, Alexei. This isn't unexpected."

My reckless, idiotic, brother's hateful stare glues to the girl. "We have peace. We already have a treaty. There's nothing more we need," he whispers. His whispers, though, are always threats.

I throw him a condescending look, still in disbelief that after all these years by my side, he still doesn't get it. "There's always more, brother."

"I'm never going to like it."

"Then just watch my back."

He turns to me, folding his arms and frowning as he says, like it's very obvious and needn't be said, "Always."

I clap him once on the shoulder. "Good. Now, excuse me. I've got a girl to woo."

I throw him a wink before leaving to chase down Sage DeMarco. We may have no idea why Dimitri DeMarco would've wanted me to marry his daughter, but I won't waste a good opportunity. More status, more power, and a beautiful girl to boot. Win-win-win.

***

The Prince boy stiffens before he sees me approaching, giving me pause as I file away a note that his instincts are sharper than they seem.

Sage is still sitting in the garden, with the sun shining on her dark hair, but now one of the other men has joined her. Freddie Fallon, another higher up in the DeMarco empire.

I bet the innocent girl has no fucking idea what he's capable of. I'll give it to him that he comes across as charming and lax. But he isn't. He's their number one hitter, and there isn't a room that Freddie Fallon leaves without painting it red.

He's an absolute sociopath. But, like everyone in this DeMarco mansion, he's an absolute sociopath with heart eyes for this one girl.

My brother is probably right. Deep down I know that. These people willing to give away their precious daughter? Definitely strange. Yes, they have no choice. The legalities are set in motion. The surprise is that they haven't started all-out war to prevent it.

"Shouldn't you be settling in?" The Prince boy says, his shoulders tightening as he turns to block my access to Sage, who has yet to spot us.

"I brought one bag, Prince. It ain't hard to settle with that," I say, folding my arms as I paste a smile on my face and square my shoulders at the fucker. If we're in for a showdown in the middle of a rose garden while the sun shines and birds chirp overhead, then so be it. I love a little juxtaposition.

Prince's jaw grinds as he narrows his eyes at me. We stare each other down for a beat longer before it becomes obvious he can't think of a reason to limit my access to the girl.

"Glad we cleared that up," I say, keeping the smile on my face. "Excellent job on the tough guy stance though, bodyguard. Bet you come highly recommended." I look back long enough to catch him bare his teeth at me.

I head up the cobblestone garden path with my hands in my pockets, finding the girl where she sits on a red bench between the roses and hedges.

Fallon is the first to spot me, his soft heart eyes turning murderous. Ultimately, that's what tips the girl off. She flips her head, dark hair twirling as she spins to face me. Her eyes widen before she turns back to Freddie and tugs on his sleeve to get his attention.

"Freddie, give me a minute?"

Fallon isn't so trusting. He runs his tongue over his teeth, an evil spark in his eyes, and goes to speak. But the Prince boy appears out of fucking nowhere. "Don't worry, Freddie, I'll be watching them."

I don't miss that that's said for my benefit, not hers.

Fallon leaves. But not before he gives me a cruel smirk, like he's trying to tell me I'm lucky to have missed his wrath. Watching to make sure he's gone and will no longer be a bother to me, I turn and face the Prince boy. "You can watch from over there, bodyguard."

He's not going to listen to me, either. Unsurprising. I have adopted the bulldozer approach after all. That rarely goes down well.

Sage gives him a nod which sends him reluctantly walking out of earshot, but not out of sight. Finally, it's just me and the girl alone.

"May I?" I ask, gesturing to the empty seat beside her.

"Please," she replies, scooting up the bench to allow room for me.

I hike my suit pants up at the calves to get into a comfortable sitting position and then sit with my arms rested on my thighs.

"Victor Rushkoff." I hold out my hand for her to shake.

The girl doesn't blink twice, hesitate, or eye me for a second before she grabs my hand in a death grip and squeezes as she shakes it. "Sage DeMarco."

Jesus, she's got tiny hands, but they're choking the fucking life out of me.

Most grown men shit their pants when I even look at them, but considering her father is Dimitri DeMarco, it shouldn't be impressive that she doesn't cower when confronted with one of the most dangerous men on the continent. Still, it is. Even when between me and her father we've killed more men than we've ever let live.

I pull back with a winced smile.

"You know it's fucking weird to propose *before* you've properly introduced yourself, right?" She folds her arms.

"Well, I wouldn't know." I lean back on the bench, stretching out my arms. Her eyes watch my biceps. I smirk. "I've never done it before. In fact, I've never had a document arranging me a marriage before."

She lifts her chin but turns her eyes away. "Well, that makes two of us."

"The proposal was a formality. I apologize if it bothered you. It had to be done."

Her eyes soften, and she nods her head once.

"And since we didn't get much of an introduction before, I thought I'd introduce myself privately."

She tilts her head to give me an amused look. She truly is a gorgeous woman. Bright, big, green eyes. Lusciously full lips that are painted nude to blend into her tan skin. Long legs crossed and peeking out of that delicate, lacy sundress. "It's nice to meet you, Victor."

I search her eyes and find nothing. I really can't tell what she's thinking. Though from her childlike mannerisms and behavior, mafia politics may be a little over her head.

"Well, I'll cut to the chase," I say. "Since we have a slew of events before our inevitable marriage-"

"As was directed in the document, I'm aware," she says with a roll of her eyes. I school my features before my brows can jump to my head. Surely Anton didn't show her the document?

"Right... well, I thought we could take the time to get to know each other."

Sage nods slowly, like she's waiting for the other shoe to drop. Her mouth opens on a false start before her brows crease. "You want to woo me?"

A genuine smile spreads across my face. So wide that I can feel it pressing against my eyes. I rub my hand along my beard in a nervous tell. "Well, I suppose when you put it like that."

She uncrosses her legs and turns to face me, waving her arms wildly at me with a confused little frown on her face. "You actually *want* to marry me? Like put me up in your house and treat me like a wife? What? No bedroom locked in a tower already prepared for me at your place?"

I choke out a burst of laughter that brings a smile to her face. From the corner of my eye, I see the Prince boy glaring at us. She smiles at me again. Those eyes just as beautiful and hard as gemstones.

"No tower, I promise," I say. "I want a wife. I want you."

"Why? You don't even know me."

I take a deep breath and try not to smile. She's brash. Straightforward. It's interesting.

"Despite our obvious differences and tenuous relationship, your father was a good man," I reluctantly admit. "If there was one thing Dimitri DeMarco was known for, it was loving you. You were the most important thing in the world to him. So, if he really wrote that document, I have to assume he did so for something more than peace or power."

Her face, once again, gives me nothing of her thoughts.

"I'd like to get to know you, and find out what that something more is," I say.

"Noted," she says, turning to wipe a stray tear from her eye, but frowning like she wishes it weren't there. "And accepted."

"Good," I say as I stand. "I hope we can speak again soon."

I smile as I walk away.

Fucking nailed it.

Eight

ALEXEI

s soon as my brother's back is turned, I bare my teeth again, my rage tearing away from its short leash. It took my fucking moron of a brother all of two seconds after spotting that girl to rush down to the gardens to see his bride.

He's wasting no time.

Proposing four seconds after meeting her. Heading off to woo her before his bag is even unpacked. It's pathetic. And stupid. Two things my brother usually isn't.

I'm still at the window, knuckles clutched on the sill, watching as he approaches and gets blocked by one of their men. The one with something needlessly possessive in his eyes as he mouths off at Victor. Prince.

Ultimately though, Victor gets his way and I deflate, both Fallon and Prince retreating as he takes a seat on the bench next to the girl.

Of course, I can't know what he's saying to her. But if I know my brother, he'll melt her. As icy as she might want to be, Victor is fire, and he'll burn away all her defenses. That's what he'll expect to do. My eyes are laser focused on them, with my finger pulling at my lip as I frown.

The girl, she is of no consequence. Merely a beautifully packaged pawn in a game being played by larger men.

She *is* breathtaking. That's not up for debate. When I first saw her earlier, she took my fucking breath away. Her green eyes locked on mine the second I exited the car. I swear the windows weren't transparent, but I hooked onto her like a honing missile.

I watch their conversion in the garden as Victor shakes her hand. Jesus. Proposal first, introductions second? My brother has lost his fucking mind. It is *not* the girl we should be focusing on. But it's like Victor doesn't even see Prince watching him, steam rising from the man's head like a kettle. He probably doesn't even see Fallon still lurking nearby in the hedges, listening at an even closer range as he fiddles with a flick knife.

Yeah. My brother is a fucking idiot.

To walk us into enemy territory was unintelligent. But to draw all his attention to her and ignore the threats around him, that's just reckless.

The girl levels Victor with an icy glare as she grabs his hand in an obvious death grip. I almost smirk. She looks like she'll be a lot of work, and sure, Victor loves a chase, but I'll never understand why one girl is worth all this.

Then, my brother does something that makes her laugh. I feel a thaw in my chest, watching her mouth open wide, head tipped back on a laugh. Suddenly, the world that I've always seen in a black, white and gloomy gray comes rushing forward in color.

Fuuuuuuuck.

No. That can't happen. I haven't had a heart for eighteen of my twenty-nine years. I don't plan on having it start beating now.

I shake my head. One of us needs to retain clarity if we're going to survive here without getting murdered in our sleep. An option that admittedly has crossed my mind more than once.

Victor doesn't stay in the garden long, thankfully, and when I see him retreat, I break from the window to follow him. I know he's probably trying to avoid me. I've got a legendary temper, and I have been loose with it ever since Vic told me we'd be coming here. I've given my brother a piece of my mind constantly over the last few days, and since he doesn't even notice

Fallon stalking him as he walks away, I plan on tracking him down so I can serve him another slice.

I come down the mansion's historic stairs, my brother's men still carrying shit up and down, and head towards the back of the house. I'm rounding a back corridor near the kitchen when I collide with someone in my haste.

It's her. The girl.

Sage DeMarco stops in front of me. The corridor is dark, barely wide enough to fit both of us through. She startles when she finds it's me blocking her path, eyes locking onto mine as her mouth rounds in a little 'o'. I look her up and down, a snarl on my lips.

We both just stand there as I wait for her to get out of my fucking way. I do not have time to busy myself with her, someone of absolutely no importance, when I'm writhing in the middle of a pit of snakes.

I arch a brow. I don't want to, but if she doesn't move out of the way in the next three seconds, I will move her myself.

"Hello," she says. I expect her to be breathless, but she's not. Despite the innocently surprised look on her face, her voice comes out hard and sultry. I frown but brush it off.

"Watch where you're going." I attempt to brush past her, but she jumps back in my path. That fucking white dress drawing my attention where it swishes over her thighs.

"Whoa, rude much?"

Is she still talking? Jesus. I don't have time for this. Still, I narrow my eyes on her. "What? Were you expecting me to fawn? Kiss your hand maybe?"

She frowns and raises one eyebrow, as if she's saying: well, yeah. She shakes her head once before affixing a smile to her face.

"I'm Sage," she says, giving me a cute little wave. I fight the ridiculous urge to smile and attempt to push past her again. I knock her shoulder against mine, but she doesn't budge, a surprising amount of strength in her stance. Something prickles against my skin. Awareness. Intuition.

Okay, temptress. I'm fucking listening.

I sigh. "And?"

We're trapped in the tight space, locked in place by pride which forces me to wrestle to assert dominance. I turn my head to her, finding her already watching me. Pride shines in her eyes too. Interesting.

"You know," she grates out, holding me hostage with her shoulder in the tight space. "It's polite and normal to introduce yourself back."

"You already know who I am."

"Yeah," she sniffs. "The other Rushkoff. The bat shit crazy one."

My mouth tilts up at the corners. "That sounds about right."

"Yours *is* the kind of reaction I was expecting from your brother. But he just-"

"Fell at your feet?" I smirk. "Forgive me, but I won't be doing the same."

Why the fuck am I still standing here? Why won't my feet *move*, dammit?! In the big picture, she's trivial and insignificant. No amount of beauty can automatically make anybody worthy. I drop my voice to a whisper and lean into her. "Why are you accosting me in a hallway? Did you drop your silver spoon, princess? Can't pick it up all by yourself?"

Something goes hard in her eyes and I barely contain my surprise before it shows on my face. Her eyes, which had previously been innocent and demure, suddenly turn rough and calculated. As if, before, there was a wall behind her eyes and now, it's dropped.

"What the fuck did you just say to me?" She knocks her shoulder against me, jostling me back a step.

"I don't have time for introductions or any of your childish, spoiled games, *princess*. I won't be getting to know you, and I do not plan on letting my brother tie his life to yours."

I slide past her and stomp away before she can respond.

"Hey!"

I pick up my pace, finally finding the exit. I push open the door at the end of the corridor and come out somewhere around the side of the house. I can smell chlorine, so the pool must be nearby. Looking back, I see vines crawling up the side of the house.

I go to move again, but she grips my elbow and pulls me back around to face her. I do. Not. Like. That.

I turn to her slowly. Venom on my tongue. "Let me the fuck go."

She just grips my elbow tighter, twisting until the skin burns and I pull it back from her.

"You're a prick, actually."

"Oh," I pout. "How will I live with myself knowing the DeMarco princess thinks so little of me?"

"Oooft, I don't like you."

"Yeah? I'm cut up. Fuck off."

I roll my eyes and go to turn away before I see her stomp her foot. Actually *stomp* her foot.

I freeze.

Her movement is slightly robotic. I see it on her face before she makes the move that she's decided she's going to. Like I'm watching an actor play out a line in their head before they say it. I can see the decision so clearly. It wasn't drawn by emotion, but by some trick of the mind. That ember of awareness from earlier suddenly bursts into full on flame.

She groans and stomps off, irritated little breaths huffing out of her.

I do not follow. Instead, I watch her. Halfway back to the house, her gait changes. She's not storming off, but walking tall and proud. Steady. Does she think I'm out of her line of sight? Before she disappears into the house, she turns to look back at me too. There's a little snarl on her face, but her expression is glistening.

Holy fuck.

I see it then.

Like every day, threats are boxed up into packages that we don't expect them to come in. Traps are traps for a reason. For their intention to fool until it's too late. Despite what Victor thinks, I see more than most, and now I understand why my eyes locked onto *her* the second we got here.

In a room full of killers, murders and criminals, she's the one who my intuition was drawn to. Body language a paradox to her behavior.

Everything about her, from her attire all the way through to that look she wears on her face. She's designed to look delicate. Designed to look feminine and small. Designed to make men like my brother think with their dicks. To think they could shelter her and coo her and save her like a damsel. Long, tan legs. Arms toned and deadly. Her breasts full, on display enough to entice but not tease.

And now I'm sure of it. Sage DeMarco is not a damsel, despite the front she puts on to look like one.

When she sees me watching her, she fixes her expression and slams the door to the house. She locks it too. Like that one act of childish defiance is going to halt my assessment.

The real threat is sitting right here in front of us, dressed in white lace.

It's not the marriage document. It's not any of the men.

It's Sage Fucking DeMarco.

The siren with doe eyes.

Nine

SAGE

"Pass the olives."

Freddie shoves the olives across my body straight to Nic, making me drop my cutlery onto my plate. Nic smirks at me and takes the offering, popping an olive in his smug mouth.

I absolutely hate these family dinners and he knows it. We haven't had one since before my father died. But alas, the arrival of my future husband appears to be cause for rolling out the good china.

"How was the drive across the city?" Anton politely asks, smiling curtly at Victor as his voice echoes in the space. Since our formal dining room is a space large enough to seat twenty-four, we look absolutely ridiculous with only the six of us gathered at one end. It, too, has been brought out like fine china for the Rushkoffs. Not even a speck is allowed to taint the wooden floors, high ceiling or chandeliers, which light the room in a faint glow.

"Only took about two hours to reach you here. We made good time, especially with all those bloody security checkpoints you lot have in place," Victor says.

Freddie chuckles obnoxiously along with him. "You saying you don't have security checkpoints buried all around that lakeside mansion of yours, Victor?"

"Touché," Victor smirks, saluting Freddie with his fork.

I've never seen the Rushkoff part of Bradford before, so I have to assume this means Victor's home is on the outskirts of their part of the city, just as ours is.

"The lake is beautiful this time of year. Perhaps we can spend next Christmas there." Victor shoves a playful elbow into Anton's side and then shoots me a gentle smile that I return.

Victor is different from what I expected. If this is what's in store for me to secure my family's future, he's not the worst.

But he's not Nic.

Anton presses a hand to Victor's shoulder and squeezes. "I will hold you to that invitation." With that, the two men laugh. After a frosty reception, it seems they've found a way to get along. It's kind of unsettling, and it's clear I'm not the only one who thinks so. Nic is cutting his chicken so hard that the knife is making marks on the plate.

I definitely wasn't expecting Victor to be so charming. Not to me or my family. From him, I was expecting the kind of reception that his brother is giving me.

Alexei Rushkoff.

The god-like man who looks like the devil.

Despite our meeting, where our eyes locked so fiercely it stole my breath, he seems to have taken an instant disliking to... well, everyone. But me especially. We've had a total of three interactions so far. This one included. So I'm not sure why he's looking at me like I personally skinned his cat.

With my head down, I shift my eyes to sneak another look at him, only to find that his are on me again. Hatred rioting within them like jagged waves on a cliff's edge.

"And what do you think, Alexei?" Nic says.

I missed the question. Alexei falters for a moment, making me think that he has too. He drags his gaze away from me in a way that looks painful before he faces Nic.

"It wouldn't be my choice," Alexei says. He stretches out, arm resting up on the back of his chair, leaving his hand to drape loosely by his hip.

"Not a fan of the lake, Alexei?" Anton asks, popping a slice of chicken in his mouth with a political smile.

"I prefer the countryside."

Nobody misses the fact that our territory contains the countryside. A few throats clear, but no one pulls him up on it. I frown as I look down at the half eaten food on my plate, unable to believe that nobody is going to confront him. Is this man really *that* terrifying?

"And what's so appealing about the countryside to you?" I survey him up and down with purpose. "You don't seem like someone who enjoys picturesque rose gardens and a quieter pace of life."

Alexei sniffs, his upper lip twitching as he regards me. I chance a look at the rest of the table and find them watching me with quiet contemplation before they turn their synchronized attention back to Alexei for his rebuttal.

I don't give him the chance. "There's not a lot to be done out here other than ride. And you don't look like much of a rider. Though I wouldn't mind seeing you get tossed on your ass."

Alexei looks almost amused, though he's gripping the armrest so hard his knuckles are going white. He doesn't reply. Content to let me stew. The silence is rejecting. The lack of noise creates a ringing in my ears.

Victor shatters the sound-vortex, chuckling as he pats his brother on the shoulder. "She's got you pegged, brother." Victor gives me a wink and then jumps back into conversation with Anton.

Alexei spares only a sidewards glance for his brother before he looks back to me, sliding his arms from his relaxed perch and placing both elbows on the table as he leans toward me. He whispers for my ears only, "I'm an excellent rider."

I lean in too, surprise in my tone when I quietly reply. "You ride horses?"

He smirks at me until I get his double meaning. I gape back in shock, and a little disgust, before I narrow my eyes back on him. I lean forward a little further so that what I say next is for his ears only. "That does not impress nor intimidate me. I ride cock better than a fucking pornstar."

Alexei's eyes widen, his mouth parting slightly.

"Your brother's gonna be walking funny for a week after I'm done with him," I smirk and then raise my voice to say a little louder, "Just ask him." I lean back in my chair and pop a green bean in my mouth, tearing the strip off with my teeth.

"Oh, she's right," Victor agrees. Alexei's head jerks as if it's glitching, neck stiffening as he turns to his brother. "The range at the back of the property. Sage showed me there today. You'd love it."

In a huff of relief, Alexei drops his gaze, pursing his lips in what is either solace or annoyance.

Freddie leans over and chuckles softly in my ear. "Oh, *bella,* you are so lucky your uncle didn't hear you say that." He pulls away with a smile. "Someone else might've, though."

I follow his eye line and find that Nicholas is now eating with a fork that's bent. He should know that my brag was all truth.

Maybe playing with these boys is going to be a little fun.

***

After the lovely *family dinner,* Anton and Victor retired to the lounge to play a game of cards and shoot back whiskeys. Or something. I'm not sure what men do when they go to the library. But there's leather lounges, cigar holders and looks all man cave-y so I have to make a guess and that seems like a reasonable one.

I slipped away early, convincing everyone that it'd been a big day and I needed to get my beauty sleep. Victor saw me off with a kiss to the hand, which did, embarrassingly, make me blush. There were more than one set of eyes that followed me up the stairs to my bedroom.

I don't plan on staying in my room long, though.

I'm adept at sneaking through, around, and out of this mansion. It's a necessity when you're a mafia princess.

It's too dangerous, Sage.

You can't protect yourself, Sage.

Freedom cannot be afforded in this family.

These walls may be my home, a sanctuary for my family. But they're also my prison. Sure, *just take someone with you, Sage,* is the party line. But that sounds a lot like having a babysitter. And I'm twenty-two for the love of God. How many times does that bear repeating?

I shouldn't need someone around all the time. I *don't* need someone around all the time.

It's just after two in the morning when I slip out of bed and stand in front of my mirror to dress. I can't risk turning a light on, so I rely on the glow of the moon shining through my windows to guide me. I brush my hair and put on a speck of makeup.

I dress in a short dress that has long flowing sleeves, pairing it with red high heels and my white clutch bag. From the dresser to the door, I'm calculating with my steps, avoiding the creaks in the floor to get to the door and make sure it's locked.

It takes nothing to get out of the window, even in the heels, but I wince the whole way, hyperaware of every sound I make. It's only been about a week since I've been able to get away, so my escape isn't dire. But it soon will be, and I'm not sure how many opportunities I will have now that Nicholas is breathing down my neck hotter than usual.

Everyone in the house has even taken to calling him 'the bodyguard' as a tease for how close he's sticking to me. I can't decide if it's hot as fuck or makes him look like an absolute tool. Especially when he stands at attention in the corner of every room I'm in.

Sticking to the shadows, I trot from the edge of the house to the gardens. When I'm on the lawn, I turn to look back at the property. All four floors are lit up, even at this hour, which they haven't been in a long time. I'm yet to decide what I think of Victor, and I *know* Alexei is a cunt, but I secretly like the bustle of people. It makes the house feel fuller and more alive than it has in years.

I shake the thoughts away and trudge across the grass, getting to call a ride on my phone.

I'm halfway across the grass when someone grabs my wrist and pulls, heaving me backwards in a spin.

"Going somewhere?"

I slam into Nicholas's chest.

Fuck.

I snatch my wrist back from him and sigh as I put some distance between us. "How did you know I was down here?"

"I'm not giving up my secrets that easily, Sage," Nicholas smiles.

"I don't suppose you're going to wander back inside and pretend you never saw me here?"

Nicholas gives me an incredulous look and then shakes his head.

"Am I barred from leaving?" I straighten my spine.

"Alone? Yes. Yes, you are."

"Well, I don't want you to come where I'm going," I say, giving him my best brat face.

"Then we're going back inside."

I shake my head, unwilling to give in just yet. This isn't over. He's found me, but he hasn't caught me. Not yet. If I can just draw this out, lend myself a distraction, I can try to outrun him.

"Sage," Nicholas warns, tongue running over his teeth as he watches me with quiet anger like he can read my mind. "It's either we're going together, or not at all."

I pace a few steps backward to keep my distance from him, slowly slipping off one of my heels.

"What are you doing?" he warns, trying to take a step towards me.

When I hold my hand up, he halts.

"Complying," I lie. "Since I'm out of options... I suppose... you'll have to fucking catch me first!"

I kick my second heel off, right into his chest, before I spin and bolt across the grass. Hoping to hell I don't step on something sharp since I can't see where I'm going in the dark.

I hear a groan when my shoe lands, but footsteps quickly follow and *shit*, they sound fast.

I whip my head around to check. He's gaining on me. Can I outrun him? I swear I used to be able to.

I pick up my pace, pushing my thighs to burn as I bare my teeth. I'm not un-athletic. I've spent my life locked up in a house with nothing much else to do but keep in shape. Feeling strong has been an imperative, especially after the incident which gave me my scars.

Unfortunately, though, it's the months of moping in my bed mourning my father that ultimately catch up to me and make me slow. That's... ironic.

Nicholas takes the opportunity and pounces. Running up alongside me, he finally slips in front of me and barely gives me time to halt as he stops dead. I slam into his solid chest, bouncing back and knocking myself onto my ass with the force.

"Nice," Nicholas admits, through his breathlessness.

I sit up on my elbows and lift my head in triumph.

"Now, you gonna show me where you were running off to? Or are we going back to the house?"

Wet, sticky grass clings to me when I stand, leaving stains across my dress. Great. I like this fucking dress. I don't deign to give him an answer as I turn back to the house.

I start to walk away from him again when he grabs my hips and pulls me close to him. "Don't," he snaps, palming my hips. "I'm not in the mood to chase you again."

I swat at his chest to get him to back off, but he bends and wraps his hands around my calves, hauling me up over his shoulder where I can do nothing but struggle.

"Put me down!" I seethe, my head bouncing and my ass exposed as he hauls us both back to the house.

"I can't trust you not to run," he says, breath not even labored by my weight on his shoulder.

I kick my legs, flailing as I aim for his groin, but he secures my legs with his other hand, tightening his hold. I feel a wet pinch on my thigh.

I gape. "Did you just bite me?!"

"Couldn't resist," Nicholas says. He slaps my butt and chuckles as I growl.

By the time we ascend the porch steps back to the house, I've given in to my fate. He's caught me. Was worth a try, though. I expect him to stop and put me down, but he doesn't. He keeps me pinned over his shoulder all the way up the steps and towards the door.

"At least let me down here," I struggle. Nic pushes through the back doors of the house and heads for the stairs.

"Not until you're back in your room."

He slams the door shut with his foot and continues hauling me up the stairs. I park my hands on Nic's butt so I can lift my head. Looking around, I spot Freddie watching us from the lounge. "Freddie, help!"

"Bloody hell." Freddie begins a howling laughter when he sees us. "Is that necessary?"

"Have you met her?" Nicholas growls.

Freddie wipes tears of laughter from his eyes and gives me a shrug that seems to say: fair enough. We go all the way to my bedroom, and Nic kicks that door open too, walking right up to the bed, where he throws me down onto the comforter.

I sit up on my elbows, glowering at him.

"Don't try to sneak out again, Sage." He leans over me on the bed, forcing me down, caging me in his arms though not settling his weight on me. "It's for your own safety. Plus, I'll catch you."

"Is that a threat?"

"It's a promise."

A wicked smile spreads across my lips. "I sure hope so."

We watch each other for a moment, my breath holding as I wait for what he's going to do next. A confrontation like this one usually gets us all hot and bothered. We usually find ways to expend excess energy.

I run my hands up the sides of his ribs.

His eyes drop briefly to my lips, but he turns his head and clenches his jaw like he's in pain. He shudders, giving in, but only for a second. He takes my breast in his palm, squeezing tightly until I drop back in a moan.

When I open my eyes, he's backed off completely, and is standing over me with his arms folded. "I'm not gonna fuck you." The words grate out with a hard edge.

I open my mouth in incredible surprise. "Why the hell not?"

"You're engaged," he grits his teeth. "I'm respecting your fiancé."

He stalks towards the door. What the *hell?*

I scramble upward. "Respect my fiancé? Are you joking?"

He opens the door, but I rush ahead to slam it shut before he can leave. The only response I get is an annoyed stare, even though I can see the outline of his erection in his pants.

"Urghhh," I groan, throwing my head back. "Fine! I don't need you, anyway. I've got an eight -inch vibrator in that drawer." For effect, I point to the drawer in question and Nic's eyes follow. "And I won't be thinking about *you* while I'm coming all over it."

He visibly shudders as he pushes me aside, slamming the door to my room on his way out.

Asshole.

I slam the door a second time for good measure and cringe. Jesus, I really am pathetic.

Ten

NICHOLAS

"Breathe, man."

If it's even possible, my scowl deepens as I stare at Freddie's smug face. "I'm breathing."

"Could've fooled me."

I return to watching Sage where she sits talking to Victor. Today, they're out on the pool deck, sitting across from one another at one of the wrought-iron tables. Even shaded from the heat of the sun under an umbrella, I can see his every expression as he leans forward while she talks. I can see hers too. While she's still guarded, every small smile she sends his way makes me want to ring his thick, dumb throat.

Freddie chuckles softly and I look down at my hands to find I'd started miming a wringing motion. "You're so transparent," he says.

I shoot him a disapproving look. "I'm still your superior."

"You gonna pull rank on me?" Freddie's brows disappear into his forehead. "*Boss.*" He tacks on that last bit with a smirk.

I ignore him and go back to torturing myself as I watch them. Sage sits with her legs crossed, her arms rested on the table as she leans forward to talk to Victor. He's lapping up every bit of attention she gives him. Every time she turns away his eyes fall to her long legs, peeking out beneath her dress. Daring as he is, he even risks a peek at her tits spilling over the top of her dress. Then he looks to me, as if to confirm I'm still here and have seen it.

I straighten, folding my arms across my body in a threatening gesture.

Victor gives me a smile and a relaxed wave, which Freddie returns, and I try to contain my twitching eye before I knock Freddie the fuck out.

Freddie then turns his back on them, looking out into the gardens. "You gonna watch them incessantly this whole time?" He closes his eyes as he suns his face.

"Like a fucking hawk."

"It's creepy, you know."

"It's also our job, Freddie." I rub at my jaw. "You're exhausting me. Don't you have something better to do?"

"Nope," he smiles widely. He turns over his shoulder to look at them once more. "They're calling you the bodyguard, you know?"

"Good."

Freddie laughs. "I think it's meant to be an insult, Nic."

Victor leans across the table and whispers something in Sage's ear that makes her giggle. His afterword has her throwing her head towards the sky. I start forward before thinking better of myself and setting back in position. He's not *hurting* her, really.

"What if she really marries him?" I worry my lip as I watch them.

Freddie sobers finally, turning away from the sun to look at me with worried eyes. "I don't know." He shakes his head. "Fuck, I really don't know."

I refused to fuck her last night. And now that seems like a colossal mistake. Surely all of this would be a little easier to bear if I knew she was sitting over there with my cum still inside her.

I clear my throat. Victor is retreating into the house now, thank God. Despite what I said to Freddie, I'm thankful to finally be able to breathe.

I start to move closer to the pool when Sage stands and removes her dress, revealing the swim suit underneath. I stop in my tracks, stifling a groan, though it's pure agony I feel. Freddie cuffs me upside the head as he walks past me.

By the time I make it over to the pool, Sage has climbed onto an inflatable, her hand swatting idly in the water to steer. The suit she wears is two piece but designed to look like one where the top rests close to the skimpy bottoms. It's because she doesn't want her scars to be on display, but she hates wearing one pieces. *I hate getting naked to pee!* she always says.

She's beautiful regardless. No marks on her skin could ever dull how beautiful she is inside and out.

She throws her dark hair freely behind her; the tips getting wet in the water.

I move closer to the poolside. Heading for the row of deck chairs, I pick one in the center and recline into it, covering my eyes with sunglasses so I can pretend I'm not watching her.

She knows, though.

I know it by the way she swats her hands in the water, wetting them and then wringing them above her chest to let the drops fall down her breasts.

For fuuuuuuuucks sake.

I pull my sunglasses down and level her with a warning glare, which makes her smile.

In my peripherals, I check our surroundings. I have no idea where Freddie has gone. But it looks like he's nowhere near us, thank God.

Years. Years I've been sliding under the radar. Doing dirty things to the DeMarco princess without anybody finding out what a sack of shit I am, violating the precious girl. If Dimitri DeMarco knew what I'd done, I'm sure he'd rise from the dead to drag me down to hell with him.

And yes, hell is where I'd be going.

She slides off the inflatable into the pool. Watching through my sunglasses, I gulp as she dips under the water for a moment, slowly coming up at the edge of the pool nearest to me and letting out a mewl as she runs her hands up her hips, over her breasts and through her hair.

"Stop that," I say.

"Stop what?" She blinks wide eyes up at me, innocent and doe-like, and I know I'm a fool to have said anything. I'm practically encouraging her. Jesus Christ.

You want her, asshole.

I need to be saved from myself.

"Are you going to follow me everywhere?" she asks, as she rests her hands on the edge of the pool.

"Yes."

"Tell me something," she starts. She saunters out of the pool, not bothering with a towel, and comes towards me, dripping *fucking* wet. I try my best, I swear I do, but I can't help but stare at the points where her nipples poke through the swimwear.

She sits on her knees at the end of the chair, right by my feet. Right between my legs. I check my peripherals again without turning my head. She's dangerous to me, this girl. I can't want her. But fuck, I do.

"Does it bother you to see me with Victor?"

"You're not *with* Victor," I growl as I sit up to face her.

"Really? Because last night, you were pretty adamant he was my fiancé, and that he should be respected," she says, lifting her chin. "I belong to him now after all."

My sense flies out the window and my dick takes full control of my brain. I grab her hips and she gasps as I pull her onto my lap.

"You don't belong to anyone," I say. My hands haven't moved from her hips, but she smirks, looking like she's gotten exactly what she wants from me. With a small sigh, she runs her hands across my chest. The feel of her nails scraping across my skin is so fucking good that I close my eyes and tip my head back.

"Our secret doesn't have to be over," she says as she rocks her hips against me.

Anybody could see us here. We could be caught at any second. I doubt we'll be able to negotiate a peace deal if Victor Rushkoff catches me dry humping his new fiancée only days after he met her.

78

"Please don't tell me it's over," she whispers, right before she goes for the jugular (literally) and begins sucking on my neck.

"*Shit.*" I rear upward, leaning into the feel of her lips. But it's the raw emotion in her voice, like she needs this just as badly as I do, that has me giving in.

"Sage," I breathe out, pulling her in by her hips so she grinds over my dick in just the right spot. It feels so fucking good and she's not even touching skin.

She leans closer to me until her tits press into my chest and soon she's controlling the pace of her grinding in my lap. Her breath comes in quick, luckily quiet, pants in my ear.

"Can you come like this, baby?" I ask.

She whimpers for me, telling me explicitly that yes, yes, she can.

"Do you need to come?" I ask again. If she wants it, she needs to give me an answer.

"Yes, Nic," she whispers in my ear. "I need you to make me come."

I pull her against me, angling my hips so the head of my cock presses against her clit, until I start to feel her shake in my arms.

She grips my shoulders, head tipped back as we work together to bring her to orgasm all over my cock.

"Just like that," she whispers, her hips losing their rhythm as she succumbs to the pleasure. She doesn't cry out this time, just whimpers quietly as she shivers on top of me.

Sick satisfaction washes over me, knowing I'm the one that's made her come when all her attention should be going elsewhere. I slow down my pace but she doesn't stop; she keeps going.

"What are you doing?" I tense.

"I want to make you come too," she says, eyes wide and innocent again, and ohhh fuck, I'm in trouble. Before I can think straight, she's pulled the buckle of my belt open, unzipped my pants and has me in her hand.

"Christ," I jolt as I sit up, but she just keeps stroking me. If I wasn't close before, I am now and oh *fuck.* "I can't come in my pants like a fucking teenager."

She smirks. "I'll take care of you."

She sits up on her knees so she's above me, continuing to stroke my cock as she pulls the front of her swimsuit down, holding the panties open like a catch.

"You want me to-"

"Come in my panties, yeah," she says, like that's a perfectly natural thing to say. My eyebrows raise to my forehead as I grip the sides of the chair, muscles stiffening as she works me over. Oh, shit. Oh, fuck. This situation got out of control quick.

We're poolside in her father's mansion, with her fucking fiancé, his evil brother, and her whole fucking family able to stroll past at any point that they like. And she's got her swimsuit half down, exposing her pussy, where she wants me to come in her swimsuit bottoms and then she's just going to... going to... sit in it?

That's the thought that pushes me over the edge.

"Sage, I'm going to-"

I don't get to finish as I'm blinded by pleasure, coming hard and gritting my teeth to keep in all sounds as she strokes me, pumping every bit of cum from my cock. I open my eyes to watch it. I watch as she milks my dick, hot cum pouring out of me and landing in her swimsuit.

My mouth is hanging open and I'm panting hard, staring at the spot where my cum covers her bottoms. She lets me go and then puts the swimsuit back into place, smearing my cum over her pussy. I let my head fall back on a groan.

She buckles my pants for me, patting my spent cock once it's secured inside.

With my dick spent, my brain finally takes back the controls, looking around to see if we've been caught. There's no sign of anyone which is a fucking relief. That was too close. It's always too fucking close.

Sage finally slumps out of my lap and sits on the lounger across from mine, resting her elbows on her knees and propping up her chin as she watches me with amusement.

"You gonna get all scared and run away now?"

I frown as I sit up. I scrub a hand down my face and stare at her, watching her gorgeous green eyes glint with amusement as she looks at me. I can't help myself. I reach out and tuck a wet, stray strand of hair behind her ear.

My hand lingers down across her cheek as we stare at each other like we're only seeing for the first time. A throat clears from afar and I drop my head like it burns, though neither of us moves. We tilt our heads towards the voice.

Alexei Rushkoff is standing at the door to the house with his tattooed arms folded and an amused smirk on his face. Sage and I jolt apart like we've been shocked. Which only seems to amuse the psychotic Rushkoff brother even more. We're lucky that all he caught was her staring into my eyes and not me coming in her panties.

Not two seconds after Sage has bolted upright, Victor comes out of the house in his own swim trunks, holding towels.

"Now, I believe you were going to teach this letch how to dive off the roof," Victor smiles wide.

I glare in Sage's direction. "You absolutely were fucking not."

Sage gives me a sheepish smile. "It's not high."

"Don't even think about getting on that roof." I retrieve my sunglasses and fold back into my chair.

"I'll settle for a swimming lesson then," Victor smirks.

Alexei scowls, his nostrils flaring. "You know how to swim."

Victor elbows him and then follows Sage into the pool.

They float around for the remainder of the afternoon, tearing strips off my resolve as I watch. Funnily enough, knowing she's out there now covered in my cum, does actually help.

***

I knock on the door to Anton's study. When I don't get an answer, I make my way in, figuring I've given him enough time to object if he wants to. He's standing at the window with one hand resting against the sill and the other worrying his lip with a glass of whiskey.

"Anton?"

He jumps out of his trance as he hears my voice. "Nic, come in," he says, shaking his head before turning expectantly back to me again. "Sage?"

"At dinner with Freddie."

Anton nods and then slumps into a chair. Closing the door behind me, I join him.

"Another breech?" I ask.

He nods solemnly. He never wanted his brother's responsibility, but he got it all, and I can see it tearing at the edges of his sanity. Guilt gnaws at me. I've defiled his niece again, risked the prospect of peace with the Rushkoffs, *and* there's been another breech on the property.

"Where?"

"Not far," he says. "They got as far as the second gate this time. They're always heading in that direction. Never coming for the warehouses or the offices, but always to the east, to the residential wing."

I lean back in my chair as I mimic his pose, reclining and relaxed but looking tense as fuck.

"With the Rushkoff presence here?" I ask.

"It's changed nothing," he says. "I can't tell whether that's to distract us from the truth or whether it's genuine."

I nod. It was a risk bringing the Rushkoffs here. Better than Sage being forced to go to them. But a risk, nonetheless. An opportunity also, though, to see if it's them that's trying to get to us.

"I'm certain of it. They want her. They want Sage," he says on a deep exhale.

"Sage is the key here," I agree, though the admission squeezes my chest. "Her marriage to Victor joins two of the biggest criminal organizations in the state. Maybe someone doesn't want that to happen."

"It would be a good theory," Anton says, placing his glass down and resting his leg on his knee. "If there were anyone else powerful enough to care. The Big Five are the closest and they've always been content with the territory they hold south. They've never wanted anything North of Darton. Plus, this started well before that document showed up. Dimitri's death is proof of that."

I'm well aware of both of those things, but I've got nothing else. Well...
I have one theory. But I think everyone is too afraid it might be true to voice
it out loud. We just have to keep her close. Keep her safe.

"What do we do?" I ask.

"I don't know," he says, looking older and more confused than he did only
months ago. "The Rushkoffs haven't been here long enough to force their
hand."

We sit in silence for another moment while we continue to drink. Security
has rarely been an issue in the mansion, other than the night that Dimitri
died. But it's getting worse the longer it lingers.

"And no luck figuring how they breached the perimeter the first time?"

Anton knows what I'm asking. He blows out a breath. "How these
attackers managed to breach security and waltz right through the gates to kill
Dimitri? It's a mystery."

"You have a theory though," I say, watching his body language closely.

Anton shifts in his seat, watching me with caution. "I think someone let
them in."

My eyebrows rise, incredulous that Anton would even suggest... The men
here have been loyal for years. I can't think of one other person, staff, brother
or naught, who would even consider such a thing.

Anton sees my expression. "I know," he says.

"You think-"

"That someone who knows all our secrets is feeding information to the
outside," Anton says. "How else were they let in?"

A frown takes over my face while at the same time sweat starts to drip
down my back. "You know this means-"

"You don't have to tell me," Anton says. "If it's true, if we can't keep our
information *in*, we'll need to consider how far we're willing to go to stop any
more of it from getting *out*."

Eleven

SAGE

I'm almost convinced I'm nocturnal. Last night as soon as the sun set, my eyes glued themselves open, staring mindlessly out the window as the moon shone in the sky. If I did sleep, it was only long enough for my tears to wet my pillow. Once again, I spent the night awake. Awake for long enough to get to watch the sun rise and the mansion start its day.

When I come down for breakfast on the back porch, the day is already warm, with birds chirping as they splash in the bird baths around the gardens.

Freddie, Nicholas and Anton are at the table by the time I get there, so I plaster a cheery smile on my face. One that is bright enough to hide behind.

"Good morning," I announce, bounding towards the table.

"*Bella,*" Freddie says. He pulls out my chair for me and I graciously accept the seat next to his, surveying the breakfast options and piling up my plate.

Anton barely even notices my arrival, his brow furrowed as he stares down at his eggs like he doesn't see them. Mindlessly, he sips on his coffee.

Nicholas holds his head in his hands through tired eyes. I don't think his lack of sleep has allowed him to notice I'm here yet, either. He refused to go to bed, suspicious that I was going to sneak out, so he tried to stay up as late as possible to head me off. Unfortunately for me, it worked.

I snap a finger in front of their faces. "Um, hello??"

Anton startles, nearly spilling his coffee while Nic just groans, removing his head from his hands and going back to buttering his toast.

"Sage," Anton says. "Did you sleep well?"

"Yes," I lie. They either don't realize it's untrue or they choose not to call me on it.

"Tell me, how are things going with Victor?"

"Shit, Anton, she hasn't even had her coffee yet," Freddie chuckles.

It's been nine days since the Rushkoff brothers arrived at our countryside estate. Victor has been nothing but a perfect gentleman, and if I'm telling the truth, that makes me incredibly nervous. He's the leader of the Russian Bratva in our city. He shouldn't be a gentleman. Like my father, I assume he's killed more men than he can count.

I raise my brow at my internal monologue. It's possible he gets his brother to do all the dirty work. Keeps his own hands clean. Maybe that's why the brother is such a lunatic.

"Sage?"

"Huh?"

Anton gives me a look and prompts me again. "Victor? How are things going?"

"Oh. Right." I shake my head and give a pursed smile. "Fine?"

"Fine?" Anton scolds me.

"Things are going... well. He's been a perfect gentleman so far." I shrug. "I don't think there's anything to worry about with the peace deal, uncle."

"That's not what I'm worried about." Anton wars to catch my eyes. "The second he stops being a gentleman just say the word and we'll make him disappear."

Nic snorts and takes a bite of the toast he'd been buttering. Plain toast with butter. "Let's just throw both the brothers in the lake right now and be done with it."

Freddie chuckles before toasting with his glass. "Ain't no wars to be started with leaders bricked to the bottom of the water."

Anton shakes his head in disapproval, but cracks a smile, anyway.

"Good morning!" The hearty voice makes me jump as Victor makes his way onto the porch with us. He's a burly guy and he speaks like one. Everything he says is big, bright, and puffed up to make him take up as much space as possible. On the contrary, his brother makes all the air disappear from the room as he slinks in the shadows.

"My beautiful fiancé." Victor mocks a bow and heaps himself into a chair, piling his plate high. We watch in fascination as he fills it to the brim with an ungodly amount of food.

"I'm glad to see you're enjoying my hospitality." Anton gestures to the spread.

Victor grabs him and shakes his shoulders. "Don't be bitter! I'll be hosting you before you know it!"

Great. Victor's a morning person.

It's strange how my family seems to think we're living in the midst of enemies, but everyone is at their most relaxed when Victor is around... Weird. I can't count the number of times I've heard the name *Rushkoff* spoken like it was meant to be spit instead. Yet, here we are.

Victor gives a pointed look at Nicholas's plate. "Plain fucking toast with butter? You got a hangover or something, Prince?"

Nic narrows his eyes. "I just like the taste."

Victor chugs back his coffee like it's water, clucking his tongue at the taste before turning back to Nic. "Come on, bodyguard, put some protein on your plate. If you're gonna be jumping in front of bullets for your charge you need your strength."

Nic runs his tongue over his teeth, scoffing as he says, "Very funny. You've had your fun. Now shut your trap, *Rushkoff.*"

There it is, the name sounding like a curse.

"Anton," Victor says, voice still booming. "Talk me through the expansion plans you've got..." At that point, I stop listening. With all attention on Victor, I recognize that right now, nobody is watching *me,* and I smirk.

***

There's only a small reprieve to escape. While Anton and Victor are busy joking and jostling each other like *they're* brothers, I take my chance to bid them adieu and bolt.

I go quietly, needing the time alone. Luckily for me, Nicholas is also distracted glaring daggers at the scene that is Anton and Victor becoming friends, so he doesn't notice me leave. Once I'm inside the house, I close the glass doors and exhale a breath, shoulders slumping.

Nine days. Nine fucking days Victor has been here and he hasn't left me alone for one second of it. Well... there were those few seconds, actually. When I humped Nic and made him come in my swimsuit. Then had to spend the afternoon chilling by the pool with Nic's cum making my pussy sticky.

Christ.

Anyway.

Yes, I brought Victor here to get to know him. To make the idea of becoming his wife a little less daunting. But I thought he'd be disinterested. That I'd be free to get to know him in public settings, watching from afar.

But no. He's charming. Polite. Interesting. *Interested.*

A girl needs some space.

I take the stairs two at a time, eyes on my feet as I contemplate the situation as it looks. That is, like Victor is not a monster. I'm so busy rushing up the stairs, lost in thought, that I don't see it coming when, at the top of the stairs, I collide with something.

Someone.

I puff as the wind is knocked out of me.

"Fucking hell, DeMarco, watch where you're going," Alexei says, nostrils flaring with violence as he glares down at me. His thick tattooed hands clutch the balcony banister for balance.

"Jesus Christ," I say, clutching my chest. "The other Rushkoff brother slinking in the shadows. Great."

"Slinking in the-" Alexei huffs. "You ran into me."

"You were clearly in the way." I bat my hand at him, attempting to move past him, but he stops me.

"Not so fast," he smirks. He releases his hold on the balustrade and runs a hand through his slick black hair. The look he directs toward me is cold and calculating, and my heart moves to a gallop. I don't like it when he looks at me for too long. "Over a week here and yet we've barely had the chance to get to know each other."

Alexei smiles then and it's all malice. It's sadistic and evil. The epitome of what I would have expected from a Rushkoff. I'm quietly unnerved but I hold my ground, because I don't want him to see that.

Lucky for me my voice holds steady as I talk. "Did you ever think that may be by design? Who says I give a fuck about getting to know you?"

His nostril flares. I'm already starting to recognize some of his tells. When he's seconds from unleashing his legendary temper. For some reason, I seem to be very good at getting it to flare up.

Even as he takes a step closer to me, trying to intimidate me, I don't move an inch from where we glower at each other.

"Still," he says. "I think I should get the chance to size up the vixen that thinks she's going to ensnare my brother."

I roll my eyes and fold my arms, hoping he doesn't see my throat bob. "You're such a drama king. We've had plenty of time to get acquainted."

"You're going to be my sister-in-law. I should think we'd get to know each other, as family."

"Sister-in-law?" My brow scrunches.

"It generally happens when you marry someone's brother," he says, looking at me like he thinks I'm an absolute idiot.

He's in my way, and I really just wanted to escape, not have a confrontation. I need to end this conversation. One, because I never planned on having it. Two, because I really don't like the way he's looking at me. And three, because I really kind of do like the way he's looking at me.

"Whatever," I say, placing a hand on his shoulder that I intend to use to push him out of the way. But as soon as my palm makes contact, he grabs my wrist, wrapping his thumb and middle finger tightly around it. His eyes are hard now, blazing, and with painful slowness he drags his eyes from mine to glare at where his hands are clutching me. He looks at my hand like he wants to bite it off.

"You know," he takes a step forward, and instinctively I go to take one back, but he clutches my wrist tighter. "You'll be spending a lot of time around me, DeMarco." He takes another step towards me, and me another one backward. "All these men here that you've got wrapped around your little finger won't mean shit when it's my roof you're living under." He steps again and I back up into the wall.

He finally takes my wrist off his shoulder and pins it above my head. "When you marry my brother-"

"If," I huff, glaring at him. God, I really hate this man and his attention. *Don't look too closely at me, Rushkoff, walk away.*

"What?"

"*If* I marry your fucking brother."

His head jerks back like he's been smacked. My wrist finally falls from his grip as he drops his hold on me to fold his arms. "What the fuck do you mean *if?* There's no if. I've seen it. Vic's been the perfect gentleman."

"Maybe I don't like gentleman."

Alexei chuckles like a villain, throwing his head back to relish in the laugh. All I can see from this angle are his sharp teeth as he runs his tongue over them. He doesn't touch me again, but he does lower his head to meet my eyes. Low enough and close enough that we're sharing breath. "Oh, I believe that. That look in your eye. You want them rough."

I suck in a gasp and I can *taste* him on the air. His pupils dilate and I think he might be facing the same confronting storm as I am. I push out a breath and I swear I can see it as he breathes in and sucks it into his mouth.

His gaze darts down to my lips (holy shiiiiiiiit) and then he leans in to whisper in my ear. "You want it to hurt. Don't you, princess?"

I grind my teeth. "The only person I want to hurt is you."

"I believe that too," he says.

I almost hold my words in. I'm almost smart enough not to speak what I'm thinking. Almost. "Your brother isn't rough."

He looks back at me and gives me a sharp look. "No. He isn't." I hear everything he doesn't say. *But I am.*

I don't like the way he's looking at me. I don't like the closeness. He's rude and brash and he challenges me and I hate it.

Smirking, he opens his mouth to say something that I just know is going to be insulting and foul. Before he can, I decide I need to diffuse this situation the only way I can.

So I stomp my foot into his.

He jumps back with a yelp. "What the *fuck-*"

He charges at me. I brace, ready to be shoved back against the wall to bear the brunt of his wrath, but it never happens. Before he can reach me, he's shoved violently out of sight.

I relax my shoulders and find Nicholas standing between us.

"Everything okay here, Sage?" Nic says, his breath panting. He must have run the whole way to find me when he realized I was gone. Alexei and Nic glare at each other, and it's like it's been forgotten that I'm even here at all. That is until Alexei makes eye contact with me and Nic actually *growls*.

"I- I'm fine," I say, eyeing Alexei as he limps back, jaw grinding as he shakes out his foot.

At that moment, my monitor goes off, beeping at me for attention. Alexei's face snaps back to me, twisting in confusion as he watches me tend to the monitor. Something like recognition draws over him, hardening his features as his jaw clenches so hard it looks painful.

"What the hell is that-"

Nic steps up to me and takes my arm at the elbow, cutting off Alexei and pulling me away. "It's none of your fucking business, Rushkoff, is what it is," Nic says as he drags me up the hallway and away from the psychotic Rushkoff.

"I think that should be warning enough," Nic says. "Threats are inside the mansion just as much as they are out."

He gives me a meaningful look and I nod once, averting my eyes. I chance a look back over my shoulder, seeing Alexei in the hall, head tilted as he watches us disappear.

Twelve

SAGE

wo weeks pass like a blur in the mansion. Two weeks with Victor chasing my attention. He is charming most of the time, but the novelty of using him to piss off Nic gets old fast. A routine has formed. Victor flirts with me. Nicholas never lets me out of his sights. Alexei and I trade silent barbs at breakfast, lunch, dinner and any other time I have the misfortune of being in his presence.

I still haven't gotten the chance to sneak out. This mansion and my bodyguard have me locked down tighter than a nun's fucking cunt.

I need to get out of here. The pent up energy from my imminent need to escape burns at me, straddling me on a knifes edge. Nic's on edge too. Because I'm going to try to run again, and he knows it.

I'm thrust out of my thoughts when Anton appears near the front door, ready to address us all. I sit on the stairs amid the staff, fiddling with the hem of my dress. Anton's gathered the whole household here for some kind of announcement. The cooks and cleaners and gardeners, all the men, Victor and his entourage. We're all here. Apparently, this concerns everyone.

Anton clears his throat, which gains him the attention of the room. His chin is held high and he appears ever like the forceful leader he's meant to be, but I see the tick in his jaw. The way sweat beads at his brow.

"I'll make this short and sweet," he says.

Nic's eyes find me from where he stands stoic next to Anton. He gives a curt nod, like he's checking that I'm accounted for. It would be an excellent time to make a run for it. I can't pretend I haven't considered it.

"As of right now, we're going into a full house lockdown," Anton says. "Only essential movement in and out, and that will all go through me."

My brows shoot to my forehead as I cease fiddling with my dress. I chance a look around at the staff, but no one seems inclined to argue. DeMarco men accept the order without a word while the Rushkoff clan looks to Victor.

Mine is the first jaw that drops, watching all these pussies stay silent. Nobody is going to say anything? Nobody is going to protest? Sure, I've been locked up here and watched my whole life, but the others have always had autonomy. This should be a big deal.

The protest comes from the most likely of places and I sigh.

"What the fuck, Anton?" Alexei says, stepping out of the shadows to make himself seen. Every head turns in his direction to watch the threatening fury radiate from him. It's only the subtle tick of his jaw that gives him away, but I swear I can hear his teeth grinding.

"For everyone's safety, we're securing the mansion. Nobody goes in or out without permission. That means you too, Rushkoff."

That snaps the short chain on Alexei's control.

"That's bullshit! You think we'll agree to that?!" he roars, charging at Anton. Victor rushes to catch him, patting his brother's chest to make him stand down. But the wild Rushkoff isn't having any of that.

"Fuck that, brother! Locking us in here with our enemies? It's a trap!"

"This isn't about you," Anton assures them, but Freddie and Nic have already shifted their hands in prep for a fight.

Victor notices this too, eyeing the hands that edge for their guns. With a rough grip on his brother's shoulder, Victor forces Alexei to sit, pushing him down on the stair next to me.

I glare sidelong at Alexei, finding him cursing to himself under his breath. I muffle a snort at how ridiculous he looks doing that. He hears it, though. Alexei's eyes snap to mine, gray and full of fury and storms. I smile, and his lip curls.

"Anton, you should have cleared this with me first," Victor says.

Freddie and Nic don't move their hands away from their weapons, and Anton doesn't answer.

Victor gives him a disapproving look and then nods towards the stairs. "A word?"

With that, the rest of the staff and the men are dismissed. In the shuffle of bodies, I make an escape, losing sight of Nic. I make it to Anton's office just as he and Victor shut themselves inside. Shit. I press my ear against the wood, groaning when I hear nothing.

A scoff next to me has me stiffening. I tilt my head to check the darkened shadows of the hall. My eyes widen when I find Alexei hidden there. Clearly having the same eavesdrop idea that I did. "Spy!" I gasp. "You-"

I open my mouth to yell but Alexei's arm shoots out, hand covering my lips as he pulls me into the shadows with him.

Not a second later, my suspicious uncle opens the door and steps out. He looks down the hall, but misses where Alexei and I are pressed up against the wall in the tight space darkened by shadow.

When my uncle is gone I relax, turning to Alexei. "Spy," I whisper again.

"Coming from you." He shakes his head, pressing a device against the wall. His eavesdrop method is far more sophisticated than mine and even comes with earbuds. They're both in his ears, but I snatch the right one and place it at my ear.

"Hey," he whisper-shouts, wrestling me to stop me.

"What? They didn't want to let you into the big kids meeting? Kicked out of the clubhouse, other Rushkoff?" I swat at him.

"Fucking hell you're an infuriating little heathen. I'm not sure how you've got all these assholes fooled." He manages to wrestle the device away from me and push me back a step.

I straighten my spine. "Give me an earbud." I hold out my hand.

"No." He scowls at me.

I open my mouth to scream but he covers it with his hand again and then places the earbud in for me.

The voices inside the room become immediately clear.

"What's the meaning of this, Anton? My brother's methods may be wrong but you have to admit, it's not a good look for you." Victor's voice.

"I apologize for the way things have come across. But the lockdown is a necessity."

"And are you going to explain what that necessity is?"

Alexei's fists clench and I watch him closely as he listens to the conversation like he very much wants to butt in. We're shoulder to shoulder, close as can be, and I try to ignore the burn that sizzles at all the points we connect.

"Security. Safety," Anton says. "You know the drill."

A beat passes, and Alexei and I exchange a glance before we both scowl at each other again and turn away.

"If you're under attack, Anton, just say that."

Another beat passes.

"Christ. How bad?"

Again, no answer.

"You're going to have to be straight with me here."

Anton sighs. "Come, let's take a walk. These walls have ears."

Alexei's face goes hard. I shake my head at him and whisper. "My uncle is just paranoid. He doesn't know we're here." I'm right, because when he and Victor leave the office and head for the stairs, they don't even notice us.

As if we can't take the contact for even one prolonged moment, Alexei and I burst out of the tight space with a bustle. Earbuds tear and pull at us, still connected as we try to rip away from one another.

"Get off me." I push Alexei away.

"Off you?!- Why- you... you're just-"

"What was that?" I hold a hand to my ear in a cupping motion like I can't hear him.

Alexei looks like he's two seconds away from exploding, but before he can he seems to collect himself. He closes his eyes, takes a breath, and then shakes his head at me.

"Stay out of my way and don't follow me," he says, pointing an accusing finger at me before he stomps up the hallway. Likely heading in the direction that his brother and my uncle went.

It's comical to watch him, really. I can almost see the red smoke and exclamation points with every bang of his foot onto the carpet. Pissing him off is quickly becoming one of my favorite things to do. I love how easy he is to bait.

I look back to my father's office, sighing at the space and trying to remember what it looked like when it was my father who sat in that chair. I head inside and sit, breathing in deep, like if I try hard enough, I'll still be able to smell him in here.

I miss him.

Terribly.

I swivel in the chair and look out the window, seeing Alexei storming around the pool in chase of Victor and Anton.

I, at least, don't need to follow them to know what they're going to say.

We're under attack.

Have been for a while.

And it started well before my father's death.

***

Tonight, I plan an escape.

I've let enough time pass that now leaving this place is a desperate need. No longer negotiable. I also know the chances of making it outside the gates are slim. Sneaking out of here used to be so easy.

I miss the good ol' days.

My hair is styled mostly down, but with the top half pulled into a ponytail so it's out of my way. I wear shorts and a cardigan, pairing it with running shoes because I can't let sparkly dresses or high heels hold me back. The jig is up anyway. They know I'm not sneaking out to party.

Forgoing the window, since I'm sure Nic's figured out that's my usual point of exit, I sneak from my bedroom, all the way across the house to the library. The heavy doors click closed with a thud and I wince. Hope no one heard that. I cross the space. This window is heavier, but I've used it before. It's one that's a lot easier to get into for when I'm sneaking back in, rather than out.

I block the sensor and climb down the side of the house, dropping into the garden bed.

Then, I run.

Fast.

I don't try to be quiet. I don't try to be sneaky. I bolt for my life across the lawns. My arms pump furiously, breath laboring and my legs burning as I clear the pool, rose garden and make it onto the lawns.

I'm halfway to the gates, convinced I've made my escape undetected and without even seeing Nicholas. When I slam into a hard chest, my excitement is halted, punishing me for celebrating too early.

I curse as I slam into Nic and stumble back with the rebound. "Fuck!"

He merely chuckles.

"God dammit," I hiss.

"I knew you wouldn't listen," he says, shaking his head.

He makes a pointed look towards the house with his eyes, and then narrows them when he realizes I'm not going quietly. His brows raise, face twisting, like he wants to ask me if I'm seriously going to fight him on this.

I am.

We eye each other for a few long moments, predators sizing the other. When I move, he moves with me, and soon we're slowly circling each other.

"I deserve to have some fun," I say.

"See, I don't think that's what you're doing at all," Nic says. "You're hiding something." We still circle each other. But I don't confirm or deny what he suspects. There's really no point anymore. He already knows something. Which is dangerous. For him and for me.

I fake a move forward, and Nicholas flinches as if he'd been ready and willing to chase me. "Don't," Nicholas says, his voice rough. "I'm tired tonight, Sage. Don't make me chase you."

"Why *do* you chase me?"

His face brightens, and he tries to hide his amused smile. When he speaks, he looks me directly in the eye, crushing me under the weight of his stare. "Because you want me to."

My mouth opens, ready and waiting for me to issue a denial. But I find I can't. The clarity and accuracy of that statement rings in my head like a gong has been struck. Shit.

"M-maybe I'll just fight you to get away then," I say, crossing my arms. My cardigan slips, dropping the sleeve down and exposing my bare shoulder. Nic doesn't miss the movement.

"You don't have the skills to disarm me."

"Perhaps not, but what you forget-" I turn and run. Before I can even finish my sentence, while he's waiting for me to speak and not expecting it, I run like the wind. My legs carry me as fast as they can, heading in the direction of the stone wall at the side of the property. It's much farther from the road, but I hazard a guess that he won't be able to follow me if I can make it over.

"Where are you running to? There's nowhere to go over there, Sage!" Nicholas yells. The location of his voice tells me he's closer than I thought he would be, but he's still not close enough to catch me.

I smile as I run, nearing breathlessness. All my attention goes to that stone wall. Just make it to the wall. Make it to the wall.

"You're going to run right into the wall if you don't slow down," he yells again.

When we're close to the wall, I hear Nicholas' footsteps slow their pursuit behind me. I assume he's decided he doesn't have to pursue me so relentlessly when I'm heading towards a dead end.

But I keep my momentum, pushing, barreling for the wall. When I nearly reach it, I veer slightly off course. There's a raised bed of stone blocks encircling the garden beds and an overhanging trellis made of high wooden poles off on the right. It leads back towards the house and into the rose garden. But tonight it's going to lead me over the God damn wall.

I jump up onto the raised garden bed, feet nimble and skipping as I run along the tiny paved wall. I don't slow down or stop as I reach the end, instead leaping to the overhanging trellis and catching the first rung. It's far too high to reach usually, but with the height from the garden bed and my momentum, I just make it, swinging on the bar as my hands clutch for purchase.

Using all the strength in my core, I connect the bar with my gut and swing around on its edges until I reach the top of the trellis and can pull myself up to a standing position. Scaling the rungs like they are stepping stones, I pick up speed again.

"Sage..." Nicholas's voice becomes laced with alarm.

I continue to step along the rungs, now at the same height as the stone wall. Nic must see that my leap to freedom is nearing, and I know he has nowhere near the skills or the mobility to follow me.

"Sage!" Nicholas bellows.

I make the final leap of faith and glide through the air. I slam into the wall hard, securing my grip on the edges but knocking the air from my gut. With an exhaled breath I hurl myself up then scramble the rest of the way.

My breath comes in harsh pants when I finally stand up and steal a glance down at Nicholas. He's standing directly below, staring at me now that I'm far out of his reach. His eyes are wide and vicious.

"Get down off that wall," Nic breathes with deadly fury.

"Don't think I will," I smile.

"Get down or I will come get you down."

I laugh and throw my head back. "I'd like to see you try."

I sit down on the wall and dangle my legs. Even with that temptation he isn't able to reach me. He doesn't move, either. As if he knows it too. I rip off my running shoes and throw them down at him with a chuckle. He has to sidestep to dodge the blows each time.

The aggressive look on his face sends shivers down my spine. It is incredible.

"How's the view from down there?" I laugh, strapping on my heels and brushing out my hair with my fingers.

"Don't do this," Nicholas begs, and God does it pull at my heartstrings. His eyes are full of worry and sincerity and I think if I asked, he'd get down on his knees and actually beg me not to do this. My heart pulls me elsewhere tonight, though. Not towards Nic. My safety is not the most important thing in the world right now.

I stand on the wall again and ready for the short jump down to the other side.

"Sage, please!" He yells again as I turn my back on him.

"Don't wait up," I say, and then leap.

Thirteen

ALEXEI

"You have got to be fucking kidding me. You're actually agreeing to this?" I try to tamp down on my rage, but I just can't hold it in. Everything I say these days seems to come out in either a growl or a yell.

I blame my brother. If he weren't being such a fucking idiot, then I wouldn't have to yell at him for it.

It's not wrong that my brother and I are very different people. Not just different, but residing at the opposite end of every spectrum we can compete on. Victor is a closed book. I've never seen him raise his voice or give away an emotion. Even when he's killing. Me, though? My voice is permanently raised, every thought voiced, every emotion suffocating my very existence.

I don't know how we ended up so different.

That's a lie. I do know. Victor was showered with our father's attention, readying him to take on the role of *pakhan*. I... wasn't.

"Calm down, Alexei," Victor says with a sigh, rubbing his brow from where he sits in the armchair in his room. He's got a glass cradled in his left hand, and he's looking at me like I'm nothing but hard work and I fucking *hate* when he acts like I'm difficult.

I throw my hands in the air and pace. The room is lit only by the lamp next to his bed, and so my shadow follows me on the walls. "Calm down?!" I rage, eyes bulging out of my head. "How can you agree to this?"

I followed Victor and Anton around the estate for about twenty minutes this afternoon but I couldn't get close enough to hear the rest of the conversation. If I ask Vic directly, it'll look like I don't trust my own brother. I'm waiting for him to tell me. Every second that he lets me rage and says nothing convinces me that he's not going to say anything at all.

"You're not paying attention," Victor says, leveling me with a disappointed glare as he stands up and comes to my side, placing his hand on my shoulder. "Look at them. They're running scared."

I narrow my eyes at him.

"Whatever is going on, they're not doing this to fuck with this. They're freaked out."

"How?" I ease my shoulders. Where I'm impulse, he's strategy, and I owe it to him to listen to what he might see that I don't.

Though, I see a lot of shit that he fucking doesn't and maybe he should listen to me sometimes. My nostrils flare but Vic squeezes my shoulder, anchoring me once again.

"Locking down this mansion. Various alarms. Bringing us here? They're not locking us in, brother, they're locking someone else out."

Victor sinks back into his chair to relax and I resume pacing with my hands on my hips. "You think they're under attack?"

"Isn't it obvious?" Victor says.

I give him an annoyed look and shake my head.

"They're not trying to fuck with us. They're trying to figure out if we're fucking with them."

Was that the summary of his conversation with Anton? Are they under attack and trying to determine if they should lay blame on us? Maybe.

"So you're going to bow down to their whims just to prove that to them? When they don't trust you?"

"They don't have a reason to yet. And yes, when marrying that girl practically makes me the leader of the entire city. Yeah, I'm going to bow down. For now," he says, giving a little smirk at the end.

I still don't like it, but Victor is done with this conversation. He stands up and claps me on the shoulder, telling me not to worry, that he's got it all under control, and to stop fucking pacing before I wear out the floor. Then he leaves me alone in the bedroom.

I stand at the window, resting my hands on the sill as my mind turns circles. Are they running scared? Their behavior does seem to indicate that something is wrong. Honestly, I'd just assumed that the 'something wrong' was us being here at all.

But if they really are under attack, it makes them weak and vulnerable. Do we have the power to crush them now where we never have before?

I'm chewing on my lip when something outside the window catches my attention. Sage is with the bodyguard on the back lawns. I can barely see them under the cover of dark, but through the moonlight I recognize her form and his sulky one nearby.

They start circling each other. Like lions on the prowl. Why the fuck are they circling each other? The show gets even more curious when she bolts towards the edge of the property and he chases after her in a fast pursuit.

It looks like a possible training scenario, but something tells me that it's not. They have no need nor intention to train the little princess. They want her sheltered and cooed over. That much is both obvious and sickening.

I smirk, understanding now. Vicious princess. She doesn't like being sheltered. She's trying to escape. But she's playing a losing game, because there's no *way* she's escaping him. She's heading for a dead end and he's gaining on her fast.

Then, out of nowhere, she surprises me. She runs across a paved garden bed, jumping onto the overhanging trellis that leads into the rose garden. She scales it, going full on parkour, as she uses the rungs as stepping stones and makes a final leap to freedom. She lands on a perch atop the wall, and Christ, she's one step away from freedom.

My brows raise when I realize that he's not going to be able to follow her. She just outran him. She throws her shoes down to a very annoyed bodyguard and my lips tilt up at the corners. When I realize what I'm doing, I frown. I did not just almost smile.

She disappears over the edge.

I let out an amused huff, but I relish in the knowledge that I am absolutely one hundred percent right. And this is all the proof I need to confirm what I've known since the first moment I saw her and she stomped her delicate little foot.

Sage DeMarco is up to something... and I'm going to find out what it is.

The bodyguard whips around suddenly, like he's going to charge into a run to the front gates and follow her, but then he sees me standing at the window and stops cold, frowning up at me.

I offer him a smirk and salute.

Oh, yeah. Sage is hiding something. And he doesn't know what it is.

Fourteen

SAGE

It takes half an hour to get to the dive bar on the outskirts of town. The whole time I'm on edge, chewing at the edges of my fingernails and then chastising myself for it. The drive is plenty of time for Nic to have rounded the front gate and charged after me with God only knows what kind of arsenal. That I've made it this far is a small miracle.

The car drops me off on the street corner; the pavements blackened by wear and the streetlights flickering. I pull my cardigan tighter as I head up the sidewalk to the bar and push open the door.

The air inside is pungent with sweat and body odor. Scrunching my nose and trying not to gag at the smell, it takes a moment for my eyes to adjust to the room. The lighting is purposefully low, patrons quiet and murmuring secrets to each other, a heavy fog of cigarette smoke polluting the atmosphere almost whimsically.

By the time my eyes come to, I spot Angie smirking at me from across the bar. She's sitting at her regular booth, completely alone and swirling a cocktail in her delicate but deadly hands.

I cross the floor and slide into the seat across from her.

"Miss DeMarco," Angie smirks, tossing a row of her flame-colored hair over her shoulder. "I thought you'd never make it."

I roll my eyes. "There's been unforeseen obstacles."

Angie's eyes alight with joy and she removes the umbrella from her drink before taking another sip. "Yes, I heard your uncle had locked down the entire estate."

When I don't respond, Angie raises a brow at me. But there's nothing I can say to her that she won't file away for later, so I stay silent.

"Did you bring what I asked for?" I ask, nervously tucking my hands under my thighs to stop them shaking and desperately hoping that she doesn't notice.

She slams the cocktail glass back down on the table. "I'm afraid we've a more pressing matter. Your uncle is behind on the payments."

I gape incredulously. "*What?*" Angie is brutal, but she's one of the few people we can trust. One of the few people outside of my father's organization that wouldn't dare to betray us. Of course, it's all a pre-paid arrangement. But her loyalty is bought fiercely. "Check again. That's not possible."

I know Anton and my father never used her discreet services for much. But I also know for sure that Anton wouldn't forget this payment. It's one of the few things we agree on.

"The payment for your-"

"Yes, yes, I know what you mean." I hurry to cut her off. I don't need her projecting our biggest secret to anyone who might dare to eavesdrop. "I'll write you a fucking check."

I don't care if we double pay her. I can't afford to have this slip through the cracks. She makes a show of eyeing me off until it becomes clear we're not moving onto other business until there's a signed check in her hands.

Grumbling, I grab my checkbook from my clutch and write out the funds to her. She accepts with a smile before reaching into her own purse and handing over the technology I've requested.

"As you wish. If you can get close enough to plant it, this should be able to spy any device you like."

I take the small package. "It needs to be untraceable."

Angie scoffs. "All of my pieces are."

I cautiously unwrap the package and study the contents. There is a tiny card that looks like an ancient SIM card, and a bunch of other miniature pieces and wires.

"Need a lesson?" Angie smirks.

I straighten my shoulders and pretend to be cool about it. "If you insist."

A hearty laugh leaves Angie's mouth before she clicks at a bartender and orders us a round of drinks. For the next several minutes, I enjoy a cocktail on her tab while she teaches me about the device I've purchased. Specifically, once I've got a hold of a phone, how to install the untraceable spyware and then how to link it back to my own device so I can follow along.

Once she's sure I've got it, she pulls away with another smile. The red of her lipstick hasn't even smudged half an inch despite the glass at her bottom pout.

"This is pretty dangerous stuff you're getting into, you know," she says.

"Don't pretend to care, Angie."

She smiles tightly before putting on a serious expression. "Paired with what you're paying me to do and the *other* side request you had... I can see where you're going with this."

"And your point is?" I fold my arms.

She regards me briefly before lifting her chin. I have to assume it's a sign of respect.

Hopefully.

"Nothing. Just interested to see how it plays out for you." If I think my secrets are dangerous, the ones Angie is privy to must be lethal.

I nod my head. I'm interested to see how this plays out for me too. I've never been very lucky and I'll need a hell of a lot of luck for this to end up how I intend. I thank her for her services, declining her offer to stay longer for drinks and instead order another private car to take me home before Nic has my head.

***

I have the car drop me off at the neighboring property, which means a slog up the dirt road to get to our expansive countryside estate. But it's much better than them being able to interrogate and likely murder the poor driver.

I don't plan on sneaking in. Nic has already seen me rush off, so I'm perfectly happy to stroll right up to the front gates and face my beating head on. I'm a big girl, after all.

When I approach the front gate, the guard tower light is on and a gentle waft of smoke is coming from nearby. Getting closer, I see a figure dressed in all black on the other side of the gates, a cigarette hanging between his lips. When he sees me approach, he stubs out the cigarette with his toe and turns to glower at me.

My eyebrows jump to my forehead as I'm sure my obvious surprise registers clear on my face. "Alexei?"

"Well, well... the prodigal princess has finally deigned to return."

I curl my fingers around the bars of our front gate as I regard him. "Where's Nic?" I frown. "Or Freddie? Or... anyone?"

Alexei gives a cruel smile. "Half are out looking for you. The others are perched at the perimeter walls waiting for you to try to sneak back inside."

"And yet you're at the front gate?" I can't help the fire that clips out in my tone.

"You'd already been seen sneaking out. It made no sense that you'd sneak back in. I hazarded a guess that you'd waltz right up to the gate... and here we are."

I smother a sigh and kick the dirt from the ground in frustration. "Yes, here we are. Can you open the fucking gate then?"

He gives a throaty laugh, the tone deep and raspy, before he regards me with a cruel gaze from the other side of the gate. "Nah, might leave you out there for a while."

I push my hands through the bars and claw at his chest, getting more enraged each time he steps out of my reach with a laugh. "Open the *fucking* gate!"

The briefest jump of his eyebrow is the only outward tell of his surprise. "You know, you've got a nasty mouth," he says. At least he does what I ask, going to the guardroom and opening the gate. I don't dare ask where the guards are.

The automatic doors swing open for me and I slip inside before securing them closed behind me. I don't want to let any weakness show in front of this asshole, but my anxiety gets the better of me. I tug on the gates, rattling them back and forth as I test to make sure they're secure and are actually locked.

Alexei raises a brow at me, but says nothing, only joining me at my side as we walk up the gravel path to the front door.

"You've got the whole property on edge with your stunt."

"I just needed to clear my head."

Alexei gives a dark chuckle that sends a shiver up my shine. I turn to look at him. "What?"

"You don't expect anyone to believe that bullshit, do you?" The cruel glint in his eye remains. I huff a breath as I tilt my head skyward. Were I with anyone else, I'd consider this night romantic, underneath the cool glow of the moon with a star filled sky.

"It's the truth." I pull my cardigan tighter around my shoulders. His eyes track the movement and I'm sure I've inadvertently given away some kind of tell.

"Sure it is. Just like the role you play is true?" He folds his arms over his chest as we stop in the circular driveway, his biceps bulging against his black shirt. This time, it's me who tracks the movement.

"Role?"

I freeze as he stalks slowly into my space. Just as I think he's going to press right into me, he turns and starts to circle me as if I'm prey. His voice seems to come from all angles as he sizes me up. "Weak. Flimsy. Delicate."

I keep my stare forward and try to school my features so it looks like I'm bored and undisturbed by this dance he's doing. But Alexei Rushkoff has a reputation as a psychopathic torturer and now I see why. Not only is he doused in rage, but I feel a psychological war being ignited.

His next words come from behind me, his breath skating over my ear. "An almost convincing role of the damsel. Little DeMarco princess."

He stares at me side on and I can't help but turn my wide-eyed stare on him.

"I'm not weak," I half-heartedly protest, shrinking from his gaze.

"Yeah. I don't think so, either." His jaw grinds on that last part as he runs a heavily tattooed hand through his slick black hair.

I can't look away from the crazed look in his eye. We stand there for what seems like an eternity, sizing each other up. Every encounter with this man is stranger than the last. But I find myself intrigued by the notion that he thinks I'm playing some kind of *role.* The weak mafia princess... scared look in my eyes... somehow I get the impression that's not what Alexei Rushkoff sees when he looks at me.

And if that's the case, he might be the only person I've ever met that can see right through me.

We only get two beats of warning, gravel crunching under boots, before our stare off is cut short when Alexei is shoved violently out of my eye line. He staggers, righting himself before he can fall.

"What the fuck do you think you're doing, Rushkoff?" Nic shouts, chest puffed up like he's marking his territory as he attempts to charge at Alexei again. Alexei begins to charge at him too, his nostrils flaring like a raging bull.

"Shit," a voice sounds near my ear. Another body joins the fray and Victor places a hand on both Alexei's and Nic's chests to stop them just before they throttle each other.

"Got something you want to fucking say to me, *bodyguard?*" Alexei seethes.

Nic pushes against Victor's hold on his chest, the larger man bracing hard to keep him in check. "Several things come to mind, *Rushkoff.*" Nic speaks the last part as a curse again.

"Enough!" Victor shouts, pushing them back harder so they both stumble away from each other. He cracks his knuckles and then his neck, the threat clear.

Nic points a finger towards Alexei. "I don't know what you're up to, but stay. The fuck. Away from her," Nic snarls in Alexei's direction, sparing a glance for Victor like he means to say the same thing to him as well.

Nic grabs me by the shoulders and redirects my attention to him. His eyes are sunken in and worried, his brow furrowed as he looks me over and pats me down as if he's checking for injuries.

"I'm fine, Nic," I say.

When he's finished patting me down, he pulls me in close, wrapping me up in his arms and sinking into me like I'm saving him from drowning just by being alive.

My heart stills. Caught completely off guard by the way he possesses me so openly. I wrap my arms around Nic's shoulders, hugging him back as I bury my head in his neck. I can feel his breath against my shoulder as he sinks his head against me too, and it makes my stomach drop *low*. So low that I have to suppress a groan.

When he pulls away he gives me a look that takes my breath away. Something completely unguarded. Something Nic has never been around me before. His eyes dart to my lips and I widen my eyes, wondering if he's really going to kiss me right here on the front driveway.

We're reminded of our audience when someone clears their throat. I turn my eyes over Nic's shoulder, where I see two very scary Russians glaring at me. Victor and Alexei are both watching us with equally confusing but completely different expressions. Victor's brow tenses as he watches me with a question in his eyes. Alexei looks at me like he already has the answer.

Victor's eyes shutter for a moment before he turns to his brother. "Come on, you need to ice that jaw so you don't swell up."

Victor goes to move, but Alexei doesn't immediately follow. He scowls at Nic before turning his angry stare onto me. "I'm fucking watching you, *princess.*"

Nic clears his own throat and stands up tall again, clasping his hands behind his back as if he's resumed his own role. The warmth from his eyes is long gone. So hidden now that I question if it even existed in the first place. The loss makes me cold.

"Your uncle will want to see you. You're in big fucking trouble," Nic says.

Great.

Fifteen

VICTOR

The sounds of Anton DeMarco ripping his niece a new place to shit from can be heard all throughout the second level of his enormous house.

It's clear the girl has a habit of sneaking out. She's a slippery one. As if I didn't already fucking know that. I wouldn't need to be here if she wasn't.

I open to the door to my suite, only to sigh when I find my brother already inside and pacing along the windows again.

"Shit, Alexei, not again. I'm tired."

He has an ice pack pressed to his face that he throws halfway across the room when he notices my expression. He rushes into my face, and I simply raise an eyebrow. My brother gets more leniency than I'd give any of my other men. Or that any brother in my position should give another. I'm still the *pakhan,* and he is a second son. A spare heir.

Lucky, because the entire city would be ash if it was left in his incapable hands.

"That fucker hit me in the jaw. He deserves a bullet!"

"You might have to settle for the satisfaction of knowing you got under his skin." I side step around my brother and go to the dresser. I don't look back at him, only watching myself in the mirror as I remove my watch and undo my tie.

Alexei's temper has not yet fizzled, and I surrender to the fact I'm going to have to let him run himself out. Though his insolence and tendency to bite at any poke in his side are quickly getting in my way.

"Bull fucking shit, brother." He stomps towards the door, and I check him in my periphery, ready to go after him if he's going to do something stupid. I smirk as I watch his eyes shudder and his pride take a hit as he picks up the ice pack and presses it against his face again.

"You really need to calm down," I stress, turning to him and folding my arms across my chest. "It's like you've forgotten what it is we've come here to do."

The fist holding the ice pack clenches, as does his jaw. "The problem with that is that I do *not* agree with your reasons for bringing us here."

"Peace versus power. I don't expect you to understand it. Understanding it isn't your place." I pin him with a meaningful look, reminding him that only one of us is in control here. Reminding him of the leniency given to him simply because he is my brother. And, admittedly, warning him not to fucking push it.

"I feel like I'm going insane," Alexei whispers, but I don't respond, because I'm not certain he meant for me to hear it. I eye myself in the mirror, noting that my beard needs a trim. I'm a good-looking man, I acknowledge that, so I can't help admiring my form in the reflection for a moment. It's enough to put me in a better mood when I turn back to my unstable brother.

"They have welcomed us into their home. Be cordial and do not fuck this up for me."

"Oh, for fuck's sake!" Alexei says, pulling at his hair. "I hate how willingly you're walking into a trap."

I pinch my nose. Alexei just lacks the forethought to see the bigger picture. He's a ruthless killer and an incredible asset, so it's usually worth tolerating these temper outbursts, but fuck, they really grate on my nerves.

"Drop it before you give me a fucking headache." This time, I let him hear the tightness in my voice. I beg him in the only way I know how and hope he doesn't force me to make it an order.

He drops his hands to the windowsill, looking tortured, before he turns his eyes on me. "She's diabetic, Victor."

I slowly turn my head towards him.

Of all the fucking things to have come out of my brother's mouth. I feel my skin tingle, body hardening. "Careful."

Alexei raises a brow. A calm demeanor settles over him, like his has returned because he can sense he's ruffled mine. He speaks slowly and deliberately, finding his head. For a moment I bare my teeth, thinking it may have been better if he'd kept his head firmly up his ass instead of nosing into my business. "I'm just watching *your* back, brother. She's not the pretty princess you make her out to be."

I choose to say nothing. Because it feels like he's getting too close to things he shouldn't know. Not that I don't trust my brother. But it's established he's a loose cannon. He would give away every secret entrusted to him just from the look on his face alone.

"I called Isla here."

It's my turn to lose my shit now. My anger rises to the surface like a wave, crashing into me and taking me under. "You fucking what?!" I barrel towards him from across the room, hands twitching at my sides, begging me to unleash my fury on his fucking face.

He stands up, straightening his back in direct confrontation with me.

"I'm losing my fucking mind here, Vic," he says, giving me an honest, sheepish look. "The way they're trapping us in here feels wrong. I need backup."

"You know how I-"

He cuts off my anger with a wave of his hand. "I don't care what you think about Isla. She's coming. So if I have to stay here with DeMarco trash and their vicious little princess, then Isla comes too. That's final."

Yeah, this is the exact fucking opposite of remembering his place and position. When he leaves the room and closes the door behind him, my glass smashes against the wood behind him.

***

"You really think letting this girl in here is going to tame your psycho brother?" The hitter, Freddie, laughs as he slaps his cards down. "I've never met a girl with a magic pussy, but I suppose there's a first time for everything."

Cigar smoke fills the air in Anton's library. We're seated around a green felt-lined table playing *twenty-one.* The sun is still up and streaming through the windows. But in our world deals are rarely made in the darkness. Here in this room is where chess pieces are shuffled around the board. All in broad daylight.

"Isla is harmless. Just consider her another member of my staff." I chuckle, pasting a bright, friendly smile on my face. I'm putting on all the charm and just hoping they don't see through it.

Not only did my fuckup brother invite his petty little girlfriend here, he's now got me *negotiating* with the DeMarcos to allow her through the God damn gates. To say I'm pissed off is an understatement.

Isla will most definitely rattle Sage. There's no getting around that. As much as I hate her fucking guts, she's a head-turner. I doubt that Sage, the girl who's used to being the center of attention in every room she's in, will take the competition lightly.

But, Isla will calm Alexei.

And right now my brother is much closer to fucking things up for me than he either knows or cares.

"One girl surely can't do much damage. Just let her in, Anton," Freddie says. "It's not like you haven't let half of them parade through here already."

Freddie sucks his lip. It means he's losing. I can't wait to play him at poker.

"One girl," Anton reluctantly agrees, shuffling his own cards. His tells are a little harder to read, but they're there. In the subtle way he holds his cards between two fingers instead of four when he has a draw he doesn't want. "Unarmed."

I laugh, puffing cigar smoke into the air. "Isla doesn't know how to use a gun."

Despite a decent card game with my soon-to-be in-laws, I can't help but notice the glaring absence in the room. The Prince boy has yet to emerge today. Likely guarding the girl.

"Where's your resident bodyguard today? Sore loser at cards?" I ask, chucking my cards on the table when I realize I, too, am losing.

"Sticking close to my niece. She's refused to leave her room so far today," Anton says, getting a faraway look in his eye. Something about the man screams unprepared. From that simple look in his eye, I know he doesn't have the gut to run this business without Dimitri DeMarco.

"The whole house heard you biting into her last night," Freddie says.

Anton's gaze flicks to me but I shrug. Pretending this is none of my business. Everyone heard the verbal lashing she got from her uncle for sneaking out. It's no surprise she's hiding away to lick at her wounds.

"Don't mind me, Anton. I don't mind a bit of unruly in my woman."

They both curl their lip at me. They might be growing to like me, but they positively hate that their precious daughter is meant to be mine. I can't help but picture how her thick lips will look wrapped tightly around my cock before I fuck her even tighter pussy in every position I can think of.

Anton deals another round. "You really think bringing this girl here will cool off your brother?"

I clench my jaw and I hate that they see it. "Isla is an annoyance, but fortunately, she seems to temper my brother."

Anton nods. "He's aggressive at all the wrong moments. I imagine that's an asset in the right ones."

I smile and chuckle. "You relate to the little bro position, do you, Anton?" I shake at his shoulders, coaxing an exhausted smile from him. "Don't tell me you have some sympathy for the psychotic Rushkoff?"

My tone is playful, making Anton laugh and shove me back. Setting the course of our friendship back on track long enough for him to forget about all the things I'm going to do to his niece.

***

Isla arrives too quickly for my liking.

It's only that afternoon when Alexei tells me she's here, waiting for us at the front gates. Him. She's waiting for him. Isla hates my guts as much as I fucking hate hers. But I am damn well going to be there when she struts her way in here. If only to remind her who is in charge and who is responsible for allowing her to keep breathing.

I stomp down the gravel path from the mansion's front doors, cigarette at my lips and a scowl firmly on my face as I head for the gates. Alexei is already well in front of me, playing on his phone as he waits for her. I see the twitch in his leg, though. He's anxious for her to get here so he can relax, knowing his back is covered.

I throw the cigarette out of my mouth, stopping when I get to his side.

"Thought you said she was here," I quip, hearing the bitterness in my voice.

Alexei rolls his eyes at me. "All cars to be left outside the gates. You know that," he says. "Just another brilliant way for them to trap us in here without escape."

While we're busy scowling at each other, the gates push open just long enough for Isla and the two duffel bags she has slung over her shoulder to slip through.

She drops them on the ground, brushing herself off. Her blonde hair is long and styled straight, her legs are wrapped in black leggings, and she's wearing a crop top that shows off the tan plains of abs on her stomach.

"Miss me that much, hey?" she smirks, looking back and forth between Alexei and me.

"Like a hole in the head," my brother says, giving her a smile that turns into a smirk when he looks at me.

118

He walks toward her and gives her a quick hug, patting her back loudly before he picks up one of her duffels, leaving her to get the other one.

She hefts it over her shoulder and walks right up to me, Alexei pausing behind her to watch the exchange. "Long time no see, Vic," she says, giving me a tone that is full of icy venom and just a bit of something menacing.

"Don't push your luck, Lenkov," I warn. "The second my brother pulls his brain back into his skull and out of his cock is the second you're fucking gone."

I pin my brother with a glare, telling him he better put his evil ass back in line now.

The ring of Isla's hysterical laughter follows me all the way back to the house.

Sixteen

SAGE

Nic has barely spoken a word to me since I snuck out. It's like the intimate moment on the driveway never happened. Like he's angry with me for defying him. Which I can't blame him for.

Still, his coldness burns me. Especially as he still insists on guarding every room I'm in.

Nic and I are already tense by the time he escorts me to the dining room for dinner. It's not just the sneaking out. It's the waiting for him to touch me. It's all the tension that being promised to marry someone else brings. We're balancing on an unstable pile, and I'm not sure whether I should be angry, or horny as fuck.

Horny is currently in the lead.

When we finally make it to the dining room, everyone else is already seated. Anton sits as usual at the head of the table, but everyone else is oddly out of order. Freddie sits on Anton's left instead of Nic. Victor is still on Anton's right, but there is a spare seat next to him that is usually occupied by his brother. Supposing I'm meant to sit next to my fiancé, I start towards Victor.

A scoff comes from next to me and Nic narrows his eyes at me as he takes the choice away, sliding in next to Victor.

Unfortunately for me, that only leaves one other spot. The place between Freddie and a smug as fuck Alexei Rushkoff sitting on my other side.

Whoever has done the seating arrangement is getting a kick in the head.

"Are you okay?" Freddie whispers to me, ignoring the greetings and conversation going on around us.

"Fine," I say, but it comes out as a hiss. Freddie's brows jump to his hairline.

"Right. Forget I said anything then..." Freddie says, but he seems to lose his train of thought, his words slurring off as he focuses on something else. I narrow my eyes, noting there *is* one other seat that's left empty. A place is set next to Nic, across from Alexei. And someone is coming in to fill it.

The doors to the dining room open with a flourish and we all turn to look.

Frowning, I watch as the most beautiful woman I've ever seen strides in and confidently takes the seat next to Nicholas. Like she's been personally invited. Like she's not at all out of place. She's wearing a red top with puffy off the shoulder sleeves, and jeans, but she looks ethereal. Her blonde hair hangs down her back in straight lines. Her smile is wide, her lips framed with blood red lipstick.

She shakes out her napkin, flattening it on her lap, and her blue eyes sparkle as she looks around the table.

I follow her gaze to find I'm the only one who seems able to take their eyes away from her. Vic is choking the life out of his fork as he glares at her. Freddie's jaw practically unhinges from his face and Anton purses his lips.

Everyone is looking at her.

Even... *Nic.*

My heart drops out of my chest onto the table, where it feels like a knife is slicing me. As if my desecrated heart is about to be served on a platter.

The person who did the seating arrangement is now getting an axe to the fucking throat.

"Princess." It's a tiny, quiet breath that only I hear.

My head jerks to the left and my breath catches.

There is one person in the room not looking at *her*. Alexei Rushkoff. And he's looking at me.

He gives me a small smirk and then deliberately clears his throat. "Ahem!"

The others snap back into motion, taking Alexei's cue to stop fucking staring, as they go back to their conversations as if the world didn't just stop for a second.

But I'm still stuck staring at the bombshell wondering *who, what, when, where, WHY?!*

"You must be Sage," the blonde smiles at me. And fuck it comes across as genuine. She looks like a threat, though, so this is very confusing for me.

She is undeniably beautiful and confident in the way she carries herself. It's not surprising she commands the attention of a room.

"I've heard a lot about you," she says, still attempting to draw me into conversation.

She pats her hand across the table, unclenching Alexei's fist and laying her palm on the back of his hand. His body visibly relaxes at her command. I can smell the intimacy between them from here.

With one quick glance at Victor, I confirm he's still glaring at her like he's going to slit her throat with his butter knife.

"Uh... yes." I recover not at all smoothly. "Sage DeMarco. And you...?"

"Isla. Isla Lenkov. But you can just call me Isla." She smiles again and I swear it's like sunshine radiates out of her skin.

"What the fuck are you doing in my house Isla?" I say.

Freddie nearly chokes on his drink, spitting whiskey across the table. He coughs in the aftermath, to the point where Uncle Anton has to pat his back to make him stop. Victor's shoulders perk up and he grins. It's almost comical. The way he straightens with excitement. I can feel Anton's heated stare boring into my back, but there's no way I'm turning to look at him.

Isla just raises her brow, patting Alexei's hand again like she's his master, telling him to stand down. She releases her hold on him and faces me. "I'm just another guest. A Rushkoff family friend. We go way back. Don't we, Victor?"

Isla gives him a saccharine smile and Victor goes back to looking like he's trying to work out how to plot a murder.

"Right," I say. "How long are you staying?"

"Is that code to ask when you can kick me out?" she laughs.

I just raise my brow in challenge.

"She's fucking staying," Alexei seethes.

Tension brews in the air. Ever the diplomat, Anton chimes in to dissolve it. "Of course, she is. Excuse my niece. She means well. Shall we serve the entrée? *Quickly.*" Anton addresses that last bit to our staff.

Entrées are placed and the guests devolve into quiet and polite chatter. Victor and Anton chortle between each other, while Nic turns to introduce himself to Isla, pulling Freddie into the conversation.

"Well, well, well. Look at the way your bodyguard is watching her," Alexei says, grinning as he leans closer to me.

I clench my jaw, trying to ignore him. But of course, he's right. Nic is conversing with Isla, his whole focus on her being.

"He's assessing her as a threat," I bite back.

"Oh, she's a threat," Alexei chuckles. "To you."

Without thinking, I react first, kicking Alexei's leg under the table.

He jolts and makes a whimpering sound, before he turns a heated look my way. "What the fuck?"

"Next time I hit your crotch, fucker."

Alexei's utensils clammer down onto his plate, and everyone stops to stare as he shoots to his feet. They look predictably alarmed at his outburst. Especially since, from the looks and the little gestures, Isla is here specifically to calm him down.

I do my best to copy their shocked expressions.

Alexei stares devils at me until he looks around the table and must realize that he doesn't have the support of the room. That he looks crazy as hell.

He sits back down, his knee bouncing while the rest of the table tries to move on with conversation. They still shoot him glances every now and again, but Alexei being crazy isn't news, so everyone does move on eventually.

"You set me a trap," he says without looking at me.

"Nope," I smile. "I just really want to fucking kick you."

His utensils clammer down again and I struggle to stifle my laugh while Isla does her best to calm him, running her hands over her face and looking very ashamed.

"Playing with fire, aren't you?" Freddie whispers from my other side, smirking at me.

"He's just so easy to bait," I say, smiling back.

Freddie chuckles. "Too easy." He clears his throat. "And you are right. Nic is just assessing the threats. For as long as I've known him, he's only had eyes for you."

I turn to him in shock, nearly dropping my own cutlery, but Freddie just stares ahead like he hasn't just dropped a bombshell on me. I'm jolted out of my shock when the entrées are cleared and the main is served.

"Before we eat, I have an announcement," Victor says.

Ugh, I'd just picked up my fork to eat. I settle it down and smile politely. Alexei is the only one at the table radiating with tension. Does he not know whatever surprise it is that his brother has in store?

I like that.

Victor stands, his chair scraping across the floor.

"Sage DeMarco," he says, and that's when I realize he's moved and is now standing behind me. Freddie reluctantly pulls his chair back a little to give Victor room. His lips purse like he's displeased, but also like he's not going to interrupt this display either.

Victor pulls my chair around to face him.

"You deserve much more than what I presented you with when I first arrived," Victor says.

"Wha-"

Victor drops to one knee.

Shit.

"Fuck." My thoughts are echoed as both Alexei and Nic speak the word in time.

A new ring box is presented in front of me, clasped between Victor's hands. It's-

"Tiffany!" I let out a delighted squeal.

The reaction causes a scowl from most everyone around the table. Except Victor, who smiles, and does he...? He... yeah, he has tears in his eyes.

Oh, shit.

He opens the turquoise box and presents me with a pear-shaped diamond that has to be at least seven carats.

My jaw drops. It's fucking gorgeous.

"A girl like you deserves a ring every bit as beautiful and unique as she is. We may have skipped a lot of steps, *prekrasnaya devushka,* and I know we've already done this once. But... Will you marry me, Sage DeMarco?"

My eyes widen. Sure, we've been "promised" for a while now. But, with the intent of getting to know each other. Discussions of peace and drawing out our time together so our families can mingle.

Not... not with wedding planning.

And not with a *ring*.

My heart jackhammers, and I turn my tortured eyes on Nic, who looks just as pained as I feel. Victor is still smiling when I turn back to him, but now with a noticeable tic in his jaw and a twitching eye.

I hesitate. For the first time, I want to take this back. But still, I say, "Yes." And then nearly choke on a swallow.

Victor takes my hand in his and slips the ring onto my finger. I look across to Anton as Victor places a chaste kiss against my cheek.

My uncle gives me a sad smile. "Looks like we have a wedding to plan. Congratulations, *anima mia.*"

***

When you consider that dinner included *another* surprise proposal, the rest of it was alarmingly uneventful. Everyone was quiet. Even Alexei. Not even Isla's arrival outshone the fact that there's a DeMarco-Rushkoff wedding to plan.

Victor offers to escort me back to my room, and Nic allows it so he can stay behind to talk with Anton and Freddie. The fact that he's letting Victor take my hand and lead me away from the dining room guts me. It's as if he's finally handing me over to Victor and my fragile heart can't handle it. I can't ignore my aching want for him.

Is this what it looks like when Nicholas Prince gives up?

All because of a gaping diamond on my finger.

We reach the bottom of the stairs. "I can escort myself back to my own room."

"Prince doesn't seem to think so," Victor says, waggling his eyebrows. Nic has cemented himself firmly in bodyguard status and the men are having a riot teasing him about it. Okay, I enjoy teasing him about it too.

I stifle a smile as I groan. "Yes, he doesn't seem to think I'm capable of much now."

"Well, it is your house. So I'll leave you here."

"Thank you," I say.

We stare at each other for a moment and I tense as I wonder if he's waiting for some show of affection from me. We're going to be married, probably soon if tradition has anything to say about it. A hearty pat on the shoulder as goodbye feels like it'd be the wrong thing to do.

Victor either senses my discomfort or doesn't care, chuckling as he leans over and plucks a kiss on my cheek. He lingers with his lips against my skin, tearing them away slowly as his beard lightly scratches at my cheek.

My eyes shutter as I look back at him. He smirks, saying goodnight before he walks away.

It's strange, how different he feels, and I curse my luck. Nic makes me feel warm inside, and Alexei's touch heats me to my core. But with Victor, I feel nothing but the ache of a place where something is missing.

I shake my head of the strange encounter. The longer this goes on, the less sure I am of anything I thought I knew before. I climb the stairs in quiet contemplation. All I wanted was a little freedom. Not to be guarded. But since my father's death all the pieces I thought were in play have left me perplexed.

So much so that I'm not even sure I know the game being played anymore.

When I reach the top of the stairs I hear hushed voices. Turning, I find Isla and Alexei are deep in conversation down the hall from me, standing intimately close. He appears angry, but when doesn't he? Isla laughs each time his eyes bulge like he's fighting to keep control of his demons.

If there was any doubt left, it's all gone now. This girl must be his girlfriend.

And he's parading her around for what?

They're standing in front of one of the doors to the guest bedrooms. The room isn't Alexei's. Or any room that had been assigned for that matter.

So it must be hers. But why would she need a separate room?

She pats his arm once and he relaxes again. She opens the door behind her and together they go into her room.

Well, that answers that question. But it also poses another.

Alexei has been hot-headed, distrustful and vague. Unlike all the other pieces of my life that have changed shape, molded to something new, he's the one I never really saw coming. The only piece on the board that isn't meant to be there, and I can't decide if he's pawn or king.

It's only a split second decision that makes me decide that tonight I should try to plant the cloning device on Alexei's stuff, rather than his brother's. Tonight. While he's distracted by his annoyingly beautiful girlfriend.

"Sage?"

I turn around and find Nic jogging up the stairs behind me. He stops a short distance away from me. Putting much more space between us than was between Isla and Alexei.

"Can we talk?" he asks.

I scrunch my brows but nod anyway, pointing a thumb over my shoulder in the direction of my bedroom. I walk inside and sit on the end of my bed, only hearing as Nic gently closes the door behind us and comes to stand in front of me.

When I look to him, his arms are folded over his chest and his face raggedly torn. I've never seen this much raw emotion on him before. It feels like nails scraping on my skin.

"Nic, what-"

"Are you really pursuing Victor? Really considering it?"

I close my eyes and look away. God dammit. He's asking for much more of my hand than I'm willing to give away.

"Right. Say no more." He moves away from me to stare out my bedroom window, turning his back on me and therefore the conversation. I make my way slowly towards him, desperate to turn him back to where we started. Back before there was no Rushkoffs. No marriage. No engagement ring and no wedding being planned. Where we were just a boy and a girl. With flirting and soft touches across my sensitive skin.

"Nicholas," I say, touching my hand to his back.

He shakes the touch away, his eyes hardening after just a fraction of softness that I'm now not sure was only my imagination.

"It's not what you think," I say.

"It clearly doesn't matter what I think," he says, turning to face me with a challenge.

I know there's nothing more I can give him. No answer that will satisfy this curiosity. So I have to leave that statement out there no matter how much it pains me.

"And I suppose it shouldn't," he says, pushing away and heading for the door.

"Please," I say.

I inwardly cringe at myself. The amount of times that I've stood in front of Nicholas Prince and begged him is shameful. Begged him not just to fuck me, but to fucking love me. All the times he's rejected me feel as bad as the times he's given in. Because he's never really given me him. There's a wall between us. I'm just not sure if it's his or mine anymore.

"I can't do this with you," he says, his jaw hardening.

My heart cracks. *Love me, please. All I've ever wanted was for you to love me.* "Why?" I say, my voice coming out as barely more than a squeak.

"Why?" he repeats, whirling to face me, his hands restless and his eyes wilder than I've ever seen them. This isn't what it looks like when Nicholas Prince gives up. It's what he looks like when he becomes unhinged. "I want you so fucking bad, you know that? You torture me. You *like* to torture me. Until all I can think about is getting back inside you. You have made my life a living hell every single day I've worked here, Sage."

Oh.

Ouch.

"A living fucking hell." Suddenly he's in my face, eyes wild. "I worked for your father and yet every single day all I could think about was you. Parading around trying to get me to come to bed with you. Fuck, if I were a better man I'd have had some self-control." He runs his fingers through his hair as he takes a step back.

"You had perfect self-control." My voices goes hard. "You've turned me down. Just as many times as you've said yes, you've said no more." I turn my pleading eyes up to his, but he doesn't return my gaze.

"It was not from lack of wanting to." Nicholas clenches his teeth. "Never from lack of wanting to."

"You know how I feel. I've never exactly hidden it," I say.

That lights some kind of fire inside him. His eyes snap back to mine and he grips me roughly by the shoulders. Before I know what hits me, his lips are on mine. They are hard, bruising even, and they devour me. He kisses me like his life depends on it, so hard and rough that I'm afraid he will swallow me whole, or I him.

Just as quickly as he started it, he uses his grip on my arm to pull me away from him, as if he has to physically push me away from him because his lips refuse to disconnect. "I know how you feel," he says. "You want to give me your body, when I have always wanted so much more."

For a moment, I'm stunned into silence, before his words sink in.

I give a disbelieving scoff. "You're an absolute fucking moron, Nicholas Prince."

I kiss him again, jumping up into his arms and deepening the kiss. He grabs my hips as my legs wrap around his waist. We're in my bedroom, but somehow going to the bed still feels too intimate. Too close to what we really want to say.

Nicholas backs me towards the dresser, balancing me in one arm as he swipes the contents off the top and sits me on the wood. Our hands are blurry with speed, shaking as I tug on his belt and he pulls at my panties.

We keep bumping into each other, our hands blocking one another as we try desperately to undress so we can connect where we most want to.

Nicholas drops to his knees with a growl. "Are these fucking panties sewn on?" He tugs my panties, searing my skin as he rips them from my body and throws them across the room.

He pushes my dress up my thighs, hands squeezing as he goes. Settling his hands on my hips, he presses his nose to my center and inhales. He's right there, so close, and I just want him to touch me. To take me.

I feel his tongue swipe across my slit and I buck up wildly. My hands pull and scrape across his skull, tugging at his hair. Each time he tries to move away I thrust my hips up and push him back into me harder.

He rips away from me suddenly, cringing with hesitation, and I swear I could throttle him. His indecision threatens to destroy me, especially when I'm on the cusp of an orgasm.

"We shouldn't be doing this. You're marrying someone else." He averts his gaze and shakes his head. I nearly scream from frustration. I can see the hard outline of him from where his pants hang on. I swear to fucking sin itself that if he doesn't take me tonight I'm going to kick him so hard in the balls he'll never be able to fuck again.

"Victor is-"

Nic turns back to me with a sneer on his face and renewed determination. Who knew another man's name was the right thing to say?

"Never say his name again," he breathes. He grips my hips and I yelp as he pulls me closer to the edge of the dresser, diving back in to pick up where he left off between my legs. "Come on my tongue. And never fucking say his name again."

I don't. I don't even think about anyone else as Nicholas gives me everything he's got. I clutch at him, my legs trembling and instead I scream his name as I do, as promised, come on his tongue.

I sink back against the mirror with my legs spread. I'm wet, panting and wild as I come down from my orgasm. There's no time to recover as Nic rips his belt free and pulls himself out, stroking up and down.

He kisses me as he traces his crown over me, soaking himself in my release. A release that I can taste on his lips as well as he can feel it on mine. When he guides his cock inside me, parting me as he sinks easily to the hilt, we both stop to gasp.

Fuck, it's been so long since we've actually had sex. I forgot how good it feels.

As much as I want it to be, this isn't going to be some grand act of lovemaking. We're frustrated, with excess energy to burn and feelings that neither of us have any fucking clue what to do with.

"Please, move," I moan in his ear when he's been still for too long.

He comes back from wherever he was in his head. His eyes move from the ceiling to me, and in unison we both drop our heads to watch the place where we connect as he starts to move. To watch as his cock disappears inside me and comes out glistening over and over again.

Nicholas has never felt so good. Never felt so unhinged and I love it. I love the way that this time, unlike any of the others, he grips me like he could ruin me. I grasp at the mirror behind me, hanging on as he clasps my hip and starts to really fuck me. Hard enough that the dresser slams against the wall, narrowly missing my fingers curled around the mirror. The noise of the dresser slamming against the wall is loud and crazy. Irresponsible and reckless and asking for trouble. Right now, neither of us cares.

"You're going to be the God damn death of me," Nic says, holding my legs wide as he slams inside me. He hoists my leg higher, securing it over his hip to get a deeper angle. "You're going to cost me everything I've ever worked for."

"Oh, fucking hell," I moan, feeling it as he hits the exact right spot inside me. "Right there... right there... right there."

"I know." His teeth are gritted. "I know."

I start to tighten, clawing wildly at him as I beg him not to stop, moaning loud enough to wake the whole house. This time, Nic doesn't silence me. He groans too. Loudly and in a deep tenor that is so fucking sexy. His voice in my ear, hearing the sounds he's making and knowing that it's me doing it to him, is what sends me over the edge.

"Oh shit," he says, his thrusts starting to become jerky as I come all over his cock. Our skin slaps obscenely as he buries himself to the hilt, thrusting home with punishing certainty and coming deep inside me. He presses his fist into the mirror, rolling his hips while his warmth floods inside me.

As we both finish, reality sinks in and my body goes cold. Even though my pussy is still spasming and his cock is still twitching inside me. My heart hurts as I anticipate the inevitable running away that comes with any ounce of vulnerability from Nic.

Being right about something you very much don't want to happen is incredibly bittersweet.

Nic pulls out of me slowly, barely able to look at me and the shattered remains of my love and pride that he leaves behind. In fact, he doesn't look at me. I sit like a fuck toy on the dresser full of his cum while he fully redresses. I feel like a fuck toy too, being discarded one too many times to not be burned alive by his regret. His regret of me.

Not even when he goes to leave does he look at me. Not in any of the steps that he makes to leave the room. I'm so disappointed, so cut by his actions, that I don't even move. Not even to close my legs.

He pauses with his hand on the doorknob, shadows streaming over his face. "I can't do this, Sage. I'm not supposed to want you. I'm not *allowed* to want you."

"I don't care what you're supposed to do."

"It's not that simple," he says, shaking his head. "We can't do this. We're *not* doing this anymore, okay? I don't... I don't want you enough to jeopardize everything I've worked for."

He leaves, closing the door gently behind him. I cover my mouth with my hand to suppress a sob. It doesn't work.

It. Does. Not. Fucking. Work.

Seventeen

SAGE

I open my eyes at two in the morning.

Once Nic left my room I showered, scrubbing hard enough to erase any trace that he ever touched me from my skin. The humiliation hurts like hell, his harsh words like teeth ripping my organs open.

After six years of loving Nic, I'm no stranger to pushing down my pain and picking myself back up. He's made it clear how very little I mean to him. Whatever is left of my pride refuses to let me waste another second of it on him.

I've got things to do. Things of my own.

I've got to get the cloning device on that fucker Alexei's phone while he's still holed up in the other room banging his girlfriend.

This is a perfect opportunity to be sneaking out of the mansion, especially knowing that Nic will be giving me a wide berth. This time, however, my priorities inside the mansion fall on much higher regard.

I tiptoe to my dresser, grab the cloner and then I'm off again. Sneaking across the landing, I make my way to the guest wing into Alexei Rushkoff's lair. The man might not be as built as Victor or as stern as Nicholas, but he is creepy and crawly and sneaky like a snake. He'll strike up and pounce. He is, in his own right, downright terrifying.

Not that I'd ever let him see I think that.

I slip through the door into the guest room where Alexei is staying, shutting it behind me with a sharp exhale and wide eyes. With feet as limber as a cat, I slink throughout his room. He's already well decorated it for himself, spreading out and making the space his own. So much so that it doesn't even look like it's part of my house anymore.

His things contaminate the space. Trinkets are littered on every surface. Clothes are thrown about haphazardly. The furnishings are covered in black linen.

Even his own pillows are on the bed. They're memory foam, which we don't have, and the pillowcases are black silk. I run my hand over them, feeling for evidence that I wanted to collect. Nothing. But the unmade bed and the sheets still smell like him. Like spirits and geranium.

It is... gross. Yep. Gross. Yuck.

I force myself to stick out my tongue in a grimace.

In his walk-in-closet I expect to see a collection of neatly pressed black shirts lined up in pedantic symmetry. But no, the man is a slob. There are clothes and accessories strewn about in an unintelligible fashion. If it is a pattern, I'm not seeing it.

Underneath some of the discarded, and worn (ugh), trousers I find several guns. That isn't exactly a surprise, though. He's a well-known mobster. He would have guns. That doesn't prove a thing.

I slide open one of the drawers and find a package of condoms. Gross. The package is unopened, though. Huh.

In another drawer I find shirts. Again, not neatly pressed or folded, but scrunched and messily wrapped up. He really is an absolute mess and an insane slob. I don't know why I expected his space to be neat when his head is obviously a mess.

Shaking my head, I open the next drawer and find his wallet.

Not the item I'm looking for but it'll do.

I open it, but to my surprise it's light on cash and cards. Light on anything worth looking at other than his driver's license. Alexei Grigori Rushkoff. He looks like a criminal in his picture.

Of course, he does. He is one. I'm an idiot. I stifle a groan and try not to physically face-palm myself.

The only interesting thing inside his wallet is the picture.

There's a color photograph, an actually printed one, sitting inside the little plastic sleeve. Three little kids. One boy with dark hair on the left, one boy with golden hair on the right and a pretty little blonde girl in the middle.

The picture is whitening at the edges, so it can't have been recently printed.

The blonde girl has her arms around the little blond boy, their cheeks pressed together, smiling brightly. The dark-haired boy is close too, but neither of the others are touching him. He's smiling, but it's easy to see he's really meaning to frown. Like he's been forced to smile for the picture despite the fact that he didn't much feel like it.

I understand that look all too well because I've felt it myself many times. The outsider. Outcast. Watching everyone else's smiles and being unable to understand why it's so easy for them. Why it's so easy for everyone else to connect. To grin. To get along. It is, however, easy to see someone else's pain when it's a reflection of your own shining back on you.

"And what *the fuck* do you think you're doing?"

I let out a little girly squeal, nearly dropping the wallet as I whirl to face the intruder. My heart beat thumps in my chest like galloping horse's hooves.

Shit.

"Alexei," I say, my eyes surely so wide that I'm actually worried they might fall out and run away.

Fuck. Shit, fuck, shit.

"Princess," Alexei says, leaned up against the door with one foot crossed over the other and his arms folded over his chest. His muscles bulge against his black shirt and his brow raises as he eyes his wallet in my hands. "Going through my things?"

I steel my nerve.

"Seemed only fair," I shrug. "You've barged into my personal space. I thought the offer was mutual."

I put his wallet down on the dresser.

"Find anything interesting?" He's smirking. My shoulders drop from the look on his face. I'm not going to find anything in here. He knows it. Whatever he thinks I was looking for, I now know I won't find it here. He's too careful for that. Even if it's just something that I can hack a cloning device onto.

"What are you even doing here? Shouldn't you be sleeping with your girlfriend?"

His eyes brighten like I've said something surprising, a full smile forming on his mouth. "Maybe I'd prefer to fuck her in here."

I blanch. That is not the answer I was expecting, and I'm not quick enough to have a witty remarked prepared.

"Or maybe my cock is so massive that impaling her on it over and over has left her ruined and dead," he says, looking amused as all hell as he tries to shrug nonchalantly. Jesus fucking Christ. I'm drowning here, and he can clearly tell because he breaks out into a chuckle when I have to turn my head to hide my pink cheeks. I'm not a virgin by any standards. But everyone gets a little nervous with the surprise mention of cock.

I clear my throat as I concede I've lost that round and instead I gesture to the picture in his wallet. "Who's in the picture?"

Alexei looks over at his wallet, finally peeling away from the wall and coming to stand next to me. His fingers trace over the faces in the photo and I try not to notice that our shoulders are touching from how close we stand. Or how warm and imposing his form feels standing next to mine. "Me, Isla, Victor."

That I had guessed, but from how Victor and Alexei were acting, it seemed like Isla was a recent fling. Probably one they fought over. I didn't realize how deep their roots went.

"Happy little photo, isn't it," Alexei says.

I give an amused smile, one that says I know something he doesn't. It takes him a second to notice, but he frowns when he does, immediately going on the defensive. "Something to say?"

"Well, happy. For Victor and Isla, at least. You look..." I keep my eyes on the picture as I try to convey to him what I see when I look at this picture. I grin when I find it. "*Murderous.*"

Alexei gives me a strange look and then checks the photo again. As if I've ruffled him so much that he has to make sure. "I'm smiling."

"Not with your eyes," I say. I lift my gaze to his, finding his stormy gray eyes watching me. The same look in the photo is in them right now. I cock my head, wondering how I haven't seen it before. There's an angry exterior, but one that is meant to hide something deeper. "You look...sad." I whisper the words.

Alexei looks back at the picture once more, his eyes softening before he turns them back on me again.

"Lonely," I say, choking on the word.

Alexei frowns at me. There's a crease between his brows. One that hasn't left his face the whole time I've known him. Inside me, there is a desperate need to be the one that smooths it over. That feeling bubbles up like water boiling over, taking me in a rush of emotion.

I reach my hand up, and he doesn't stop me as I smooth the line with my thumb. His posture relaxes, our eyes not leaving each other, and when I pull my hand back the crease is gone.

"You love her," I say.

He grits his teeth. "Yes."

"And Victor-"

"Doesn't," Alexei snaps.

I smile.

"Stop smiling like that."

"Why?"

"I don't like it," he whispers now too.

"You don't like anything." God, we're close now. How did we get this close and what the hell am I doing? Is this my lonely heart reacting to Nic's brutal rejection? Or is it... something worse.

Alexei is quiet for a moment, but his voice is full of intent when he speaks again. "You think you see me, princess. I see you too. All the secrets. All the lies. There's a wall behind your eyes. Right now, it's down."

I swallow, but I can't bring myself to blink. There are walls around me. There has to be. I want to put them back up, worried that he really can see past them, but right now I'm not sure how to do it.

"Right now, you would let me. If I were to kis-"

An explosion sounds abruptly in the background, shaking the floor underneath our feet, stiffening us and shocking us back to reality. My wide eyes meet his frown as I see Alexei look more pissed off than I've ever seen him. What's more, he looks alarmed. That only terrifies me further.

"Wha-" I start, but a bright flare pushes up the window outside until I see fire blanketing the entire lawn.

We both rush towards the window, not even bothering to shove at each other in our haste. On the grass there is a hoard of men with guns, vests and black masks on their face, swarming in at all angles.

I burst out in a cry as I use both hands to cover my mouth. "Oh, my God. What's happening?"

"Shit."

I look at Alexei. He watches the scene outside with predatory calculation, a muscle feathering in his jaw. When he looks over at me, his face drops, obviously seeing the terror etched over every part of my being.

The sound of smashing glass soon follows and I barely hold in a scream.

Renewed determination shadows his features as he turns to me and says, "Whatever you do, princess, stay behind me."

Eighteen

SAGE

I stand in shock as Alexei rushes to his closet. I remember the litany of guns I had seen banking the space and assume he's gone to collect them. When he comes out of the walk-in, he's got a vest on, two guns already strapped over his shoulders and a pistol in his hand.

I can't seem to look away from the lawn. The men are coming in swarms, fires igniting everywhere as they smash their way through our windows. It's that night all over again. The night I opened the gates and ruined my entire life.

I look down at my hands, wondering if I'm hallucinating in my panic.

Blood. Mine? Not mine. I can't tell. I can't see.

"Princess." Alexei grabs my face in both his hands and twists me towards him. On reflex, my hands snap up to grip at his. "It's gonna be okay. Put this on."

I stand there, numb and useless, as he helps me into a bullet-proof vest and my frame drops with the weight. The once dark night gets brighter and brighter as fires spark outside.

"We can't stay here," Alexei says, though more to himself. He can't be talking to me because I am obviously acting embarrassingly pathetic in my shock. I watch him load his guns, clocking the ammunition in place as gunfire sounds on the lower levels.

He swings open his bedroom door and Isla comes bursting through from across the hall.

"What a fucking welcome," she says, shaking her head like she's disappointed and annoyed by the whole situation. "Closet?"

Alexei continues rushing about the room, preparing somehow, but I don't catch the exact nature of the movements. Because I don't understand what he's doing. I'm frozen still, listening as the sounds of gunfire intensify. Isla comes out of the closet wearing her own bullet-proof vest, locked and loaded with a multitude of weapons as well.

She looks incredible. She's not scared. She's not fazed. She's about to do business.

Begrudgingly... I can see it. She's the whole package.

"What's the deal?" she asks Alexei. His eyes shift sideways to me, and I know that they're talking about me though neither of them acknowledges that I'm in the room.

"Help the others. You know what to do," he says.

She doesn't once question him, just gives him a silly salute and then heads out into the hallway with a rifle at the ready.

He just sent her into the line of gunfire? But he loves-

Before I can process that fully, he's back in front of me again. "Okay, princess, we need to move."

I nod but I can feel the tears running down to my chin.

"Jesus, fuck. Don't cry." His voice hardens as he wipes the tears from my face with his thumbs. "Look at me."

Numbly, I do. I'm going to die here. I barely made it through the first ambush on our estate. Now, with a panic attack looming over me from my previous trauma, I know it's enough weakness to kill me. Especially standing here in front of this man. Our families have hated each other since before I was born.

"Show me that siren's face you did when I first got here," he says.

What? I can't think. I can't breathe. I look at him blankly.

"You are the daughter of Dimitri DeMarco. And you might have all those men out there fooled but I know what you are." He presses his palm to my chest. "You're a devil in disguise. A warrior and a siren. And this heart is made of steel. Which means no one out there can tell it to stop beating. Take what you want, and no one stops you."

I close my eyes and nod, warmth flooding me from within. It's a pep talk I didn't know I needed. Giving me back some of the power that I lost each time Nic tore my heart from my chest. Or perhaps, power that I have never been given before. Perhaps, power is something I have to take.

"Who are you?"

I frown, as it takes me a few moments to clue in to what he's asking me to do. "D-Dimitri DeMarco's daughter?" I stutter.

"What are you?"

"A warrior."

"And who's gonna stop you?"

I pull up short, wondering if it's the right thing to say, but at the same time feeling in my bones like it is. "No one."

"Good girl." He presses a small pistol into my palm. "We're getting out of here. Stay close to me."

I cock the gun and give him my best devil's stare. His lips twitch before he schools them. His attention is promptly stolen by gunfire that echoes on our floor. I follow Alexei to the door but before we get there, a man kicks it open.

He's not expecting us, and Alexei puts a bullet in his face, his head cocking back with the shot before he dies.

Alexei doesn't stop, doesn't think twice as he pushes into the hall. I follow him, keeping alert, but staying behind him as he made me promise. His gun is up and smoking. Two more men who were coming up the stairs are shot dead at Alexei's hand before I can blink.

It feels so hot and so bright for being the middle of the night. All I can hear is the searing sounds of gunfire and fighting. More bullets come for us.

Alexei backs up and pushes me against the wall, his back to my front as he shields me. At perfectly timed intervals, he leans forward and opens fire on our attackers until I hear bodies drop and gunfire stop.

Alexei reloads his gun and steps away from me, motioning with his head for me to follow him. We head across the landing and down the hall again. He's taking me to my bedroom.

Suddenly, he stops short and I nearly slam into his back.

I wonder what the hell has got him stopping dead, but then I see a group of men exiting my room. At least six of them by first count.

"She's not there," one of them says to the other.

My eyes widen.

"We can't leave here without her. Boss's orders to get the fucking girl."

One of them notices us then. "There she is!"

"Fuck," Alexei says.

We barely outrun the gunfire, rushing into one of the rooms on the other side of the hall. Our heads duck low as we run, slamming the door closed behind us. We're in my father's media room. Rows of plush black theater seats line the untouched space. There's a movie screen on the far wall and a projector above my head.

Alexei ignores me as he races to the window.

He doesn't see the man about to get the jump on him.

Like me, he's assumed the fact that the space is untouched means that there's no one in here. I can't breathe. I can't make my brain work fast enough to warn him. All I do is scream. Scream and fire my gun.

Alexei hears me, turning just in time to see me shoot the guy in the stomach. He drops like a sack of potatoes and a row of blood spatter slashes onto the previously pristine wall.

"Shit, princess," Alexei curses. The guy on the floor cries out in pain. Alexei presses his foot onto the guy's chest, shooting him.

There's a thud at the door that jolts me from my thoughts. I can't think too long about the fact that I pretty much just killed a guy. My feet carry me toward Alexei as I realize they're trying to kick the door in.

Alexei rushes forward to me too, and grabs my hand, putting me behind his body, holding a gun in both of his hands as he gets ready to defend us.

"Is there another way out of here?"

I stammer, trying to think on my feet. I'm going to need to get harder than I am, because I'm not cut out for this. And I *need* to be.

"I - there's... there's another door behind the projector screen."

Alexei looks at the screen next to us and nods, bracing as the thuds on the door get louder.

The wood shatters, and I barely suppress a scream as several men push through. I'm livid by the fact we're standing out in the open as they ambush us, but I stay behind Alexei as he told me to. I don't move from where he tells me to stay.

Alexei shoots the first one dead, and then the second, before they get the hint.

I poke my head above Alexei's shoulders and he gives me a warning look before we turn in time to see surrendered hands from either side of the door, but no more brave faces coming in.

"Whoa, whoa, whoa," a voice says. "Calm the hell down, we're not here for you, Rushkoff."

Alexei shoots the guy's hand. "Don't fucking care who you're here for."

"Fuck!" the voice shouts. "You're in the fucking way, man! We're not here to hurt you. Just hand over the girl and have at it."

H-hand over the girl....?

They want me. They want him to give them *me*.

Oh, shit.

He's going to do it. He has to do it.

Alexei has no reason to defend me. In fact, he actively hates me and wishes away my presence for the safety of his brother. Of course, he's going to hand me over. There's no reason for him to help me.

"Not fucking happening," Alexei grits out, his voice the toughest and angriest I've ever heard it. "You're not getting the girl, fuckers. You'd have to go through me first. And you're not getting through me."

I gasp, shivers overtaking my body as I peer over Alexei's shoulder and look him in the eye. He only spares me a brief glance, but one that feels like it lasts for an eternity, and says so much, before he turns his attention back to the threat.

Alexei... he's going to *help* me. I can't imagine on what planet this guy would want to help me. Would want to stand in the way of someone trying to take away his biggest problem.

But he's going to.

"Get ready to run," Alexei whispers to me.

I barely even have time to consider the request.

"Come on man just-"

They don't have time to finish their sentence either, as Alexei open fires with a rifle. He grabs my hand and suddenly we're running, diving behind the projector screen and just getting to the next room to get the door barred before we're followed.

The room is tiny, and we've just taken the one entryway into it. It's not meant for anything other than storage for the media room. Sooner or later they're going to find out that we're in here, even with the projector screen acting as cover.

Can Alexei really take down all these men? On his own?

Alexei sees the look on my face. "Yeah, I can take them all down, princess."

"But not while you have to protect me." I read the subtext, and he doesn't deny it.

"Just-" There are barely there voices nearby, distracting Alexei from me.

He frowns, searching the space until he finds the window. Instinctively, he knows what to do next and goes to the window, opening it as he peers down. He lets out a soft curse before he calls out to the people below. "Look up and don't shoot, asshole."

"Rushkoff?" Nic's voice.

"These better not be yours." Anton's voice is a growl.

"Do they fucking look like mine?" Alexei scoffs at the insult.

I rush to the window and he lets me push up next to him.

"Uncle Anton!"

Nic's eyes shoot up to me. "Oh, thank Christ."

"Sage?" Freddie.

"Anton, Freddie, I'm here."

Nic doesn't miss the fact that I'm not addressing him. You'd think a life or death situation would be enough to thaw my annoyance towards him. After all, it usually doesn't take *anything* for me to forget my pride and run right back into Nicholas's bed.

They're sitting ducks out there, idling in the garden. But we're sitting ducks in here too. I panic, looking between my family down there and the boy who saved me up here.

"You need to jump down to him, princess." Alexei's voice is soft as his lips brush my ear, pushing back an errant strand of hair.

"Sage, jump to me," Nic says.

I look down at him before turning contemplative eyes on Alexei.

"What about you?" I whisper.

"I'll be good. Go," he says and I see the linger of a smile on his lips. "I'll paint your little theater red for you. You just watch."

He nudges me towards the window. Nic opens his arms for me and I cannot believe I'm about to do something so incredibly stupid. My legs tremble as I slip out of the window and onto the ledge. Closing my eyes with little bravery, I yelp as I leap down, and Nicholas catches me, effortlessly cradling me in his arms. I don't even get enough time to look up to see Alexei, to ponder if he's okay, and will be okay, before the three of them are on me.

"They're here for her again," Freddie says.

"Again?!" I blanch, still being held bridal style in Nic's arms.

"Take her until this is over, brother," Anton says. "We'll clean up this fucking mess."

I don't get the chance to protest. Nic doesn't put me down, he just runs across the lawn at full speed. I can see where this is going. There's a storage cellar under the stables. It's supposed to be our secret evac point.

"Thank fuck you're okay," he breathes as he exerts himself with the run. He could just put me down, but I don't mention that. Despite my pride, I feel safe in his arms and still, even though he humiliated me again, that's exactly where I want to be.

"There were men coming out of my room," I say.

"You weren't in it?" he asks.

"No, I was bothering Alexei."

"You weren't where you were supposed to be."

I hear the subtext. You weren't where you were supposed to be, and it might have saved your life.

***

Nic shuts the door to the underground cellar above our head. Securing it with a bolt and pressing the panic button to seal it with steel before he climbs down.

I sit with my back against the wall and my arms hugging my knees, surrounded by bottles of expensive wine and the stale smell of damp stone.

"That should do it," Nic says, brushing the dirt off his hands and coming to sit down against the wine rack across from me.

"Will they be okay?" I ask.

"They know what they're doing," Nic nods. "We just need to convince them that you're long gone and the attackers will either die or give up."

"Because they're after me." It's not a question. It's an accusation.

Nicholas doesn't say anything, and I can see him visibly sharpening. I'm not getting any answers out of him tonight. If ever.

I scoff out loud. "Whatever."

We sit in silence for a moment. I can't hear any of the noises of fighting or see any bursts of light from the fires, so the cellar must be well insulated. My mind wanders to what we've left behind at the mansion. I left Alexei alone, with no less than five men still chasing him. Five men who think he was protecting the very thing they'd come for.

For some incredible reason that I cannot fathom the motivation of... I worry about Alexei Rushkoff.

I don't want to go back to that mansion and find that he's not in it.

"It's quiet," I say.

"The cellar is soundproof," Nic confirms. He sits with his legs stretched out in front of him and his arms folded, not looking at me. This whole time, he's jumped at the chance to be my bodyguard. To keep me close and to keep me safe. Now he looks reluctant to be here, and I wonder if I should tell him to just piss off. To leave me and go fight alongside his brothers. Even though being trapped inside another cellar makes the scars on my back and belly tingle with nervous energy. So badly that part of me thinks being out in the open would be a less painful reminder of my trauma.

"How will we know when it's safe?" I ask, watching the ceiling like I can see right through it.

"Anton will come and get us. He knows where we are."

I nod and a tear slips down my face.

Nic sighs, erasing the space between us. "Don't cry, Sage." He comes closer still and wipes a tear from my face. When he sees I'm not going to stop crying, he settles for sitting beside me with his back against the wall too.

He wraps his hand around my shoulder and pulls me in tight to his side.

"Why are you so hot and cold to me, Nic?" I ask, the words coming out on a restrained sob.

He sighs.

"We're obviously compatible," I say, the most tactful way to point out that we're really good at sex. "What's the problem? Do you not-"

"That's not," Nic sighs again. "That's not the problem, Sage."

"I have feelings for you," I say. "Can you not see it?"

He's silent for a long time. It's only when I think he's not going to answer me that he finally does.

"I know," he whispers. "I have feelings too. Doesn't change what I said."

"This is still because of my father?" I clench my fists.

"It's more complicated than that," he says, resting his head on top of mine. "It's just complicated, Sage, for lots of reasons. One of which is... *was* your father. Now, Anton. Victor. It's not appropriate for me to be chasing after you. We both know that."

"Who cares what's appropriate?" I roll my eyes.

Nicholas says nothing, which only makes me angrier. "You do," I huff. "You care what's appropriate."

"I'm not right for you," Nic says, jaw grinding and voice tense. "Just leave it at that. We're not a thing, Sage, and we don't have a future."

He blows out a breath that I feel skating across the top of my hair from where he cradles me. "Please, accept it. Please stop making me say it."

Nineteen

SAGE

*N*ic and I spend another hour in the cellar before Anton finally comes for us. When I get back to my room, I can smell enough bleach to know it's been cleaned within an inch of its life. There are people all over the property patching up windows and repairing the damage, but the window in my room is crack free.

It's only the fact that the glass is an inch or two thicker that tips me off that it's new.

"You good?" Uncle Anton asks, standing at my door with Nic behind him.

I spin to face them. I was lost in my thoughts, thinking about how easily that window could or would be shattered.

"I'll be okay," I lie. I had a hard enough time sleeping before all this. I'm not getting a lick of sleep tonight.

"You'll be safe tonight," Anton says.

I smile and nod, sure that my feigned smile is more a grimace. I look behind Anton to Nic, who won't look me in the eye. Given what he said... yeah, I'm not surprised. I wrap my arms tightly around myself.

Anton moves to leave but I stop him with my words. "Is... um," I stutter. I cannot believe I'm about to ask this, but something inside me demands that I do. "Is, uh, Alexei okay?"

Nic and Anton both stiffen, shoulders straightening as their spines go rigid.

"Since when do you care about Alexei Rushkoff?" Anton narrows his eyes on me as he licks his lips.

"I... don't. He just - he saved me," I say. From their cautious expressions I know I'm getting nothing so I just roll my eyes. "Never mind. It's not important."

"Yell if you need anything," Anton says, happy to leave the conversation there.

Nic doesn't look up from the floor but his jaw clenches as Anton closes my bedroom door, the soft click enough to make me jump. Once again left alone with my thoughts, I turn back to the glass and sigh.

After a long, weary shower, I turn off the lights, undressing quickly and crawling into bed. I still refuse to shut the curtains, allowing the light from the moon to brighten the inside of my room as if that will somehow help.

I settle down into the blankets, tugging the cover up over my shoulders and watching the night sky out the window. Exhaustion tugs at me, trying to pull me under into sleep but I resist. I can't convince my mind it's safe enough to sleep.

After a while, I close my eyes. I wake feeling like only seconds have passed but knowing by the wet puddle under my face that I've been lulled into another nightmare.

I sit up, wiping the tears from my cheeks and slightly gasping as I try to get my breathing under control.

There's a sharp bang at my door. I jump, the noise doing nothing to slow my breath. My hand rests over my heaving chest, drawing sharp gasps. The banging persists, and I realize I'm going to have to answer it.

"I'm coming," I grumble, kicking out of the warm bed. I hurry to the door, wiping at my eyes as I go.

Ready to scowl at whoever is on the other side, interrupting an already fitful night, I swing the door open.

Alexei leans over the threshold, his arm braced on the frame.

"Alexei?" I exhale in a gust of relief.

His eyes snap up to mine as I say his name. They're narrowed, but soft enough for me to realize the relief must show on my face. He falters for only a moment before he puts his own mask back on and returns to teasing me.

"The Prince boy managed to keep you alive. Guess he's not totally useless," Alexei smirks.

"What time is it?"

"Almost five," he says, grunting. He flexes his tattooed fingers and then steps back from the doorway. His jaw clenches before he speaks, like his brain is fighting the urge for the words to come out. "Are you alright?"

"I - did I make a noise?" I brush away the stray hairs that have become stuck to my wet cheeks.

"No."

I look him up and down, from where he's wearing freshly shined black shoes, crisp black pants and a shirt that hugs him tightly. He's freshly showered too, hair slicked back and not a strand out of place.

"Are you gonna let me in or are we both just going to stand here looking stupid?"

I sneer, but for some reason, I do open the door. He walks in and makes the place his own, strutting in like he's been in here a hundred times before. All I can do is stand and watch him in confusion.

"They patched this up quick, didn't they?" Alexei says, tapping on the glass. "It's thick."

"Like your head," I whisper, meaning the words to come out as an insult but my fear still hangs fresh in my mind and I can't muster the ability to make it sound as mean as I'd like.

Alexei looks back over to me but doesn't respond. He watches as I curl my arms around my body again before he averts his eyes.

"You've changed clothes."

"Yeah," Alexei says, heaping himself into the chair by my window and settling in. "I painted your theater red for you, princess. Got a little *paint* on my clothes."

A soft laugh escapes me as I walk back to the bed and climb under the covers. Settling into the warmth, I rest my head on my hand as I lay on my side to watch him. He looks comfortable from where he sits. His head is leaned back in the chair and his feet are crossed at the ankles.

I don't understand my reaction or his. But we both lay there, on opposite sides of the room, watching each other as silence descends again. Like we've been here thousands of times before. Like the way we watch each other in the dark is completely natural.

Alexei takes a deep breath. His fingers steeple under his chin, pointed tattooed fingers on his lips in contemplation. He looks as tormented and bewildered as I feel. This connection that draws us together seems to be one that neither of us wants to give in to but can't resist all the same.

I shuffle under the covers, getting warm. "Shouldn't you be protecting your girlfriend? Pretty traumatic night."

"If you haven't noticed, Isla can take care of herself." He doesn't look at me as he delivers an easy smile with the words.

I shake my head at my own stupidity. Of course, she can. She was rushing off like a warrior princess earlier in the night. Of course, she doesn't need help. She probably sleeps like a baby and definitely doesn't cry herself awake.

It's only princesses like me that dig themselves graves they can't climb out of. Another rush of self-loathing cascades through me, amplified by tonight's events.

"You must really hate it here," I say. "You know, to have called in your girlfriend as backup."

"Here does suck," he says. I smile into my pillow, turning it over because the side I'm on is still soaking with tears. I swear there's no way he could know that, but his eyes track the movement like he does.

"What were you looking for in my room?" he asks.

"Nothing."

From the look on his face, the slight raise on his brow, he knows I'm lying.

"You were doing something," he says, thumbing at his lip. "You really think I'd bring secret evidence into my enemy's house? How dumb do I look?"

"Very dumb," I smile.

He bites his lip, which I suspect is to cover the urge to smile.

I sigh, and my eyelids try to flutter closed of their own accord. I snap them back open. I won't let myself go to sleep.

"You tired princess?"

"I don't want to sleep. I'm..." I'm afraid. But I'm not going to tell him that, am I? Even if I am far too drained to remember he's the enemy.

In the end, I don't even need to say that I'm too afraid to sleep. Somehow he knows anyway. He settles deeper in the chair, making himself very at home and comfortable. From somewhere out of nowhere, he pulls out a book and reads by the light of the moon. His eyes scan over the pages, and without looking at me he says, "Go to sleep, princess." I'm on the precipice of sleep when I swear I hear, "I've got you."

***

Morning sun heats my face, and I instinctively cup my cheek, feeling for the telltale tackiness of dried tears on my cheek. When I feel nothing but smooth skin, I smile.

My eyes open slowly, but when I take in the room fully and realize I'm not alone, I falter. I sit up in bed, staring wide-eyed at the form sleeping peacefully on the bed right next to me.

The person I was expecting to be there isn't. But someone else is...

Nicholas is sprawled out on top of the sheets. Still wearing last night's clothes like he fumbled into bed next to me when his body couldn't take it anymore.

I chance a glance at the chair by the window, finding it empty. My heart does an inexplicable twist as I wonder if I dreamed the whole thing. But then

I notice there's an open book sitting on my windowsill and I know that what happened was real.

I watch Nicholas where he sleeps, his chest barely rising and falling with his breaths. What the fuck is he doing here? After what he said, I cannot imagine why he is here in my bed. He said himself that we couldn't be anything. That we had nothing.

Less than twelve hours ago he was inside me, telling me I mean nothing to him. Now he's back in my bed. I scratch at my brow. Which one of us is it that's pathetic? Him for falling back into my bed so quickly after being a fucking coward? Or me?

Because I'm weak too. Because he smells so. God damn. Good.

Isn't that pathetic? All it takes is a smell. One whiff of my Nic and I don't care what he's said. I'm dying to convince him that what we have *is* something.

I furrow my brow when a smirk forms on his lips, with his eyes still closed.

"You're watching me."

I widen my eyes. "You're not asleep?"

"I was." Nicholas opens his eyes then and smiles. "Until someone interrupted me."

I gasp. "You didn't even have your eyes open!"

He laughs then, full and bright, the first laugh of his that I've ever heard sound so genuine, since he spends most of the time acting like a big grump. "I'm trained to be alert at all times."

"I'm not buying that." I fold my arms over my shirt. I'm not wearing a bra and sitting upright like this puts my nipples on display... and yeah okay, I want to pronounce them by puffing up my chest. "Maybe you were watching me."

"What if I was?" he says, reaching up to tuck a loose hair behind my ear, then stroke his thumb longingly up and down my jawline. I melt into him and then instantly hate myself for doing so. If this is his form of an apology, then now is the time that I need to stand my ground and tell him it's not good enough. I can't forgive him this easily.

"Then that's rude," I say, but it comes out breathy. Fuck.

"I agree," he says, looking from my eyes to my lips. Instead of leaning into him like I normally would, my lip curls. He's giving me fucking whiplash. I turn my head so that his hand falls away from my neck.

With a sigh, he pulls away. As much as it hurts, I know I've done the right thing by respecting myself this time. Sitting on the edge of my bed, he runs a hand through his hair. His eyes catch on the book by my windowsill and he turns a curious gaze back on me.

Oh fuck. Please don't ask me about the book.

"Ahem," a voice says, purposefully loud.

I whip my head towards the doorway, finding Anton standing there with his hands behind his back, looking murderous. "Thought I'd find you in here."

Nic scrambles off the bed, tripping over his own feet in his attempt to straighten up and smooth over his clothes. "Anton." He says it with the same admonishment he'd say the word '*fuck*'.

"Come on," Anton says, his lips pinching. "Crew just finished the cleanup. Freddie's refusing stitches. Need you to help me hold him down."

Anton walks away and Nic heads towards the door, stopping at the last second and poking his head back around the corner to me. "Coming?"

I give him a raised brow and a sniff. But yes, I am coming. So I dress and follow him out the door.

***

"I swear to fuck if I feel one more sting!"

Freddie sits laid back in a green armchair in the library, creating crescent circles in the upholstery from where he grips the arm. Victor chuckles, not looking like he's taking any extra care as he wipes a gauze over Freddie's exposed wound.

When Victor comes back with the needle to patch him up, Freddie leaps forward like he's going to claw his face off.

"You need stitches Freddie, shut the fuck up," Nic grumbles, holding Freddie's arms and forcing him back in the seat so he can't punch Victor as he's treated.

"It's fine, leave it!" Freddie says, teeth gritting as the needle pierces his skin again.

"It's a gunshot wound, Fallon," Victor laughs. "Sit still."

I fiddle with the necklace at my collarbone, watching from where I sit at the opposite end of the library. It seems the worst that happened last night was the gunshot wound through Freddie's thigh. Which is superficial and treatable, but the idea that the wound was inflicted in pursuit or defense of me makes my skin sticky.

My mood has been somber. It's not my first gun fight. But now I know for sure they were after me. Have they been this whole time? The knowledge sits like rocks in my gut.

Victor moves his skilled hands against Freddie's skin, not hiding the fact that he wants to laugh. As I watch my fiancé's hands sew together my friend's leg, my mind drifts. To other hands. Tattooed ones. Tattooed fingers pressing on my chest over my heart. Tattooed fingers being licked and then used to turn pages in a book.

My blood heats and I forcefully shake it off in a shiver.

What the fuck is wrong with me?

"Your brother up yet?" Anton drawls from where he nervously shuffles a deck of cards.

"Sleeping in. Had a big night," Victor says, frowning as he concentrates on Freddie's wound.

I'm told Alexei and Isla took down more men than anyone else last night. They clearly don't call him the psychotic Rushkoff for nothing. As if speaking of them has summoned her, Isla comes sauntering into the room, a gun still loaded on her hip. Her blonde hair swishes behind her, left unbound, and her smile is mega-watt bright. "I bet you're glad you invited me in when you did, Anton," Isla smirks.

Anton shakes his head, glaring at Victor. "I thought you said she didn't know how to use a gun?"

Victor glares daggers at Isla. He really fucking hates her. That much is clear. From what I learned in the moments before the attack, I can only assume that there was once a battle for her heart, and that Alexei won.

Does she ever look at the ring on my finger and wish it were hers?

"Can't use a gun? I'm offended, Vic. Especially since I gave you your first one."

Victor grumbles but he says nothing in response, his sole focus on stitching up Freddie's leg. He's high roading her. I think.

Alexei struts in shortly later, eyeing me where I'm laid out on one of the lounges, a cigarette hanging from his lips.

"What a shitshow," Anton says. "I've never seen so many fucking bodies."

"I've seen more." Freddie and Alexei say those words at the exact same time, causing Freddie to smile and Alexei to frown.

Isla sniffs at the exchange and then steps up to Alexei, taking the cigarette right out of his mouth and inhaling before she places it back between his lips. I feel my breath hitch, the feeling strange and foreign. I look at Victor, finding him watching them with poorly restrained anger and probably jealously.

What the fuck have I gotten myself into here?

"You're a shit doctor," Freddie curses as Victor finishes patching him up.

"You're very welcome," Victor says. He smiles and snaps his blue rubber glove off.

"Another attack, another mystery as to how they got so close in the first place," Anton says, throwing away his cards and taking a long sip of whatever amber liquid is in his glass. I've never seen him drink so much before.

"You better not be accusing us again," Alexei drawls. It sounds calm, but we all know he's ready for a fight if one breaks out. He always is.

Anton sighs and then concedes as he slumps into the lounger across from mine. "I'm not."

"But you don't know who it is, do you?" Victor says.

Anton clenches his jaw. Nic and Freddie watch him closely, I assume gathering the status quo. Whatever Anton says next is going to set the tone for whether we trust the Rushkoffs with our family business.

"No," he says quietly.

"Attacks happen often?"

Anton eyes me before he answers Victor's next question.

"A lot. But they never get through the gate."

Victor nods and the room goes silent. The idea that an unknown party can get into the mansion to challenge not just us, but the Rushkoffs in here with us, doesn't bode well for anyone's status in the city right now.

It feels heavy with tension. A fog building in the room as each person draws their own conclusions from what Anton has said.

It's Isla that breaks the tension.

"Right. Well, problem for another day," she says. "We fought them off this time. Go team. Now, who am I besting in cards today?"

Nic flops down next to me on the lounger, brushing hair back from my face.

"You look like you could use a break."

I narrow my eyes on him and fold my arms.

He sighs. "You're sulking."

I lift my chin in indignation. "Rightfully so, I'd say."

He stands and holds out his hand to me. "Come on, let me apologize."

I refuse to take his hand, instead raising my chin another few inches to make my defiance clear. Nic just smirks and shakes his head. "Come on, give me a chance. I'll answer all your questions away from prying eyes."

Twenty

NICHOLAS

"Alright, you've got me out here. What do you want?" Sage asks, folding her arms and pouting as we walk through the gardens together. She remains a respectable distance away from me as I lead her through the rose garden and to the lawns on the outskirts of the property, making sure to insolently kick at the dirt every few feet.

I'm not surprised she's responding to me this way. In fact, I probably deserve more disdain than she's given. She couldn't possibly hate me any more than I hate myself. It was a slap across the face and a wakeup call for me, personally.

All this time I've been worried I'm doing the wrong thing by defiling her. By going against her father's orders and my own, touching her when I shouldn't be. Thing is, my heart is so tightly wrapped up in her now that no amount of cutting would ever set me free.

I thought I was saving myself by pushing her away. Seeing her at Victor's behest ruins me, driving me to act impulsively rather than rationally. I can't take another second of it. With her wedding coming up, and her likely going through with it, I'm not sure I'll survive if I don't make this right.

Because I've now realized there's a third player in the game. Victor's brother. Alexei Rushkoff.

Funny thing is, I don't think neither he nor Sage realize that he's in play, but in every room they're in together they move close. Like they're drawn to each other and just can't stay away.

"Just a few more steps," I say, and Sage huffs from where she's walking next to me. As we turn around a row of hedges onto the lawns, I watch her face.

Her breath catches, but her eyes narrow. Conflicting reactions and not exactly what I was going for but it'll have to do.

"You set up a picnic?" she says, turning to me with a hand on her hip and a raised brow.

"Too cheesy or not cheesy enough?" Not waiting for her reaction, I head for the quaint setup. I've put a red and white checkered rug out here to enjoy the sunshine and had the kitchen staff put together a basket.

I'm hoping that the alone time together will allow me to plead my case, but by pleading in the gardens instead of her bedroom I'll be able to avoid pouncing on her and ruining my point.

She follows me but doesn't join me as I sit down on the rug and lean back on my hands, getting comfortable. "Sit down, Sage."

"No," she says, folding her arms and lifting her chin.

Sighing, I open the picnic basket, knowing I'll have her here. "There's a bottle of Moscato and chicken Greek yogurt tea sandwiches in here."

"Really!" she yelps, smiling as she falls onto the picnic rug and begins hunting for the little sandwiches that I know are her weakness. I smile up at the sky, closing my eyes to enjoy the sun as I leave her to heap into the food.

"So, what am I out here for, Nic?" she says around a mouthful.

I immediately feel cold, even in the sun's light. "I uh," I say, clearing my throat to buy time. "I... this is, it's my apology."

She swallows and purses her lips, giving me an unimpressed look.

"Didn't hear you say it," she says.

My eyes shutter. "I'm sorry," I say, my heart hurting as I lay it out on the line for her. But I know I put myself in this position and have no room to hold on to my pride. "All those things I said, they were harsh and I didn't mean any of them."

She wipes her mouth with her thumb. "You said you didn't want me enough to risk everything you ever worked for."

I shudder, closing my eyes so I don't have to look at her. I'm such a sack of shit. I can't believe I decided to hurt her instead of hurting myself. What the fuck is wrong with me? Protecting her interests over mine, taking the bullets that are meant for her, is literally my job description as her bodyguard. Which, let's face it, in spite of all the teasing, is what I am.

"I did say that," I admit. "And I'm sorry. I didn't mean any of it. I don't have an excuse. I'm just a shit who wanted to save myself when I should've been thinking of you."

She takes another large bite of the tiny tea sandwich and watches me wearily. I feel like I'm on the stand about to be sentenced.

"It wasn't very nice," she says.

I nod. "It was despicable and horrible. I'm horrible."

She sighs, her shoulders dropping as she puts down her food haul. "You're not horrible, Nic." She bites her lip. "Maybe an emotionally stunted fuckwit," I laugh at this, "but you're not horrible."

She smiles over at me and I smile too, feeling lighter but also undeserving of her forgiveness. Her green eyes sparkle at me, even as she wipes crumbs off her hands onto her knees. She's wearing a rose gold sundress that has fluffy sleeves and exposes a generous amount of her tanned thigh.

She's been wearing a lot of easy access dresses lately. Specifically to drive me crazy? Fuck, I hope so. I want them all to be for me. I try to avert my eyes and get my breathing under control. I really do not want to get a boner right now.

Though the ship is already sailing at half-mast.

"You said you'd answer my questions," she says, voice soft like she's being cautious in asking.

"I did say that," I agree. I get comfortable and lie down on my side to rest my head on my hand. "Have at me then, gorgeous."

Her lips tilt up at the corners, her face warming at my compliment, but she's a master of pulling herself together before acting upon it. The air settles heavily around us for a while, her eyes closed as she soaks in the sun. When she opens them to look at me, the mood is somber again.

"How many times have they come for me, Nic?"

"Too many to count." I go for brutal honesty. She now knows someone is after her. How many attacks have we stopped? Too many. Far too fucking many.

She blows out a breath.

"Is it that bad?" she eyes me through lowered brows, her fingers fiddling with the hem of her dress and pushing it further up her thigh.

"However bad you think it might be, assume it's worse."

"Wow," she shakes out her head. "Cryptic much."

"Everyone is holding back a secret, Sage. Doesn't matter who they say they are, there's always something."

She answers too quickly. "Amen." There's a brief pause before she continues her line of questioning. I've got a lot of ground to grovel over, so I have no choice but to wait patiently.

"How long have you known they were after me?"

"Not long. A month," I wince. "Or two."

She nods.

"Took us a while to figure it out. But they keep coming to your room. They're not after the storages, the business. It's you. Always you."

She looks at me like she knows I mean several things with those words. "*That* night? Do you think they were after me?"

I let my silence be all the answer she needs. Whoever came here, that night, wasn't trying to get Dimitri DeMarco. But they got him anyway. Anton continues to think, against my better judgment, that this all materialized as a result of a plot against Dimitri but I'm not convinced. I'm sure even before Dim died, it has always been about her.

"So it's all about me," she says, echoing my thoughts and I smile, wishing she could see how in sync we are. So she would agree to fuck off Victor and his psychotic brother.

"Hasn't it always been?" I joke.

She sends me a devastating smile before she hides it again. She brushes her long dark hair back over her shoulder.

"Is that what this is about? The secret *you're* so intent on hiding?" I ask. "Some sort of retribution for your father's murderer?"

"Who says I'm hiding anything," she shrugs, nibbling into a little tea sandwich like she's being casual even though she can't look at me.

I give her a dry look.

She slumps her shoulders. "Just trust me, please."

I bite back a sigh.

I want her trust more than anything.

"Fine," I bite out, realizing asking for forgiveness and trust on the same day is definitely asking too much.

She regards me warily before giving a nod and taking out another sandwich. She eats quietly for a while as I pretend not to watch her, giving her all the space she needs to let me back in.

"Nicholas?" She looks up at me with inquisitive eyes, unsure eyes. And I wonder if she's about to cross the threshold and give me what I want also.

"You've killed people before, right?"

What the hell?

I try to hold back my shock but I'm sure some of it shows. My eyes widen, my brows trying to shoot up before I gain control of my face. Hoping that she hasn't seen me react. "Yes."

"What should it feel like?" She sits up on her heels and leans in to me like she's hanging on my every word. Alarm bells go off in my head.

"A life in defense of another is the easiest life to take." I mull on it a moment. "And give."

"That doesn't answer my question."

The question takes me back to places that I don't wish to revisit. Every life is hard to take. And while necessary most of the time, it's always something that wears a heavy mark on my soul.

"Not like you'd think. These mobsters running around taking lives like it means nothing... They make it seem easy, but it never is. Not for me, anyway."

She takes a deep breath and studies the landscape, deep in thought. The people we associate with make it seem like human life means nothing. It is their way to discard life. Like it's trash that they'd put another load full of out the next week, anyway.

It is the way of this life. Though I'm not sure anyone can escape the toll it demands on your soul. It always hurts.

Even Freddie. Our notorious killer with a psycho streak to rival even the most tempered Rushkoff brother. He feels those kills under his skin. In his heart. I've watched as his eyes became heavier each time he snuffed another life at Dimitri or Anton's command.

"You do it anyway?" she asks, snapping me out of my memories.

"When I have to."

The alarm bells in my head grow to a full on blaze, but I keep my breathing under control. What does she know? Or what is she going to do? Why this information, and why now?

I run my tongue over my teeth. "Do you think you could do it?" I ask. "Kill in cold blood?"

"Yes," she says, without hesitation, but stutters through her next sentence. "I'm sure that if I had to, I could. People always say you can't know until you're in the situation. But trust me, I don't need to be in the situation to know. If I had to kill, I could do it."

"That's a big responsibility," I reply.

"Is it?"

"Yes," I say, sitting up to look at her and hoping to stress the seriousness of my words. "The most important thing to know about killing, Sage. It is a responsibility. Every time it is possible to spare a life, then you must. Only kill when there is no other option."

"Only when there is no other option?"

"*Only when there is no other option,*" I repeat. "That's the only way to kill and still keep your heart. If you break that rule, you don't just kill the other person, you kill a part of yourself."

"How will I know if it's the only option?"

"You'll know," I say, whispering. "Trust me, you'll know."

She nods once, letting me know she's taking the advice I'm sharing seriously.

"Come here," I say, holding out my hand for her to take. She frowns as she hesitantly accepts, holding her hand delicately in mine. She gasps when I pull her into my body and start running my hands along her side.

"You're giving me such mixed signals," she whispers.

"I know," I say. I'm ashamed to say I'm doing it. I know I am. I know I'm hot and cold. I recognize I'm a hypocrite for asking for all of her secrets when I won't give her even a fraction of mine.

"I'm supposed to let you go with Victor. I'm supposed to do that. But every time I try, I can't do it. I don't want you to belong to him." *Because you belong to me.*

She raises a brow at me.

"I'm sorry. Always. For all the dumbass things I keep saying."

"You'll have to do more earning it," she says, but she wraps her arms around my neck anyway, giving me a deep kiss.

"I can do that."

"I mean it," she says, pulling back to pin me with a serious glare. "This doesn't make us a thing. You're gonna have to earn it."

"I know I-"

She puts a finger over my lips. "I'm serious, Nic. You know I want you. But I can't keep playing this game with you where you destroy me every time you change your mind."

My heart drops.

"We are *not* a thing," she says again, pinning me with a serious look. "If you really want more from me than this stupid game we've been playing, then you'll need to earn it."

"I know, Sage, and I'm so-"

She scoots down over me, putting her face close to my crotch.

"Wait, what?"

She kneels over me, pulling apart my belt before she glares up at me again. "This doesn't make us a thing."

I nod furiously even though I hate the idea that I've hurt her enough that she feels like she has to guard her heart around me.

I'll have to tell her. I'll have to tell her the truth about-

She takes my cock in her mouth. "Holy fuck!"

I grip the back of her hair, looking down at her as she smiles wickedly up at me, maintaining eye contact as she takes me to the back of her throat.

All of my words run together as I lose all sense. "Sagewe'reoutinthemiddleofafield- whatisitwithyouandpublic- Jesus Christ!"

She sucks me deep, running her tongue along my cock and massaging my balls as she deep throats me. "Oh shit, shit, *shit*."

I'm losing the tentative control that I have over the situation. I brought her out here so that I wouldn't get tempted to do *this*. So she'd know I was serious about wanting to win her heart and her trust and not just because I wanted a place to get my dick wet.

She slurps and releases me with a popping sound. "Feel good?"

Internally, I cringe. I have a chance here to stop this. To not allow her to finish me, and prove to her that I'm after her heart, not just her body.

"Fucking fantastic," I say instead. "Don't stop." I gather her hair into a ponytail and guide her mouth back to my aching dick, moaning and dropping my head as she takes me again. She's so fucking good at this. The way she licks and sucks, and how she uses her hand to massage me and stroke me while she does.

"Sage, I'm going to-"

She grips my hips and forces herself onto my cock, pushing me further down her throat than I thought possible. Then she swallows, and the muscles at the back of her throat tighten around me.

Holy fucking shit.

I yell loudly as I spill into her.

When I come to, she's still kneeling in front of me. I shake my head to clear the fog and wonder if I'm seeing things. Nope. Yeah, she... she has her mouth open and her tongue out so she can show me the cum sitting on the end.

She makes sure I'm maintaining eye contact, then she closes her mouth and swallows.

I drop my head back to the picnic rug. "Fucking hell."

She lays down next to me and smiles over at me, giving me a smug expression that she more than deserves. I lace my fingers through hers.

She accepts but gives me a meaningful look. "You and I. Not a thing. Got it?"

"Even though I just came down your throat."

She smiles. "Yep!" Then she laughs at the look on my face.

***

Eventually, the sun gets low and we have to come back from our picnic. Sage leaves me alone to clean up the mess, still sitting in her righteousness that we are not a thing, and that I'm going to have to prove to her that she means something to me.

When I come back up to the house, dirty rug and picnic basket in tow, my head is a mess. A nightmare of confused, jumbled thoughts that I can't make sense of. I knew I didn't deserve instant forgiveness. That she wouldn't tell Victor to eat shit just because I'm ready to open up. But still, a guy can hope.

The thing that cuts the deepest is that Sage is guarding her heart from me. As she should. I can admit that. Even if it hurts.

In the past, every second that I spent wanting her I also spent fighting it. Convincing myself that my only concern should be keeping alert to keep her safe. Not indulging in fantasies I've had for as long as I can remember. Not lending myself to distraction.

I'm not allowed to want her.

That hasn't changed. But I don't really give a fuck what I'm allowed to do anymore.

I leave the kitchen and head for my room on the bottom floor of the house. I'm coming around a corner when someone else slams into me at speed.

"Rushkoff," I say to the tempered brother. "Where are you off to in such a hurry?"

Alexei glares at me. "None of your fucking business."

Despite the circumstance that I can't quite wrap my head around - he *saved* Sage last night - I still can't seem to find common ground with this imbecile.

He continues in a fury driven rush around the corner. I'm about to stop him when the blonde girl, Isla, runs into me in her pursuit of him.

"Oh!" She slams to a stop, hand over her heart. "Sorry I didn't expect to run into anyone."

She surveys me with interest. Not in a sexual way. But like she, too, is trying to work out if I'm a threat.

She was certainly an asset last night. A force to be reckoned with. I can't fault her for that. She jumped into the fray without really knowing whose side she was on. All for her allegiance to Alexei.

"What's up his ass today?" I frown, looking to where Alexei disappeared.

"What isn't?" she says, but she says it with a smile, like she's thinking of him fondly. She didn't exactly give up much of herself or him in the little time I got to talk to her at dinner last night.

"You're Alexei's... girlfriend?" I ask. It's not a question that I would usually dare nor care to ask. But I feel something unpleasant brewing in my gut. Every time I watch that psychopath look at Sage. Every time his eyes survey her with interest. Like he wants to pretend he doesn't see something he wants in her. Like he's trying far too fucking hard to hate her. It burns me. Every single time I see him glare across the room at my girl.

My. Fucking. Girl.

Who I drove away.

Isla laughs. "No...uh, no. We're very good friends. Platonic. Very platonic."

My stomach drops.

That's not what I wanted to hear.

I look up the stairs, following the direction that he went, as if I can sense him out from just where I stand. When I turn back to look at Isla she is watching me curiously.

"Why do you care?" she says with a smirk on her lips.

I chuckle and shake my head. "Forget it."

"Miss DeMarco doesn't seem to have taken a liking to me," Isla grins. But I just frown at the abrupt turn of conversation. "I think she thinks I'm a threat. To her relationship with you."

"We don't have a relationship," I answer. Cringing when I realize how bitter that sounds coming out of my mouth.

"I've only been here a day and still, some of us aren't blind," Isla says, starting up the stairs but turning back to look down at me. "Everyone seems to be so worried about me being here," she too looks up in the direction that Alexei disappeared, "when there isn't an eye in this house that isn't on *her*."

I raise my brow, watching her as she walks away. Wondering if what I just heard was a threat.

Or a warning.

Twenty-One

SAGE

You wouldn't think there'd be a positive to being attacked and hunted in the middle of the night. Alas, I seem to have found it. I can safely wander around my own God damn home without Nic shadowing me. They must have decided the Rushkoffs are trustworthy after all. At least trustworthy enough to not kidnap or murder me in broad daylight.

The downside to that is that Nic is nowhere to be seen. No longer does he stand stoically watching me from the corner of every room I'm in.

I sigh as I stand in front of my floor-length mirror, brushing out my bed hair. As I dress for the day, I check my CGM for any issues. Watching myself in the mirror from over a shoulder, I run my hands over the scars on my body, lifting my shirt to see the scars that run right across my back. Still there. Still raised. Even after what feels like a lifetime.

They cover a significant portion of my lower back and stomach, but I've become good at hiding them. There are enough garments in my wardrobe now that I can dress to show skin without ever showing my scars.

You'd never even know they were there if you hadn't seen them before.

I tug my shirt down and smooth out my hair one final time before leaving my room for the day.

On my second pass of the ground floor I conclude that Nicholas must be holed up in Anton's office with the rest of them.

As I head up the stairs, I pause, listening to the sounds that pass through the office door. The sounds are jovial. Bursts of male laughter drift through the door, getting louder the closer I get. When I'm directly in front of the office, my hand involuntarily presses against the door, as if I can somehow be a part of the fun if just through touch. I let my fingers skim along the door as I leave them be.

The air is fresh and crisp when I step out onto the second-floor balcony. The one that overlooks the pool and has the best view of the edges of the property. I've mapped many an escape route from this position before.

My smile overtakes me as I lean up against the railing and look out onto the property. On my right is the rose garden; the first place Nic kissed me in secret. The first time he gave me that horrified 'just kicked a kitten' look.

There's the fountain far off on the left. Where Freddie used to play water games with me in the summer. When he taught me to shoot water pistols like they were real weapons. Where he, Anton and Dad used to gang up on me, but always end up falling to their water-pistol deaths against me.

I think they let me win.

I watch the spaces nostalgically, able to see the shadows of memories play out like ghosts. Idly, I wonder where I'd be if the things that happened to me when I was nine, just never happened. Would I have been less sheltered? Would I know what it feels like to have friends that don't work for my father? To have people whose allegiance is solely for me and not because of my family?

My eyes drift directly downward towards the pool. The sight there is new.

Alexei and Isla sit side by side at the pool's edge. Neither touching, but looking totally relaxed in one another's company.

They seem too intimate to not be together, but I haven't seen them constantly touching like they can't keep their hands off each other. And while he says he loves her, I can't see Alexei look at her like the galaxy exists only to sustain his love for her.

I wonder if it's friendship that I'm witnessing, unable to recognize it for the fact that I have nothing to compare it to.

A longing opens up in my chest. There is a hole in my heart that misses that. Mourns for something I've never had. I've never had a girlfriend to tell my secrets to. To share in hers. To laugh together at all the silly things we do. Though I've fucked many men, I've never had anyone to tell. And somehow I suspect gossiping about it might be part of the fun.

"Sage."

I turn around at the voice, ripped away from my melancholic thoughts. "Uncle Anton."

Anton watches me from the doorway with his hands resting in the pockets of his suit pants. He never started dressing in full suits, like a leader, until after my father's demise. It never looks right on him.

Anton slides up against the railing with me. His eyes fall to the pool, where mine had been only seconds earlier. "Isla. Alexei was quite insistent on seeing her," Anton says, side-eyeing me for my reaction.

I sigh, resting my hand on my chin as I continue to watch them, though they haven't spotted they have an audience. I drum my fingers over my chin.

"Do you think we'll ever find out what happened to Dad?"

Anton chuckles and leans against the railing with me, his shoulder drooping. "I don't know."

"I don't like that answer." My lips purse as my eyes tighten.

Anton turns serious eyes onto mine, leveling me with a warning. I roll my eyes when I realize what he's going to say before he's even said it. "You promised me you weren't going to pursue this anymore."

I turn my head so that he can't see the guilty answer written all over my face.

"Sage," Anton says, hand reaching to run through his hair before he stops himself. Seeming to remember not to mess with his put together appearance. "I'm serious. I told you I would handle it and I am."

"By missing payments?" I turn my sharp glare on him.

"What are you talk-" he says, rearing back before he stops and stutters, his eyes widening as he drops his voice to a whisper. "*Fuck* - tell me you did not go to see Angie."

"I did not go to see Angie."

Anton glares. "Now say it without lying."

I tip my chin up in defiance.

"Sage. You have got to trust me here."

I throw my head back and huff an annoyed breath. "I'm sorry. You know I trust you. I just can't sit around and do nothing."

Anton scratches at his chin, not looking at me, but down to Isla and Alexei as he speaks. "Whatever *is* going on, in spite of what happened last week, you know those brothers are at the center of it. Even if they're not the cause of it."

"I know," I say, worrying my lip. "When I marry Victor, though, imagine what I can learn when I'm actually there. In their territory."

Anton pinches the bridge of his nose. "Jesus, you're not an infiltrate. I want your father's... *killer* caught. The second you marry Victor, the perpetrators lose. And you don't flush out players that think they've lost. Only the ones that still think they have a chance to win."

I pause, biting the inside of my cheek as I try to come up with a decent argument against that very excellent retort.

"Though Victor is pretty intent on rushing things along," Anton says, shaking his head, losing his own train of thought and saving me from a reply.

My eyes drift to the insanely large ring on my finger. "I noticed."

"On that note," Anton says. "We're throwing an engagement party for the two of you this weekend. Here."

I jerk my head towards him, mouth dropping open. "What? Why?"

"Victor needed some kind of event, now that we're *wedding planning*. It was an engagement party or the wedding itself. I'm stalling as much as I can."

I go to open my mouth to yell at him, but I stop myself, frowning as I process his words. "You're trying to stall? Why? Wasn't I clear about my decision? To both you and Victor?" I swallow as I say the words, and Anton doesn't miss it, his eyes following the curve of my throat as the lump passes across it.

He seems to read the thoughts on my face. "Victor doesn't seem... unreasonable," Anton says, grimacing. "I could work something out."

I scoff, biting at my lip a little harder, and just now noticing I've been fidgeting with this ridiculous ring on my finger. I twirl it around my finger a few more times for good measure.

"I can't risk it." But I want to. I want to risk it. I want to risk it so fucking badly. I can't let Anton give me hope. "Besides, you know that's a lie. Victor is not reasonable."

Anton smiles. "Well, yes. Victor is a man who gets what he wants. Doesn't mean he gets you."

"Maybe." I do my best to smile but I'm sure I haven't done a very good job. With little else to say I find myself eyeing Isla and Alexei again. They're laughing like old friends again, but still never touching. I'm not sure why I keep seeking them out to watch them interact.

"I will get rid of her if you want," Anton smirks.

"Isla?" I shake my head, even though I do kind of consider it. She's beautiful and threatening and... I'm all out of excuses. "No. No, she's fine."

"You're watching her like a predator," Anton smiles.

"You sound proud."

"I am."

I burst out into a laugh. He's such a fucking weirdo. We smile at each other and I watch Anton's eyes soften like he's reveling in a sight he hasn't seen in a long time. When was the last time I smiled and meant it?

"You don't have to get rid of her," I say as my smile fades.

Anton nods. "Just say the word."

Without saying another word or even bothering to look at me Anton strides away with his hands clasped behind his back.

When I look back to the pool to continue my viewing, gray eyes stare back at me. Alexei watches me now too, his eyes latching onto mine and giving my body a visceral jolt.

Things have been stupid weird between us since the night of the break in. We'd reached a healthy level of mutual disrespect and now our dynamic has been flipped on its head. Things between us seem calmer on the outside, but more chaotic than ever inside my head.

Alexei says something to Isla and then gets up like he's coming right for me. But that's stupid because I'm on the balcony and he's two levels below me. There's no way- *Uhhh....?* Oh!

Shit. Is that possible?

Alexei, like a fucking terminator, jumps and grabs onto a drainpipe, which he then proceeds to scale. When he reaches balcony-height, he leaps from the drainpipe onto the side of the balcony, gripping the railing as he hauls himself over to stand right in front of me.

With my hand clutched to my chest in a very '*oh my stars*' kind of way, I chance a look at Isla. She has an amused smile on her face as she walks away.

"Isla thinks you don't like her," Alexei says, thumbing his lip before he folds his arms. "You being vicious again, princess?"

"What? No. I'm... I'm nice."

Alexei smiles and shakes his head. "You gonna put that back on the right finger?" He gestures to where I've fidgeted my engagement ring onto the wrong finger.

Sheepishly, I put it back on the right finger. Alexei narrows his eyes as I do, glaring at the piece of jewelry like it's personally offended him.

"So," Alexei says as he folds his arms. His black shirt tightens over his muscles and I have to force myself not to follow the movement. He's still the stormy gray-eyed devil I saw when he arrived. I must muster contempt back or I will lose control of everything.

You hate this man. Fucking act like it.

"You gonna give Isla a chance?"

I curl my lip. "Who says I'm not?"

"Ah, so you are being vicious again," Alexei smiles cruelly, one that turns into pure competitive joy when my lips turn up in a smile and I have to bite my cheek to stop it.

I roll my head and stomp my foot. "Fuck," I say. "Who gives a shit if I give Isla a chance?"

"I do." He pauses, face twisting as if the next words are physically hard to get out. "She really wants to be your friend for some dumbass reason."

I frown as I watch him warily, my mind on the hunt for ulterior motives. Is this a future sister-in-law thing? Wants to be besties with the girl who's gonna marry her boyfriend's brother?

"Why?" I say, slowly enunciating each letter.

"Fuck if I know," Alexei smirks.

I purse my lips as I smile. With an aggrieved, childlike sigh, I straighten my shoulders. "Well, what's in it for me, then?"

He raises a brow at me in an incredulous look. "Besides the obvious?" He shoots a pointed look towards Anton's office where more sounds of male camaraderie burst free. As if he knows what it is I long for. "All you gotta do is let her be your friend for the short while we're still here, alright?"

I wipe the sad look off my face before I face him. "You forget when you and Victor leave here. So do I."

"Not necessarily," he says, almost in warning.

It's my turn to return his incredulous look.

"Let me make something clear. I *don't* want you marrying my brother."

"Yes. Thank you Captain Obvious." I roll my eyes. "I mean, how could I guess? You were being so subtle about it."

Alexei's jaw tenses but he shakes away the look. "And you *definitely don't* want to marry my brother."

"You heard me just now?" I wince.

"No, Lieutenant Obvious," I don't miss that he's promoted me above him in the obvious-ness department, "you've been so careful with the Prince boy."

"You're the worst." I blow out a breath. "Fine. I'll stop being vicious if you stop being a psycho."

"Can't make too heavy a promise," he replies in a grumble.

"Shake on it." I raise my chin and stick out my hand.

Alexei shakes his head, regarding me like a petulant child before he grips my hand in his own.

And *fuck*. What a mistake that is.

The chemistry of touching him is like an explosion. Just the small parts where his warm hand connects around mine feel blistered and burnt.

He squeezes his hand, and it's as if he's squeezed my breasts instead. He's close now, and smells like geranium and spirits. I have this revolting urge to sniff him.

Holy *shit*. Shit. I need to let go. I need to let his hand go right now before-

He tugs me forward slightly by our conjoined hands. His face is now inches from mine, his lips rough and his mouth open. "Vicious little princess."

"Psychotic Rushkoff," I breathe directly into his face.

His hand remains clasped around mine, and my eyes drop to his rough lips again.

He rips his hand from mine with a hiss, stepping back like he's been electrocuted. I have a feeling he's done us both a favor by being strong enough to pull back.

He winces, like he was thinking the same thing, and then walks away.

He's almost gone when he stops, pausing as if he's about to say something. His fists clench at his sides, but he does walk away. Which is probably for the best.

Fuck.

Twenty-Two

VICTOR

I have a long list of people I have to kill. A long list of people I am going to kill.

Standing against the stone wall of the house, watching my brother by the pool with that fucking blonde bitch, is making me wonder if I have to add him to the list.

My fucking brother. Loyal to a fault. An excellent weapon but proven destructive.

Alexei and Isla are sitting by the side of the pool, chatting idly, their feet dangling in the water as they lean into one another.

My brother and I are as different as any two people can be. That's no secret. But I understand my brother. I understand what drives him. I understand what motivates him. And I use that to our advantage as often as I can.

But this... this is the one part of my brother that I don't understand. The one part that is out of my control.

He loves that girl. I know he does. It's probably one of the only reasons I haven't killed her. I will never understand why he won't just marry her if he feels so strongly about her. Or why when I fucked her on-and-off for four years, he didn't even bat an eye.

That ended badly to say the least.

I could gladly put that girl in an early grave.

She's too close to my brother. I wish I knew how to separate them. Or at least get him to marry her, so we won't look so weak when she keeps infiltrating our inner circle thanks to said brother.

She knows far more than she ever should because my annoying as fuck brother trusts her. We have history with her. As a family, of course. We grew up with her. Her father was an enforcer for mine. Our mothers used to be close.

Which is probably why Alexei is closer to her than I am now. He was always Mother's favorite. While I was Father's.

I'm still watching them when all of a sudden my brother's eyes get hard, his fists clenching as he glares up to the balcony above. I follow his stare and find Sage staring down on him as well. I unfold my arms in surprise. I didn't even see her there.

My gaze ping-pongs back and forth between them.

Until my brother suddenly jumps up and begins scaling the fucking side wall to get to her. He scales the drainpipe and jumps up onto the balcony right next to her. Those are the kind of skills I'm talking about - the ones that make his insolent temper almost worth it.

I sigh as I watch him with her. I can see them talking, faces hard, likely hurling insults back and forth between them. They got off on the wrong foot. They haven't spent one second together without trying to filet each other's skin off.

Once again, my fucking idiot brother is paying attention to the *girl* instead of the priority.

I tilt my head. They're coming to an agreement of some kind. She holds out her hand for him to shake and he accepts. But they hold that position for what feels like forever. Then my brother pulls her in, and they bare their teeth at one another.

God. Fucking. Dammit.

I run a hand over my face and grunt as I watch them, realizing what is happening.

My own brother.

Fucking Christ.

Marrying her is going to be a lot harder with my reckless, unpredictable brother making his version of googly eyes at her.

That will complicate things. I need him on my side.

This is a moment that I would usually call in for backup. But right now I can't use my phone.

One of these DeMarco fuckers planted a cloning program onto it. I'm not going to take it off, though. Whatever they're looking for they won't find on my phone.

It had been my priority to befriend Anton while I was here. But I fear I've now made a mistake. My priorities have been wrong and they need to shift.

Anton was skeptical about jumping straight into wedding planning. So we've settled on an engagement party this weekend. Held here. It's not the endgame but it suits my goals just fine. The power players in this city will soon be shown exactly what Rushkoffs and DeMarcos can do when there's an alliance.

I hate myself for admitting it, but I need to take a page from my brother's playbook.

I need to focus on the women.

My first priority *should* always be Sage DeMarco.

She's my future after all.

One thing needs to be made clear, though. She is *my* future. *Not* his.

***

I tighten my tie in the mirror, liking how it sits in a way that pronounces my chest muscles. My blond hair is slicked back and I've neatened my beard for the occasion. I check my watch and decide to head down the hall to make sure my brother is ready and is going to pull his head out of his ass.

181

None of this is going to go the way I want it to if he puts his head where it doesn't belong.

Sage DeMarco is my fucking business. Not his.

And this will never go my way if my idiot brother decides he wants to save her from her fate.

I push his bedroom door open to confront him. What I don't find is Alexei. What I do find is fucking Isla.

"What the fuck do you want?" She sneers, fiddling with some sort of necklace, looking openly hostile.

I. Fucking. Hate. This. Woman.

"What have you done with my brother?"

She gives me an evil smile. "He's already down at the party."

I clench my jaw and shake my head. Alexei has already forgotten whose side he's on once already. I need to pull him-

"You're not gonna pull him into line, Victor." Isla goes to the dresser and grabs a tiny sparkly purse.

"What the fuck is that supposed to mean?"

She stops in front of me and glares at me. "Exactly what I said. Whatever you're planning here, and I *know* it's something, Alexei isn't going to fall into line and follow you."

"You don't know my brother."

"I know your brother is a smart man in every area except one. Trusting you. For that, he's a fool."

"Then there's nothing keeping you here, if you think that little of him."

"Oh, I'll be here," she says. "Every single day, making sure that whatever it is you want, you don't fucking get it. And that you don't drag Alexei down with you."

We stare off at each other.

I knew this bitch was going to cause trouble. That's what she does best. A fucking thorn in my side.

Maybe I don't give a shit what she means to my brother. Maybe it's time-

"Just fucking try it," Isla says. "I dare you."

She gives me an evil smile, watching me for the whole time that she walks away.

When she's out of sight, I run a hand over my mouth. This is getting far too complicated. I don't like it one bit. Sage DeMarco needs to be mine. Now.

Every extra second we spend here is another second waiting on disaster. Too many moving parts.

No. This needs to be finished.

Twenty-Three

SAGE

$\mathcal{I}$t occurs to me now that I've never seen over ten people in a room at once. Not since I was nine years old have I had to be too long in crowds. The most people I've ever seen in one place were the men storming our compound to kill either me or my father.

My very large and very public engagement party is an inopportune time to discover this. Similarly so, a terrible time to discover crowds might actually scare the shit out of me.

I hide around the corner for a moment longer, my body refusing to cooperate and just go down the fucking stairs into the ballroom. I'm wearing a silk, olive cocktail dress that stops a generous amount below my knee but has a slit in the side that runs up to my thigh. The silk clings to me like wrap, the corset-like top hugging my breasts and dipping in between my cleavage. I've left my hair loose, but falling in dark waves down my back, and have lined my green eyes with a shimmering rose shadow and dark liner.

I smooth down the front of my dress as I try to reason with myself.

All I have to do is walk downstairs into a party. Nobody is going to stop and stare at me. Nobody will even notice me nor care that I'm there. Are there possibly hundreds upon thousands (okay maybe not *thousands*) of people here? Sure. That doesn't mean they're paying attention to me. This can all be over in minutes. All I'll have to do is walk. Down. Stairs.

I take a deep breath and dive in.

I step foot onto the top step and the murmuring stops, heads twirling in my direction.

Oh, I was dead wrong. *Every*-fucking-*one* is looking.

I melt under the pressure. Feeling like I'm under the harsh stare of a spotlight.

Not a conversation in the room continues as I will my poor feet to walk. Victor steps forward to wait at the bottom of the stairs, unbuttoning his suit jacket and placing a hand in his pocket. I want to anchor myself to him; I do. But I can't look at him. I can't look at fucking Victor Rushkoff right now.

When I descend, it's obvious everyone has been waiting for this entrance. For me. Specifically. But I don't know half the people in this room. Whatever tonight is, it's my uncle's game. Not mine.

I cling to the banister like it might save my life, walking down one step at a time as the party guests watch me. I survey their eyes, trying to feel what they are thinking. The appreciative gazes of men and flaring nostrils of women tell me enough.

Anton and Freddie are on one side of the crowd. We lock eyes and they give me their best version of encouragement, sheepish thumbs up. *Thanks, guys.* But it's not enough.

It's not enough.

I can't move into a crowd of people, some of whom probably want me dead. Are they the ones? Are they ones who are after me? Sweat beads at my temple and my skin dampens.

I can't. Can't. Can't. Can't.

I feel myself sinking. I'm seconds away from running. Alone, eyes feel like loaded guns and me, prey for the slaughter.

A pair of stormy gray eyes catch mine.

Alexei's eyes lock onto mine, more intense than any other eye in the room. But somehow settling. He holds eye contact with me as he takes a visible deep breath that reminds me to do the same. I let the air into my lungs.

My wobbly feet get steadier.

I center myself in the storm cast behind his eyes, and his throat bobs on a swallow.

It's as if the edges of the room glitter away into dust. Lining us up together like we are covered in a spotlight. The faces around his blur until they fade to black entirely, like each slow step that I take, I take it only to be closer to him.

His fingers twitch at his side. To hold himself back? To reach out and touch me?

I brush a lock of hair behind my ear, becoming more and more aware of how close I am getting to the bottom. And what I might do when I reach that bottom step.

When I cry, I cry silently. He knows, and he hears my silent cry right now.

He moves then too. Towards me. He jostles several people out of the way in his haste. His haste to make it to me. It's then that I make the mistake of looking down. Victor watches me with confusion, which turns into a glare when he looks over his shoulder and makes eye contact with his brother. Alexei stops in his tracks.

I turn my head in shame, only to find Nicholas. He's standing off to the right and from the horrified look on his face he has just witnessed absolutely fucking everything.

I nearly trip on the last step, but Victor's arm is ready and waiting for me, catching me and disguising my stumble as he helps me upright.

"Hi," I say, looking up at Victor, only sparing a brief glance to watch Isla corral Alexei back into line.

"Sage, you look wonderful," Victor says.

"You clean up well too," I say. I press a kiss to his cheek - chaste, of course - and he softens. Thankfully, it seems he is willing to drop whatever the fuck he's just witnessed.

"Come, let me dance with you."

As Victor tries to lead me to the dance floor, Uncle Anton appears out of nowhere to block our path. "Actually, I think I'm owed first dance." He smiles curtly at Victor and then levels me with a look. My deviant fiancé looks like he wants to argue, but Anton is technically the one giving me away. So, in our world, it *is* his right to the first dance if he wants it.

As the music begins to warm the atmosphere, I notice that there's a spot cleared in the center of the dining room. Now that the table has been cleared away, it comes off more like the ballroom it was meant to be. There are already several people paired up to dance.

Without saying a word, Anton grips my hand and leads me to the dance floor, spinning me into position before beginning to guide me in the movements. When Anton doesn't immediately say anything, nerves start to flutter inside me. Subtle glances to the crowd show me their wistful smiles as they watch us.

"Anton?" I ask, clearing my throat.

"I need a minute," Anton says. "To think of what I'm going to say to you without pissing you off."

"Excellent start," I deadpan.

Anton sighs, spinning me into a slow twirl before drawing me back into frame and leveling me with a look. "It seems some attentions have strayed your way."

My heart sinks and I nervously drop my head. "It's unwanted."

"Is it?" He raises a brow at me as I lift my chin to regard him again. His eyes tell me a story of what he sees. I don't even know what *I'm* seeing. But Anton looks at me like he certainly does.

"Whatever is happening with Alexei it needs to stop. This is life and death, *anima mia*."

I tense my jaw and my hands tighten on his before he hisses. I grimace as I loosen my grip.

"There's nothing going on there," I say.

"Not right now," Anton says, agreeing. "You're supposed to be marrying his *brother*, though, Sage. These people can't see you fawning over anyone other than Victor." His lip curls on the last part as if he doesn't like it any more than I do.

When I don't respond, my feet moving limply, Anton gives me a knowing look. Full of regret, I nod. Anton nods too, like he doesn't really trust me but knows his message has hit its mark regardless.

He brushes a lock of hair behind my ear and the song ends.

"Ah, Anton!" A voice calls out from somewhere in the crowd.

Anton gives them a wave and a smile before lowering his voice to say to me, "Try to look like you're having fun, hey?" He gives me a smirk and then disappears.

I flinch as a new song starts up and I'm left standing in the middle of the dance floor alone. Pairs start to spin around me, but my nerves are shot to hell. I shake my head to dislodge an errant train of thought and turn abruptly. When I do, I turn straight into a hard chest.

My eyes shoot upward, past tight muscles bound in a dark suit against a black shirt and black tie. All the way up to blacker hair and gray eyes.

Alexei looks down on me with an expression more intense than I've ever seen from him before. For a moment, we hold like that, chests pressed together as my lips part on an inhale. He extends a hand to me, his tone breathy. "Dance with me?"

I look down at the hand he has pressed between us and bite my lip. Anton literally warned me to stay away from Alexei no less than five seconds ago. I can't be caught dancing with him now. Especially after my grand entrance. Especially before I've danced with my future husband.

"Sure," I say.

Alexei's lips tip up in a smirk as I place my hand in his much larger, firmer one. His gaze seals on mine as he walks backwards, tugging me along gently with him. We reach the center of the dance floor and he pulls me into him, eliciting a sharp gasp from me when he settles his other hand at my hip.

It takes me a moment to realize he's constructed the perfect dance frame and my hand that he isn't holding hangs limply.

He leans in, lips brushing my ear. "Hand on my shoulder, princess."

I scowl. "I know."

He chuckles as he leads me around the dance floor. We step into a waltz pattern like the others around us, but we're far too close to be holding a proper frame. The dance feels like a battle of wits as we each move more fiercely, regarding only each other as I follow every complicated step he leads each time he ups the ante.

As the song progresses, the innocent hand he had on my hip moves to my waist and curls around my back. The one I had at his shoulder moves around until it's cupping the back of his neck.

Our movements get faster. More passionate. The other people on the floor with us look amateur in comparison. We glide across the space at speed, turning and turning until my hair starts to twirl with us. All the while there's no sight for us but one another.

Like we're being sucked into the center of a vortex, we continue to spin as the velocity pulls us closer. Our feet whirr at speed in expert time, never stepping out of place.

I hear the music build to a crescendo, but it only spurs us on higher. Spurs us to get closer, to orbit further into the other's embrace.

I see *no one* else.

In this moment, I am suspended in time. All that exists here are lightning storms set behind gray eyes. Tattooed fingers clutching at my waist. Soft strands of silky black hair twisting around my fingers.

Just when it feels like we can't get closer, like the next step is only to fold into each other forever, a rough hand grasps Alexei's shoulder. He jerks hastily. Our movements stop as we both jar at the intrusion.

Alexei drops me like I burn.

Victor uses the grip he has on his brother's shoulder to pull him farther away.

"Thanks for holding down the fort, brother, but I'll take it from here," Victor says, dark menace evident in a tone I've never heard him use before.

I struggle to catch my breath, panting heavily, and Alexei fares no better. Though he does give in first, giving his brother a nod before storming off into the crowd.

Victor regards me with a raised brow and then offers me his own hand. Through my stuttered breathing I nod politely and take his hand.

He pulls me into a dance that is much simpler than his brother's, but with an intention of intimacy that is no less lacking.

He holds me together as we sway back and forth in a basic hold. He pulls me in until my head rests on his shoulder. It's literally the closest we've ever gotten. If Anton felt the need to forewarn me, then I suspect this is a show of power from Victor. To remind everyone who I am meant to belong to.

"That was quite the dance," Victor says.

"Was it?" I say.

"My brother is an excellent dancer. So are you, I see."

"I try," I shrug. Pulling back from Victor, I do my best to give him a smile and redirect the conversation to lighter topics.

"You enjoying the party as much as I am?" I ask.

"I do hate a good party," Victor smiles, though I doubt that is true. "Too much posturing."

I can't help but laugh. "Why do I feel like you're in your element?"

He sways us a bit more. "I suppose I am," he says, smiling out into the crowd. "I'm good at networking."

"No better than a politician," I joke, shaking my head.

He gives me a laugh and we settle into a comfortable silence as we go through our movements. I relax, assuaging myself that Victor wasn't bothered by what he saw.

As we move around the dance floor, I find that we're being watched. Intently.

At the far corner of the room, Alexei stands leaning against a pillar with his arms folded tight and one leg propped over the other. He's nearly hidden in the shadows, but he's just visible enough that I can see his angry glare.

Next to him, Isla looks stunning in a floor length red dress. She follows his line of sight to us and sighs, saying something passionate to him that he ignores. They continue to argue until something she says has Alexei glaring at her instead.

And then he charges across the room. Coming right for me. Again.

She grabs his hand back, stopping him. His eyes are still locked fiercely on where Victor and I dance. Even as Isla desperately tugs at him still. Even as she pulls him forcefully until he stumbles.

When she lets him go, he charges for us again and my breath hitches.

Isla folds her arms, looking annoyed as she says one word that I can't make out. But that's all it takes. Just one word. Alexei stops. He turns over his shoulder to her, then looks back at me with pained eyes.

I watch it as he hardens, curses and then levels me with a dark look before he storms off completely, shoulder checking Isla on the way.

My gut plummets.

Did I *want* him to come to me?

Oh *no*. No. No. No. This won't do.

I fucking hate it when my uncle is right.

The music stops and I pull away from Victor as fast as I can. "Thank you for the dance," I say.

"Save me another before the end of the night," Victor says but I barely hear the reply as, against all rational thought and better judgment, I rush off the dance floor in search of Alexei.

***

I narrowly miss shoulder checking Isla on my way through. I brush past her as I stomp after Alexei, swerving through the party until eventually I find him alone, pacing in the darkened kitchen.

"What the fuck is your problem?" I sneer.

He startles, shocked to see I've followed him. "I've got no problem." He looks like he wants to be calm, but his teeth are clenched and he's nearly shaking with anger. "I've got nothing for you, actually."

"Stop looking at me then," I whisper-shout, arms-flailing to make my point. "Just, whatever it is you're doing. Stop it. All of it."

"Me?" He launches forward. "*Me?* You're the one giving me 'fuck me eyes' in front of the whole room."

"Are you insane?" My eyes nearly bug out of my head.

191

"Possibly. But you're giving me a run for my money." He scoffs, turning away as he puts exasperated hands on his hips.

"I was *not* giving you 'fuck me eyes'. You wish," I scoff and roll my eyes as I fold my arms.

Angry eyes snap to me. "I wouldn't fuck you if you were the last woman left on this planet," he says, spewing vitriol as he steps right into my space, backing me up against the counter as he does. Though I don't think he means to do that. "I'd rather chafe my own fist tugging my cock for eternity than put it anywhere near you."

Dick!

I slap him and his head reels from the contact, his jaw contracting.

He slams his palms on the counter either side of me, boxing me in, and looking like rage embodied. Like he could kill me by ripping apart my gut with his bared teeth. He leans down further into my space.

"You. Dare. Touch. Me."

I try to slap him again.

Harder. He deserves it. But his hand snaps up to grip my wrist instead. He growls, dropping my wrist like it burns and instead grabbing my hips like he's going to move me out of his way and out of his mind.

Instead of pushing me away, like I'm sure he intended, he lifts me. He parks my butt on the countertop and my dress rides up as he smoothly steps between my open legs.

His eyes bulge and I'm sure mine do too.

What the fuck am I doing? I've lost my mind.

In my mind, I beg for this to stop all the while begging for more.

He looks down to where his hands fist on my hips in the dress. Silk curling around his tattooed fingers. We both stare down at his hands until his thumb starts to draw strokes and - fucking kill me for this one - I arch into the contact.

My breasts brush his chest and his hands come slamming around me to grasp my waist in full and drag me against him.

We are so. Fucking. Close.

It feels like I'm suffocating.

I clasp at his shoulders and moan as his hips press into mine. I can feel a very sizable bulge pressing where he stands between my legs.

"Shit," he whispers. He holds me close and strokes down my spine. In response I begin embarrassingly massaging his muscles. Not for his pleasure, but for mine.

Alexei is ripped and dangerous and fucking sin embodied.

He isn't sweet and gentle like Nicholas... or even Victor, rather everything he does hurts. Even the things that feel good.

I throw my head back and he takes the invitation, leaning his head into the crook of my neck, his breath fanning along my collarbone.

Something in my chest starts to break.

"You feel..." he breathes along my neck like he's drinking me in, and I moan.

We're still only touching. And yet, it's like we both hold back because we know any more friction than this and we will both die. We both know, before we have even tested it, that we are nuclear.

He pulls back and looks at me with a pained, horrified expression. Like he can't fucking believe what he is doing and to be honest, I can't either. I'm sure that confused, horrified expression is mirrored in my own gaze.

A flash of blonde hair catches my eye and over Alexei's shoulder I find Isla standing in the doorway, arms folded and smirking. Alexei's head snaps up and he follows my gaze, stumbling back to drop his hands away from me like I'm diseased.

Alarmingly, my first thought is that the absence of his hands *hurts*.

"You," Alexei says, wistfully like he is just remembering where he is. He steps back another few paces, practically tripping over himself. His gaze locks on mine and turns venomous. "Stay the fuck away from me, princess."

Then he storms from the room, pushing past Isla as he does.

"Well," Isla says, laughing as she approaches me. "That was interesting."

"I-" ... have no fucking idea what to say to her. Sorry for dry humping your boyfriend? I'm not sure why I liked it when he repulses me? I sheepishly close my legs, step down from the counter, and go with the truth. "I - I'm sorry. I don't know what to say. That was-"

Isla smiles knowingly, leaning against the bench as she sing-songs happily. "Well, I'd say if you had half as much chemistry with Victor as you do with his brother, this marriage wouldn't be such a problem."

"What?"

"Watching you with Victor is like watching someone who hates kids hug a baby." At my obviously stunned expression, she chuckles. "You know? They want to like it, think they should like holding the baby, but really they're just disgusted."

I can't help turn up a small smile at that. "Victor is...fine. *Alexei* is repulsive," I say. "Fuck, I'm sorry. I didn't - ugh, that was rude. I know he's your boyfriend."

She frowns.

"Alexei isn't my boyfriend." As if she's just worked something out she gives me an incredulous look, followed by a smirk as she shakes her head in the direction Alexei just went. "Did he tell you that?"

I ignore her. "Fuck buddy then?"

"Why do you *care*?" She raises a single brow at me. *Touché.* "It's actually neither. That's fucking disgusting. He's like my brother."

"What? He... made it seem?"

She smiles again. "Oh, he's such a devious little fool." With that, she comes toward me and links our arms together. "Come. Let's walk back together."

Twenty-Four
ALEXEI

I want to rip my fucking skin off. I want to filet my skin and burn it for betraying me. Punish it for lighting up when *she* touches me.

She's the enemy.

She's fucking the bodyguard.

She's engaged to my brother.

She might be marrying my brother.

I tear through the party, my feet slipping from beneath me as I run towards the porch for air. I grip the railing and gag over the edge, bile rising in my throat as I do. I almost choke on it. Good.

I scrub a hand over my sweat soaked face. I've never felt so out of control and off plan ever before. I'm not sure how long I've been out there when I sense someone approach.

"You're royally fucking this up you know," Isla says. I turn and scoff at her before facing out into the night again and lighting up a cigarette. Hoping it might burn away some of the anguish.

"What would you know?" I spit back at her, my stomach threatening to come up through my throat as I inhale the smoke.

"Everything," she chuckles and rests on the railing beside me. "Or did you not call me here because you were losing your mind?"

I rub at my head.

"She's the fucking enemy. She... wraps herself up in a delicate little package like we're supposed to think she's not capable of anything," I say, thrusting my arms into the night air. "But she'll be the one to take us all down. I don't trust her. Victor shouldn't trust her."

Isla rolls her eyes. "Not this shit again."

"I know you don't like my brother-"

"That's the understatement of the century," Isla says. "Be concerned with your own actions for once. And ignore Victor's. Besides, it's not Victor she's looking at."

This time, I chance a look back into where the party goes strong. My eyes find her instantly, as if I've got radar on her. I see her far in the distance, surrounded by Fallon and her uncle, but smiling up into Prince's eyes.

"Does it matter?" I ask, inclining my head to where I see Sage and then turning to look over the gardens because I can't watch her give him those puppy dog eyes.

"She's in love with the bodyguard," Isla nods, voice turning solemn as the wind picks up and crickets chirp in the distance.

"And if she weren't, she'd marry Victor," I say. "Hell, she might even do that anyway."

Isla worries her lip, studying Sage closely. "She won't go through with it. That would be stupid. And she's not stupid."

I throw the cigarette down and take a deep breath, feeling as if I've gained a semblance of control over my sanity again.

"Victor has more than failed to capture her attention," Isla says, stubbing my cigarette out for me with her red pump.

I huff a laugh, thinking of my brother. "I don't think Victor realizes that."

"I think he does," Isla says. "It worries me what he'll do with that knowledge."

"Do you have to always think the worst of him?" I ask, glaring at her. It's always something with these two. I hate being put in the middle. To both of their dismay, I will not choose between them. I could never give up Victor. I could never give up Isla.

"He's given me reason to," she replies.

"He's my brother," I say.

"Yes, and that is the only reason I haven't slit his throat," she says, turning angry eyes on mine. So full of hatred for him. Even though they've slept together numerous times.

I groan. "That's not the real issue, anyway."

"What is?" Isla asks.

"She planted a cloning device on Victor's phone. She's up to something. Hiding something." I fold my arms as I turn to watch her too. She's still laughing with her family, giving Prince those heart eyes. I clench my teeth as I watch her hand curl around his arm. He looks at her like she makes up his whole world.

Isla pauses for a moment, her brow furrowing as she sees me react. "I like her," Isla says.

I huff a laugh. Of course, she does.

I, though, cannot have the luxury of *liking* her.

I have to forget her. Forget niceties. Forget olive silk dresses, green eyes, dark hair. No. All of it is designed to distract me and I've let it. I will not let myself be as blinded by her as the rest of these fuckers are.

That's it. That's all it is. Just like I said. She's a pretty package, designed to be a distraction. I can't let myself get caught up in her bed. Web! I mean... caught in her *web*. Jesus.

"She's just playing me like she's playing the others," I say, watching Sage as my vision darkens.

Out the corner of my eye, I see Isla shake her head. "God, you're such a fool," she laughs. "You usually see everything. How are you so incredibly blind?"

I give her a strange look, but she just smirks at me. "When you pull your head out of your ass come find me." She winks, rushing into the party at a skip where she settles in alongside Sage, linking their arms like they're the best of friends.

Sage smiles, arm going around Isla as well, and they start to engage in conversation. Enough of one that has Sage tipping her head back in a laugh.

When I see Isla subtly tug Sage's hand away from Prince's, I bite my cheek to stop a smile.

Twenty-Five

NICHOLAS

J leave Sage at her engagement party in Freddie's reliable hands, my heart in my throat as I take the short walk across the mansion halls to get to Anton's office.

When I get there, I don't bother to knock. Instead, I just barge inside, where I find Anton already waiting and sitting in one of the armchairs, eyes vacant and a whiskey clutched in one hand.

I watched him escape the party about five minutes before me. I know he's seen everything as clearly as I have. But I bet his heart doesn't splinter because of it. I bet there are no tattooed Rushkoff hands reaching into his chest to rip his heart out.

"Nic," Anton greets, slurping down the last of his whiskey and gesturing for me to sit across from him.

"Anton," I say, resting down into the chair like the weight of everything that's resting on my shoulders right now.

"Couldn't stand it either?" Anton asks.

I nod. "Yeah. Freddie's covering her for now."

Anton shakes his head. "I'd say there's a lot more than just Freddie covering her."

I run a worried hand over my mouth and lean forward in my chair. "You don't have to tell me that." Believe me, I already fucking know. I watched her with him. The way she honed in on him when she came down those stairs. How they pressed together when they danced, eyes glued together like they were the only sight worth seeing. When she finally made her way to me, her eyes still shone with the admiration she's always given me. Yet still, I can't shake the feeling that wants to sprout.

Anton watches me curiously, his head tilting back and forth like he's trying to bore my brain open and extract all my secrets. "I think we can both agree that things are getting out of hand."

I nod. Though I'm not sure what he's referring to. Because there are so many things that are out of hand. The presence of the Rushkoffs, any impending arrangement between Victor and Sage, myself and Sage... then there's that *fucker* Alexei. I stifle a laugh. "It depends on which thing you're talking about."

Anton gives a tired laugh too, and scrubs a hand down his face. There's a shadow of stubble on his chin, his tired eyes sunken in. "All of it," he finally concedes. "The Rushkoffs... are becoming a problem."

"I agree," I say, trying to stop my excitement sounding through. "This marriage, I don't like it. Anton, I don't give a fuck what was written in any kind of will or contract or document. I won't ship her off to him." I lean forward and barely let myself think of the repercussions of my words as I launch them at him. "Please. Please don't make me." I cut myself off and worry my lip with my thumb.

"Because of what's going on between the two of you?" Anton says.

My startled eyes find his. But he gives me nothing.

"Or because of whatever is going on with her and Alexei?" Anton finishes.

My heart goes off like a cymbal, clanging loudly enough to create a ringing in my ears. He's noticed it too. Which means I'm not just seeing things, and I'm definitely not making it up in my head. There's something about the hatred that they pour into each other that is starting to come across much more like...

"I don't think they have any idea what they're doing to each other." I smile through the hurt.

Anton eyes me warily as if I'm a gun primed to fire. "That must be hard for you."

"I don't need a therapist," I say, giving him a chuckle. "But I'll have whatever she gives me until she tells me otherwise."

Anton nods again.

"She..."

"Loves you," Anton finishes. "That much is clear. As it has been ever since you've been around here." He stands and makes his way towards his desk to sit behind it. "You're the only dumbass that didn't realize."

I laugh and let out a groan, praying that is still true before I run out of chances. She's given me far too many as it is.

"I've figured it out far too late," I admit, going to stand at the window. "Whatever is there between her and Alexei may be too far gone now."

"Could be nothing."

"It doesn't feel like nothing. It feels like the beginning of *something*."

"Nic, you know that girl means the world to me. Whatever she chooses... I..."

"I know."

"If she chooses Alexei?"

My face turns to solid stone as my blood heats. I level him with the angriest glare I've ever felt in my life. "Then he'd better fucking deserve her."

Anton raises his hands in a surrendering gesture. He watches me for a moment, maybe to sense if I'm calming down. I'm not, but he must think I have because he continues. "Would that change anything for you? Here?"

"No," I say, shaking my head. It would tear my heart in two, rip my guts out from my throat, but it would change nothing. "I'll die for her and this family regardless of whether she loves me back."

"Good," he nods and then he levels me with a harsh glare of his own. "Because when it comes to her, *all* of us are expendable. Dimitri would say the same if he were here."

"We just need to get rid of the fucking Rushkoffs," I say instead. Meaning more to whisper it to myself but grateful for the opportunity to say it to Anton. I miss the days when it was just Sage and me here. No fiancé. No brother-in-law. Just the days that I took for granted.

Anton barks a laugh. "Understatement," he says. "They need to go."

"Sage planted a cloning device on Victor's phone. He knows," I say.

I hear a thud and turn to find Anton banging his head against the desk. "For fuck's sake," he says. "She won't leave well enough alone will she?"

"Probably not," I reply. "I don't trust Victor either. Something about him is off."

"I know." Anton raises a brow at me.

"I can't put my finger on it. Even with the psycho Rushkoff running around here, Victor still seems like the bigger threat."

"Did Sage find anything on his phone?"

"I don't know yet," I say. "I'll keep an eye on it."

"I doubt we'll have any luck convincing Victor to go quietly," Anton says, thinking out loud to himself. Though I have to agree. I turn back to look at Anton to find him watching me again. "She doesn't want to marry him. But she won't say no to him, because of the threat to us if she does."

"So don't give her a choice," I say, heart plummeting even as I do. I know taking the choice from her is a betrayal. But she's choosing wrong. "As I've said all along."

"You can't be serious," Anton says, huffing out a breath. "She'll kill us."

"Victor might beat her to it," I say, smiling at him. His lips twitch even as he tries to remain annoyed. "I'll death promise Victor if I have to. He has too much honor to back down from that."

"You're not death promising Victor," Anton growls.

I just shrug. "Victor is friendly with you now, Anton. He might back off and then I won't have to."

He looks away, staring off into space like he very much doubts that I'm right.

"I'll keep her safe," I say. "You just get the fucking Rushkoffs out of here. Both of them."

I leave him with the particulars of figuring out how the fuck to do that. I turn back to the window, watching the lawns. Wondering if I've used up all my grand gesture chance cards to win her over. I'll need them once she finds out what we've done. Especially if it starts a war.

As I'm looking out the window, I spot a figure in the distance. A familiar woman in an olive-colored cocktail dress running up the driveway in her heels.

"Fucking Freddie!" I launch into a run out of Anton's office.

***

Sage grunts and flails comically, like her legs have turned to jelly. She's halfway up the fence, struggling to get over without the motion sensors going off. It's got to be a nightmare in that little olive dress. She can't even lift her leg properly to haul herself over.

I fold my arms across my suit, holding in my laugh as I watch her.

God, she's funny. I don't think she even means to be.

She continues on without noticing I've spotted her and am watching. She tries one foot and then the other, but that death grip she has on the fence will not make an ounce of difference if she can't lift her leg.

"You're kidding me right?" I say, and she pauses her climbing, head turning slowly over her shoulder. She sighs when she confirms, that yes, I have found her. Gravel crunches under my feet as I approach her. "You're trying to scale the fucking fence? In the middle of your own engagement party?"

"How do you always know?" she groans, throwing her head back in a grimace.

"It's my job to know," I chuckle. I move closer to peer up at her as she continues to cling to the fence for dear life. "You gonna come down?"

She shakes her head.

"Am I gonna pull you down?" I ask, standing up straight and readying to do just that.

She shakes her head again.

"How is this going to go down then?"

She closes her eyes, and I think that's where we're going to leave it. This will be where she comes down and I live another day wondering what the fuck she's still hiding from me.

She purses her lips as she thuds her head against the bars and says, "I'm going to trust you." It physically hurts her to do this. To trust me. She's either gotten herself in some really deep shit or I've fucked my chances more than I thought.

"I'm getting out of here tonight, Nic. And if you must come with me to make that happen, then so be it."

I take a step away from the fence. This is big for her. I know that. But I look back up the driveway to where I can see the party still raging in the ballroom all the way up to the second floor.

Am I really going to run off with her in the middle of her God damn engagement party?

Fuck.

I am. I'm gonna do it.

I check my holsters to make sure I'm equipped with enough ammo. Checking all my weapons up my legs and then my arms, making sure they're all there and loaded before I roll up my sleeves and step up to her. I place my hand under her foot and she gasps as I launch her easily the rest of the way up the fence.

I hurl myself over after her and land perfectly on my feet. "Okay, now where are we going?"

Almost on cue, a black sedan pulls up in front of the gates. I raise my brow at her but she just grimaces, opening the door and giving me a sheepish smile when she gestures for me to get in.

***

We end up way downtown. As in, a drive into the city downtown.

The area we're in, while technically DeMarco territory, is the absolute worst part of it she could have chosen.

"Here we are," Sage says as we stop in front of a nondescript dive bar. She grabs the handle with enthusiasm, but I pull back her elbow and she scowls at me.

"Are you serious?" I curl my lip at the neon sign. "Is this where you've been coming the whole time? This is so fucking dangerous."

She gives me a flirty smile. "Haven't died so far."

"Oh My God."

"Come on, get inside." She yanks herself out of my grip and pulls open the door faster than my arms can reach out to catch her. With a growl, I follow her inside.

It's worse in here than I expected. Smelling of body odor and filled with shady men who don't hide their interest as they look at Sage with open lust.

It honestly couldn't get any worse.

That is, until Sage waves at someone. Someone sitting in a booth far near the back of the bar.

Scratch that. It just. Got. Worse.

Sage drags me over to the booth where I come face to face with a thorn in my side fiery redhead.

"Really?" Angie says, glaring at Sage. "You brought him?"

"Yeah?" She looks back at me.

"Angie." I dip my chin.

Sage gives me a look, and I dread the fact that I'm going to have to explain this later. I always avoid doing business with Angie when Dimitri or Anton asks.

"Nicholas," Angie smiles with all her teeth, like a movie villain. She looks me up and down and smirks. I level her with a warning look but her eyes just twinkle with mirth.

"Oh. *Please.* Sit," she says, slowly and casually. But even Sage picks up on it as we slide carefully into the booth.

I don't take my eye off Angie the whole time.

She has the power to erupt and destroy me within a second. She knows it too.

Angie has two men flanking the booth behind her, watching the room for potential threats. Ridiculous really when Angie could probably kill everyone in here whilst sipping her drink and without ripping her dress.

I hate the fact that whatever Sage has hidden has to do with her. What has she gotten herself into, what hole has she possibly dug, that she needs Angie of all people to bail her out of it?

"Well, I'm surprised to find you brought a guest along tonight, Miss DeMarco."

"Am I not entitled to bring friends? I thought it was open invitation." Sage gives Angie a sassy look. I try not to grimace. *No one* talks to Angie like that.

"Well," Angie smiles as she swirls her drink. "You sure he's a friend?"

I clench my jaw.

This meddlesome bitch.

"Yeah." Sage rolls her eyes. "Yeah, I'm pretty sure."

Angie looks back and forth between me and Sage. I see when she starts to get it. That Sage means something to me. That I, hopefully, mean something to her.

Angie normally keeps a cool poker face, but even she has a micro-reaction to this. A tiny twitch of her brow. One that only lasts a fraction of a millisecond before her face returns passive and calm.

She licks her lips once. "You really going to bring *him* into this?"

"It's my business," Sage says, lifting her head in defiance, all the while giving me a curious side-eye.

Angie considers a moment before she shrugs. "It's your funeral."

"So... about what I asked for then?" Sage prompts, her leg bouncing under the table.

"You know the rules. Favor for me first." Angie's eyes dart to me. "Miss DeMarco, go to the bar and order me a drink."

"Seriously?" Sage groans.

Angie just levels her with a look.

"Guess you are," Sage sighs. She steps out of the booth, pressing a kiss on my cheek before she goes. I go to follow her but Angie halts me with a hand in the air.

"Not so fast."

"I'm not taking my eyes off her."

"Calm down, Nicholas," Angie says. "You can see her from here."

I look over and see that I can, in fact, see Sage from here. Not only that, but Angie's guys have moved in behind her in defense, glaring at all those creepy, lusty assholes. I almost can't believe what I'm seeing, Angie showing favor to Sage. But if anyone could tame the fire-queen, it'd be my girl.

"So," Angie says, smiling cruelly. "You're the Prince and you've snagged yourself a little mafia princess."

I'd laugh at that if I found anything about Angie amusing.

"Too bad that's not your real last name," Angie grins.

I run my tongue over my teeth. "I'm warning you, Ang-"

"I'm surprised to find you in the same position after all these years," Angie says. "The work you've put in."

"I swear to fuck Angie if you ruin this for me-"

"I'm not here to ruin anything," she swirls her cocktail glass before taking a sip. "But I can see now why you've stayed for so long."

"Watch it," I warn.

"Gosh, you're so hostile. Your secret is safe with me, *Nicholas Prince.* Nobody is telling little Sage DeMarco-"

"*Anyone,*" I warn.

"Right," she smiles. "Nobody is telling anyone about what skeletons you've got hiding in your closet."

I slink into my chair. I need to get us out of here and back to the mansion as fast as possible. "What do you want?"

"Nothing," she says.

I raise my brow.

"Just good to know you're still... doing the things you do."

"You always want something, Angie."

She contemplates for a second. "A favor. I always like being owed a favor."

I slump into my seat. "This is why I never agree to come anywhere near you, you extortionist."

She smiles.

"You'll leave this alone?"

"I'll leave it alone," she says sincerely. "She's gotten herself into a world of shit on her own. I won't add your bombshell onto it."

"What does that mean?"

"You'll see."

With that, Sage slams Angie's drink down onto the table and gets down to business. "Now. Give me what I came for."

It turns out that what Sage wants is for Angie to blindfold us and lead us to our deaths.

Okay, that may be slightly dramatic.

But Sage doesn't look one bit surprised to see the blindfold appear swinging from Angie's finger.

"What? No. Jesus Christ."

"Nic, come on," Sage clasps my hand, giving me those puppy dog eyes. "This is how it's done."

I point my finger at Angie. "No."

"Yes." Angie gives me a saccharine smile.

Sage obediently closes her eyes.

I cannot believe it when I allow Angie to place the blinder over Sage's eyes and then mine. I clutch tightly to my girl's hand, not letting her go now that I can't see her.

I can't fucking believe Sage has been sneaking out this whole time to be blindfolded by crazy killer redheads and lead into unknown danger.

It was so much worse than my imagination possibly could have conjured up.

"I swear to God, Angie," I growl as I feel hands on me lead us away from the bar.

"Oh, calm the fuck down already, Nicholas. The act is getting old," Angie says.

I keep my bearings enough to realize we make it to a car. Which could be great or horrific depending on how much I choose to trust her. I'm not trusting Angie, though. I'm trusting Sage.

I take a deep breath and step into the car, taking Sage inside with me.

"I'm really going out on a limb for you here," I whisper.

"I know," she whispers back, and places a kiss on my hand.

I must really, really be into this woman.

All the while we drive, I count each turn in my head. It's after the fourth consecutive left that I realize we're being driven in a pattern designed to distract me from being able to tell where we're going.

For me, that's the final straw, and I'm done playing along.

I struggle, ripping my hand from Sage's as I start for the blindfold.

"Nicholas, don't," Angie warns.

"Nic, please," Sage says grabbing for my hand again.

But I'm so done. I put up a fight, struggling even as Angie's guys jump in to hold me down. My body thrashes against theirs, fighting for control while Sage begs and pleads for me to stop.

"Nic, please, stop," Sage begs.

"Where the fuck are we going?" I shout, not ceasing my thrashing long enough for them to get the upper hand.

"You'll see," Angie says. I can hear the smirk in her voice.

"Fuck this," I say, reaching for my gun, the click audible even over the protests from Sage and the fight from Angie's security.

"We're going to see my father!" Sage shouts. It's the words that she whispers, afraid to be heard, which stop me dead. "He's alive."

Twenty-Six

SAGE

*P*redictably, Nic doesn't take the news that Dad is still alive well. Though he does quieten down and stop trying to fight Angie.

The blindfolds aren't taken off until we're inside the building and Angie disappears, only leaving behind one guard. As usual, only one stays behind to see me home safe. Even I don't get the privilege of knowing the actual location of this building.

That's probably for the best. I'm breaking a hundred rules and even more promises just by being here. And a thousand more by bringing Nic.

"Come on," I say, gesturing to Nic to follow me down the familiar corridor.

The inside of this building looks like the set of a horror movie. Whether that's to help Angie's cover or not, it's still creepy as hell. The sound of a gun clicking echoes and I turn behind me to find Nic has drawn his weapon. I suppose this does look like a place people come to get chased down by killer clowns.

We climb two flights of stairs until finally coming to our destination. I pause with my hand on the door, gathering my courage before I swing it open and we step inside.

Just like that, Nicholas knows my biggest secret.

"Oh." There's a nurse sitting next to a hospital bed, reading a magazine. She places it down when she finds us in her space, smiling gently at me. "Visitors. Sage, you brought a friend."

Nicholas's weapons clang to the floor. My eyes first go to where they've dropped and then up to him, as he looks at the hospital bed in horror.

"I didn't actually believe you."

Nic's eyes dart frantically over the room. I watch them as they land, taking in one unfathomable sight after the next. The nurse, the medical equipment, the heart rate monitor beeping steadily in the background.

The patient in the bed.

"Holy fuck," Nic says, doubling over. "Holy fuck, Sage!"

"Ssh, way too loud," the nurse scolds. She gives me a questioning look, her hand reaching for the panic button but I just shake my head. Her returning look is judgmental, but she lets it go.

"Dimitri," Nic says, dropping to the floor beside Dad's bed. "He's alive."

Confusion blooms across his face, before tears begin to form in his eyes. I don't think I've ever seen Nicholas cry.

"Yes," I nod. "My father is still alive. And if you want to keep it that way you will keep this to yourself."

"Well, he hasn't woken from his coma since the accident," the nurse chimes in, giving Nic a sympathetic smile. "There's no way to know if he ever will."

"I'm optimistic."

"Doesn't sound like you," she jokes and I smile.

"How? How have you kept this secret?" Nic asks, his jaw clenching. "Why would you keep this a secret? Your marriage to Victor is predicated on your father being dead. Which he is not!"

I shift nervously on my feet. This is an angle I hadn't considered. I'd anticipated Nic's anger about being kept in the dark. But not once did my thoughts stray to Victor and what Dad being alive means for us.

"Anton and I decided to keep him alive in secret so that whoever wanted him dead would leave him alone."

"Anton? Anton's in on this?" Nic says, giving an annoyed puff and shaking his head. "So Anton is well aware there's a trump card to your fucking wedding sitting in this hospital bed."

"Are you serious?" I say, remaining deadly calm. He must hear the warning in my tone. "Dad's life is not a fucking trump card. It's safer for him here. And it's safer that the least amount of people know."

"Fucking Angie," Nic seethes. "Of course, she'd be behind this."

"Hey," I snap, stepping towards him and pushing my finger into his chest. "The only people in the world who know about this are me, Anton, Angie and now... you. Don't waste the trust I'm placing in you, Nic."

Nic purses his lips as he looks between me and where my father lays. "I am undoubtedly grateful that Dimitri is alive," he says, jaw grating hard. "Don't get me wrong, I am. But why? Why would you keep this a secret? You'd never have to marry Victor if you hadn't."

I have nothing to say to that. These are all facts that I know. All facts that Uncle Anton knows as well. Yet we've still made these choices. Still set ourselves on this path.

He drops into a chair next to the bed, looking exasperated and unsure. A look I've never seen from him. "I can't believe you hid this from me."

I gulp, but find the answer forming in my throat to be raw, rude, and completely honest. "It had to be done."

***

By the time we sneak back into the mansion, the party is long over. If anyone noticed the guest of honor missing, the commotion must have long since drowned out.

Nic has not calmed down even slightly on the drive back home. The one guard left to blindfold us and take us back ended up with one black eye. I don't know what I expected from him finding out that Dad is still alive. It wasn't this, though. It wasn't that he'd be so angry with me that he'd barely be able to look at me.

In my heart, trusting him feels like the right choice. I don't want to listen to the devil on my shoulder that is telling me to doubt his intentions.

The whole way across the back lawns towards the house, Nic stomps ahead of me without even stopping to check that I'm following him.

"Well, well, well, look who has deigned to return," Freddie says, stepping out of the shadows on the back porch and scaring the shit out of me.

"Jesus!" I clutch my hand to my heart. "Don't do that."

Nic goes to open the back door to the house, giving Freddie a stern look. "Yes, we're back. And you're in big fucking trouble."

Freddie cringes. "Only took my eye off her for a second."

Nic raises his brow. "She only needs half a second."

Nic continues into the house and Freddie gives me a pleading look. The best I can give him is a bright, bratty smile. I follow Nic through the kitchens into the foyer, pressing my back up against the wall in an attempt to tiptoe upstairs without him seeing.

"Oh, no you don't." My wrist is grabbed and I'm tugged away from my escape route with a pout.

"Where are you taking me? You can't kill me! I'm important!" I feign, as I struggle against him.

Nic makes an amused sound. "Back to my room. You're with me tonight."

"Oh," I say, my voice taking on a flirty tone.

We stop in front of his room on the ground floor and he raises a brow at me as he opens the door, gesturing for me to step inside first.

Curious mind getting the best of me, I rush inside and look around.

His room is tucked on the first floor with a beautiful view over the back gardens. It's small with only a double bed pushed up against the wall, a desk and a door that I assume leads to a private bathroom.

My fingers are itching at my sides to touch everything that I know he owns and sniff his sheets. I might wait until he's asleep to do that last one.

"I know you're eager to snoop, but can it wait?" Nicholas says.

"Can we fuck first and fight later?" I grimace.

Nic runs a hand over his face, but he does smile at me from where he stands across the room. In a few steps, he's in front of me and holding both my hands in his.

"I'm sorry for what you've gone through," he says. "All of it. But it can all stop now. With your father. You need to use him."

I pull my hands away from his and step away. "How can you even ask that of me? I could never."

"He'd want you to," Nic says, eyes pleading. "If he were awake, he'd tell you to."

Tears build in my eyes, pouring out the overflow from my aching heart. "But he's not awake, is he? Sure, he's alive. But he can't tell them this isn't what he wanted."

"Risk it."

"No," I say, spinning on Nic. "Anton won't risk Dad and neither will I."

"But you'll risk you?" Nic shouts, giving me a wide-eyed stare. "Unbelievable," I hear him mutter under his breath.

I storm past him, but he catches me on the way, spinning me back to him. When I turn around, he's right in front of me and I gasp. Gone, though, is the hard angry glare. What I see in his eyes is someone who looks... scared.

He licks his lip. "I know you planted a cloning device on Victor's phone. Which I assume now that you got from fucking Angie, but-"

"Nic-"

"Ssh, it doesn't matter," he says, staring earnestly into my eyes. "I know you think it's the Rushkoffs behind this. I don't."

I frown. How could he possibly-

He runs a thumb over my cheek before his hands drift down my back, slipping to the place where the olive dress parts and running his palm over my scars.

"How'd you get the scars, Sage?"

My body chills.

It's incredibly strange. How I can go months, sometimes years, without thinking of the night when I got my scars. How I can feel nothing. And then, just like that, one reminder, and I'm back in that cellar with florescent lights flicking over my head. Losing all sense of time as I lose my mind.

Tears brim in my eyes.

"Someone has a vendetta to finish," Nic says.

Goosebumps take hold of my skin and I suddenly flush cold.

"You think *he* has come back to finish what he started?"

Nic nods solemnly.

"What?" I say. "How could you possibly know that?"

"Anton, Dimitri and I fended off multiple attacks before your father was hurt. Whatever this is, it didn't start with the marriage contract."

I already know that. But I don't say it.

"Dimitri had a death promise with *him*," Nic raises his brows meaningfully. "He had spent the last few years trying to find him to exact revenge for you. You know what a death promise is?"

I nod. "In our world it's like signaling war? Black roses are exchanged to signify the two people are going to fight to the death."

"Half right," Nic explains. "The exchange means a fight to the death with no interference. Neither party can use their army or any backup. It's barbaric," he shakes his head, "but it's a challenge of strength and honor."

"You think *he* was after me, because of this death promise? That makes no sense - then his vendetta would be with my father-" I clutch a hand to my chest, breaking the contact with Nic as my breaths start to come in harsh. I'm hyperventilating.

Nic places his hand over mine where it lies on my chest and stares deep into my eyes. Calming me down as he breathes in sync with me. "Maybe I'm wrong. But whoever it is, I will *never* let them take you. Any of them."

It feels like a promise that etches onto my skin.

"I love you," he says. "And I'll never let anyone hurt you."

I still can't breathe. I still can't get it under control.

"Hey," he says again, now clutching my face in his hands. "I'll never let them take you. Nobody is ever going to hurt you again. I fucking swear it."

He kisses me.

It's harder than the other kisses, and I can feel it like a thread snapping in my back as I push myself into his arms. Like the ropes that held us apart have splintered, coming down around us like fireworks as we kiss.

I'm a sad, stupid fool. I know I am. I know he's been cruel. I know I haven't made him work for his place in my heart. But he has one, nonetheless. I couldn't change that if I wanted to.

I love him.

I jump into his arms. He holds me at my thighs while I literally try to climb him like he's a tree. He is -

"-so tall."

Nicholas pulls away with a chuckle.

I cringe. "I said that out loud."

He tightens his hold around my thighs. "I didn't realize tall-ness was such a turn on."

"Absolutely." I push my weight into his with renewed fervor and he grunts as together we fall onto his bed.

"And I love you," I say.

His eyes grow tender and he shifts a lock of hair away from my face, cupping my cheek as he stares into my eyes. "I've waited so long to hear you say that."

I smile and kiss him again before my lust takes over. Like, embarrassingly takes over.

I am usually graceful, I swear. Right now, though, I maul Nicholas like a cat in heat, mewling like one too. He groans as I rip my shirt over my head and grind myself against him, pressing rough kisses down his neck.

"Sage. Sage-sage-sage," he says.

"Mmm?" I pull up with a start, flicking my hair over my shoulder.

He doesn't have to say he wants to slow down. I know he does, but after everything I'm not sure if I can.

He flips us so he is on top and settles between my thighs.

216

"Relinquish control," he says. He begins an agonizingly slow roll of his hips and oh. Oh fuck. Gripping my thigh, he continues slowly grinding into me while he kisses down my neck and then removes his shirt.

My eyes nearly bug out of my head. Ripped grating lines of stomach muscles clench in my vision, drifting down to the perfect V that's pressed against me between my legs. Muscled corded forearms rest on either side of my head, and above me Nicholas smirks.

His hands slide all over my body as he peels the dress away from me until I lay before him completely bare.

He sits back to admire me, tilting his head with a hungry gaze. Posing, I arch my back and extend my legs, drawing attention to their apex.

Nicholas pries my legs open and throws them over his shoulders.

"What-"

The words disappear from my mouth when his tongue brushes along my slit.

"Oh."

He traces lazy circles between my legs, gripping my thighs over his shoulders as he feasts on me. My head falls back to the pillow, my mouth wide in a silent scream. He doesn't let up, knowing exactly where to touch me to make it count. He's *so* good at this.

"Yes!" I writhe. "Yes. Yes. Yes!"

I come, squeezing my eyes shut so tightly in bliss that stars speckle around my vision.

Before I can come down, before I know what is happening, Nicholas is on me, kissing me, and I taste myself on his mouth. When he settles back between my thighs, he's somehow lost his pants. His bare skin brushing up against mine.

"God," he says. "You're so wet."

"Don't tease me anymore," I beg. Yes beg. I've misplaced my pride.

Eh. It's not that important to me anyway.

He grips his cock and positions it between my legs, pushing at my entrance.

He slides inside one inch, his head rolling back as he pushes in another. Then another. And when he presses in so far that we were fully joined, he stills.

My breaths puff, chest heaving as I wait for him to move. Again, with a slow roll of his hips he pushes out and then back inside me. Over and over. Burying his face in my neck he keeps his momentum.

"You're worth everything, Sage. Everything. I should've never let you think otherwise."

This might be the first time we've ever had sex in an actual bed. What we're saying to each other now has gone beyond words. I've been waiting since I was seventeen years old for Nicholas Prince to love me. With every thrust into my body, he tells me that he always has.

A low build starts against my belly. Chasing with every press of him inside me. With each thrust it grows closer. He holds my legs open and keeps the pace.

"Nicholas, I'm going to - oh!" My orgasm tightens again and I am lost in wave after wave of sensation. Crashing down around me.

Through it, Nicholas keeps his thrusting. "God, Sage. You're so-"

When I open my eyes, his teeth are clenched. Eyes tightening like he's pain. Though judging from his groans, it is a pain he rather enjoys.

"I'm going to come," he says.

"Come inside me," I say. "Please, come inside me."

"Christ."

He thrusts a few more times before stilling. I feel his warmth flooding within me. After a few more ragged breaths, he collapses beside me and pulls me into his arms.

This time, he doesn't run. He looks me right in the eye as he cleans me up, pampers me and holds me in his arms as he tucks us both into bed.

As we drift off to sleep, nothing exists but Nicholas and I. Exactly as it was meant to be.

Twenty-Seven

SAGE

y eyes open of their own accord, commanded from somewhere else in my brain. The room around me is unfamiliar and the pillow is hard as a fucking rock. Oh. Not a pillow. I sigh as I sit up against Nic's hard chest, quickly wiping away the drool that rested there.

He's out like a light. Snoring gently while I'm wide awake again.

With his sheets pressed against my naked front I turn to look at the clock on his bedside. Only two-twenty-seven in the morning. I scrub a hand over my face and tiptoe out of the bed on silent feet, slipping on his shirt as I go to the door and leave his room.

His door closes with a small click and I breathe a sigh of relief in the hall as I whip out my phone, dial and press it to my ear.

I glance nervously back at the bedroom door, extra jumpy about rousing Nicholas right now. "Pick up, pick up, pick up," I chant, bouncing on my feet as I wait for the phone to connect.

"Miss DeMarco," Angie answers. "Again so soon?"

"Angie, thank God," I sigh.

I hear light chatter on the other end of the phone. "An emergency?"

"No, nothing like that," I say, blowing out a breath. "I just wanted to check with you..."

I check over my shoulder again, unable to voice the request.

"Spit it out, Miss DeMarco. We both know you've got more money than sense. You can afford me."

I roll my eyes. "The marriage contract, Angie. The one between me and Victor-"

"Yes, that is the only marriage contract I'm aware of."

"You're interrupting!"

I swear I can hear her smile on the other end. "Go on."

"The marriage contract, is there any way, you know... *out* of it?" I nibble on my nails.

Angie chuckles. "You having second thoughts about marrying Victor Rushkoff, girl?"

"That's putting it lightly," I admit, checking over at the door *again.*

"You've been so ambitious," she says. "You want to give up now?"

"Maybe."

"Because Prince is making moves on you?"

"Is that really any of your fucking business, Angie?" I say, raising my voice a little and then nervously looking around to make sure no one has overheard.

"It's not," she admits. "I'm sorry, Miss DeMarco. There's no way out of the contract. As it says, there's only war."

"Really? Nothing? Nothing you can think of?" I beg.

"Come on, Sage," she says, addressing me by my first name for once, which throws me off as I suspect she intended. "You've got your trump card sitting in a hospital bed-"

"I won't use that," I growl.

She sighs. "Then the contract is air tight. You should know. You wr-"

"I know, I know," I say, waving my hand and whispering as if that will quieten down the noise on the phone and shut her up. "So there's nothing?"

"I don't know what you want me to say," Angie says. "Get Victor to agree to get out of it without war. That's your only option."

The phone goes silent for a moment.

"Or start one," Angie suggests. "Start a war for all I care."

I groan.

"Make sure your payments are on time from now on, Miss DeMarco."

"Yeah, yeah," I say, hanging up the phone and clutching my gut as nausea builds in my stomach. I can't use Dad. And I won't start a war.

As much as I wanted there to be another way, it seems my luck has run out. I have to finish what I started. I blow out a breath and chew nervously on my fingernail.

I frown as a muttering voice drifts to me from somewhere else. Not from behind Nicholas's door. Farther away.

The voice gets closer, and I spot a figure rounding the hall corridor, pacing as he mutters like he's trying to talk himself off a ledge. He doesn't seem to even know that I'm here. But he still comes closer to where I stand. Instant panic is my reaction. Until I see who it is.

"Alexei?"

He startles, frowning as he looks from me to Nicholas's door and then finally takes in my attire with a pursed lip.

"What are you doing here in the middle of the night?" I ask.

His recovery is swift, trademark sneer branding on his face. "I could ask the same of you. You've been missing since the fucking party. I thought you were taken." Alexei grumbles before clenching his jaw. "And you weren't in your room."

It suddenly dawns on me that he's here to check on me. It should be weird, but it isn't, and that may be the strangest thing of all. "How did you know I was here?"

"Please," Alexei says, his lips curling in distaste. "It's blindingly obvious that you've been spreading your legs for the bodyguard. It was not a leap to check here, princess."

I roll my eyes. "You are foul."

"You skip out on your own engagement party to bang someone else? That's tasteless. Even for you."

"Who I fuck is none of your business."

"You're marrying my fucking brother!"

"And you don't want that to happen. So once again, I repeat, what does it matter to you who I fuck?"

Alexei glares at me, but in his eyes I see indecision. His gaze drifts endlessly between me and the closed door and his mouth opens several times as if he is debating against himself somehow.

"It... doesn't," he says, eyes hardening. Whatever indecision had been running through his head trickles out at the last moment.

"What do you want?" I say. "As you've noticed, I'm kind of preoccupied." I gesture at the door behind me with my thumb, folding my arms underneath my breasts.

Alexei's eyes drift away from my face and take in my attire, resting on my chest for a few seconds before skimming my bare legs. I uncross my arms and look down, displeased to see that my nipples are pointing straight through the shirt.

When I meet Alexei's eyes, he smirks.

"You're done," I say, moving to turn away.

He growls, peeling back his lips to reveal his teeth, seeming to remember the original reason for his visit. "Someone planted a fucking cloning program on my brother's phone."

Oh fuck.

I feel my face go white as a sheet but I try not to react.

"And who do you think could've done that, princess?"

I glare at him. "This is a middle of the night problem?" I ask, throwing my hands out. "This is a middle of the night, follow me to another mans bed kind of problem?"

"Don't pretend to be innocent."

I gulp but keep my composure as he stares into my eyes for answers.

"You just have to keep reminding everyone why you're the enemy, don't you?" I scoff.

"We are enemies. It's in our fucking blood to be enemies." Alexei looks at the door, his eyes growing hard and painful. "Given that it seems my brother has no chance at winning your heart, I don't see that changing anytime soon."

I bite my lip, looking back at the door to Nicholas's room.

"Does he, Sage?" Alexei asks, head turned down from me as he softens. "Does my... *brother* have any chance of winning your heart?"

The question, though simple, feels complicated. Like if I answer it, I'm actually answering something else.

In the end, once again, the easiest thing is to do nothing.

"We're done here," I whisper, trying to brush him off. I turn to open the door but he pins me with a glare, staring at the door like it's the real enemy here.

"Do not go back into that fucking room, Sage."

"You can't stop-"

"We're so not done. Do not-"

I raise my chin. "I will do-"

He thrusts his hands against the wall beside my head, caging me in. "Don't. Go back. Into that. Fucking. Room." He stares down at me with black eyes, intense and telling. Yet he renders me speechless.

His chest is heaving.

Mine is too. And with each brush of air my breasts press against his chest. But we don't dare blink. Don't dare break eye contact.

Please, no. Not again. I don't want this. I don't want him.

I do. Fuck, he smells good.

His eyes dart down to my lips. He presses forward further as my tongue darts out to wet them.

"Sage?"

Alexei's gaze snaps away from my lips back to my eyes. That wasn't his voice. That one was farther away. In another room?

"Sage?"

Nicholas's voice.

Alexei pulls away from the wall and straightens his shirt. I look toward the door and he follows my eyes, gulping in understanding.

"I... gave my heart away a long time ago," I say, even though I'm not sure why I do. It doesn't even scratch the surface of the answer I should be giving him.

I watch as all the air leaves his lungs. He closes his eyes, and when he opens them, they're rough and stormy once again. "Understood." He walks away, and I have the stupid, uncontrollable urge to stop him. I don't have to, though. He turns around anyway, looking over his shoulder as he whispers to me. "Sweet dreams, princess."

Alexei disappears just as the door to Nicholas's room swings open.

"Sage?" he says.

I turn to him with the best smile I can muster. Which is crazy, because smiling should be easy. But it feels like Alexei just walked away with a piece of something that should belong to me. That I should get to decide what to do with.

"What're you doing out here?" Nic's voice is gentle and trusting.

"Sorry. I thought I heard a noise," I say. I just lied. Why did I do that? "It was nothing."

He smiles and pulls me into his arms. "Come back to bed."

He leads me inside and closes the door behind us. I settle into bed with his form pressed up behind me, my hands under my head on the silk pillows. Trying desperately not to cry.

What the fuck is wrong with me?

I have everything that I've wanted for so long. Nic loves me. I've begged for that for as long as I can remember. That he'd finally see me, look at me, the way he has tonight.

So why is it that when I try to close my eyes, I only see stormy gray ones staring back at me?

I did give my heart away a long time ago. I gave my heart to Nic, even as he stomped on it repeatedly. He's the one who has it now... But...

A sinking feeling settles into my gut.

Over the past few months, someone else might have stolen it.

Piece by piece.

Inch by inch.

So slowly that I didn't even realize it was happening. That I didn't even realize my heart was no longer mine to give away. I never even considered that maybe, in the process, I stole a heart that didn't belong to me too.

Twenty-Eight

NICHOLAS

"It's a good deal, Victor. Take it."

Anton means business from where he sits behind his desk. I stand behind him like a sentry while Freddie lazes on the lounge in the background. Strategically placed in case there's any bloodshed from this risky encounter.

Luckily for us, Victor doesn't have any backup. Alexei and Isla are both nowhere to be seen this morning. Which is fine by me. As long as they're nowhere near Sage. I'm getting really fucking sick of people trying to steal her out from under me. Rushkoffs. Masked men.

She's *mine*.

Still, Victor doesn't look happy from where he sits in front of Anton's desk. His shoulders are tense and rigid, almost as if he's steeling himself for a fight, even as his eyes drift over Anton's shoulder to me.

"Give up the marriage contract?" Victor seethes. "Do you hear yourself, Anton? Need I remind you it's the only reason I'm here in the first place?"

"I'm aware. I revoke it," Anton says, chair squeaking beneath him as he shifts.

Victor leans back, resting one leg on the other and steepling his fingers under his chin. "You don't have the power to do that."

We're well aware we don't have the power nor the right to do that. But look at us, doing it anyway.

"I don't care what I have the power to do. It's what I'm doing. I revoke it."

In one swift movement, Victor stands, and as I tense I see Freddie shift slightly to do the same. We watch Victor warily as he paces about the room. My fingers itch for a fight. I want to throttle this motherfucker. Funnily enough, though, not as much as I've come to want to throttle his brother.

"How dare you! You want to start a war?"

"You'd start a war to fight for a girl who doesn't want you?" I smirk, even as Anton throws me an annoyed look over his shoulder.

Victor's eyes cut to me. "I fight for the right to what is mine."

"She's not yours," I say, arms flexing involuntarily.

"Enough," Anton says, standing now too, and coming between Victor and myself. "The fact remains Sage is now mine to give away. And I won't do it. She's not marrying you, Victor. That's final."

Victor smiles cruelly, one full of his white, wolfish teeth. "That's not *really* up to you is it, Anton?"

Anton narrows his eyes. "Dimitri is dead-"

"Oh, I'm not talking about Dimitri." Victor stalks forward, pointing a finger down on the desk. "I'm talking about her. You tell that girl it's me or a war. What do you think she'll choose?"

"That's blackmail," Anton seethes.

Victor raises a brow, the threat clear. I'm going to rip that smug look right off his face.

"You don't care?" Freddie sits up, eyes furrowing. "Even if you have to blackmail her?"

Victor looks back over at him and folds his arms. "She comes with me."

Nobody moves as we contemplate the gravity of what he's saying. He won't go quietly.

I only give one warning sound, a harsh grunt, before I tear across the room, diving across Anton's desk and knocking shit astray as my vision reddens on Victor. "Oh, fuck you, Victor you fucking cu-"

I'm almost over the desk, waving my arms wildly and swearing my head off. But Anton grips my shoulders and hurls me back before I can do any real damage. The whole time, Victor just laughs, and that only fuels me to fight harder against Anton's grip.

I struggle and finally throw Anton off, cooling down and stretching out my shoulders.

"I do what I need to in order to take what's rightfully mine," Victor says.

"I swear to fuck if you keep referring to her as property-" I nearly dive again but Anton gives me a look.

"Tell the girl, Anton," Victor grits out. "Tell her to choose."

All eyes fall to Anton for the answer. Especially Freddie's. And I can't help but feel like he's going to be disappointed in us when he finds out we're not giving Sage a choice in the matter.

Anton must see it too, because he grimaces at Freddie before shaking his head and regarding Victor again. "What she says doesn't matter. She doesn't get a choice," Anton says. Victor won't see it, but I do. How his eyes shutter in sadness when he says those words. He hates taking the choice away from her. Even if it's for the best. "I'm making the choice, Victor. And I'm saying no."

Victor's nostrils flare. "Don't do this, Anton. You're gonna regret it."

"Maybe," Anton smiles sadly. "But I am really hoping we've built enough of a friendship over these months that you won't make me."

Victor huffs, pushing too much air out of his nose as he refuses to look at us. Hands on his hips as he shakes his head. "You've got no fucking idea what you've just done."

With that, Victor storms out of the room. When the door smashes open, Alexei is standing on the other side, obviously having heard the whole thing. He spares one second to look at us like he wants to kill us before he's off trudging after his brother.

"What the fuck have you done?" Freddie says, sinking further into his chair.

I have a feeling it doesn't matter whether Dimitri is alive. Victor is set on Sage, and if he can't have her, he's going to have his war.

Twenty-Nine
VICTOR

I only get a second to pause, a slight falter in my steps, to register that my brother is standing outside the door and has listened in on that whole conversation, before he spins on his heel and stomps up the hall in front of me.

Growling, I storm after him.

As I pass the landing, a set of claw-like, red nails dig into my arm to halt me. My teeth bare as I face Isla. Only I find that her teeth are bared too, while she gouges crescent circles in my skin. "You lost Victor. It's over. She doesn't want to marry you. Listen to your brother for fuck's sake."

I tear my arm from hers and she flexes the fingers that were just gouging holes in my forearm. "You don't need territory. You don't need more power. Forget the fucking war. Let the DeMarco girl go and go home."

The competing burn of frozen ice and scorching fire slices through me, variants of rage warring within me for control. My traitorous *fucking* brother has spilled his guts to this girl again. I swear to God I don't even know where his loyalties lie anymore.

I push past Isla and storm to my bedroom. I've had enough of this.

I've had enough of playing the nice guy.

It's never been who I am.

I throw my bedroom door open and leave it to smack against the frame. When I get inside I find Alexei already sitting on the bed, folded forward with his tattooed hands resting between his legs.

I've always envied my brother for his ability to show his inked skin so brazenly. I have plenty of tattoos too, but mine are all hidden under suits and business shirts in the name of appearance. I certainly can't afford to have ink crawling up my neck the way he does.

His eyes lift to mine and he gives me a look that tells me he knows exactly what I'm thinking. "Don't do it, Victor," he begs. "Let's just go home."

"You have got to be fucking kidding me!" I shout, kicking at the carpet. "You as well?" I pull at my hair, whispering under my breath, "what are they putting in the fucking water here?"

"She's not worth this, Vic. Let's just go home."

She's most definitely worth it. A fact I'm sure my brother knows too, given the way he looks at her. At this point, even if I got Sage where I wanted her, I'd have to convince my brother to back off. And now, I'm not sure I could.

"They're disrespecting us." I grind my teeth. "This is a massive show of disrespect!" I'm shouting now. "The DeMarcos have always held one over our head! Like they're gifting us the fucking universe just by allowing us to exist!"

Alexei's eyes snap up to glare at me. "Why the *fuck* do you want this so badly, Victor? What the fuck has Sage Fucking DeMarco got to offer you?"

"Power! People! Everything!"

"We already have all of that." Alexei stands, tightening his muscles like he's preparing to fight. Preparing to fucking fight me on behalf of this fucking girl!

I growl, throwing all the items off my dresser and only feeling a mild pinch of satisfaction as they shatter aimlessly on the floor.

"Stop it. Now, brother," Alexei begs. "I see what you're doing. Stop it now before it gets out of hand. Even more than it has."

He touches my shoulder but I shrug him off, putting distance between us. My brother puts up a fight, though, gripping my shoulders and pulling me in until our foreheads are touching.

The uncharacteristic move is enough to give me pause.

"Please," he begs. "Please. Don't do this."

I let in a sharp breath. I have never in my fucking life seen my brother beg for anything before. Even when our father held a gun to his head when he was sixteen, he didn't beg for his own life.

I watch him carefully as he pulls away, my chest heaving.

I run a hand down my face. "Fine. Fine, have it your way, Alexei," I say. "I'm listening."

"Good," he nods, swallowing hard.

"Then we need to get out of here. No point in staying," I say.

He nods solemnly, but his eyes go hard like he hadn't considered that. I go to the closet and pack my things into duffel bags to illustrate my point. Even as he stands at the closet door, he only watches me, making no move to stop me.

"You're going now?"

"Like I said, no point in staying."

"Okay," Alexei nods.

"You coming?" I clench my jaw, pausing the packing to watch him over my shoulder.

"Yeah," he says, his eyes becoming glassy and distant. "Yeah." A beat passes. "We'll need time to wrap up, so, I'll, uh, I'll stay tonight and pack up with Isla and everyone else tomorrow. We'll come home, Vic."

I turn away so he doesn't see the rage manifesting on my face. He doesn't want to leave her.

"Good," I say, holding my tone. "See you tomorrow."

My brother recognizes the dismissal, thankfully, because he doesn't seem to recognize my commands these days.

He presses the door closed behind him and I bare my teeth.

With my fucking idiot brother out of the way, I'm set to have things my way. Finally.

I settle into the armchair by my bed and I wait.

I wait hours. The whole day. Further into the evening.

When night falls, I stand, jumping up with a start.

Under the cover of night, when I know almost everyone will have retired for the evening, I round up our men. Gathering our guns and charging my way across the premises.

I've got eight guys in tow with me by the time I kick open Anton DeMarco's office door and aim my gun at his head.

Within seconds, my men have surrounded the room.

Anton doesn't look at all surprised to see me. He puts down his pen, eyes pinging around the room to survey the damage.

"Really, Victor?" He shakes his head. "That was fucking quick."

"I get what I want, Anton," I growl.

He stands, turning off his desk lamp and shrugging off his suit jacket before approaching me.

"So, it's come to this?" he asks, facing me head on.

I smile cruelly. "It's come to this."

And then I cock the gun.

Thirty

SAGE

An errant strand of sunlight hits my eye and wakes me. When I open my eyes I find the curtains closed, and a smile forms on my face when I remember that I'm in Nic's bed. More specifically, with his arms wrapped around me and my head resting on his chest.

I stroke up and down the plains of his abs, smoothing over the chest hair.

As my mind wakes and I remember my predicament, dread pools in my stomach.

I've confined myself in a hole I'm not sure I'll be able to crawl out of. Half of me wants to forget the name Rushkoff ever existed and see the both of them out of this house forever. The other part of me can't let it go. The part of me that feels like they're involved somehow in the plot against me. The part that still doesn't want to ignite a war with Victor.

The part that comes alive when his brother looks at me. Even though whatever floats between us feels like passion disguised, but he looks at me like I disgust him.

I hate how it makes me feel.

Everything is simpler loving Nic.

I want simple.

Nic grumbles, his chest vibrating underneath my head as he comes to. I pat his chest with a smile as I slip out of bed, wrapping a sheet around myself and opening the curtains in full.

Nic hisses as the light hits his face. "Devil woman," he groans, rolling out of bed onto the floor to hide, but I just laugh.

I stare out the glass doors onto the back lawns as Nic grumbles somewhere behind me. My smile slips when I notice men carrying crates and suitcases back and forth up the driveway.

"What's going on out there?" I ask Nic, pointing to the men.

Nic stands, following my stare before he gulps and looks away. "Just moving some merchandise around."

I frown. "Those are Rushkoff men though?"

"Yeah, I don't know. It's their merchandise. Just getting a head start on their move I suppose."

I want to question it further but when I spin, Nicholas is there and suddenly his lips are on mine. Kissing me stupid and I smile as I forget all about what I was just thinking.

"I'm going to shower," Nic says, winking. "Someone should surprise me in there."

I chuckle. "Give me a few minutes." He slaps my butt before he walks away.

The shower starts running, only as background noise to me while I watch men carry things up the driveway and load them into cars.

I shake my head, ignoring the funny feeling stirring in my gut.

I'm about to join Nic in the shower when I hear a faint buzzing. A buzzing that feeds the anxiety in my stomach like tiny sparks of lightning.

After a few moments, it stops, but then starts again. I frown. I can see Nic's phone sitting on the dresser. It's not where that's coming from.

I move throughout the room, running my fingers along each surface. Past the bookcase, dresser, and finally coming to his desk. Like a game of hot or cold, my skin warms when I sit down in his chair.

The buzzing rings against the pads of my fingers.

Something's here.

When I open a drawer it gets louder. I rifle through the contents unashamedly.

The intensive drawer search turns up nothing, but I can still feel the buzzing against the bottom of the wood. I bite my lip as I continue to run my hands over the surface, certain that I can feel the vibrations beneath.

I press my fingers to the bottom of the drawer, but there's something strange about how it sits. Too small for its height. I curl my fingers around a thread of loose ribbon.

I know what will happen if I tug it.

I know what I will find.

Here, I contemplate shoving the drawer closed and ignoring what I see. If I stop now, I can blissfully get into that shower with Nic. He'll probably kiss me. Make love to me against the shower wall. And I'll never think about what's in this drawer again.

Only I know that isn't true.

I'll never be able to forget it.

I scold myself for the blatant violation of privacy, and then I rip the ribbon up. The bottom of the drawer lifts out to show me a secret compartment.

God dammit.

I peer inside the drawer.

There's the source of the buzzing. An older phone that can only be described as a burner for all the lack of personality is has. The burner phone has several unnamed missed calls and one message that says: *call me now.*

My heart starts to gallop in my chest. I pull the rest of the contents out and start to flip through them, lacking dignity and feeling righteous in my search.

There's old cashed cheques. Too many payments to count. But hardly a mafia man's money. Why would he need to hide this?

There's more paperwork inside. Nothing that means anything to me. Underneath it all, though, at the very bottom and hidden under everything else, there's a black flip book about the size of a card. The kind that people usually keep ID cards in.

The black card isn't heavy but it feels crushing in my hand. I lick my lip. I shouldn't open this. Nothing good is going to come from-

I flip the black card open and my body chills.

Icy poison slices within me, tearing up my insides.

No. Please no.

I hold my hand over my mouth and barely hold in the sob that chokes me when my ears start to ring.

Yet I can't let go of the book. I can't stop staring at it, even as the world fades around me and darkens to gray with the weight of all the lies.

It's not an ID. It's a badge.

Nicholas *Baker.*

FBI.

***

The shower water stops running, abruptly throwing me back into reality.

Instinct takes over and I burst into action, messily shoving everything I found back into the secret drawer before Nic can see me. My fingers slip multiple times, even as they clutch the badge like they're not going to let go.

Tears pour down my face, but as always, I cry silently.

He was supposed to be my prince.

"Sage?"

I look over and I just know all my emotions are written on my face by the way Nic's jaw clenches. His fists ball at his sides and his eyes go cold as he looks me over and then looks over to the drawer, which is very clearly askew. I'm bad at covering up my messes. Nic clearly is not.

"You weren't supposed to see that," he says.

The words tear bullets through me. I sob, backing up and clutching the sheets tighter over my chest. Suddenly I feel more vulnerable than I ever thought I would around Nic.

Nic.

Nic makes to step toward me. He wears only a towel hung low on his hips and I'm only wearing a sheet. We're not dressed appropriately for the eruption that is surely to follow.

"No!" I hold out a hand in front of me. "Don't come near me."

"It's not what you think," he says, raising his hands in a placating gesture and giving me the sincere eyes he's always had. Now, though, I'm not sure I can believe them.

"Tell me what I think, Nic. Tell me what I fucking think!" I yell, tripping over the length of the sheet. I chance a glance to the door, my escape route and Nic looks over his shoulder too, following my eyes. He's blocking the door. There's no time to get past him.

"Look, yes, okay. Yes I'm FBI. But if you'd just let me-"

"Let you explain?" I yell. "Let you explain!"

I stumble backward, tripping over my own feet until I fall into the glass door and remember that it opens out onto the courtyard. An escape hatch. I reach for the handle of the glass door, when something occurs to me. I turn back on him with murder in my eyes. "What are they really doing out there, Nic?"

His jaw clenches.

"Nicholas?" I cry, my heart tearing in two. "Nicholas, what are they really doing out there?"

Nic purses his lips, huffing, and he really doesn't want to tell me. "The Rushkoffs are leaving. Anton broke the marriage deal. You're not marrying Victor fucking Rushkoff."

"What?!" I cry, seeing the packing with fresh eyes. I don't have to marry Victor, but. "What about the threat of war?"

Nic gives me wide panicked eyes, and when I thought I knew him, I'd say he's thinking how unlucky he is to be having these two hard conversations at once. "We can take them."

"No," I cry, sobbing into my palm. "No!"

My brain struggles to deny it. They... Isn't this what I wanted? They broke the marriage deal.

But they did it behind my back. It was meant to be my choice. I was meant to be *my* say.

"It was meant to be my choice," I whisper.

"Yeah? Well you were choosing wrong. Had to take matters into our own hands."

"You betrayed my trust," I whisper, then turn to shout. "And you're the fucking FBI, Nic!"

He takes another step.

"No!" I cry out, sobbing. "Don't come any closer."

"Sage, pleas-"

I pry the curtains apart and open the door, slamming it shut behind me. I struggle to hold the sheet against my breasts as I gather a deck chair and press it up against the handle to hold the door shut.

And then I run.

Not like I've run before. This time, I bolt around the side of the house, pavement nearly burning under my bare feet. My hair and the sheet fly wildly behind me as I struggle to keep myself upright.

I nearly gave up everything. Sacrificed my family. For a liar and a *fed.*

I'm not sure where I'm going, just that I need to get away from here. Just that tears are streaming down my eyes. Just that my heart is lurching in my chest. Just that I need to find a way out.

I feel like I'm going to combust.

I race around the side of the house. I look over my shoulder, not watching where I'm going as I turn a corner, only to slam straight into a hard chest in a black suit. The both of us stumble backward, but tattooed hands grip my shoulders. Alexei finds his feet first and rights us both.

"Fucking Christ! Watch where you're-"

I look up into his eyes and he pauses, the hatred melting off his face like it was only there to hide the layer underneath. "You're still here," I whimper.

"What's happened?"

The sheet slips out of my grip as I falter, gripping onto his shoulders too.

"Fuck," Alexei curses, pulling the sheet back up to secure it in place. "You're naked."

"Take me to your brother."

His eyes darken. "Excuse me?"

"Where's Victor?"

Alexei shakes his head. "He left last night."

"Take me out of here," I beg him, but he just gives me a stunned look. His eyes that remain fixated on my face, also look like they're taking a lot of energy to remain there. It's like he can't even hear a word I'm saying. "I know you know how to get out of here!" I yell. He blanches but still holds the sheet in place as I wave my arms frantically. "Please! Get me out of here."

I need to fix everything before it's too late.

Starting a war between my family and the Rushkoffs is exactly what a *fed* would want. Way to kill off two birds with one prince.

"Fine. Jesus," Alexei says, huffing at me. He pulls the sheet tighter around me and secures it in a knot around my waist. He holds out his hand and I take it, twirling our fingers together. I only have a moment to appreciate the strong calluses of his palm gripping my small hand in his large one before we're off.

He leads me and we run across the yard, the sheet flapping aimlessly in the wind but secure around me from the knot he tied. We run past the pool deck and away from the rose garden, until we're sprinting full speed on the lawns next to the driveway.

"Sage, no!" I don't stop running but I do turn to look over my shoulder and I see Nic standing at the front door in only his pants. Nic starts at a run and I gasp as I focus my attention forward once again.

"Come on." Alexei tugs at my hand and we continue to run, him pulling me along and my legs working as fast as they can to keep up. We stop when we reach the front gate, and I turn to see Nic coming up fast. Alexei clenches his jaw as he looks to see Nic chasing us. A stray hair of black hair falls across his forehead and his eyes lock on mine for only a second before he's back in action.

Alexei pulls out a gun and shoots the lock on the gate. Once, twice, then a few more times until it starts to sag and loosen. Nic is close. Coming up so close.

With his expensive oxford-shoed foot, Alexei boots the gate open and takes my hand again. Then we're running out onto the gravel road. I wince, feeling prickles of sharp rock dig into my heels. It's hell on my feet but I don't stop. I can't stop.

Alexei looks down on me, then to my feet, barely even stopping his run as he scoops me up into his arms. He pulls me up with one arm under my legs and the other under my shoulders and I instinctively wrap my arms around his neck as he keeps running for both of us.

We come a ways down the road and Alexei leads us behind a bush where a black car is hidden and waiting.

"Get in," Alexei says.

The car unlocks and I don't hesitate, jumping into the back seat while Alexei gets into the driver's side and tears off.

The gravel peels dust up off the road as we scream away, fishtailing before the car rights itself. When I look out the back window, the last thing I see is Nic standing barefoot and bare-chested in the middle of the road, pulling at his hair.

Thirty-One

SAGE

alfway toward town Alexei finally pulls off the gas and slows our speed, conceding that we aren't being followed anywhere Nic could find us. The interior of Alexei's car is exactly as I expected. Luxury, leather and everything in midnight black. Just like his hair and the ink in his colorless tattoos.

"Want to tell me what that was about?" Alexei asks.

"Not really," I quietly say, turning my head away from the back window to look at him.

"Isla has some clothes stashed under the seats. They should fit you," Alexei says, watching me in his rear-view mirror.

I wipe the tears from my eyes and reach under the seat where I find a gym bag.

Isla doesn't skimp on the goods. Inside there's a black crop top, leggings, black sneakers and a refreshment bag.

"Don't look," I say as I untie the sheet.

Alexei scoffs but his jaw hardens. "As if that's something that I'd want to see."

He shoves the rear-view mirror askew with a ridiculous level of aggression and keeps his eyes forward even as his hands clench on the wheel.

As I thumb through Isla's things, my heart cramps.

I can't believe Nic is FBI. I can't believe I trusted him. The feds have been after my father for years. And Nic was right under his nose. Was it Nic that I led right to him that night? He was supposed to be my father's protector? And yet, he wasn't there on the one night my father needed him the most.

It all makes so much sense now.

I sigh, changing into the clothes Isla has and then opening the refresher bag. There's a little mirror inside. Using the tissues, I clean up my face, putting gloss on my lips and mascara on my eyes. I brush my long dark hair back into a ponytail and secure it with the ties she has.

When I finish with her gym bag, I go to place it back under the seat, only to see a shining glint of metal. At the very bottom of the bag is a small knife. Makes sense she'd have a weapon. I look up, satisfied that Alexei isn't watching me, and pocket the knife. Just in case.

"I'm done," I say, feeling much better now that I'm refreshed.

Alexei adjusts the mirror again and looks at me but doesn't say anything. Though the storm in his gray eyes always seems to say it all.

I fold my arms and stare out the window. There are many things I could do now with the information about Nic's betrayal. Though like a song on repeat, my mind keeps tripping over the fact that he may have started a war with Victor to get me out of the marriage. Jeopardizing everyone I care about.

"Where are we going?" Alexei asks.

"To your brother."

"You were serious about that?" Alexei says, raising his brow. "Your family put on a hell of a show to get you out of that you know?"

I eye him in shock, scoffing as I contemplate that I'm clearly, once again, the last to know about matters that concern my own future. I don't bother replying, and he ignores me too, as I climb through the middle to plop into the passenger seat.

"Phone," I say, holding out my hand.

Alexei narrows his eyes on me, barely concentrating on the road. "What do you want my phone for?"

"Need to make a call."

He shakes his head but reaches into his pocket and hands it over. "Course you do."

I dial up the number by heart and press the phone to my ear. Anton's number rings out, and I curse him for not bothering to answer right now when I need him most.

I try again, frustration building as I get nothing but voicemail.

"Problem?" Alexei asks.

I shake my head, sighing as I type in a different number. I direct Alexei to stop at the local pharmacy for insulin supplies. I'll be needing all my strength when I proposition Victor after what my family has done.

I bring the phone to my ear and this number only takes one ring.

"Angie, it's Sage."

"Miss DeMarco, what a surprise."

"Yes, hi, hello, I need..." I say, hesitating when I remember whose company I'm in. "I need you to guard... the *asset* until I can get to... *it*. People might be coming for it."

"Hmph," she says, tone sounding very high and mighty. "Mistake in who you trusted?"

"Don't rub it in," I reply, side-eyeing Alexei who is trying very hard to pretend he's not interested in this conversation.

"We can guard the asset, but it's gonna cost you."

"Like I give a flying fuck what it costs."

She chuckles. "Okay, firework, calm down. We'll take care of it."

"Thank you," I say and hang up the phone.

"Wanna tell me what's going on?" Alexei asks as he pulls over in front of the pharmacy.

"Nope."

I leave him idling while I go inside and retrieve the few things I'll need. Insulin supplies and other important items I imagine will come in handy.

It'll be a pain to manually check my levels and administer insulin but I suppose I lost my brain when I was bolting away from my house in a sheet.

Alexei is patiently waiting in the car once I get back and I slide into the passenger seat beside him.

"To your brother," I say as I secure my seatbelt.

"You sure?" he says, letting genuine worry and indecision show in his features for once.

"I'm sure."

"Okay," he says and he starts the car. "My brother has gone home to our side of the city. It's a fair drive."

"He left. I know." I wipe at my face and lean back in the seat, resting my feet on the dash as I get comfortable. Then I remember that Nic said all the Rushkoffs had left. Yet Alexei was still there even though his brother was gone. I give him a look. "But *you* didn't leave."

He gulps, averting his eyes from mine to check his blind spot even as there is no need to. "There were some things I found I couldn't bear to leave behind."

I watch him for a moment, but when he gives me nothing further I decide to drop it. More important things and all.

I attach the insulin monitor and deliver the dose via needle to my stomach. Definitely a pain to do this manually. I wince as the needle disappears deep into my stomach, highlighting the scars that run across my abdomen.

The whole time, Alexei's eyes dart to the movement, nervousness crinkling his features.

"Got something to say?"

"No," he shakes his head. But he looks over at me again like he wants to say something. It's as if he's talking to himself in his head. With the way his eyes dart around, his head shaking and his teeth nibbling his lip. In the end he says nothing.

I let it go and we complete the rest of the drive in relative silence. Alexei looks over at me every now and again, but still doesn't ball up to whatever he wants to say.

When we make it into Rushkoff territory, I can't help but stare out the window. Even pressing up against the glass in curiosity. I've never been this far across the city before. Their lake side is just as beautiful as our country side, if not more. Sprawling woods envelop both sides of the road and the air smells crisp.

Eventually, some two hours later, we pull up to the infamous Rushkoff compound and Alexei smirks at me as I fail to hide the wonder in my eyes.

The compound presents similar to my own house with a big iron gate, but the front lawns are manicured with native vegetation and the driveway is paved all the way up to the wooden mansion. The lake shines off to the west of the house, water glistening in its depth. It's rustic and majestic and wonderful.

I can't imagine why they would want to stay at our estate when their place is as beautiful as this.

Alexei enters a code at the gate and then begins to drive. I watch in fascination as the house and the lake come closer into view. I don't even notice that Alexei has exited the car until my door opens and he's standing in front of me with his rough tattooed hand held out.

A curl of indecision unfurls inside me, but I ignore it as I take Alexei's hand. He stares into my eyes and we stand frozen in the driveway with my hand in his. He licks his lips, his eyes warring with indecision.

"What?" I breathe.

He sighs, the look melting off his face. "Nothing," he says. But he doesn't let me go.

"You do have something to say."

"No. *Fuck.*" He curses as he corrects himself. "Yes." He lets go of my hand and gestures down to my stomach as he folds his arms. "How did that happen? Were you born diabetic?"

"You... you want to know if I was born diabetic?" I raise my brow and gesture to the front door of his house. "Right now?"

He clenches his jaw and nods.

I'm ridiculously confused, but I answer anyway. "No, I wasn't born diabetic."

Alexei's eyes shutter but he keeps staring at me, and I can see why he's so good at interrogating because before I know what's come over me I'm speaking to fill the silence.

"Uhh, when I was nine, one of my father's right-hand men attacked me. He mutilated my stomach. Sending strips of my skin back to my father and Anton to antagonize them. I'm surprised you haven't heard about it."

Alexei's eyes stay locked on mine, worry and indecision pouring out of them and again, I'm talking. To fill the silence or earn his approval, who knows.

"The mutilation took 4 inches off my colon and destroyed my pancreas. That's, um, that's why I'm diabetic."

Alexei's face drops, his breath leaving him all at once. He takes a faltered step back from me, hand running over his face. When he looks back at me, his eyes grow angry. He grunts in frustration, rushing forward and landing a punch against the car door as he shouts.

"Get back in the car. Don't go in there," he says, grabbing my elbow.

"What?" I rear back in alarm. "Why?!"

He points towards the car door, getting in my face and yelling. "Get back in the fucking-"

"Ah!" We both turn towards the steps to see Victor coming down to greet us. "Sage. Changed your mind so soon?"

Thirty-Two

SAGE

Victor stares expectantly down at me and Alexei as several of his other men surround him. Apprehension swirls inside of me as Alexei's hand slips from the vice grip it had on my elbow.

That was really strange, but I shrug it off and I take the steps up to greet Victor. My feet clicking against the stone amplifies in the silence. When I reach Victor, he steps aside and sweeps his arm wide to gesture for me to enter his home.

The inside is even more beautiful than the outside. The theme of a wooden lodge continues, with all the ostentatiousness of luxury furnishings and modern black trimmings.

Victor says nothing more as he moves throughout his home, and I follow eagerly behind him. We end up somewhere around the back of the house, in a sunken living room with large windows that overlook the glowing lake. Drawn to the sight, I rush forward, pressing a hand against the glass as I admire the beauty of the water.

What a beautiful place to get to exist.

"To what do I owe the pleasure?" Victor says. I turn to find him settling into a chair and buttoning his suit jacket. More of Victor's men fill the space too, spreading about at various points of the room. Alexei takes up a quiet corner in the back, his brow furrowed.

"I had to let you know it wasn't my decision to call off the marriage agreement," I say, frowning as I take in the space again. The way his men place around the room, in front of every exit, is making my skin tingle.

"They went behind your back," he says. "I know. They weren't shy about telling me." Victor smiles, but the warmth that was once there is gone.

"Well I -" I stutter, suddenly feeling under confident with my decision to come here. Alexei didn't want me to come inside. Why? "I came here to talk," I say.

The side of Victor's lip twitches, and he gestures for me to take the seat across from him. I perch just on the edge of the armchair opposite his, all too aware of the company.

"So talk," Victor says. "But I will say I'm surprised. I thought the situation was clear."

"The situation?"

"Your interests seem to have strayed elsewhere."

He gives me a hard look and despite myself I look to the back of the room where Alexei has dropped his head. It's to my horror that I realize he must have been talking about Nicholas and not his fucking brother.

"I didn't ask for them to call it off," I say. "I was hoping you'd take me at my word. And, you know, not start a mafia war."

Victor bites his lip, leaning forward until our faces are only inches away. A thick finger trails down my cheek and he whispers, "You want me to help you. Defy your family? Marry me?"

The twisted whisper of his voice makes ice curl in my veins and my heart stop to a standstill. Victor pulls away with a smirk and I finally get a good look in his eyes. A good, close up, look.

For the very first time, I see the storm in his eyes that I see in his brother's. Victor's though, is evil.

Alexei steps forward carefully from the shadows. Victor doesn't even acknowledge his brother when he places a hand on his shoulder. "Brother," Alexei says. "Let me get rid of her for you."

My eyes snap away from the sinister depths of Victor's and into Alexei's. He looks... worried.

Fuck.

The world comes crashing in around me and realizing my mistake feels like being hit by a bus.

"Unnecessary," Victor says, shrugging his brother's hand away even as his gaze remains glued to me. "I think Miss DeMarco is right where she needs to be."

Oh, God. All the air evaporates from the room and I'm seconds away from hyperventilating. I don't do well in crowds. Or life and death situations, apparently. Now I'm here, in the home of my enemy, with no backup. Didn't I call Victor a fucking idiot for doing something similar not long ago?

Should've listened to my own advice.

I gulp, forcing my breath to steady as I focus on the now. As I focus on becoming the person that I set out to be so long ago. Someone who wasn't scared or weak. Someone strong, with the wit and power to out manipulate a man at his own game.

"Tell me something," I say, hearing the breathlessness in my voice that I hope doesn't translate to them.

Victor grins, and I feel it all the way down to my bones.

"Did you ever thank me?" I ask. Victor's smile drops minutely and I continue on. "After all, you wouldn't have been able to get through the gates and onto the property to kill my father, unless I'd opened them for you."

Alexei's mouth drops open and he glares at his brother. Victor raises a single brow and then lets out a menacing laugh. This one all too like the charm he exuded when he was trying to woo me.

I came here to negotiate for my family's lives. To marry Victor so that there would be no war. Now I see the truth. Victor never needed to marry me. He just needed me here, right where I am now.

Question is, why?

"Well," Victor laughs, clapping his hands together. "Here I thought I was so discreet. Tell me, how did you know it was me?"

I smirk. "I didn't. Until right now."

Victor's laugh ceases abruptly and his teeth clench as his gaze bores into mine, regarding me warily.

"It was you, all this time, that's been after me," I say, shaking my head. Victor looks very proud of himself indeed. That's okay. He won't soon.

"Dimitri was simply in the way, darling Sage," Victor smiles. "It's always been you."

Alexei sinks back into the shadows in horror, and I swear I see him sizing up his own men. I can't make out his features but his chest is heaving. Something tells me this is news to him too.

"I guess they've done me a favor after all, by trying to get rid of me." Victor stands and begins obnoxiously pacing. "Months of trying to get close to you. Months of trying to snatch you up. And now... how interesting that you would walk right up to my door."

Victor smirks, pouring himself a drink before he comes to stand behind me. He leans over me, stroking a hair off my face in what now feels like a vile touch. "All of these perfectly laid plans of Dimitri's, to keep you safe. And then this document shows up and leads me right to you, and thus you right to me."

Exactly.

"That does seem like a coincidence, doesn't it?" I say, shaking his hand away and doing my best to keep my voice even. "Strange that all those pieces would fall into place to allow me to get close to you."

His hand stills in my hair.

I stand and turn to face him. "That all these turns of events would put me face to face with the person I most want revenge on."

Victor narrows his eyes, pausing mid sip. He watches me with questions and calculations in his eyes. Like he can't quite put his finger on what is off about this situation. I straighten my shoulders and steel my nerve.

But I don't take my eye off Victor.

All the time I spent looking into Alexei, only to realize that someone so reckless would never have the forethought to plan this. While Victor was too perfect, with an answer for everything at every turn.

Nicholas *Baker* might have given me the final turn in this direction. But all along, I've been the one driving the car.

"You should really see about stopping this nasty habit you have of walking right into my traps, Victor," I say. "Dad didn't send the marriage contract. I did."

"Wha-"

I pull the knife that I got from Isla's bag and launch across the armchair straight for Victor, sending us both tumbling to the floor.

The first stab goes through his shoulder while my weight pins him to the floor. The second slash down of my knife goes through his ear as he dodges to resist the stab to his face.

The room erupts into chaos, men shouting, weapons drawing, as I'm swarmed from all angles.

I rear my arm back to stab again, ready for a kill shot, but I'm halted mid-air when my wrist is grabbed. Alexei hauls me off his brother and pulls me into his arms, holding me steady while I struggle to wrench myself free and go after Victor again.

"Fucking hell!" Victor screams as he gets off the floor clutching his shoulder. "You stabbed me."

He waves off his men and puts pressure on his own wound.

"I wrote the fucking marriage contract. How do you like that, Vic?!" I scream and flail in Alexei's arms, trying to get back to Victor. "I fucking *knew* it was going to be you."

Alexei's arms grip me roughly, pulling me back as I scream and lurch for his brother. The men surround us, gearing for Alexei, but he just grips me tighter.

"Hand her over brother," Victor says. "We need her alive."

Alexei pulls me back closer to him again. "Why?"

"I'll tell you everything after!" Victor says in exasperation, eyes going wide. "Stop thinking with your fucking cock and hand the girl over!"

"Come and fucking take me Victor! Let me get close enough to slash your thick throat!"

I hear Alexei lick his lips though I don't see it because I'm honed in on Victor like a nuclear weapon and I'm ready to destroy the second that Alexei's grip slips.

"You were the one after her this whole time?" Alexei asks. "Trying to break into their estate to take her? Why?"

Victor snarls and throws his hands in the air, letting the blood from his stab wound seep out onto his probably stupidly expensive suit. "We don't have time for this, Alexei! Hand her over. That's an order."

I feel him hesitate, his hands gripping me tighter instead of letting go. Alexei leans his head into my neck and whispers just for the two of us to hear. "If I let you go, if I hold them off, will you run?"

"Do you want me to lie to you?" I whisper back.

"Please don't do this," he says into my neck.

"I wish I had a choice," I growl.

"God dammit," he says, the puff of his breath teasing my neck. He sniffs once, straightens and then releases my wrists to push me into the arms of Victor's men. Alexei stays silent, eyes on the floor, the whole time that I struggle back and forth as the men secure my wrists and wrench me from the room.

"This isn't over Victor!"

I'm shoved through the house and down into the basement where I'm thrown into a dank cell and a metal door is locked behind me.

Fuck.

That could've gone better.

Thirty-Three

ALEXEI

"What the fuck was that about, brother?" Victor snarls at me as he flops onto the couch.

"Let's get you some aid for that stab wound," I say, ignoring his question and going to the bookcases to find the medical supplies that we keep there.

"Don't avoid the question, what the fuck?"

I take the supplies out and sit in front of him to put pressure on his wound with the gauze. "She sure stabbed you good."

"You were going to let her go," he shoves at me. I might have gone a little rogue and have a lot to answer for. But so does Victor.

"Don't *fucking* test me!" I yell. "Don't act like I'm the one that's keeping something from you. What the actual fuck was that? You've been after her all this time? *You?*"

Victor sits back and scrubs a hand over his face. "I couldn't tell you my plans."

"You couldn't trust me."

"Must you make me say it," he says.

I shove the medical supplies on the floor and in my rage sweep all the bottles of alcohol off the bar, leaving a mess of raining glass. "I will ask you this only one time. And you will not lie to me!"

I take a heaving breath and my brother finally looks at me like he's starting to take me seriously. I cannot believe he kept this from me. I'm meant to be his right-hand man. Not only did he fucking *kill* Dimitri DeMarco, but he led a plot against our enemy's daughter, bringing us right to their doorstep in pursuit of a plot he never told me about.

I think back on Sage's wounds, trying to tamp down on my rage as I face my brother and ask a question that could destroy us. "Is this about Chet?"

Victor sighs and holds his head in his hands. The heart that I thought had long frozen over drops through the floor. "What have you done?" I scream at him. "What have you fucking done?"

"Calm the fuck down and sit!"

"We agreed we would let that vendetta go after Dad died. We don't fucking need Chet!"

He levels me with a glare and I sit as his stare commands me, even as our world turns on its axis.

"The DeMarcos are everything that is wrong with the world, brother. You've said it yourself many times. What Dimitri took from Chet... he wants retribution. Retribution that we can deliver to our best benefit. That's what family does."

"Chet stopped being our fucking family the day he hurt a nine-year-old girl!"

"Dimitri drove him to that point! Do you not see that?!" Victor shouts. He curses and then drops his head. "It was a mistake to bring you there. First you couldn't shut up about Sage being the enemy, and now she goes and proves it by fucking stabbing me and you still can't see further than your cock."

He may not be wrong, but I'm beyond caring at this point.

"She's a threat, brother. She's the same threat that you thought she was all along," Victor says. "She's the danger here. See? She said it herself. She set up the marriage contract. She put this entire plan in motion just so she could bring us to her."

He's grasping at straws. Sure, Sage has proved herself to be a bigger threat that even I anticipated when I first saw her stomp her dainty little foot, but *Chet?* There are some lines I don't think I can cross.

"She's been the real threat all along. That's why we need to be rid of them. Don't you see? It's us or them," Victor says, his eyes wilder than I've ever seen them. Is this the hidden side to my brother that Isla has been warning me about all these years?

I shake my head. "I won't stomach working with Chet, Vic."

"It's a necessary evil brother. To rid the world of unnecessary evil."

"Please don't pretend to care about that shit with me."

Victor rolls his eyes. "Chet's powerful, Alexei. He's built his own army. He's got men that we never could. Once we give him Sage, we join our forces with his, and raze the DeMarco empire to the ground to have this city for our own."

The only thought that runs through my head right now is that I should've known. I've known my brother my whole life, and I should've known he was never really intent on marrying that girl.

"Look at them, brother. They're the *enemy.* We have to stop them."

To prove his point, he pushes his hand against his shoulder so the blood flows out of it from where Sage stabbed him. I feel the aching from his wound like it's my own. I love my brother more than anything on the planet. In a childhood constant with abuse and danger, my brother has always shielded me from it. He's been the one to get me this far in life. My only reason for living.

I cannot and will not live without him.

"I've always got your back, Vic," I sigh. "But this? Seriously? You want me to agree to hand her over to Chet as leverage so we can what? Kill them all? Anton? Freddie?"

Vic bares his teeth. "Do not tell me you have gone soft for them. She's shown her true colors. Look at what she's done to me. She wants to kill me. And if you let her, then she will do just that."

I hang my head.

"She will *kill* me, brother. That's been her plan all along. You want to watch me die?"

I shake my head.

And then punch my fist right though the wall. Trapped and caught between two impossible places that I never wanted any part in. Sage, who I hate with every fiery passion in my bones, and want more than I could ever describe. Then my brother, my only family. The only person in the world I'd gladly die for.

I look back at my brother. Victor smiles.

"Chet wants her alive. I'm going to call him to come and take that bitch off our hands."

Thirty-Four

SAGE

I bang my fist on the metal door. It only takes me one hit to work out that banging my hand on solid metal fucking *hurts* and I'm definitely not going to do it again.

I scowl at the door as I rub my fist and walk away feeling like an idiot.

"Sage-"

I gasp as I whirl around in shock, clutching my hand to my chest. Sitting against the opposite wall with his hands zip-tied in front of him is none other than Uncle Anton. He rests casually against the wall, even as his lip furiously bleeds, one of his eyes is swollen over, and his nose is raw and purple.

"Oh my God," I say, rushing to his side. "Uncle Anton?" I crouch down next to him and he reaches out and takes my hand.

"Sage, what are you doing here?" His voices croaks painfully and I notice the bruising around his throat too.

"Me?! What are *you* doing locked down here?"

"Victor was going to use me as leverage to get you," he says. "It seems that has worked."

I duck my head in guilt but I figure now isn't the time to tell him that I ran away from my bodyguard right into the arms of the enemy without thinking.

"I just saw you last night..." I say trying to piece it all together in my head.

"Victor ambushed me right after dinner," Anton explains. "Zip-tied me." He lifts his hand to show me exactly that.

I show him my identically zip-tied hands as well and give him a half-smile. It makes him chuckle.

"Does this hurt?" I ask, fingers reaching out to poke at his wounds before I think better of it.

"Surface wounds," Anton says.

I slide down the wall to sit cross-legged next to him. "It was certainly nice of them to room us together."

Anton chuckles, which turns into a full laugh. We sit in silence for a few moments when he cups both my hands in his, the limited movement all that can be allowed with both of our wrists fastened.

"You obviously figured out that Victor is behind all this?" Anton asks.

"Yeah, he kind of admitted it," I say. "I did get to stab him twice though."

He gapes at me in bewilderment. "You stabbed Victor?"

I nod proudly.

"That's my girl," Anton smiles, before raising a brow. "Fatal?"

I sigh. "Not likely."

"Shame."

"There's something else," I say. He furrows his brow as he watches me. Watches as my heart tears apart with the words I'm about to say. "Nic - he's... he's been lying to us. He's FBI."

I wait for the outburst. For the eruption. I watch a flurry of emotions cross my uncle's face. But the overarching one I see is not surprise. It's guilt.

Oh, fucking hell.

Anton drops his head. "Sage..." Regret fills his look, as well.

"Fuck, what have you done?" I ask.

"None of that matters, *anima mia*."

"Did you not hear me? He's FBI, Anton. Victor may be something but that's the real enemy. Feds? Absolutely not."

Anton gives me another pitying look. "Nic confessed everything to me a long time ago. Right after your engagement party."

My eyes widen.

"I'm not happy with him about it, obviously," Anton sighs. "But he laid down his head on the platter. All for the chance of having you. Of stopping Victor from taking you from us. I knew then that he was one of us. Regardless of where he started."

I shake my head and hold my eyes closed, as tears start to form and my throat burns with the effort to keep them in. What have I done? He told me to let him explain.

Jesus. I should've.

"He *was* FBI. But, he hasn't been with them for a while." Anton gives me a knowing look.

"Fuck! Why wouldn't you tell me that?"

"You have plenty of secrets we've kept from him."

"I told him about Dad," I say, throwing my bounds hand up. "And then I found his badge, freaked the fuck out and ran straight into Victor's arms. Because some asshole called off the fucking marriage contract and started a war without telling me."

"Oh, Sage," he says, using his bound fingers to stroke a lock of hair away from my face.

He purses his lips, sighing as he slumps back against the wall.

"What do we do now?" I ask. "Just sit here and wait for them to kill us?"

Anton scoffs. "They want you alive, at least."

"Why?"

"I wish I knew." Anton shrugs, before frowning. "Did you say you ran from Nicholas before coming here?"

I nod.

Anton smiles as he pats my knee. "Then sit tight and wait. There's nowhere on earth that he wouldn't chase you."

I smile too then. Because I know firsthand that is undoubtedly true.

***

Sometime later - what feels like hours, but I'm sure isn't very long - a heavy banging pounds from somewhere above us. Just on the verge of sleep on Anton's shoulder, I jerk awake, gasping at the jarring roughness of the sound.

"What was that?" I ask.

Anton stands, frowning up at the ceiling as he helps me off the floor too, pushing me behind him. "It's either Nic coming to our rescue..."

"Or?" I ask.

"Or..." he says. "It's Victor coming to kill us."

"Great, perfect. Love those odds."

The banging and screeching in the house gets louder. Closer. Preceded by footsteps pounding on the floor above us. Multiple sets of footsteps. But one pair stands out above the rest as it draws nearer, the sound beating down the stairs until they're right outside the metal door of our cell.

"Brace yourself," Anton warns.

The door bangs several times from the other side and a little kernel of hope sprinkles inside me. Hope that is crushed when the door clicks opens and the lock turns. A key.

As the door is pushed open, Anton straightens like he's readying himself for a fight.

The door bangs against the cold wall of the cell and Alexei stands on the other side, unmoving and unwilling to come any closer.

He blinks, only sparing a single look of surprise for Anton before he scoffs and narrows his eyes at me. "Come on, Sage," Alexei says. "Gotta take you to Vic."

"Fine by me," I growl, ready to take another shot at that motherfucker.

Anton reaches out and blocks my body. "What? Why?"

Alexei looks back and forth between us, surprising me when he actually decides to answer my uncle. "Victor's handing her over to Chet in exchange for his army," Alexei says.

I swear my very blood freezes.

Chet.

That's not a name I've heard spoken aloud in a very long time. I shrink into myself. Oh, fuck. What was I thinking? Victor is one thing. A big, scary thing. But Chet is something worse. All of my fears, the reason I've been sheltered the way I have, the reason I've stayed inside my house, never leaving and never having friends. They're all packaged up into the trauma that Chet gave me when I was only nine years old.

"I will fight you with my bare hands tied, *Rushkoff*," Anton says, going eerily quiet and scary calm. "Chet will *never* get his hands on my Sage again. I swear it."

Alexei's eyes shutter, like he was expecting just that answer. His eyes flick to me. Instinctively I know what he's saying. He wants me to come with him, or he'll have to take me and risk hurting my uncle.

"Stay here, Uncle Anton," I whisper.

"I am not-"

Anton charges forward but Alexei pulls out his gun and aims it at him.

"Come on, Sage," Alexei says and I slowly tiptoe around my uncle to get to him. When I reach him, Alexei takes me by the arm and backs out of the room slowly. The whole time watching Anton like he's about to charge at us.

When we exit the room, Alexei straightens, running a hand over his tired eyes as he takes a second to breathe. He pulls the door closed behind us. But I don't see him secure the lock. I don't hear it click.

I raise my brows at him, looking back the door. He gives me a withering look in return, daring me to challenge him, but I'm not going to say a fucking thing. I quickly look away.

Alexei places me in front of him and grips my shoulder to lead me through the house. We start up the stairs until we're back on the main level. Even as I'm being led to my slaughter in this place, I can appreciate its beauty. Open floor plans with high wooden ceiling beams. Fireplaces galore. It's a heavenly retreat.

As a place to die? It'll do.

"So, this was about Chet this whole time?" I ask, gulping.

"It seems so," Alexei says.

"You didn't know?" I ask.

"No," Alexei confirms.

We move through more beautiful rooms, open-plan kitchen, living room, dining room before continuing up a flight of stairs to the second floor of the house. Alexei leads me through a maze of hallways until we stop in front of a closed wooden door.

Alexei moves from behind me to stand in front of me, torn eyes boring into mine as he grips my shoulders.

I open my mouth to speak but he stops me. A single tattooed finger against his lips signals me to be quiet. Then he shakes his head, like he's disappointed in himself.

He unclips a weapons belt from his waist and lifts the front of my shirt, revealing the litany of mutilated scars on my belly.

"Jesus Christ," he whispers, a horrified expression pinching his features as his finger traces the lines of raised flesh over my body. The whole time, I watch him, feeling oddly comforted at the touches he gives as he surveys my darkest damage. He takes the clip and secures the belt around my waist.

I go to open my mouth but he pins me with another hard look, telling me again to shut up. He slides a knife into the belt, his eyes warring with indecision as he unclips his spare gun, checks the bullets and then slides that into the belt too.

He pulls my shirt back down and slides around the top and the leggings until he seems sure that he's concealed what he's done.

I go to speak, but *quietly*. "What are you doing?"

His lightning storm eyes glare into me, a crease forming between his brows before he drops his gaze to his feet. I wonder if he's not at all sure what he's doing. He probably can't even tell me. Instead he says something very strange indeed.

"I'll do anything for my brother." Stormy eyes snap to mine. "Except, apparently, give him *you*."

My heart stills.

With a sudden rush that burns my wrists, he tightens the zip ties to the point of pain. I wince but still keep to only a breath when I say, "Psychotic Rushkoff."

Alexei's lips tip up at the corners before he grabs my arm and turns me so I'm pressed against his chest. The pose is not unlike he's been manhandling me the whole way here, but it's also not unlike he just wants to feel me against him. "Don't let him take you," he whispers finally. "Vicious little princess."

He takes a deep breath, opens the door and then shoves me forward into the room.

"Here she is."

Thirty-Five

SAGE

I fall to my hands and knees. When I look up, Victor smirks at me from where he stands near the window. The playful facade he built while we were in my mansion is gone. He looks every bit like I expected him to when we first met. Powerful. Terrifying. Out to hurt me.

Not the playful, charming person he pretended to be. In hindsight, it's obvious, and I'm an idiot for not seeing through it.

I look around the room. We're in a lounge. Plush green sofas and armchairs line the space. There's a fireplace on the wall with a stupidly big TV hanging over it. I know why we're in this room, though. The view is over the front of the property. You can see the lake and all the way up to the front gate. If we're waiting for someone, this room has the best vantage points to make sure Victor can see them coming.

There's a variety of Victor's men about the space too. Which I only notice for the first time when one of them grabs me and pushes me into a chair. Alexei, like usual, slinks to hide in the shadows.

He's given me everything he can at this point. That's the best I'm going to get from him. I'm on my own now.

"What am I doing up here?" I ask.

Victor's jaw clenches, but he doesn't answer me.

One of his men comes up to give some sort of report. "They've ambushed the whole side gate. We've directed Chet through the front."

"What's going on?" I ask.

"Your fucking family," Victor seethes, "have somehow worked out exactly where you are and launched an attack. You didn't want me to start a fucking war?" He shakes his head. "Too late. They're already starting it."

I breathe out a sigh of relief. Nic is here, and probably Freddie. They just have to get to me before Chet does. I just have to use the tools I have to defend myself until they get here. I just have to not let myself be taken by Chet.

Victor's minion clears his throat. "The, uh, the blonde girl is with them."

Victor whips his head around. "Isla? Isla is fighting with them?"

"It appears so, sir."

Victor sends a scathing look Alexei's way. He obviously thinks that's his fault.

There's a rumbling sound from somewhere nearby. Victor scowls as he grabs a remote and turns on the compensating-for-something-TV, folding his arms as the security footage shows.

Live, I have to assume.

The camera sits on the side of the house above a wooden deck with a view over the lawn. DeMarco men are launching a siege on the compound, taking out every Rushkoff that comes in their sights.

I let out a soft whimper of relief which Victor shoots me a scathing look for.

Leading the charge is Freddie, Isla and my Nicholas.

They fight like they were born to fight. Nicholas doesn't hesitate with every bullet. Every person he takes down. Every man he kills. He's not thinking about morality or the consequences on his conscience. He's coming for me.

They breach the house. Isla doing the bulk of the heavy lifting as she takes an axe and shatters the floor-to-ceiling window, signaling the others and they begin to pour inside.

"They're coming for me." I smile to Victor. "Or you."

Victor's jaw grinds as he checks his watch.

We both know what this means.

If they get to me before he can get me to Chet, he's done for.

Victor signals at his men. "Go! Stop them from getting to us."

The countdown begins.

Thirty-Six

NICHOLAS

I wipe the sweat from my brow.

I have to hand it to Victor. It's been a pain in the ass to breach his property. Victor's defenses are just as good as ours, if not better. If it weren't for Isla taking the lead, we would never have gotten as far as we have.

Even so, we're already many bullets down and we've only managed to get onto the deck outside the house. It does have a fantastic view of the lake, admittedly, but what I really need is to get inside the fucking house. Since it's made almost entirely of wood and glass, that should be easy. But like I said, Victor's defenses are top notch.

I duck as I'm charged by another person. I roll the guy over my back, pushing him off the deck and down into the depths of the lake.

Freddie, at this point, is in his element, bathed in blood and killing for sport as he chuckles like a maniac.

I hear glass shatter as Isla, *finally*, smashes the floor-to-ceiling window to the house and signals us to follow her. Freddie and I rush inside the house behind her. We push into the kitchen through the sharp opening, ducking behind the, surprise, all-wooden counter as we regroup.

"God damn, they're definitely prepared," Freddie says. "I really don't want to go to war with these assholes."

"This isn't good," I say. "She better be here."

But I know she is. I know Sage is here. It was pretty fucking obvious when Anton went missing. Then to see Sage flee the property with that psycho Rushkoff. Yeah. She's here.

Isla rolls her eyes at me. I'm being pretty harsh to her, considering. But I'm in a world of pain right now. Sage found out I'm FBI and then she ran from me, right into *Alexei's* arms. And now to Victor's. I should've just told her. I was going to. But... it never seemed like the right time. I had to clear the air with Anton first, before I could feel safe clearing the air with her. He was the one that I needed forgiveness from most.

After all, I wasn't assigned this job so that I could make best buddies with him and Dimitri.

When I started this assignment, I didn't expect to find the one place I truly belong.

"She'll be here," Isla says. "Look at the assault they're launching at you. I knew Victor was up to something."

Freddie starts reloading weapons while Isla covers us with a slight of practiced, perfect fire.

"You think that fucking hurts?!" A voice comes from afar, and I frown as I realize it's familiar. "You think that even stings, asshole?"

Freddie frowns over at me as well like the voice is familiar to him too. "Anton?"

We pop our heads above the counter and see Anton, his zip-tied hands cradled around the neck of a man who he is strangling to death. The man keeps trying to punch backwards but Anton doesn't flinch, acting like he barely feels it.

"Anton!" Freddie shouts.

Anton startles as he sees us, releasing a sigh of relief before he expertly snaps the man's neck and rushes over to us to crouch behind the counter too.

"Fucking hell, am I glad to see you," he says. Fuck, he looks like death. His eye is nearly half swollen over and his nose is bright purple. He looks over at Isla and tilts his head. "All of you."

"What the *fuck* is going on, Anton?" I shout.

"Can you get these off me?" He holds out his zip-tied hands. Isla smirks as she pulls out a flick knife and scissors through his binds.

I shake my head. "You can pull those apart with enough force, you know. You just have to tighten them first."

"I don't mind saving you, Anton," Isla smirks. "I'm always here for the damsels in distress."

Anton gives her a look before turning to us. "It isn't good, Nic. Victor has Sage as a fucking hostage."

"Fuck," I say, at the same time that Freddie says. "We figured."

"What's the deal here? He wants to marry her that badly?"

"No," Anton bares his teeth. "He's been after her all this time. He's made some deal with Chet. Hand her over and Chet gives away his army to help take us down."

My skin pales.

Chet. I knew it. All along I've felt this has something to do with that asshole and his sick obsession with getting revenge on Dimitri through his daughter.

"Chet's on his way here," Anton says. "We have to get to her before he does."

"How did you get free?" Isla asks.

Anton narrows his eyes and I know from the look on his face that he doesn't want to answer her. "I don't even know," he says. "Alexei came to take Sage to Victor and he just left the fucking door open."

Anton leaves the conversation there, and doesn't notice when Isla smiles wistfully to herself. Proudly, I'd have to guess.

"How are we going to get to her?" Freddie asks. "Where would he take her?"

I survey the lay of the land. There's a heap of Rushkoff men coming from the stairs. So much more than we ever could have anticipated. There's hundreds of them. I had no idea Victor's army had amassed to this size. If he has Chet's too... Well, this is definitely not a war we can win.

"*If* we can get to her," I growl.

"You're outnumbered by a lot," Isla admits.

"We might not get to her before Chet gets here," Freddie whispers. "We should prepare for that."

"Like hell," I growl. I won't let her be left alone to be taken by him. I won't do it. Not again. Not when I've seen up close and personal the physical and mental damage he left on the woman I love.

"Victor is trying to clear a path," Isla says, eyes brushing calculatingly over the fight. "The odds that we'd make it through all this shit before Victor gets her where he wants is slim."

"All this God damn way and we lose her anyway?" I shout.

"Nic-" Freddie tries to calm me with a hand to my shoulder, but I brush him off.

"We'll do everything we can," Isla assures me. "If she fights a little, she may buy us enough time."

Absolutely not. I won't allow her to go through this alone. Not like she's had to go through everything else alone. There is no scenario in this world where I am letting Sage get taken by Chet again.

I say as much.

"Fuck this," I say. "She's not going through this alone."

"What?" Anton starts.

"I'll buy you your time. Come and save us," I say to Isla. Her eyes shutter as she nods, understanding where Freddie and Anton haven't caught up yet.

"What the fu-" Anton yells. But he doesn't have time to stop me before I'm running out into the open to be captured like bait.

Thirty-Seven

SAGE

Victor paces the floor like a wild animal, TV remote clutched tightly in his hand. He lost sight of Nic, Isla and Freddie as they got into the house. Every few seconds, he checks his phone and his watch, while I prepare myself mentally for what I'm going to do if they try to take me to Chet.

There's a thud outside the door that makes us all jump.

"What the fuck was that?" Victor says, pacing stopped.

The incessant banging continues with renewed purpose. With a growl, Victor changes the channel on the TV, to the one that's obviously just outside the door.

On the screen, Nicholas looks up into the camera, his hands in surrender as a Rushkoff goon pounds on the door with a closed fist and a gun to Nic's head.

My heart stills. Nic. He's here. He's here for me.

"Open the fucking door, Victor," Nicholas seethes.

"You think I give a fuck about some random guy?!" Victor shouts. "Give me a fucking break. Kill him for all I care!"

On the TV, Nic shakes his head, moving like lightning speed as he regains the upper hand and swipes his knife across the guys throat.

Victor shuffles on his feet, clearly unimpressed that Nic called his bluff.

Nic comes for the door next, flying into an insane rage and tearing chunks away from it with the knife. I turn over my shoulder and see the blade protrusions through the wood where Nicholas is forcefully breaking down the door.

"Fucking hell," Victor says. "Stop him!" The men in the room fumble, unsure how they're going to stop Nicholas from getting in here at the rate that he's breaking down the door.

"Jesus, Alexei, get in there and restrain him!" Victor yells.

Alexei doesn't do as he's told, slowly slipping from the shadows to face his brother. "Vic, let's think about this," Alexei says, hands clasped behind his back as he continues to ignore the rage Nic pours into their door.

"Are you fucking joking?" Victor says.

"Come on, Vic. Chet? Surely we can work out another way," Alexei says, moving forward with pleading eyes.

"I do not have unlimited pep talks to give you!" Victor yells, spit flying from his teeth. "Pick a fucking side! I will not ask again."

I realize now, in this one tiny moment, that no one is looking at me. For the first time in months, I'm not at the center of attention of one of these men. Nobody is even sparing me a glance.

It's an opportunity I can't afford to waste.

"Vic-" Alexei starts.

Victor rushes to Alexei and grabs him violently by the back of the neck, pulling him so they're eye to eye. "You want me to die brother? Is that what you want?" Victor hands Alexei a knife. "Because if you're backing them you may as well stab me yourself."

I tighten the zip ties with my teeth, watching carefully for the moment that someone's attention lands back on me. Using all my might I slam my bound hands over my body, down and against my hips, willing the ties to break.

"Go on. Make a choice." Victor opens his arms wide like he's inviting Alexei to stab him.

Alexei shivers, taking a stumbled step back from his brother.

Finally, the zip ties snap and I stand up slowly. Not a single eye lands on me as I free myself and take the gun at my waist, stalking carefully forward towards Victor.

I do it now. While the men are still trying to stop Nicholas from breaking in. While Alexei still can't look at his brother in the eye. While Victor is vulnerable.

I step forward and raise my hand, pressing my gun against Victor's head.

"Get on your fucking knees, Victor." The whisper of my words shoots through the room like a missile.

Everyone freezes.

The only sound left is Nicholas finally smashing through the door.

Victor bares his teeth at me, but he raises his hands slowly in surrender. Even though I asked so nicely, he doesn't kneel.

I won't forget that.

Nic stops, his eyes flitting across the scene. He reaches for his gun but Alexei is there a second sooner. He knocks Nic down with a kick to his calf, drawing his own gun even as he kicks Nic's away.

My heart sinks. For all his training, Alexei has the one up on him.

I whimper as I realize it's a good old-fashioned standoff.

I've got Victor in surrender. Alexei has Nicholas in surrender.

"Do it, Sage," Nicholas says, his eyes still trained on Alexei. "Kill Victor. Now."

"Everyone just take a breath," Alexei says, the calmest and most scared I've ever seen him, "and this think through."

Victor starts to lose it, shaking violently from where he stands with my gun trained at the back of his head. "That's enough! I've had it with you, Alexei. This ends now. For whatever fucking reason, you brother, seem to think this girl's pussy is worth more than my life."

Alexei doesn't dare to move long enough to shake his head and deny it.

"Kill him, Sage," Nicholas says again, eyes unwaveringly confident even with a gun pointed at him. Water burns my eyes. I will not shoot Victor if Alexei is going to be right there to hurt Nicholas.

"No," I say. "What about you?"

"I'll be okay," Nic says. "Do it."

"Don't fucking do it Sage!" Alexei yells in my direction, still watching Nic carefully.

"Shoot the Prince boy, Alexei," Victor says, hands still in surrender and eyes holding a similar eerie confidence to Nic's. "She doesn't have it in her to fire the weapon."

"Don't you dare touch him-"

"Do it brother!!"

"Sage, stop, it's okay-"

"Prove whose side you're on! Kill him brother!"

"Don't make me do this, Vic-"

"Sage, it's okay, stop crying-"

"Fucking do it brother! You insolent little cock-"

"Shoot Victor, Sage, you have to do it-"

"Don't fucking touch my brother!"

"You want me to fucking die?!"

"Shoot him, Sage!!"

Adrenaline floods my body, shouting ringing out in my ears, tears blurring my vision. Before I can think, before I can stop, before I can second guess myself, I cock the hammer back on the gun. The next movements are fast. But they *feel* slow.

My gun clicks, signaling that the bullet is ready in the chamber.

Alexei's eyes shift minutely to me, hearing the tiny sound.

He turns the gun my way. His eyes panicked, reacting on pure emotion. On instinct. On survival.

He's going to save his brother.

He's going to be faster than me at pulling the trigger.

Alexei fires his gun.

My eyes widen.

The bullet pierces the wind.

Next thing I know I'm on the ground. A heavy body panting over mine.

But.... But. My stomach gets warm. Really warm.

Adrenaline pushes breaths through my lungs. When I look down I see only blood, my hands twist in it, fingers running through it as I try to work out where it came from. Is it mine? Am I hurt? Why is there always so much blood on my hands? The ringing in my ears gets louder, dots sparkling in the corners of my vision.

It all comes blurring back into sharp focus simultaneously.

"Ouch," Nic says.

And then he collapses off me and lolls to the side.

Thirty-Eight

SAGE

Victor laughs.

The booming, bent over at the waist, kind of laugh.

Nicholas gapes, lying flat on his back with his hands resting unnaturally by his sides and his bloodshot eyes on the roof. Not even an ounce of energy spared to pressure his own wounds.

My horror-filled eyes cloud with tears. I sit on my butt, hands supporting me as I stare. I can't move. I can't breathe. I can't speak. I can't look away from the sight of Nicholas's eyes clouding over and the steady drip of blood that seeps out of him, soaking his shirt like a sponge.

Alexei just *shot* Nicholas.

"Nic," I whimper, finding myself. I rush forward, kneeling at his side to pat at his face. "You're going to be okay. It's okay, it's okay."

"Jesus, that was brutal." Victor still laughs, but I can't take my eyes off Nicholas. I'm convinced if I move for even a second then he's going to leave me. Nic's eyes drift slowly from the roof to look at me, interrupted when he's kicked away from me, clutching at his ribs.

Victor steps into the space he just kicked Nic from and takes my gun, throwing it away. Next, his hands are in my hair, lifting me by the ponytail to hold me upright as I cry out. Even as I lash out and scream and scramble to get back to Nic, he tugs harder.

I pull until it hurts. I just need to get to something. The gun. Anything. Anything that will save us from this. Anything to get Nic to move again. When he's curled over on his side I can't see his face. I can't see the reassuring rise and fall of his chest.

"Nice one, brother," Victor says, amusement coloring him.

I cut a glance to Alexei, who still hasn't moved. His mouth hangs open and his gun still points as he stares in open shock at the spot I just vacated. He hasn't even looked down. He drops his gun like it's on fire, and sinks back into the shadows, turning his back on me once and for all.

I have to do something. I grasp Victor's hand and bite down hard.

"Bitch!!"

He drops my hair to shake out his hand and I fall to the floor with a thud. I start to crawl to Nicholas on my hands and knees but Victor's boot is fast in my back, sending me flat to my face.

"Nic..." I whisper.

I reach out my hand like I'm going to be able to make it to him.

"Chet should be here any minute now," Victor says. "Brother, go let him in."

Alexei stands frozen, frowning and looking at me.

"Did you hear what I fucking said?" Victor shouts. "Go and let Chet in."

Alexei closes his eyes in pain, not sparing anyone a look as he takes Victor's remaining men and leaves.

All that's left is me, Nicholas's dying body, and Victor *Fucking* Rushkoff.

My body goes cold, flooding me with something that draws all the breath from my lungs. Adrenaline, fire-like rage bubbles slowly over me.

"Shouldn't be too long until you're back with Chet, little girl," Victor says. "Such an oversight you know, him not taking care of you properly the first time."

I push myself up from the ground, snarling at Victor the whole time I do.

I still have a fucking knife.

"Ridiculous really," Victor keeps monologuing. "You were so small, should've been easy to kill."

I rip the knife out of my belt and scream. "You're fucking dead!!"

Victor only has the chance to raise his eyebrows before I'm flying across the couch, screaming in rage, knife clutched in my hand. And even though I'm rushing ahead at full speed, I'm not even sure if I have the upper body strength to pierce his skin.

Our bodies collide once I'm over the couch, and I'm thrashing and screaming doing everything I can to get to bury my knife into this asshole.

"Fucking Christ," Victor says. He snaps out and grabs both my wrists in his big hands, pushing me away from him as I struggle. He sends me flying across the room where I hit the bookcase and bring several classics tumbling down with me.

"Nightmare woman," he says, shaking his head. I lay on the floor in pain but I'm absolutely not done. Groaning, I pull myself up on shaking legs. My discarded gun lies nearby. I snatch it up and raise it to shoot.

"Shit," Victor says, lunging at me and pushing my hand skyward as a shot goes off, leaving behind a smoking hole in the ceiling. Victor takes the gun, unloads and disassembles it this time.

I rush him again, still screaming and he backhands me away.

Rationally, I realize this is a bad plan. That I'm probably going to lose.

Yet nothing about how I feel right now is rational.

I grab his leg and bite his ankle. My teeth sink into the flesh and secure a lock-tight hold as he shakes his leg in an effort to dislodge me. When he kicks me away like a dog, I come away with a mouth full of blood that I feel dripping to my chin.

While I'm down, he kicks me in the ribs. I'm sure he doesn't need a weapon to kill me but sure enough, he goes to the fireplace and pulls a hidden gun from underneath the mantel.

"You are so fucking frustrating you know that," he says, he paces the floor while running one hand over his jaw and waving the gun with the other. He's not taking this fight one bit seriously. Why would he? No one ever has seen me as anything but in the way. A nuisance. Nothing but a pretty face to push to the sidelines. "I hadn't planned to kill yo-"

He doesn't get to finish the sentence because I jump onto his back. My legs wrap around his waist and I secure my arms around his head in a lock, pulling tight in a wild effort to strangle him to death.

He stumbles, losing his footing and sending us both crashing down.

I let go just long enough for him to take the brunt of the fall and then I'm on top again. I knee him in the crotch, satisfied by the way he howls. I scrape my nails down the side of his face in a vicious arc, feeling the skin peel beneath my fingernails. But I don't stop there.

Animalistic, feral urges consume me as I straddle him, grabbing his chin in one hand and forcing my index finger into his left eye as hard as I can with the other. Slimy texture melts against the pad of my finger, giving way to goo as I breach the surface. Like sticking my finger into a peach, the juicy blood drains from his eye.

It. Is. Fucking. Gross.

But it's so satisfying too, and the wild grunt I let out confirms it.

I'm running on pure rage. Fueled by every misdeed that has come my way. I'm fueled by the image of the tubes running out of my father's nose and mouth. I'm fueled by the blood that came away on my hands when I thought he died in front of me. I'm fueled by the look on Nicholas's face when he went down with a bullet to the chest. The way he gaped. The way Victor laughed.

I'm fueled by the rage of a nine-year-old who was held down in a cellar for thirty-seven hours while Chet drew knife scars across her back and abdomen. Eventually leaving her to bleed out, thinking she was dead.

I'm also fueled by love.

Alone they're powerful. But combined?

My finger goes way too far into Victor's eye but I wiggle it around while it's in there, giving as much as I can before he eventually bucks me off and discards me. My back hits the corner of the coffee table this time, sending sharp spikes of pain up my spine.

For the first time, I consider not getting back up again. I consider laying here to die. I look down at my body, finding my own knife sticking out of my thigh. Victor must have stabbed me in the struggle to get me off him. But I didn't feel it at all. I might have a stab wound, but I also have most of Victor's eye on my pointer.

"You bitch!" Victor growls as he struggles to stand. His eye is a mess, dripping blood everywhere as he hobbles towards me. "You'll fucking pay for that you little cunt!"

"Just... try... and-"

I don't get to finish as Victor hoists me off the ground with one hand at my throat. He pulls the knife from my leg and plunges it right into my abdomen. In the exact same spot that my pancreas should be. The exact same spot that Chet left the worst of the scars.

I gasp as he slams me down into the couch. Then he's mounting it and straddling me. His fingers grip my throat and rob my breath. I grip his wrists as if I can pull him off by sheer force. But I can't. He's too strong. Too practiced. His fingers dig in fast and deep.

"Your father was a pleasure to kill!" He growls as he continues tightening his hands and I gape for air like a fish.

"And the rest of them? Uncle Anton? Fucking Freddie?" he laughs. "I'm going to enjoy gutting them too."

I'm fading now. I'm almost gone. I can feel death gripping me. I pull at his arms, tearing scratches down them as I try to bring him down. My nails only find purchase gouging into his skin, but it doesn't stop him.

"You're not supposed to... kill me," I rasp out.

"No, but you'll pass out and then it's over to Chet for you bitch," Victor says. He squeezes harder. If there's one thing I know, it's that I'm not going back to Chet. Not now. Not ever. And if I have to work my way around the entire city's underworld to get at him myself, then so be it. Because I'm gonna kill Chet too.

"Always too fucking late. Always too fucking slow," Victor says.

I'm fast, though, not slow, when I rip the knife from my gut and stab it right into Victor's side. He only falters momentarily, eyes widening almost imperceptibly, but I stab again.

And again. And again.

And again and again and again.

He finally releases his hold, and I realize now I'm screaming. Covered in blood that might be my own. But I'm sure is his.

He slips up, hesitates for a moment. That's all I need. I only need half a second. It's then that I stab the knife into his heart.

Nicholas can teach me all about killing with honor all he wants. The fatal mistake in this fight was that Victor wasn't aiming to kill. But I certainly am.

I grip the hilt again, twisting the knife further into Victor's chest. He gurgles, blood seeping at the edges of his mouth with no other path for it to escape.

I wish I could enjoy it, but I can't. Because I'm fading too.

And it's with the last of my strength that I pull the knife out of his heart and stab it into his neck.

He coughs blood all over me as it's removed.

Victor Rushkoff dies, dead even before his body finishes collapsing on top of mine.

I don't have any fucks left to give for him. I push him off of me and run for Nicholas.

Thirty-Nine

SAGE

The room alights back into focus, and without the rage and adrenaline driving my actions I'm left with only aches, pains and the sharp brightness of light burning my tired eyes.

"Nic? Nic!"

Victor's body slumps off me and I fall off the couch with him, crawling through his blood as I rush on my hands and knees for Nicholas. He's still curled over in the same position as he was when I last saw him. I turn him over to face me, huffing in relief when his *alive* eyes meet mine.

"Sage," he says, voice choking. His warm, comforting hand is clutching a wound on the left side of his chest and I cover my mouth to gasp. I pull his hand away and see blood pooling in the precise spot on the left of his chest.

It's not his heart, though. It's not his heart. It can't be his fucking heart. His heart is mine. It belongs to me. I get a say on when it stops beating.

"Nic, can you hear me?"

"I hear you, gorgeous," he says, but it comes out weak. And with a side of blood surrounding his mouth.

"You took a bullet for me," I say as tears fall down my face.

"Isn't that," he coughs and more blood makes its way out, but he smiles, "isn't that what a good bodyguard does?"

"No," I cry. He looks pale. Nic never looks pale.

Nic removes his hand from his wound and places it on my cheek. I don't care how much blood is on my face. I'll take it all. I sob as I sink into his hand.

Sure, the bullet wound is where his heart is, but it won't have hit his heart. There's no way. No. There'll be some kind of miracle. It'll have missed anything vital by merely a hair and he'll live. And we'll live. Happily ever after.

"Please help!" I yell so loudly, turning my eyes to the doorway expectantly. But there's no one there. I turn my panicked eyes back on Nic. I did everything I was supposed to. I chose my first love. I killed Victor. I - this isn't how it's supposed to end.

"Sage," Nic whispers, his eyes crinkling in pain.

"No," I whisper. I never got to bitch at him for the FBI thing. We would've resolved it.

Could've.

Can. Can. *Can.*

What's left of the door bursts open and I muffle a scream that turns into a sigh of relief when I see my family has finally made it to us. Everything will be okay.

"Help," I cry. "Freddie, he's-"

Freddie drops to our side as Anton freezes next to us.

I vaguely register that Isla is here too, watching from the doorway with her hand over her mouth. I see the moment her eyes finish searching the room and land on Victor.

"Nic, brother," Freddie says. "Let me see it."

Nic's hand slips from my cheek to give Freddie access on his other side, to his wound. I clutch his free hand in mine.

It's cold.

Freddie puts pressure on the wound, inspects it once, and then puts pressure on it again.

He looks at Nic, pain filling his eyes, then he shakes his head.

"What? What does that mean? Why are you shaking your head?"

Nicholas looks over to me, but it's slow. It's so slow. A painfully sedate turn of the head and croak in his throat.

"Nic, I love you. Nic, I love you so much. No. No, please," I shout. "Anton, help! Help please! I didn't yell at you about - I didn't get to say - I didn't mean it Nic, I promise. I didn't want to run. I'm sorry, I'm sorry, I'm sorry."

"Ssh," Nic says, but it's so soft it's almost a gargle.

"No, I'll do anything. I'll do anything, I swear it. What do you want? I'll do it. I'll do it. I'll do it."

Nic presses a finger to my lips, the heavy pools of blood sliding away with a drop of water. I frown. Wiping at my face as I find my tears nearly drenching the impact of his blood.

My heart cramps.

So much that it hurts. Everything hurts. Much more than a stab wound.

"I love you, Sage DeMarco," Nic says, the ghost of a smile on his lips. "I'm sorry for lying to you. I never wanted to. It's just... well, everything changed the moment I first saw you. Whatever life has put me through and where it has led me... I'd do it again, over and over again forever, because it meant I got to have you. Even if it was only for a moment."

I stroke his cheek and kiss him. Deep. Deeper than I could've thought as the sobs wreck my body. I bury my head in his shoulder and hold him tight, compressing him in my arms.

His gentle whisper meets my ear. "I don't see my life flashing before my eyes. All I see is you."

Beneath me, I feel him relax.

I hold him close to me, and when he dies, I feel it, both underneath my hands and inside my soul.

This time, I don't cry silently. I scream.

Forty

SAGE

"Sage, he's gone. We have to go." Anton's despaired voice pounds at my head. But I'm not fucking moving. My throat tears new raw skin as I scream. "Shit, we have to stop her screaming."

"Chet's supposed to be here any second," Freddie says.

I vaguely register them moving around me, but all I'm focused on is the lifeless form in my arms. Nic's body is getting cold. He's not meant to be cold. I have to keep him warm. I hug myself into him. I'm not letting him go. I won't.

"Chet's not here," Isla says. "Look."

She's got control of the remote. I turn my tear soaked face on Nic's body, continuing to rest my cheek against his abdomen as I watch the scene play out on the screen.

Isla rewinds slightly, so I can tell this has happened in the past. A limo pulls up to the gate, a singular hand coming out of the back window to buzz the front gate.

The gates don't open though. What happens instead, is an enraged Alexei sprinting down the driveway at full speed, beaming for the car and firing off endless amounts of ammo. He avoids all the carnage of DeMarcos fighting Rushkoffs and instead charges straight for Chet's limo and starts screaming through the fence.

Eventually, someone gets out of the car and comes to the gate, putting out a calming hand like they're trying to tame Alexei. Looking like they're at least exchanging words. We can't hear what is said but it gets heated. Alexei clearly doesn't like what he's being told. He reaches through the bars of the front gate, pulling the guy in and snapping his neck.

The limo disappears quickly after that.

"Guess Chet's not coming," Freddie says.

I'm still sobbing over Nic's body. Nic's body... Nic, who *Alexei Rushkoff* killed. I see red. My love. My light. Left this world. Because of that fucking *cunt.*

"Someone else is," Isla says. She forwards the video this time. Minutes later, Alexei is sitting to the side of the front gate with his back resting against a stone pillar and his head in his hands. A barrage of other vehicles pull up, red and blue flashing lights with the FBI logo on the side.

Alexei looks over his shoulder, shakes his head and then presses a button above his head. The front gates open and the FBI vehicles speed in.

That mustn't have been long ago because the flashing lights now start to come through the window.

"He didn't let Chet in, but he sent the fucking FBI," Anton grates out.

"I have to go," Isla says, running out without saying another word.

I clutch onto Nic, crying and wailing.

"Sage, we have to go," Anton begs, reaching for me but I bare my teeth at him, ready to bite if I have to.

"I'm not fucking leaving!" I scream.

Boots pound up the stairs and then there's shouting. Men in tactile gear file into the room and FBI rifles train on us. I can briefly hear the sounds of them arguing with Anton and Freddie in the background while I hold on to Nic. Though I don't care enough to listen.

"You've got a traumatized girl and one agent down, back the fuck off!" Anton yells, his hands in surrender.

Someone else comes into the room then, someone who's clearly important because when he tells the men to put their rifles down, they do.

He goes right to Anton. "Is it?..."

Anton chokes slightly. "Special Agent Baker," Anton says. "He's down."

"He's gone," Freddie adds through a tight throat.

"We'll have to take him," the man says.

There's a moment of silence while I hold on to Nic's chest. The bleeding has stopped now. He's gone completely cold, his eyes still open looking at the ceiling.

On a whimper I close them. And then press a kiss to his mouth, but it feels cold. It lacks the life and passion that Nicholas poured into me every time we touched.

"N-no," I cry out, slobbering all over the place. "*Please come back.*"

I think about the last time we kissed. It must have been last night, before we went to sleep. Did I even kiss him this morning? I ran from him. I gasp in horror at what I've done. If I'd known the last time was the last, I never would've... I - I would've savored it. If I had my time again, I'd listen. I'd never get out of that bed and look in that fucking drawer. I'd never run. I close my eyes on another sob. I wish I could go back. I'd do anything. I'd do *anything*.

"Nicholas belongs to us now," Anton says. "What's it gonna take to make this go away?"

"Let's have a conversation," the man says and the guys who were in the room move away, leaving me and Nicholas alone with Freddie watching over us.

"I'm so sorry, Nic. I never should've doubted you," I cry. "Please, I need a second chance. I'm sorry. I l-l-love you."

Freddie sits down on the other side of Nic and strokes my hair as I sob into Nic's empty chest.

Forty-One

SAGE

When they lower Nicholas Prince's body into the ground, they take my heart along with it. Anton and Freddie carry the head of his casket. I watch him go into the ground. But all I can think about is that his perfectly selected coffin looks too small to hold him. It doesn't reflect the size of the life he lived.

I close my eyes and a tear drips down my cheek.

The day is overcast, and silent as we sit in the open air around the cemetery, listening to everyone pay respects to Nic. I barely hear a word of it. It's only by some miracle that Freddie managed to get me out of the house for this.

Only because he convinced me I'd never forgive myself if I missed Nic's funeral.

My father's men, our brothers, gather in mourning. Suits in sunglasses haunt the edges of the service. The devastated look in their eyes is the only thing that stops me from demanding they leave.

I wear my sunglasses the whole time, though the day doesn't require them. When Anton gets up to speak about Nic's life, my heart cracks. Did we know him all that well? Are we honoring him properly? We only have the last six years of his life. I don't know Nicholas Baker. We only *have* Nicholas Prince.

So I bury him in the name Nicholas Prince.

He will *always* be my prince. And I will always be the mafia princess.

"Sage?"

I look up to find Anton standing over me. Suddenly aware that the funeral is long over, I see the grounds are cleared and where there was once a coffin, there's now a fresh line of dirt.

"The service is over. Are you ready to go?"

I shake my head.

Anton nods and returns to his seat next to me, caging me between him and Freddie.

I stay until it's cold. Until the sun turns orange and disappears from the skyline. My thoughts drift endlessly through all the things I could've said differently. All the things I could've done differently. Everything that seemed big before now feels tiny in comparison.

"Anton?" My voice sounds listless and distant even to me.

"Yeah, *anima mia*?"

"You must know what this feels like." I turn my tired eyes on his and he cringes, sympathy coating his features. He just nods. Anton was married once. A really long time ago. The day that Chet turned on us and tried to take me, it was only Aunt Emma and I in the house. I never knew my mother, but if I had one, I would've wanted it to be her.

She died when she was only twenty-five. Chet killed her. She was trying to stop him from taking me.

"You've never moved on." I state. It's a fact.

"No," he agrees, whispering.

"I won't either," I say, shooting upright in anger. I don't know why I'm upset with them, him and Freddie, but I am. I sit down in the fresh dirt above Nic's grave, wishing I could bury myself underneath it with him.

***

I can't even get out of bed.

For the next several weeks, I sink into myself. Our love was so young before it got cut.

Yet on some level, I know this is my fault.

I started this. I drew up the marriage contract. I forced myself towards Victor Rushkoff. I was always going to kill him. Whoever was after me, whatever they wanted, I wanted them dead for it. So I could prove to my family I could hold my own. So they'd let me out of the shelter they created for me and let me stand on my own two feet. I was always going to secure my freedom and my future this way.

I may have earned my freedom, but my future has been viciously ripped from me.

I now fail to see the point that I was fighting for. Was being locked inside the house, guarded, sheltered, really all that bad when it was Nicholas I was locked inside with?

Now, I'd give anything for it.

Nicholas's goodbye is a hurt that lingers. It lingers deep in my chest.

Several times over the next few weeks I even try to rip it out. I dig into my skin as if I'll find it and be able to relieve myself of it.

Freddie stops me. Anton stops me.

But here is a place I don't want to be anymore.

Because this earth no longer has Nicholas in it.

I make them bring the sheets from his room and put them on my bed so I can sleep in a place that smells like him. The thought that the smell is already beginning to fade sends a coldness to my limbs.

I push my face into my pillow as it grows wet again. There are water stains plaguing it at this point, but I won't let the staff come in and change it. If they so much as try I threaten to gut them. And after the little mafia princess killed the big bad Rushkoff, they believe me.

I hear a knock at my door.

"Go. Away."

"Sage?" It's Anton's tentative voice but I bury myself in the covers.

I feel the bed dip and I pull the covers off my head, shooting him a vile look. He hardens his jaw. "That look may scare off the maids but you're not scaring me, *anima mia.*"

"Get. Out." I flick the covers back over my head.

Anton's tentative voice follows, a lot softer this time. "Do you want to let me brush your hair? You haven't gotten out of bed in weeks. Your hair isn't doing well."

My lips curve up at the corner but I stop them and frown. I love my family, but I hate them all for not being able to save him.

And I hate him for taking a bullet for me. For being the one person who isn't getting a miracle. I felt Nic's heart stop beating, I held his cooling corpse for six hours. I kissed his cheek before they lowered him into the ground.

Nic is dead.

He's gone. He's never coming back. He's never going to be here to hold me. He'll never be able to make anything feel better ever again.

And I'm left here alone.

And fuck, I wish I could join him.

"Sweetie?" Anton is stroking my cheek. "Want me to brush your hair?"

As much as I loathe to admit it, it is pretty gross. My grease has grease.

"Fine," I sigh.

A hopeful face greets me when I pull back the covers, but my scowl sends it away fast. Anton trails me to the vanity where I sit down in front of the mirror.

As Anton takes my brush and starts working through the knots in my long dark hair, just like he used to when I was little, I look at myself in the mirror.

I'm gaunt. Tired. My eyes look cloudy and fogged, my green eyes dull. Lifeless.

"I don't understand, Anton," I whisper.

His hand stills in my hair, before he picks up the soothing movement again.

"I know, I know it's hard. I wish you didn't have to feel this. If I could take it away, I would in a heartbeat."

"Why couldn't we save him?" I look away from my reflection as tears free onto my skin.

"I don't know. I wish we could've," Anton says.

"I don't know how to live with this," I admit, my scared eyes finding Anton's where I hold up my hands to look at them. "I don't know how to not see his blood on my hands."

He keeps brushing my hair, looking away as he speaks. "It will hurt. It will always hurt. Some days a lot. Some days a little less than that. But one day, you'll pick yourself up. You'll find yourself laughing again. And though the hurt will always linger, you'll find a way to smile for it."

He smiles like he's recalling a similar memory.

"One day, you'll think of Nicholas and you won't see blood on your hands. Instead, you'll see memories. You'll see the smiles he shared with you that he wouldn't give anyone else. You'll see him scowling," Anton laughs, "standing guard behind you like he couldn't ever bare for anyone else to touch you. You'll see him give up everything he knew and ever wanted because a girl in a bad man's home stole his heart." Anton's voice cracks then. When I look up, I see him fighting a tear or two of his own.

"One day," Anton smiles. "But not today."

Epilogue
SAGE

One day doesn't come.

Nicholas has been gone for six months now. Time allows me the luxury of being able to get out of bed. Being able to shower. I function. But I'm going through the motions. The black hole of grief holds my heart over my head and smothers me.

The word has spread that Victor is dead, but no word of what happens to his empire. At the very least, the attacks have stopped. I'm free and I'm safe. Apparently ripping out a guy's eye makes you a badass because the men give me a wide berth.

I stare out the window as I ride in the back of Anton's limo, watching the greenery of the countryside pass by me. Next to me, Anton scrolls through his phone, a ping here and there sounding important business.

"Another dinner tonight?" I ask.

Anton answers without looking up. "Yes, family dinner tonight. Don't be late." He smiles at me then. But I don't mind the family dinners so much now. I just wish everyone was there to attend them.

Anton was wrong about one thing. I don't smile.

From what I once was, I'm a hard shell. There isn't a room I walk into now that I don't get a tentative stare. They know I'm a threat and now I never get overlooked. The Sage DeMarco that used to be is dead and buried right next to Nic.

We pull up to the cemetery, driving through the open winding roads until we stop underneath the shade of a tree, close enough to Nic's grave to see it but far enough away for privacy. Anton and I both step out of the car. A cool breeze brushes past me, sending the smell of freshly cut grass through the air.

For a moment, I pause, memories flashing through my mind.

"Want me to come with?" Anton asks. I snap away from the memories, finding Anton has moved in front of me. I shake my head. "No. I'll be okay." I pat his shoulder and approach Nic's grave, climbing a slight hill to get there.

I look back, and Anton gives me an encouraging nod as I stand in front of the headstone. Taking a deep breath, I place my roses down onto the plot, and close my eyes while I talk to him in my head.

Just like I do every week at this time.

Sometimes I feel a breeze fly past me, or get a sharp feeling in my gut and it feels like he's talking to me. Like he's answering the unspoken questions I send out into the universe.

Sometimes it feels like a hum. In a language only the two of us know.

What I don't do, however, is cry. Once I decided to be harder. Better. More than I was before... I haven't shed a tear since. Freddie and Anton worry that I'm building my walls too high. I believe I'd always built them too low.

The wind ruffles again, blowing the hair back from my face and carrying a familiar scent on its breeze.

Spirits and geranium.

I frown. Where do I know that smell?

"Back the fuck up..." At Anton's careful warning I snap my eyes open.

What I see nearly chills my blood.

Nearly.

Truth is, I've been waiting for this moment. If they thought me setting a trap for Victor Rushkoff was something, then they haven't seen nothing yet.

I signal a hand for Anton to remain where he is.

Standing a few paces away is the devil with the God-like face and the stormy gray eyes. Alexei Rushkoff stalks towards me with a scowl. He's dressed for a funeral, a long dark coat stopping at his ankles, hands in his suit pocket and nothing but hatred in his eyes when he meets mine.

I can feel Anton's trepidation from where I stand, but I don't look back at him. There's a knife at my waist and a gun at my hip that I'm well equipped to use if I need to. But something tells me I won't need to.

Something tells me Alexei is here for the same reason that I am.

He comes to a stop next to me, stepping shoulder to shoulder with me as his eyes rove over Nic's headstone.

"Long time no see," I say.

His lips lift at the corners. "Trust me," he says. "I wouldn't come anywhere near *you* unless I absolutely had to."

I give him a smirk in return. "They said you'd be here begging for my forgiveness for what you've done," I say. "I knew better than that."

Alexei tilts his head to regard me and narrows his eyes. "I'm not in the business of asking for forgiveness, princess." He throws his head back, taking a deep breath through his nose before puncturing me again with his gaze. "I am, however, in the business of seeking retribution."

I purse my lips knowingly as I nod, disregarding his stare to instead admire the greenery of the cemetery once again. "We're on the same page," I say.

We stand in silence for a moment, not looking at one another. I, for one, relish in this moment of peace. There won't be a moments peace after this. After this encounter ends, I'm going to hunt him to the ends of the earth. I expect the same of him.

"We done with the posturing?" he says, breaking me from the silence.

"Oh, I'm ready," I say. We turn to face each other almost as if we'd synchronized the moment.

"Good," he says. He licks his lip and his eyes go hard, showcasing that psychotic streak he's always kept just below the surface for moments like this. "You killed my brother."

"And you killed the love of my life."

Alexei smirks, like he's pleased with that fact, and I suppress the urge to strangle him here and now. "May the best man win," he says.

I raise my brow but still, I take the black rose from within my coat pocket, one I've been carrying around for six months in anticipation of this moment. I place it gently on the top of Nicholas's grave without missing a second of eye contact with Alexei.

"Sage, no!" Anton gasps. Still, I don't make a move away from Alexei. The horror in my uncle's voice is clear. But I don't care. A death promise was the only way this was going to end between me and Alexei. I killed his brother, and he killed Nic. Now there's no one in the world I want dead more than Alexei Rushkoff. I have never in my life felt the blind squeeze of hatred the way I feel it for this motherfucker.

Clearly the feeling is mutual.

Alexei smirks in Anton's direction and pulls a black rose from his coat as well, placing it over mine. He smiles at me before he holds out his hand.

I shake Alexei's hand and with that we seal our death promise. As we stare into each other's eyes, baring our teeth, a bolt of lightning strikes. Neither ones of us moves. It feels poetic. That the lightning would strike now to symbolize this moment.

The next time I get my hands on Alexei Rushkoff, I'll be tearing him to shreds, just like I did his brother.

I smile as I seal my fate. "I can't fucking wait to kill you, Alexei Rushkoff."

"You'll be dead before you ever get the chance, *princess*."

TO BE CONTINUED

Sage and Alexei's story continues in 'Dangerous Promises'.

ACKNOWLEDGMENTS

Warning: Spoilers!

This book took me to a wildly different place than anything else I'd ever tried to write. Especially that cliff-hanger. If it makes you feel any better, I didn't see it coming, either. For a long time, I'd tried to write this book with Sage and Nic intently as the endgame main characters. But alas, Alexei came sprinting onto the page to interrupt me and I had no choice but to listen. I hope you fell for Alexei as much as I did. And if you didn't, well, I hope you'll give him a chance. He and Sage may hate each other more than anything right now, but who doesn't love a kill-or-be-killed enemies-to-lovers? My heart hurts for Nic, but I can't wait to show you what's in store for these two.

Anyway – onto the acknowledgments.

To my family and friends who support me endlessly in this journey by cheering me on, hoarding paperbacks, and generally being awesome. To my wonderful Dad, and to Mum, who is always the first to read my work whether she likes it or not.

To the phenomenal group of people in my writer's group—A'Mhara McKey, Bri Weir, Brigita Ozolins, Catherine O'Neill, Jason Underwood, Jenny Gibson, Jo Mitchell, Jude Anison, Kate Burns, Kate Reynolds, Kerri Flanigan, Kerry Anderson, Michelle Harris, Natasha Granath, and Shelley Dark. We have built something so special that I'm honoured and amazed to be a part of.

To the incredible reader community. In particular, every blogger, influencer and reader who helped to promote this book either by posting, reading or arc reviewing – I'm so grateful to all of you. To Wildfire

Marketing, Grey's Promo and Peachy Keen Author Services for helping me get this book out to this amazing book community.

And as always – to you, the reader. I've said it once, I'll say it again and I'll repeat it always. With every flip of the page, you're making my dreams come true. That means the world to me.

REVIEWS

I'm on Amazon and Goodreads if you'd like to leave a review!

Reviews are like gold to indie authors such as myself. If you'd be so kind I'd be forever grateful if you'd consider leaving me a review.

Review on Amazon: https://tinyurl.com/takyuh5e

Review on Goodreads: https://tinyurl.com/4nkbau6d

Follow Me: linktr.ee/amybarnettauthor

ABOUT THE AUTHOR

Amy Barnett is an Australian author of romantic suspense fiction.

First and foremost a fan-girl, Amy is obsessed with stories and the wonderful worlds created by them. You will find her forever swooning over her latest book-boyfriend, staring void-eyed off into space as she lives out stories in her head and generally going about her being as a hopeless romantic.

When she's not daydreaming love stories Amy can be found spending downtime with her wonderful family and friends, and taking endless photos of her dog napping. Visit www.amybarnettauthor.com for more.